EVERYTHING
THAT BURNS

# ALSO BY GITA TRELEASE

*All That Glitters*
(previously published as *Enchantée*)

# EVERYTHING THAT BURNS

# GITA TRELEASE

FLATIRON
BOOKS
NEW YORK

EVERYTHING THAT BURNS. Copyright © 2021 by Gita Trelease. All rights reserved.
Printed in the United States of America. For information, address Flatiron Books,
120 Broadway, New York, NY 10271.

www.flatironbooks.com

The Library of Congress Cataloging-in-Publication Data is available upon request.

ISBN 978-1-250-29555-2 (hardcover)
ISBN 978-1-250-29556-9 (ebook)

Our books may be purchased in bulk for promotional, educational, or business use. Please
contact your local bookseller or the Macmillan Corporate and Premium Sales Department at
1-800-221-7945, extension 5442, or by email at MacmillanSpecialMarkets@macmillan.com.

First Edition: 2021

10  9  8  7  6  5  4  3  2  1

*For Tim and Lukas,*
*encore une fois*

*. . . the guns shot above our heads*
*And we kissed, as if nothing could fall*

—David Bowie

# PARIS, AUGUST 1789

*RISE UP*

# CITIZENS!

---

AT LAST
FREEDOM
IS IN OUR GRASP
THE

# REVOLUTION

IS

AT

# HAND

---

LIBERTÉ
ÉGALITÉ
FRATERNITÉ
OU
LA MORT

# 1

Giselle had only two bouquets of yellow roses left.

It was late afternoon, and August's withering heat hung over the flower seller and her blooms. Like the other girls who'd stood there since early morning, selling bouquets in the shadow of the church of Sainte-Chapelle, Giselle had lined her wicker tray with evergreen branches. Not only did they show off the roses to advantage, they also kept the blooms fresh.

But on a steaming day like today, even cedar boughs were not enough.

While the other girls' flowers had drooped, the edges of their petals etched brown with decay, Giselle's had stayed perfect. As if newly picked.

Glancing at her posies, passersby couldn't help but think of a dewy garden in the early morning, its cool air alive with green perfume and the liquid trills of birds. A place where trouble and striving didn't exist. In that imaginary garden, there were no bakers strung up from lampposts for the crime of running out of bread, or children crushed beneath the wheels of an aristocrat's carriage. There were no grain shortages or rumors of aristocratic plots against the people. No vagrants or arsonists, no beggars or bloodthirsty magicians.

Amid the revolutionary chaos of Paris, this was no small illusion.

To conjure a garden from a tray of cut roses was to set people to dreaming, and if that dream cost several sous, what of it? It was worth it to hand over the coins, and to take the bouquet—its thorns snipped neatly away—and press it to your nose, inhaling all that was good and sweet while the hot reek of the river Seine, ferrying all manner of rotten things in its water, faded far away.

Giselle knew this, and priced her blooms accordingly.

"You." A man approached, a nobleman, Giselle guessed, by his fine suit and silver-capped cane. Lace spilled from his cuffs, unapologetically expensive, and above his spotless white cravat, his mouth was large, too eager.

"Oui, m'sieur?"

"I'll take the prettiest one." As he waited for her to give him a bouquet, he cocked his head and watched her.

Giselle smiled only vaguely in his direction and chose the finer of the remaining bunches. With some customers, it was best not to meet their gaze, for they took it as encouragement. She suspected he was one of those, and the sooner he was gone, the better. Curtseying, she handed over the flowers. The livre he gave her—without asking for change—she slipped into the hem of her apron. *Safe.* She waited for him to leave. Irritatingly, he did not.

"How fresh your flowers are!" He stared not at the bouquet, but at her. "What trick do you use to keep them that way?"

"I stand in the shadows, m'sieur," she replied. "Where it's cool."

Of course that wasn't the whole truth.

Her friend Margot got ice from a warehouse at the city's edge. Her lover was the night guard, and he let her in. In the gray morning, before she left, he'd brush away a heap of sawdust, chip off a shining sliver, and give it to her along with a kiss. Margot kept a chunk of that ice tucked under the oranges and strawberries she sold near the Louvre palace. And because Giselle shared with Margot the boughs she cut from trees at an old cemetery, Margot always asked her lover to cut a second shard of ice for Giselle.

The ice was a wonder. Trapped inside were thousands of tiny bubbles, like pearls. She wished she could keep the ice in the open and watch it change over the course of the day. Becoming something else. But flower sellers were poor, and a flower seller with the money to buy ice would be no flower seller at all, but a thief. So she kept it hidden under the green boughs on her tray. It wasn't magic, but it felt like it. A secret.

The nobleman had drawn close now.

*Too close.*

Behind him stood a girl her own age. Well dressed, freckled, auburn hair coiled under a straw hat, its swooping brim wider than any Giselle had seen. Tucked under her arm was a bundle of papers, tied with string. She seemed nervous, and Giselle gave her an encouraging smile. If the girl came forward to buy the last bouquet, the nobleman might move on and leave her be.

But the only smile she got was from the man, and it was a wicked one. "You are so lovely, mademoiselle—une très belle fleur."

"I'm not a flower." She shifted her wicker tray so it rested on her hip, keeping a distance between them. But he was tall enough to reach over it, and behind her was the high stone wall of Sainte-Chapelle.

Once more, Giselle glanced toward the girl in the hat standing behind him. It was too much to hope she might intervene. Wasn't she but a girl, just as Giselle was? Giselle knew there was beauty in her smile, the cocoa-brown gloss of her hair, her flowers' sweetness. But after that? She was only a poor girl trying to stay alive. If their places were reversed, she knew in her heart she would never do for a stranger what she was hoping the girl in the cartwheel hat would do for her.

"I'm naught but a flower seller, m'sieur."

"Come, come!" he cajoled. "Are you certain?" And then, as if it were the most natural thing in the world, he grasped her hand. In his palm, pressed hard against hers, was a louis d'or. She recognized its size, the shape it made against her flesh. A gold louis was more than she could earn in weeks. Enough to take her friends to a café in the Palais-Royal, where they'd dine like queens. It'd be late, the sky deepest midnight, but inside the candles would burn bright as stars. They'd order champagne and roasted chicken. There would be a rich sauce, slices of bread to mop it up. And after, stewed apples swimming in cream. She imagined what it'd be like to sit at a table with white linens and clean plates while someone waited on them, where they could laugh and talk and dream. For once, not to be striving to keep fear and hunger at arm's length. For once, to belong.

*That* was what a gold louis was.

But she wouldn't take it. She was afraid of what he wanted in return.

Tugging hard, she freed her hand and held the glinting coin out to him. Across her palm curved a red line where the louis had bitten into her flesh. "M'sieur, you've already paid for the flowers. This is too much."

Frowning, he asked, "Too much for what?"

"I'm sure I don't know," she said, obstinate. What made him think he had any rights over her? "Take it, m'sieur."

He came nearer, mouth twisted, face purpling. As he pushed against her tray, her last bouquet tumbled into the dirt. Gone. She didn't dare pick it up. Instead, she took a step backward, then another. "Please!"

"You are a *nothing*," he hissed. "You are a girl on the street, fresh one day and spoiled the next—how dare you? It's not for the likes of you to tell me what is too much." He spun, theatrically, to address the passersby. Sunlight danced on his silver-topped cane as he raised it high. "Is this what revolution has brought us? Flower sellers who think they're the equals of men?"

From behind him, someone scoffed. Was it the girl in the hat?

Giselle took another step back, and found the church wall unyielding against her back. "I don't think that!"

Though of course she *did*.

He must have seen the defiant spark in her eyes, because he thundered, "See what she has in her hand! She stole that gold louis out of my pocket!"

"That's not true!" Giselle threw the coin at him as if it scorched. Surprised, he caught it. "Now leave me be! I haven't done anything wrong."

"Can we let this impudence stand?" the man bellowed, and in the crowded street, several hatless men, their brick maker's aprons red with clay, stopped to stare. "Shouldn't she be punished?" the aristocrat asked as the crowd eddied around him.

No one asked a question of *him*. No one said: *What is the truth?*

She'd seen it before. People didn't care to know who was right and who was wrong before they joined in. No matter what was happening on the street—a circus or a hanging—it was as exciting as the theater. Better, even, because you never knew how it would end.

Then someone screamed: "À la lanterne!" *To the lamppost! String up the thief!* A dozen voices took up the blood-chilling cry. Giselle shrank back, as if she could somehow disappear. Where to go? If she slipped through the church's shadow, raced to the river and across the bridge, perhaps she could vanish in the tangle of crooked alleys and lanes she knew so well. But if by some miracle she escaped the mob, there was still the police. His word against hers. There was no question whom the court would believe.

Her breath came shallow and fast.

The terror of a prison cell at La Petite Force, the iron lock and bars. But worse, much worse was what would happen to the others: Margot, Claudine, Little Céline with her sweet smile and sticky hands. Without them, what or where would she be? Her legs trembled as the circle of people tightened around her.

There was no way out. She might die here today. Hanged from a lamppost or a tree. Her head stuck on a—

Then the girl in the hat stood in front of her, blocking the others from view. Her gray eyes burned. "You must disappear! If the crowd doesn't get you, the police will, and they won't believe a word you say." She grasped the leather strap of Giselle's wicker tray. "Leave this and run! People have been killed for less."

Giselle bent her head and the strap slid along her back as the tray came away in the other girl's hands. "But I need it—"

The expression on the other girl's face said, *Not as much as you need your life.* But somehow she understood, for she said, low, "Meet me in the little square at the end of the island, by the old oak, before six. Now go!"

Giselle choked out a "merci" and then shoved past the man, running faster than she'd ever run before. Past carriages and vegetable sellers and a juggler in a tattered costume, her breath in her throat, her heart a wild drum. Behind her came the mob, relentless as a cresting wave.

# 2

But Camille Durbonne, the young Vicomtesse de Séguin, did not run.

Instead, she stood, shaking, as the red-faced nobleman watched the crowd chase after the flower seller. Then he turned his rage on her.

"How dare you interfere with my business!" he snarled, raising his cane. "What right have you to go against me? I ought to have you whipped—"

Fear was a sudden hand at her throat, and she choked on the words she'd thought to say. Instead she stepped back and let him see her: the richly patterned fabric of her dress and its exquisite silk jacket, the lace at her collar and sleeves—unlike his, not excessive for these revolutionary times—the finest from Alençon. The straw hat that curved daringly across her brow was one of Sophie's sweeping extravagances, and there was no mistaking Camille's white fingers and smooth skin, the clean hems of her skirts, the unworn heels of her raspberry-tinted shoes. Everything she wore proclaimed money and power. Which, she suspected, were the only things this man understood.

As he took in her appearance his mouth fell open. "Mademoiselle?" he stammered.

Camille's anger at the injustice ran like a fiery river through her. Seeing the flower seller trapped, Camille felt her own fear clawing its way back, sharp and raw as ever. But now she had a title, a mansion, and fine clothes. Shouldn't she use them as weapons?

"Monsieur!" she said, disdainful as any courtier at the Palace of Versailles. "Do not speak to me of rights. If I were you, I wouldn't put myself where I wasn't wanted. The people of Paris no longer bend to your will." She added, each word as sharp and scornful as she could make it, "They are human beings and might turn on you next."

"Pardon!" he exclaimed. "I did not realize the girl was a protegée of yours! If I had known, of course, I would never . . ." He attempted a wan smile.

She wanted to kick him. Viciously. His pretend apologies and pathetic excuses were just like her brother, Alain's. Weak, but still capable of hurting others. Like this nobleman, he'd never owned up to what he'd done, but instead just took, took, took. When would people like him finally understand the world wasn't theirs for the taking? That a girl was more than a fruit or a flower to be plucked?

"A word of advice, monsieur: keep your hands to yourself and things will work out much better for you." Behind his shoulder, the street had emptied out, the crowd dispersed. "Now that the revolution has come, no one is your property any longer. We are all equals, non?"

"How correct you are!" With a fawning bow, he held out the yellow roses to Camille. "You would honor me by taking these—"

Not trusting herself to speak, she silently took them and he scuttled off.

Though Camille's performance had gone as well as she could have hoped, inside, she was trembling. Her hurt and anger threatened to consume her.

*Steady.*

She tried to breathe, still her pounding heart, and listen. The mob was far off, or had given up its hunt, for she could no longer hear its frenzied screams. For now at least, the island returned to its everyday noises. Her fury receded like a tide, laying bare the helpless fear underneath that never seemed to go away. The wild beat of her pulse that buzzed: *if not for magic, that might have been you.*

Things were better now, but each morning she willed herself to believe it would last. For wasn't that one of magic's lessons—that nothing stayed? She had lost so much before, why not the fine house, the friends, the raven-haired boy she dreamed of?

She pushed the thought away.

Shouldering the strap of the flower seller's tray, and tucking her bundle of pamphlets and the roses under her arm, Camille struck out toward the old oak at the island's tip.

Her way took her past the old palace wall, built by French kings long before the Louvre, the Tuileries, or Versailles. On it, two boys were hanging posters. The taller one balanced on a ladder, a bucket of paste swinging from his arm, in his hand a wide brush. The other handed him posters, one by one. As they went up, a woman read them aloud to a ragtag group gathering around her. Plenty of people in Paris could read. Others got their news this way, from the mouths of hawkers and newsboys, troublemakers and rabble-rousers. Each of the papers and broadsheets and pamphlets that had mushroomed since the fall of the Bastille had a tale to tell. Some of them real, some fake. Camille could hear Papa now, how angry he'd have been if he'd been able to see the lies people printed: *A pamphleteer must tell the truth!*

But what if no one listened?

Two small boys, their clothes worn to rags, split off from the group and ran to her on their bare feet. Their bellies were swollen—rumor said the poor had nothing but grass to eat—their eyes too large in their faces.

"Mademoiselle!" they begged. She kneeled beside them and emptied her purse into their hands. "Buy something for yourself first," she told them. In a moment, they had vanished, as if they'd never been. As Camille stood, she heard the woman shouting out the poster's words: *Bread. Aristocrats. Death.*

On the Quai des Morfondus, she passed a weary farmer in his wagon, heading home. Unlike last year, there was grain to be had this summer, but drought had dried up the rivers and there was no way to mill it into flour. In the countryside, hungry people were leaving their villages to search for food and work, and it made others suspicious.

All of Paris was a mass of kindling, piled perilously high.

It would only take a spark to leap into flame.

Having traversed the narrow island, she had come to the river Seine, flowing dark beneath her. Across the river lay the Right Bank, where she lived, and the infamous Place de Grève. It was in that great square, Papa had told her, that King Louis IX had burned twelve thousand copies of a religious book in an act of censorship and hate. Worse were the executions. Legend said the Place de Grève was haunted by those who'd been tortured there, their malevolent ghosts waiting to drown passersby in the river.

Despite the heat, Camille shivered.

Ahead of her lay the island's tip and the ancient oak, its limbs spreading wide. It was only August, but the dry heat had tinged its leaves with bronze. Under its shady canopy, people stood talking with their neighbors.

But the flower seller was nowhere to be seen.

Camille could only wait a few minutes. As she rested the tray against the old oak, she remembered the pamphlets tucked under her arm. Across the top of them was sedately written: *On the Education of Girls by Jean-Nicolas Durbonne.* The sight of those words made her want to scream. If only she could toss them into one of the bonfires that burned at night on the Seine and incinerate them into ash.

Her visit to the bookshop of one Henri Lasalle had not gone well.

She'd passed the store several times, working up the courage to enter. In its window hung posters announcing the latest actions of the General Assembly, which was meeting in Versailles to create a constitution and rights for the citizens of France. Through the bookstore's open door came the buzz of enthusiastic arguments. Promising, but also intimidating. Standing on the threshold, she suddenly longed for Lazare—his hand at her elbow and encouragement in his deep brown eyes.

But Lazare was elsewhere.

Taking a deep breath, she went in. The shop was not large, but clean and well organized, its patrons browsing the bookshelves or paging through newspapers. One of the men, a baker's apron tied over his long pants and clogs, was waving a pamphlet at a plain-clothed priest. From behind the counter, the man she took to be the bookseller joined in with a few choice words.

"Monsieur," he said, "how can you argue for all men to be equal under the new constitution?"

The priest looked surprised. "Are not all men equal before God?"

"Aha!" said the bookseller, as if he'd caught his friend in a trap. "Tell me then, why is the Church itself so rich? Are they so much more equal?"

"Touché!" cried the baker. "Come, Father Aubain, you must admit there's a hole in your argument."

"Not so fast," he warned. "Let me explain what the Church does with its money."

"Explain the amount of land you own while you're at it," the bookseller said good-naturedly.

As Camille listened to them debate, a smile crept across her lips. At last she had found the right bookseller. The previous three had said no, but they'd clearly been out of step with the times. *Here* was the debate she'd been searching for. Here was the place where she might step in and make a difference.

She cleared her throat. "Monsieur?"

"Ah, mademoiselle!" He smoothed the front of his coat. "Anything in particular you're looking for?"

"Not today. Instead, I have something you might be looking for. A new pamphlet."

Behind her, the conversation paused.

Camille held out a copy to the bookseller and was mortified to see that it had somehow become creased.

He barely glanced at it. "What is it called?"

"*On the Education of Girls.* By my father, Jean-Nicolas Durbonne."

"Ah!" The bookseller's attention sharpened. "What kind of education do you mean?"

"History, philosophy, Latin. Everything that boys—"

"Non!" He threw up his hands. "Won't work."

"Why not?" Camille said, flustered.

"If you'd said, 'The Education of a Girl of the Streets'? People would buy that faster than you could tell them the title."

"Scandalous!" scolded the priest.

"But it sells, Father. 'The King's Mistress'? They'd be shaking their purses upside down over the counter." The bookseller warmed to his subject. "'Murders in the rue Trianon'? They'd wait outside the shop before it opened, perspiring with anticipation! Accounts of the storming of the Bastille are still popular if they're grisly enough. Blood filling the moat, innocent citizens tortured. A head cut off with a paring knife. That did happen, you know." He leaned an elbow on the counter. "Got anything like that, mademoiselle?"

She had only Papa's words and what he'd taught her. In their printing shop, he'd shown her how to pull the lever on the press, saying: *With one stroke, ma petite, you can change the world.* She'd insisted she was just a child and what could she do, being so small? Papa had given her a melancholy smile, as if thinking of something that had happened long ago, and replied: *You will do what needs to be done.*

What this bookseller wanted was not what Papa had had in mind.

"Shouldn't people be inspired to do better?" Camille demanded. "To change the world?"

"Your pamphlet's not going to do it," laughed the baker.

"If you read it, you'd find it's well argued. Convincing."

The bookseller shrugged. "I read the first few lines. It won't sell. It is not au courant. It is not *now.*"

Frustrated, Camille said, "But it's about equality! You were just speaking of it."

"Girls—women—will, I'm afraid to say, never become true citizens. Therefore, your pamphlet is not a part of the debate. How else can I say it? It's irrelevant and dull!"

"Do we then not matter?" Her words came out choked, humiliating.

The bookseller must have seen the hurt in Camille's face, for he added, a bit more kindly, "You're welcome to leave a few of your pamphlets here, and I will try. Still, I cannot make people buy something they don't wish to read."

She laid the papers on the counter. In that ink was so much work and hope. With a curt nod to the men, she left the shop as quickly as she could, but not before she'd heard one of them laugh, "You can always use the pamphlets to light your candles, Lasalle!"

Around the corner, alone under the shade of an awning, traitorous tears pooled in her eyes. What was wrong with the pamphlets? What was wrong with *her*? Those long afternoons printing with Papa, she'd believed those black letters could launch ideas into the world and change things for the better. A *good* kind of magic.

She had used a dangerous magic to disguise herself at court, cheating at at cards to keep herself and her sister alive, even while that magic hollowed her out and left her wondering if she would ever be completely free of it. But through determination and daring and pain, she'd lifted herself and Sophie from poverty to a place of safety.

And yet?

She hefted the bundle of unwanted pamphlets. She was not satisfied with *this*.

In the fairy stories Maman had told them when they were little, the ones that had gotten mixed up in her head with the gilded stories of court life, there would sometimes be a girl who got a wish. Usually she had done something kind, like saving a trout that was really an enchanted prince or helping an old woman find a needle she'd dropped, which turned out to be the thing that released the woman from a terrible spell. And in return, the girl got a wish. Some girls wished well and others wished badly. When they could have had anything, those girls wished for sausages or for their shoes to fit. They had been so desperate for so long that they had stopped wishing for anything big. Anything that could truly change their lives.

She did not want to make that mistake.

Solemn and deep, the bells of Notre-Dame began to toll six o'clock. The dry leaves of the oaks rattled in the hot wind that rose from the river. The long afternoon was edging toward evening, and still, the flower seller hadn't appeared. But surely, Camille reasoned, the girl would return to Sainte-Chapelle in a few days, and she could bring her the tray then. As she stooped to pick it up, a flash of white caught her eye. A piece of paper, nailed to the tree. It had an unusual shape: long and narrow, its bottom edge ragged.

A notice of some kind? Curious, she began to read.

It was a list of names. Hastily scrawled, blots and spots marring the letters. Some names were misspelled. To her surprise, there were a few names she recognized from court. The Comte d'Astignac. The Duchess de Polignac.

Unease gnawed at her. Halfway down was the name of the aristocrat who'd reported Papa's revolutionary pamphlets to the censors. Below it, Germaine de Staël's, who held a popular salon on the Left Bank, which Camille had attended with Lazare and Rosier. What was her name doing on this list? But when she came to the end, and saw the names Louis XVI and Marie-Antoinette, she understood: it was a list of nobles deemed traitors to the revolution.

At the very bottom was written: *À la lanterne!*

Who gave this person the right to decide who should live and who should die?

Glancing surreptitiously over her shoulder, Camille tore the paper down.

Quickly, she left the square, heading home. As she crossed the river on the Pont Notre-Dame, she dropped the crumpled paper over the side of the bridge. For a moment, the list floated on the Seine's black water, undulating with the current, and then, like an eye winking shut, it was gone.

# 3

Home—if it could be called that—was the ancient Hôtel Séguin.

Protected by a cobbled courtyard and a tall, spiked gate, the mansion stood proudly aloof from the rabble of the streets, very much like the aristocrats who had always lived there. Built of honeyed limestone, the Hôtel Séguin's facade glittered with costly windows, its two wings enfolding a walled garden where a fountain burbled and carefully kept fruit trees grew. Between it and the gate lay the small stables and a carriage house.

From the outside it looked like the kind of place Camille had dreamed of living in. Elegant, impenetrable, safe.

It had certainly seemed that way the first time when, with Lazare at her side, she'd arrived in a gown stiff with blood to free Sophie from imprisonment at their brother's hands. The Vicomte de Séguin had planned to use her as a pawn to compel Camille to marry him, so he could in turn use her sorrow to fuel his own magic. And she had married him, though things had gone differently than he'd hoped. And upon the death of her handsome and villainous husband of a few hours, like the fulfillment of a wish, this grand house and all his other property was suddenly hers.

As if this shadowy house could belong to anyone.

As she approached the gate, she noticed something stuck in its iron bars. Reaching down, she wiggled it loose. It was a scrap of paper, printed in a cramped style, as if the writer had tried to put the most words possible onto the page. Some letters were incomplete, ghosts of what they should have been. Papa would have dismissed it as a sorry piece of work. *Leave room for the reader to think,* she could hear him say. *Give the words some air.* She was about to crumple it up when a sentence caught her eye.

> soon the MAGICIANS will flee Versailles and their
> rotting estates and come to Paris where they will insult us
> with their tricks and snatch the food from between our lips
> for this is the way that they are, a race apart, sinners and
> EVILDOERS that must be eradicated like the rats they
> are—do not the ends justify the means when otherwise we
> will be killed in our beds?

There was no author's name at the bottom, only a stamp resembling a bird. She traced it with her thumb, as if that would tell her something. What was it her friend, the Marquis de Chandon, had said to her in a dusty hallway at Versailles?

*They are frightened of us magicians, because of what we are willing to do.*

She felt a shadow creep over her, as though a storm cloud had covered the sun. But when she looked up, the street was still bright, busy with people going home. Paris was full of people printing things, herself included. Everyone wanted to be heard. Everyone wanted to shift the tide their way. This was nothing more than rubbish, blown against the gate and tangled there by accident. She wanted to let the breeze take it far away, but instead she tightened her grip on it.

*It was too dangerous to let go.*

Timbault, the wizened gatekeeper, nodded at her as she went inside. On the other side of the gravel court in whose center four pointed yew trees stood like sentinels, a low flight of shallow marble steps led to the front door. Behind it would be servants . . . and possibly Sophie. So she kept to the right, heading toward a battered servants' entrance that faced the stables.

She didn't relish going in that way, but the narrow back hallway led directly to the blue salon, which was, in the peculiar way of the house, always ice-cold. On a steaming day like today, it was her best chance. There was bound to be a fire in the hearth, and she was determined to see the pamphlet burn.

She found the door unlocked—a relief, since she never knew what the house would do—and went inside. The cramped passage was long and dim, and as she hurried along it, it began to change. Tendrils of mold bloomed on the plaster. The floorboards creaked in a chorus of complaint. And the walls themselves leaned ominously close, as if they wanted to touch her. "Get back," she whispered, but they did not listen. She walked faster. Doors on either side led to a network of servants' halls and stairs that tunneled through the house like secrets. In the few short weeks she'd lived there, she hadn't wanted to explore them. Trying to uncover what was in the rest of the house had been more than enough.

For the Hôtel Séguin was webbed with an insistent, uncomfortable magic.

She hadn't realized it, not in the first week or two. It had come on slowly, step by step, a wary animal edging closer.

The house was always changing, a corridor appearing where there hadn't been one before, a door that should have opened onto a bedroom revealing a bricked-up staircase instead. Objects Séguin had enchanted when he was alive had begun to fade, taking on their former shapes: an ornamental sword hanging over a fireplace became overnight the thigh bone of a horse. A vase of what appeared to be Sèvres porcelain turned out to be a rusted urn.

All of it made Camille uncertain, as if everything around her might turn out to be different than it seemed. Sometimes she woke with the taste of ash in her mouth or caught herself holding her breath as she went from room to room, as if someone were listening. She stayed away from the dim attic where in a great wardrobe her once-enchanted dress hung silent and sleeping. She avoided the library that murmured at night. But it was harder to dodge the wind that idled through the rooms and the sudden shadows she'd catch out of the corner of her eye that she could only guess were ghosts. Hôtel Séguin was a magician's house with its own intentions, and it didn't deign to share them with her.

But Sophie loved it.

"Imagine!" she'd said when they'd moved the short distance from the Hôtel Théron and stood in the courtyard of the Hôtel Séguin, "we own all this. Our beautiful home." And she'd thrown her arms around Camille, her blue eyes liquid with tears. "We made it here. This place, can you imagine? And now we will be truly happy."

Its unsettling magic was invisible to her.

Just last week Camille had pointed to a tapestry in the red salon, remarking how sometimes blood seemed to drip from the lance of the knight riding a big white charger. "Look, it's doing it now!" Camille tried to keep the horror from her voice. "Don't you see?"

Sophie had only blinked up from her sewing. "See what?"

Neither she nor their brother, Alain, had any aptitude for magic. Sophie couldn't see how the house's magic seemed to seek out Camille, how it clung like smoke to her hair and clothes, how it felt as if it were always trying to overtake her. For Sophie the mansion was luxury and safety, and she deserved to be happy after what she'd gone through at the hands of Séguin. Camille would do nothing to jeopardize that. Perhaps in a few months— once Paris settled—they might find a place that felt more like home.

Finally, up ahead, glowed the green-painted door at the end of the passage.

Relief sighed through her as she stepped out into the wide hall that ran through the middle of the house. Paintings and curio cabinets crowded its paneled walls. And there, just across the parquet, was the blue room, the fireplace visible through the open door. Another minute and the hateful pamphlet would be ash.

She was nearly inside when a shadow caught her eye.

It had her mother's slim, elegant form. Maman's small delicate neck, her tiny waist. She had no idea what the house could manifest—it seemed capable of anything. Her heart climbed into her throat as she whispered, "Hello?"

"Are you looking for someone?" The shadow dissolved as Sophie stepped into the hall.

A thread of loss pulled tight in Camille . . . but what had she been thinking? Of course it was her sister, whose gold-blond hair, milky skin, and deep blue eyes were just like their mother's.

"Just you!" Camille said brightly. In a minute, Sophie would notice what Camille had in her hand. As she hurried toward the fireplace, the carpet beneath her feet *curled*. She caught her toe on the edge of it, stumbled—and dropped everything. Roses and papers slid from her arms, cascading to the floor. Out of nowhere, the low persistent breeze that murmured through the house began to rise.

"Merde!" she swore.

"Oh Camille!" Sophie exclaimed. "Your beautiful pamphlets!" Though she was wearing a striking pink dress and jacket, she dropped heedlessly to her knees to gather them up before they blew away. Heat flamed in Camille's cheeks as she realized that Sophie would know exactly what had happened.

Sophie carefully laid the sheets of paper in a pile. "The bookseller didn't take them?"

"He took one, in case there was any interest. But he doubted there would be." She tried to keep the bitterness out of her voice. "He said it's not exciting enough. Not the right kind of story."

"But why ever not?"

Camille stepped on a pamphlet to keep it from drifting away. "He said it was too dull! Ideas and philosophy. But that's just the kind of thing Marat is printing in his paper all the time!"

"Is it?" Sophie asked. "I thought he had a reputation for being . . . terribly incendiary." Squaring the sheets she'd gathered, she handed them to

Camille. "I must say I agree with the booksellers; after all, you have to give the people what they want," she said with a wan smile. Sophie's hat shop, Le Sucre, was quickly becoming one of the most popular in Paris by doing just that. The people's appetite for everything blue, white, and red seemed insatiable.

"Oh!" Camille said, surprised. "I thought you didn't like selling the revolutionary ribbons and cockades—"

"How lovely these roses are!" Sophie scooped up the bouquet Camille had dropped and brought it to her nose. Then she rang a little silver bell that waited on a nearby table to summon one of the maids. "So what if those revolutionary trims aren't what I dream of making?" she mused. "Why, just today I hired another seamstress to help us, for we have far too many orders. My tricolor trims are as pretty as it's possible for them to be. You should see the horrors Madame Paulette tries to sell at the Palais-Royal—"

Sophie fell suddenly silent.

Camille followed her sister's gaze to the ragged anti-magician pamphlet that lay on the carpet like a stain. She lunged for it, but Sophie was too quick. "Give it to me!" Camille demanded. "It's just a piece of trash I intended to burn—"

Sophie gleefully held it out of reach. But when as she read it, a worried V appeared between her brows. "How can people print these terrible things?"

"It's nonsense, just ravings—" But a little voice deep inside her whispered: *Is it?*

Sophie sighed and handed Camille the scrap of paper. "My customers are breathless with the same kinds of malicious rumors. Magicians are causing the drought. Magicians are hoarding grain, so there's not enough bread. Magicians are making the rivers flow backward. Oh, and Marie Antoinette dyes her gowns red with the blood of the French. Never mind that would make her dresses brown."

"Magicians can't even do those kinds of things," Camille said with more certainty than she felt, for both Chandon and Séguin had revealed her knowledge of magic to be a very meager thing. "At least the ones I know."

Sophie glanced sidelong at Camille. "I can hardly tell them that my sister's friend the Marquis de Chandon is a very charming magician."

Behind Sophie appeared Adèle, the youngest housemaid. She wore a black dress with a starched white apron and a cap over her wavy, coffee-colored hair. The expression on her face was often one of incredulous and barely hidden surprise at something Camille had done. It was, in fact, the expression she now wore. In her hands, she held a folded length of fabric, which she laid on the little table. "Mesdames?"

"Adèle, would you put these roses in water? And while you're passing by the printing room," Sophie added, gesturing to Camille, "leave Madame's pamphlets there."

The thought of those failures waiting for her sickened her. She did not want to have to face them tonight. Or tomorrow. Or even the day after. She would never be satisfied with them, not now. Shoving the densely printed page that had unnerved her into the middle of the stack, she tucked them tight under her arm. "I'll take care of them."

"So you'll make a fresh start with your pamphlets?" Sophie said approvingly as Adèle disappeared down the hall.

Camille grasped them tighter. "I will."

"Good. And now I'm afraid I must go."

A surge of disappointment rose in Camille. But just as quickly, she reprimanded herself. Wasn't this what she wanted for her sister: happiness, independence, a full life? "I did think you were dressed too well for dinner at home."

Sophie ducked her chin and smiled. The undernourished look she had for so long was vanished, like a bad dream, and had been replaced with rosy cheeks and laughter. She wore her newest silk dress topped by a short, sapphire-blue coat, its collar and deep cuffs embroidered with chrysanthemums. Her golden hair waved becomingly over one shoulder, and the pretty flush in her cheeks showed that the ordeal she'd suffered at the hands of Séguin three weeks ago was finally behind them. *This*, Camille thought, *was something to hold on to.* And if it meant living in this uneasy, watchful house full of magic, she would do it.

"Where are you going?" Camille asked.

"First, to Le Sucre." Sophie showed her the folded cloth Adèle had brought. "A client is desperate to have this shawl for a patriotic banquet tonight. All the tricolor tassels had my fingers aching! But since it's done, I might as well give it to her, and get paid. And then," she added happily, "the Marquis d'Auvernay has promised me cake at a decadent café run by Russians. They will be dressed as Cossacks, he tells me—it will be terribly romantic."

Camille couldn't help but think of the crowded streets, the flower seller, the nobleman who'd whipped up a mob for his own benefit. "Just be careful."

"In the streets?" Sophie lowered her voice. "Or with d'Auvernay?"

"You are terrible!" Camille laughed. Though Sophie was only fifteen, since the events of the spring, she'd come into her own. She suddenly seemed capable of handling anything. "I trust your heart is in no danger?"

"Hardly! He is rich and handsome, and that is all. And fear not, the footman Daumier will come with me to Le Sucre, and when the shawl has been paid for, d'Auvernay will fetch me in his carriage."

Camille's throat constricted when she thought how overjoyed Maman would have been to see Sophie looking so well. "He will not be able to keep his eyes off of you."

"It just goes to show how getting a dastardly magician out of a young lady's life can make things so much better." In the mirror, she caught Camille's eye, suddenly serious. "All of that is behind us now, n'est-ce pas?"

"Of course." Séguin was dead, and with him, her old life. This new one was full of possibility—a couple of raving pamphlets and a list nailed to a tree did not change that.

Sophie leaned in to give her a kiss. "Oh, I nearly forgot! An invitation arrived for us a few hours ago. It's waiting for you in the printing room." With a wink in her voice, she added, "I bet it will raise your spirits."

# 4

Nevertheless the uncomfortable feeling persisted as she passed smoke-blackened paintings and cabinets crowded with Venetian paperweights and ancient coins before she reached the dining room. From its ceiling hung an enormous chandelier, dense with cut-glass crystals. Underneath it stood a wooden printing press.

She'd sought out an old one, like her father's. When she ran her fingers over the worn wood, or held the smooth iron lever that seemed to fit her hand perfectly, she thought of all the people who'd owned the press before. Had they printed invitations and revolutionary posters, like Papa? Etiquette manuals? Histories of far-off places? Or advertisements for the spectacles Paris adored? There was no way of knowing, but she imagined that somewhere inside its metal and wood, the press remembered.

Around the room stood cabinets covered with stacks of paper and containers of ink. Above her head, lengths of rope ran from glittering sconce to glittering sconce, making a spiderweb from which she'd hung freshly printed copies of *On the Education of Girls* to dry.

Failures, all of them.

Papa would have folded them into dragons or queens or boats—something to prove her work wasn't worthless. As she began to unpin the useless sheets, she could almost feel the paper warming in her hand as she imagined the words becoming compelling. Entrancing.

How much magic would it take to make it right?

*None*, she told herself sharply.

Magic was not easy to get rid of. The more she'd used it, the worse it had been, and even when she'd stopped, the disquieting hunger for more had been hard to quell. Despite everything, there was something in her that yearned for magic's dark transformations—even though it had nearly killed her and threatened the lives of everyone she loved. The way magic still tugged at her reminded her of her brother's inability to stop gambling, and its power frightened her.

But in the weeks since Séguin's death, one thing more than any other had healed her hurts: an ebony-haired boy who made her *feel*. It had been Lazare she'd turned to when her memories were too much, when she feared she might never truly recover from having used so much magic. He'd needed to convalesce from his own battle with Séguin, and together they'd ambled in the dusty gardens of the Tuileries. He brought her sweet pastries from Stohrer's, and sat with her in the shade of the fruit trees in her own garden. Leaning against the trunk of a plum tree, his long legs stretched out in front of him and his dark head tipped back, his face was alight with enthusiasm. For hours they talked of inventions and revolution, balloons and the journey they planned to take over the Alps. In his dreamy, amber-flecked eyes, she saw herself differently: not as a desperate magician, but as the best version of herself. It had gone a long way toward mending what was broken.

She wanted to hold on to that feeling of hope and possibility, of a future free of magic's dark taint. For she wanted nothing to do with its wild unpredictability, the uncomfortable feeling that it wasn't *she* who was working the magic, but rather, that the magic was working *her*.

She unpinned the final sheet and tossed it on top of the others. Perhaps Papa's pamphlets *were* too theoretical. After all, how would one of Papa's pamphlets help the flower seller? It would take years for the ideas to trickle down from debates in the National Assembly and become law. The flower seller and the starving children of Paris needed a better life *now*.

She carried the pamphlets—including the hateful one she'd found stuck to the gate—to the back of the room and dropped them into the fire. Instantly long tongues of flame leaped up to devour the pages. Soon they would be coal black, their edges gone to ashy lace, drifting up into the chimney's blackened mouth. She'd thought printing would be her future. She'd vowed it to herself at the tennis court in Versailles, when she committed to doing what Papa hadn't been able to.

She had tried, but it hadn't been good enough. Not even close. She needed to do more.

*But what?*

The breeze slithered through the room, whispering, but it said nothing she could understand. She was about to blow out the candles when she remembered the invitation.

It lay on the table, folded into the shape of a star. Sophie's and her names were spelled out in extravagant purple ink and sky-high capital letters. In her hand, it felt like hope, the perfect antidote to her failed pamphlets, violence in the streets, and troubled magic.

Camille unfolded it and pressed it flat. Inside was written:

> *Mes Amis!*
> *Please join me for the launch of a marvelous adventure!*
> *Wednesday, 2 o'clock sharp-ish*
> *At the workshop*

Just below, scrawled so boldly that the final "r" ran right off the page:

> *Charles Rosier*

And at the bottom, a final note:

*P.S. Lazare has promised to attend!*

Camille laughed out loud. Of course she would go.
Knowing Lazare had returned to Paris, she could never stay away.

# 5

From her dressing room Camille heard Sophie's light step in the hall. "You're home already? Come quickly—we're to meet Lazare and Rosier in an hour and I need help!"

"I closed the shop early." Sophie was smartly dressed in a gray-and-blue flowered cotton dress and a straw hat festooned with silk periwinkles. In one arm, she was carrying her black cat, Fantôme, who was purring loudly.

Camille lifted the lids of several enormous hat boxes. "Tired from your adventures with d'Auvernay?"

"Cake and boys are never tiring. It's my customers' choices that are exhausting," she said, giving Fantôme a kiss. "Why does no one want a hat trimmed in sky blue? Or a rich green, like you're wearing?" She sighed. "Revolutionary ribbons are *not* why I opened Le Sucre."

At least, Camille thought with a twinge of envy, Sophie made hats and ornaments people wanted. But the sad set of her shoulders made Camille instantly regret it. "I wish you could sell only your fantastical hats, ma chèrie. I hate that your original ideas are going to waste."

Mollified somewhat, she asked, "What hat will you wear?"

Camille looked despairingly around her chaotic dressing room. "I don't know!"

"I do believe you're nervous," Sophie observed.

"I'm not!"

Her gaze went to the tiny balloon-shaped music box Lazare had given her. It was a souvenir of the two times she'd gone up with him in the balloon—and that gossamer night he'd taken her in his arms at the top of Notre-Dame, the city's rooftops far below.

But last week he'd left Paris abruptly to visit his parents at their estate of Sablebois. And though he'd been away only a handful of days, his sudden absence had left her feeling unmoored. Unsure. For so long she had tried to hold on to the things she loved only to have them slip like water through her fingers. What was to say it could not happen again?

Lazare was true, she knew. He did not willingly keep secrets. Still, it rubbed at her, like a seam sewn wrong.

"Ne t'inquiète pas! I'll find the perfect hat," Sophie said, setting the cat on the floor. He disappeared immediately under the bed. "It's got to be here somewhere."

Casting a critical eye at the mirror, Camille examined her emerald-green dress, embroidered with ribbon roses in various shades of pink. Over it she would wear a pistachio cloak with a wide ruffle and shoes that matched. As she smoothed her skirts flat, she thought for a moment of the other dress, the enchanted one that always made her look beautiful and compelling, hanging quiet and alone in a wardrobe in the attic—

"You should wear this." Sophie handed her a hat she'd unearthed from a pile of Kashmiri shawls. "The dotted ribbon will go nicely with your cloak."

Just as Camille was settling it over her hair, Adèle appeared in the hall, her cheeks very pink. "Monsieur Mellais has arrived in his carriage! He wishes to offer you a ride to the workshop."

*Lazare, here?* "I thought we would walk! I'm not at all ready—"

"Apparently he couldn't wait," Sophie remarked. "I wonder why."

Camille's fingers fumbled with the hat's ribbons, but even she could see how prettily her gray eyes sparkled, how becomingly her skin flushed. She bit her lip and smiled.

"You look absolutely delicious. He will devour you like a pastry."

"Hush!" Camille swatted at Sophie with a fan. "Adèle, would you let him know I'll be there in a moment?"

When she came downstairs, the doors to the courtyard stood open. Lazare was leaning against the door of his carriage. His beautiful face was turned away, but Camille could never mistake his tall shape nor his elegant, lanky ease, the gloss of his long black hair. Lazare being in the country at Sablebois hadn't agreed with Camille, but it'd certainly agreed with him—his skin had deepened to a bronzy brown across his cheekbones, as if the sun now lived inside him. His tricorne hat tucked negligently under his arm and head tipped back, Lazare seemed to be absorbed by a flock of swallows swooping across the cloudy sky. The way he looked at things made her want to see what he saw, or, she thought, be seen by him.

Etiquette said to be coy, but she didn't care. Instead she ran across the cobbled court. Five steps away, then three. Two. One—and he turned and pulled her to him.

Her heart was pounding ridiculously fast. "You've returned," she said—and instantly felt foolish for saying this most obvious thing. With him in front of her, she was suddenly shy.

"Seeing you, I understand why each moment in the country felt like an eternity." Slowly, he kissed the back of each of her hands, one by one, before releasing them. It would have been chaste, not violating any of etiquette's rules, except for the way he looked at her. Hot, as if his gaze could kindle flames. The brush of his lips thrilled—a hand kiss from Lazare was much, much more than such a small thing had a right to be.

"Oh," breathed Camille. Why go anywhere else, when he was here? Absently, she straightened a fold of his cravat, her fingers grazing his skin.

"Do you think . . . would Rosier really miss us? Could we not perhaps sneak away?"

"There is nothing I would rather do," he said in a way that made her feel like she was flying, "though he would certainly be disappointed. But now that I'm returned to Paris, nothing will induce me to be parted from you."

Her fingers curled against the warm skin of his neck, she imagined a different autumn in Paris. Not the one that she'd been living, disturbed by the house's magic and dissatisfied by her destiny.

Instead, it could be *this*.

She pulled herself back to the moment. "And your parents? Are they well?"

She remembered them from the opera—his bejeweled stepmother's disdain; his distant father, a pale inverse of Lazare. Lazare's warm coloring and inky hair came from his father's first wife, an Indian from Pondichéry, whom he'd met while visiting his family's spice plantations. When she'd died of malaria, he and a very young Lazare had returned to France. Whatever India had been to his father, it was no more. That door was firmly closed, even to Lazare. His father insisted, Lazare had told her, that he be more French and less Indian. It hurt and bewildered him.

At the mention of his parents, a muscle in Lazare's jaw tightened. "Well enough. Some angry peasants had threatened to burn down a neighbor's château. They'd managed to work themselves into a fright by the time I arrived. Anywhere, they said, would be better than Sablebois."

Lazare loved Sablebois, she knew. "They're not thinking of becoming émigrés and leaving France?" After the storming of the Bastille last month, some noble families, following the lead of the king's brother, had fled to England or Austria. She couldn't imagine turning her back on her home, and she knew Lazare felt the same.

"They haven't gone quite that far," he replied. "But they did decide it was safer in Paris, where at least they could rely on the police. Which means they returned with me and are now settling in."

She had the feeling both she and Lazare would have preferred them to stay in the country. "You did tell them that it's hardly better here?"

"They wouldn't listen." One corner of his mouth rose up. "Perhaps they wish to keep an eye on me."

"Why would they do that?" she teased. "What secrets have you been keeping?"

"Nothing worth knowing." He took her hand, traced her knuckles with his thumb, and then, drawing closer, brought her hand to his lips.

Camille's breath caught. She found herself wishing his mouth was ... *elsewhere.* "Don't you know hand-kissing has been deemed too gothic for this revolutionary age, like wigs and rouge?"

"Or magic?" He raised one dark eyebrow, the one cut by a scar. "Though that hasn't prevented you from enchanting me."

"I didn't intend to." Though perhaps longing was its own kind of magic?

"I'll need to study you more carefully to know for certain."

"Like you were studying the birds just now? Or was it the clouds?"

His gaze traveled like a caress from the collar of her cloak and along her cheek before coming to rest on her mouth. "Not exactly."

It was like feeling the warm sun on her face. "I'm glad you're back in Paris."

"Me too, mon âme. And I am determined to stay. You will become quite sick of me, I'm certain." Camille was about to say that it was impossible when she heard Sophie coming toward them.

"Lazare! Welcome home!" she called out as she ran lightly down the stairs. Her dress billowed behind her as she kept one hand pressed to her head, to keep her extraordinarily wide hat from blowing away.

Lazare bowed. "I *was* only gone for five days."

"To some," Sophie mused, "five days can seem an eternity. Wouldn't you agree, Camille?"

The heat climbed in Camille's cheeks.

Lazare suppressed a smile. "I imagine Rosier is feeling eternity stretch on ahead of him at this very minute. Shall we go?"

Once inside the carriage, Camille took her seat opposite Sophie, who remarked, "I see you'd prefer a different companion on your bench and I wholeheartedly approve."

"You are hopeless!"

"The opposite, in fact."

Lazare climbed in and closed the door behind him. He knocked on the ceiling and the horses stepped out and away. Flinging himself down beside Camille, he stretched his legs out in front of him. "A few minutes and we'll be there."

"It was kind of you to take us," Sophie said, "when we might have walked. Perhaps you might tell us why we're going to the workshop?"

He crossed his arms and grinned. "I really couldn't say."

Thwarted, Sophie yanked back the curtain and watched the streets roll by. Lazare shifted so close that his legs tangled in Camille's skirts. In her ear, he said, "Rosier hopes to—"

"What are you whispering?" Sophie asked. "It's rude to keep secrets."

"You want me to break my vow of silence?" He tried not to laugh. "Rosier will have my head."

Diverting the conversation, Lazare asked them what they had done while he'd been away, and told them stories about the latest crop of foals at Sablebois, and the vineyards that had been planted. As they talked, Camille luxuriated in the joy of simply being next to him again, the late summer unfurling in front of them like a grand map of adventure, her worries fading to a distant hum, inaudible over the carriage wheels whispering *soon, soon, soon.*

# 6

At the far end of the lane, a cobalt-blue door beckoned.

Above it, Camille knew, was written in faded letters: L'ÉCOLE DE DRESSAGE. To anyone else, it could very well be a riding school where students cantered around a dusty ring, practicing flying lead changes. But to her, it was a doorway into dreams.

Inside was pleasantly cool and dim. Overhead perched scores of slate-gray pigeons, and a few flapped into the air when Lazare opened the door. The packed-dirt floor was as it'd been when she'd first came to the workshop, but the viewing stand, once filled with failed balloon experiments, had been cleared out. The gaggle of judgmental seamstresses was also gone, though there remained, at one end of the long space, an uninflated balloon and two wicker gondolas, as well as a table piled with books and papers. In the middle of the riding ring stood a small stage, facing a row of chairs. From the way the red curtains bulged, something—or someone—stood behind it.

Questioningly, Camille looked at Lazare.

"Don't ask me! All I can say is Rosier's been hard at work."

*Odd.* Rosier was hardly one to be quiet about anything.

The curtains twitched and, as if he'd heard his name, Rosier appeared. As always, he seemed to be in perpetual motion. From his coat pocket protruded the stem of the pipe he always carried with him. His clothes seemed an afterthought, as if he were thinking of something much more exciting than what to wear, and without a hat, his light-brown hair curled exuberantly. But his dark eyes were as searching and clever as ever.

"Thank you for coming, all of you!" He made a particularly low bow to Sophie. "Welcome to my marvels!"

"Is it a play?" Camille asked.

"I will not prejudice your reaction with categories!" He gestured to the waiting chairs. "Please sit." Once they were settled, he clapped his hands. An ethereal tune, played on a violin, rose from behind the curtains as slowly, they drew apart, revealing . . . an empty stage.

"Oh!" Sophie's face fell.

"Merde!" Rosier exclaimed. "What am I saying—forgive my mouth! Forget this happened! Scenery is forthcoming. In the meantime, please *imagine* the backdrop: a row of trees, an ancient forest." Once more he clapped his hands, and two puppets emerged. They had painted papier mâché faces and wore colorful costumes that suggested the play was set in a distant and magical land. One puppet wore a pair of gilt paper wings tied to its back, the other carried a red rose. When they met in the middle, they bowed: first to each other, and then to the audience.

"Just wait!" Rosier said under his breath.

One of the puppets—a young man—produced a box and presented it to the other puppet, who was, judging by her long horsehair wig, supposed to be a young woman. When she opened it, a puff of smoke drifted from under the lid.

"Ignore," Rosier muttered.

"But what—?" Camille wondered.

"A firework. It'll work next time." He waved his hand at the puppeteers. "Continuez!"

The play continued. At times the characters spoke to each other, but Camille could not tell whether their speaking was part of the story or directions the puppeteers were giving each other, in which case, she should be ignoring them. As the violin played faster and faster, the players too sped up their actions, until, at a blistering pace, they gesticulated, danced, kissed, pretended to sail in a boat, and finally, after stripping off their masks and flinging them away, bowed low as the curtains swung closed on top of them. If puppets could have panted, they certainly would have.

"Bravi!" shouted Rosier, applauding enthusiastically. "Well done, well done!" To his audience, he said, "Did you not think so?"

"I've never seen anything like it," Lazare said, straight-faced. "What do you call it?"

Rosier beamed. "Les Merveilleux, naturally."

"The Marvelous Ones is a beautiful name," Camille remarked. Even if the show had not quite lived up to its name—not yet.

"What about you?" Rosier stooped solicitously by Sophie's chair. "Tell me your thoughts, Mademoiselle Sophie!"

Regretfully Sophie replied, "I may never have been to the Opéra or the Comédie-Française, but dear Rosier, if you plan to use these costumes, which should be beautiful but . . . are not . . . I'm afraid people will laugh. In the wrong way."

Rosier looked at the stage and muttered something inaudible.

"It's only his first attempt, Sophie." Seeing how he'd angled for Sophie's verdict, Camille couldn't help but defend him. There was perhaps more to this than she'd thought. "You always try out your hat designs in paper first, to see how they might be improved. Maybe this is like that?"

"That's true," Sophie demurred.

"A brilliant strategy! I should have done a paper trial long ago. I'd thought to take the show to the streets in a few weeks' time, but perhaps," he said significantly, "there is no point. With things so hard in Paris, I thought

I might bring a smile to the face of a child, a happy memory to an old lady, or perchance, a bit of the marvelous, the extraordinary—"

Lazare cleared his throat.

"Some hope," Rosier said, reining himself in. "That is the most important."

"An admirable goal," Sophie conceded. "What do you two think?"

"It has a great deal of promise," Camille said truthfully. "I'm certain it could be improved in time for a performance . . . in the near future?"

"But how?" Rosier wondered.

*How strangely he behaves*, Camille thought, but Lazare remained silent, as if he didn't want to break a spell. Finally Sophie spoke up. "I might have some ideas to improve the costumes. The rest . . ." She bit her lip. "It would take a lot of work."

"You are right to focus on their clothes!" For someone who was receiving a lot of criticism, Rosier seemed strangely glad. "I had aimed for a ragamuffin je-ne-sais-quoi, but clearly my aim was dreadful. With your eye for design, the show will be vastly improved. And you'd be bringing hope to our city."

Sophie beamed. "I am rather good at things like this."

"It's true, she is a great talent," Camille encouraged. "She even works wonders with tricolor stripes."

"That will *not* enter into this!" Glaring at Camille, she rose from her chair. "I can show you what's not working with the costumes right now, if you wish. It shouldn't take long."

"I would like nothing more!" Rosier said happily. "And it takes as long as it takes, n'est-ce pas?"

As they strolled together to the stage where the puppeteers held out the puppets for them to examine, Camille whispered, "Did he make it flawed on purpose, in the hope she would help him?"

Lazare's dark gaze met hers. "The things we do for love."

The way he was looking at her—sometimes it was almost too much to simply *sit* next to him. "And will hope make a difference with everything that's happening in Paris?"

"It's strange," Lazare mused, "but I distinctly remember being captivated by a girl who made a passionate speech about the power of hope to a packed audience at a salon. Wasn't that you?"

The corners of her mouth twitched. "It was."

Searchingly, he asked, "Something's bothering you, isn't it?"

"Yesterday I went to another bookseller." She tried to keep her voice light, but still, it wobbled as she remembered how hopeful she'd been. "He said my pamphlets were dull and no one would ever buy them."

"I know how frustrating it is to try something and not have it be good enough. Think of the balloon! But another bookseller will see the strength of your work, I know it. It's just a matter of time."

"But what if time is running out? There was a flower seller . . ." She dug at the dirt floor with the toe of her shoe.

"Where? What happened?"

"At Sainte-Chapelle. A wealthy man propositioned her. She was defiant, and he became enraged." Unbidden, her fear and anger came rushing back. "I stepped between them and told her to run. And she did, the mob he'd whipped up chasing her."

"No!" he said, shocked. "She escaped?"

She nodded. "But the nobleman made me furious!"

He had done more than that. He had made her see how close she still stood to the flower seller's precarious uncertainty. Not physically, for while they had the Hôtel Séguin and enough money in the bank, they were safe, but rather in her own head. There the everyday terror of not knowing if she would survive remained. That wound had not yet healed, for it was deep, and the flower seller's plight had exposed it. Though she and Lazare had spent hours talking in the garden and telling stories, this hurt wasn't one she wanted to share.

"You were brave, mon âme."

For a moment, but what then? How could she be satisfied with the little she'd done? "It wasn't enough. I helped her in that moment, but what about today? Tomorrow? *She* is the reason I keep trying to sell those pamphlets."

She looked up to see Rosier and Sophie standing in front of them, both looking strangely satisfied. "We're ready if you are?"

She hated to leave the workshop, where so many dreams had begun. As long as they stayed here, she thought to herself, everything seemed possible. But as they got to their feet, Lazare said quietly, "You must not give up. There will be another way, I know it."

The ride back to the Hôtel Séguin was all too short. Sophie had decided to take the puppets and their costumes home with her and the gilded wings would fit into the carriage only at an angle, separating Camille from Lazare. She wanted to ask him how he could say so confidently that there would be another way. Was it because that's how it had happened for him? Or was it because that was what he wished to believe? She thought of what he'd told her about his experiments: did he know from observation—or was it a hypothesis?

But separated from him by the puppet's wings, she couldn't ask. Instead she listened as Rosier animatedly proposed ideas for how to curl the female puppet's wig and better operate the curtains. In response, Sophie promised to come to the workshop a few times a week, and if she could, find a seamstress to sew new costumes for the puppets.

"I could not be more elated!" Rosier said. "You are truly a marvel yourself, mademoiselle."

Was that a blush that rose in her sister's cheek? "You must call me Sophie, if we are to work together."

Rosier's smile dazzled. "Now that is settled, and what with Lazare's new adventure unfolding—"

"What? You hadn't told us!" Sophie chided.

"I didn't have a chance!" From the other side of the wings, Lazare said, "Lafayette is creating a balloon corps—part of the National Guard. I'll be training the men who go up." He shifted in his seat to see over the wings. "Balloons are already being sewn. There will be four or five, two aeronauts each, both capable of piloting."

Sophie gave Camille a sharp kick under their skirts and a look that said, *Say something!* "It's very exciting, n'est-ce pas, Camille?"

"Very exciting!" she said brightly. And it was. Wasn't it? "What will you do?"

"We will be a small unit of observational balloons," he added. "Surveilling the borders, that kind of thing. Gathering information. Scientific, really."

"You'll be doing a lot of flying?" Camille tried to keep loss from tugging at her voice. Hadn't he just said he'd be staying in Paris with her?

"In the training, yes."

"Tell us, how did it come about?" Sophie asked.

"Could this be more in the way?" He shifted the puppet's wings and his gold-flecked eyes, framed by the swoop of dark brows, reappeared. "The Marquis de Lafayette made a surprise visit to Sablebois when I was there. He's an acquaintance of my father's and came to propose the idea of a balloon corps."

"How flattering!" Rosier observed. "The great man himself!"

Lafayette, Camille remembered, had been interested in balloons from the time she'd made her speech at Madame de Staël's salon. There he'd thrown his arm familiarly over Lazare's shoulders, guiding him away for a private talk about the military possibilities for balloons. "He can be very persuasive."

Lazare's mouth twisted in a wry smile. "So I discovered."

This wouldn't be the demonstration flights over Paris he yearned for, but it was something. Even if it meant he'd often be away from Paris, even if it meant their own journey over the Alps would be delayed, she wished this for him. But at the same time—knowing it was selfish—she couldn't help but feel as if an open door she'd been walking toward had suddenly closed.

"Will you invite us to the launch?" she managed to say. "I should like to see you go up."

Lazare shrugged. "If you wish. I'm guessing it will be a fairly ordinary send-off."

"If I have anything to do with it," Rosier scolded, "ordinary is the opposite of what it will be! And I cannot imagine that the Marquis de Lafayette will do anything halfway." As they neared the Hôtel Séguin, he outlined in enthusiastic detail a scheme by which the balloon corps could draw a large and celebratory crowd—"which would only cast you in the best possible light, Lazare. How impressed your parents will be—"

Suddenly the carriage shuddered to a halt not far from the Hôtel Séguin.

"Can you see what's happening?" Sophie asked.

Camille peered out. "A wagon carrying bricks has blocked the road."

A flicker of movement by the iron gates of the Hôtel Séguin caught her eye. It was a girl, gesticulating at the gatekeeper Timbault. While she pointed toward the house, he gestured angrily for her to leave. But the girl did not relent. There was something about the proud tilt of her head that Camille recognized.

Camille leaped to her feet.

Lazare half stood, tussling with the wings. "What is it?"

"I must speak to that girl—she's the flower seller I told you about!"

"Wait, I'll go with you—"

But she'd already flung open the door and, grasping as much of her dress in her hands as she could, leaped to the ground. She stumbled, caught herself, and raced to the gate. But by the time she reached it, the girl had vanished.

"Monsieur Timbault, what did she want?"

"She made no sense," Timbault grumbled. "Said you had something of hers. A tray? She said she needed it to sell flowers. Did I do wrong, madame?"

*Merde!* "She was telling the truth, but there was no way you could have known."

"She'll be back. That type always is."

He thought the flower seller a beggar, a cheat. Resentment flared inside of her. Imagine if Timbault knew how the mistress of the Hôtel Séguin had been living only a few short months ago. She was not at all certain the flower seller—proud, defiant, but also wary—would return.

She hesitated. The carriage door yawned open as if in surprise, filled with her friends' alarmed faces. Could she leave the others like this, with hardly an explanation? She could practically hear Sophie calling her reckless.

But it wasn't enough to stop her. For here was a mystery and a chance to do something right.

"Tell me, Timbault—which way did she go?"

# 7

The river, Timbault had guessed. Camille struck out toward the Seine, following the glow of the flower seller's yellow dress. Walking fast, the wicker tray now tucked tight under her arm, she soon left the aloof mansions of the Marais behind and was swept up in the evening crowd. Shadows crept around the leaning buildings and narrow lanes, and she kept well away from places where people might be hiding. Driven from the countryside by villagers and farmers, vagrants had come to Paris, restless and hungry.

Another piece of kindling laid on the fire.

Far ahead, the girl's yellow dress winked in and out of the crowd. She had nearly reached the old Tuileries palace. Like a castle in a fairy tale grown over with thorns, the Tuileries had stood empty for a hundred years, ever since Louis XIV had moved the court to Versailles. There was not much there but dusty pleasure gardens, where she'd walked with Lazare these last few weeks, and a makeshift theater. So many rooms, and no one to live in them.

At Camille's left hand ran the liquid pewter of the Seine. The river was a restless, quicksilver thing . . . even more so at night. Dredgers walked its shores, searching for drifting treasure to haul in with their hooked poles. Things cast away, on purpose or not. Wood and canvas, rope and netting, crates of vegetables tumbled from barges, a well-dressed corpse with pockets to pick—all this the river provided. Above it arched the great Pont Neuf. Even at night, the bridge was busy. It crawled with promenaders and police, pickpockets and prostitutes. Silver merchants sold their wares there, as did men who made wooden legs. Acrobats performed alongside letter writers, who composed love notes for a fee. It was a world unto itself, and Camille wasn't eager to cross it alone.

Too many hands.

But the flower seller didn't join the throngs on the bridge. Instead, she plunged down the bank toward the water itself. Camille followed as best she could, but the footing was treacherous. Once at the shore, she tramped up and down for a quarter of an hour before she finally spotted girl's yellow dress underneath the bridge. Did she have a hiding place there, tucked between a stone arch and the river's edge? Camille ground her teeth in frustration. If this is where the hunt for the flower seller ended, she was out of luck. She was not going beneath that arch.

As Camille took in the muddy flats, the cold, lapping river, the tray still under her arm, a window-shaped light came on under the bridge. Then another, glowing warmly. A dwelling, beneath the Pont Neuf. All Camille had to do was go there and give her the tray back. Then why did it feel so frightening?

It was only the deepening dusk, she told herself. Only the unknown. Still, she felt uneasy as she made her toward the two golden rectangles. At first she could only make out the weathered shutters around the windows. As she drew closer, the house's hunched outline became visible. It was wedged under the arch the way that bats shrugged themselves into the smallest spaces.

The house had no rhyme or reason, but had been cobbled together from bits and pieces that, she guessed, had been scavenged from the river's banks: mismatched shingles; doors fortified with boards; a circular window set into the roof that looked out on the river like the flat eye of a fish. Smoke drifted from its crooked chimney.

Tucked as it was out of sight, it felt secret and forbidden, like a house in a fairy tale no one was meant to see. As she took in the way the river had left a dark ribbon of silt on its walls from the peak of a flood tide, she tried to imagine what it would be like to live there. Threatened by floods and the traffic on the bridge. A last resort, a house fashioned from broken things no one wanted.

It made her want to leave the tray by the door and run.

Instead, she drew closer as she heard a murmur of voices coming from inside. The flower seller didn't live alone, then. Perhaps she lived with her family, though when Camille tried to imagine them, she couldn't. All she could think of was her own brother and how cruelly he'd forced her to use magic to turn coins. How carelessly he'd sent her out into the streets to spend them, knowing the risks she took.

What if it was the same for the flower seller?

There was no way she could turn and go.

Carefully she walked along the planks that led to the front door. As she hesitated on the doorstep, the house went completely silent.

She raised her fist to the door and knocked.

The door whipped open. A hand reached out, grabbed Camille hard by the wrist, and yanked her inside.

She stumbled into a lamplit room full of girls. Some were dressed in costly secondhand gowns that had been sliced to fit; others wore pants and jackets, their hair tucked up under a tricorne hat or cut boyishly to their shoulders. Some wore bright stockings and shoes, others were barefoot. A couple had tattoos twining from under their cuffs. Almost all were her own age.

"Let go," Camille cried, trying to twist loose from the girl's vise-like grip.

"Not until you tell us what you're doing here!" the girl said. She was strikingly beautiful in a red dress that set off her light brown skin, freckled from the sun. Her wary stare took in every detail of Camille's appearance, from her too-extravagant hat to the deep hem of muck on her green dress. The girl gave her arm a last vicious twist, forcing Camille to let go of the flower seller's tray. It dropped to the floor with a rattle.

"You stole Giselle's tray!" the girl cried.

"I haven't stolen anything," Camille blazed. "I brought it back *for* her!"

"Giselle!" one of the other girls called out. "Hurry and come here!"

At the back of the room, a curtain covering a doorway was flung aside and the flower seller emerged. Beneath her large, wide-set hazel eyes her pretty mouth fell open in a shocked O. "Dieu, Margot, let her go! That's the made-moiselle who saved me at Sainte-Chapelle the other day! Remember? When I was attacked by the nobleman who thought he could have me for a louis?"

The girl in the red dress frowned. "She hasn't come to throw us out?"

Another girl, tall and black-haired, laughed. "Doubt she's strong enough, Margot. It's going to take the cavalry to drag us away. That or they'll have to pry the house loose."

"She's the fancy girl?" Margot said to Giselle. "She's smaller than I'd imagined."

Beaming, Giselle strode over to Camille. "She is as fierce and brave as any of us." Gently she pried Margot's fingers off Camille's arm. "And see, she's brought my tray."

"My apologies, *princess*," Margot said gruffly, though she did not sound sorry at all.

Camille rubbed at her wrist as she took in her surroundings. While the outside of the house had filled her with foreboding, the inside of the house was not at all what she'd expected. Instead of stepping into a fearful room from her own past with her drunk brother holding sway, she found herself in a surprisingly cozy place. Beds and trundles and straw pallets hemmed the room, and a fine, if somewhat threadbare carpet covered the packed dirt floor. There were cheerful, mismatched flowered curtains at the windows, and the walls had been newly whitewashed. Hanging on them were tiny but beautiful ink drawings in chipped frames—portraits of the girls them-selves, Camille realized—as well as other small objects. Looking closely, Camille made out a door knocker in the shape of a bird and an unusual lock in the shape of an apple, its shank the apple's stem, the key that sat in the keyhole shaped like a worm. Between the rafters ran lines of laundry hung with red and white petticoats as well as a few printed sheets.

Camille murmured, "It's so different from how it looks on the outside."

"Sleight of hand," Giselle said, pleased. Picking up her tray, she lovingly brushed it off and set it behind a chair. "Thank you for bringing this to me. I cannot make my living without it. I thought your gatekeeper would have me arrested for asking for it!"

"He's very protective," she acknowledged. "But how did you know where I live?"

She laughed. "You're conspicuous, with your red hair and your big hats. All us girls know Paris inside and out—it wasn't hard to find you. I'm Giselle, by the way," she added. "What name do you go by?"

It was a good question. Neither her title nor her married name suited her at all. "Camille Durbonne."

"Well, Camille, welcome to Flotsam House!" she exclaimed. "I noticed you were looking at what's hanging on our walls. Those pretty portraits, they were done by our Henriette." She nodded at a small girl, blond and whip-thin, who stood by the stove. "Henriette makes things what they're not."

*Like a magician?* "What do you mean?"

Her small girl's voice was proud. "I can copy anything. A painting, a will, a contract. I can make it appear exactly as it was, but altered so it says what you need it to say. Odette says there will be paper money soon instead of coins. I can't wait."

*A forger.* Camille blinked. "Pleased to meet you."

"And the apple lock on the wall?" Giselle said. "That belongs to Claudine."

A girl with wavy brown hair, cut short like a boy's, made a bow, complete with a court flourish. "That lock was my father's, and it's very dear to me."

"Did he make it?"

Claudine nodded. "I would have learned how too, but—" She shook her head, as if shaking off a thought. "I didn't. I can slit a pocket or a purse before anyone notices, though." And then, from her other sleeve, she pulled a set of needle-thin knives in a tiny flannel case. "Mostly I pick locks," she said, with a dangerous smile. "I haven't met one in all of Paris that can resist me."

The others whooped.

"Who can resist *me?*" said a tall girl with olive skin and black hair who wore a costly dress with a plunging neckline. Fake diamond earrings swayed from her ears, a collar of the same clasped round her swan-like neck.

"Meet Héloïse," Giselle said. "Best pickpocket in Paris. Tell her how you do it, won't you?"

"Bien sûr! I walk comme ça. . . ." Héloïse took a few, hip-swaying steps. "Then—oh là là, pardonnez moi!—I bump into a rich man, my shawl falls aside . . . and while he's busy ogling, he's forgotten *all* about his purse." The others roared with laughter. Camille joined in, too. There was something extraordinary about them, their pride and determination.

"And you?" she said to the girl in the red dress who'd dragged her inside.

"I sell fruit, strawberries or oranges, depending on the season. Nothing *criminal*, in case you're wondering."

Giselle gave her a meaningful look. "You're selling yourself short."

"Well, I do have a few tricks." Margot's voice had a pretty lilt to it, an accent Camille didn't recognize. "I use ice to keep them fresh—Giselle does the same with her flowers."

"It's well done, Margot," Claudine the lock picker encouraged. "We must live by our wits, for what else do we have?"

"Speaking of which," Giselle said, waving forward the last girl, who'd hung back in the shadows, "here is our clever Odette. She stayed with us once when she was in trouble. Now she's on the up-and-up, but she still visits from time to time."

Camille bit back an exclamation. She'd seen her only once before, when Odette had been a starving girl fleeing barefoot through a crowded street, a tiny roll of bread in her hand, but she'd never forgotten her. Odette was much changed. She no longer looked as if she were stealing food to eat, and as she faced Camille with her hands on her hips, a proud defiance radiated from her. Where the thin, hungry girl Camille remembered had been painted with rouge, her feet bare under her petticoats, this new Odette was dressed in black, a plumed hat on her head, and most startling of all, wore a brace of pistols on a belt around her waist. Underneath her hat, she had Camille's vivid red hair and the same gray eyes, though hers were iron-dark.

"The two of you could be cousins," Margot observed.

"I suppose." Odette made no sign that she recognized Camille. And why should she? If she remembered Camille at all, it would be as someone who hadn't helped her when she'd needed it. Camille hoped Odette had forgotten her entirely.

"Odette won't be able to visit us much longer," Henriette remarked.

"Why, is something wrong with the house?" Odette asked. "Or are you tired of me?"

"Not with the house." Claudine jabbed an angry finger toward the door, as if a villain lurked outside. "With *them*."

"That's why Margot pulled you inside like that," Giselle explained to Camille. "We're worried people will see us coming and going."

"Why? Who would care?"

"The people who want to clean up Paris." Snatching a newspaper from the table, Giselle handed it to Camille. It was worn and soft from having been read many times. She tapped at an article toward the bottom of the page. "Read. Odette hasn't heard it yet."

Camille cleared her throat.

> *Such are the Troubles in the Countryside of France that Vagrants and Brigands have become all too Common and Dangerous. Having made Themselves Known to the police in the country for their Nefarious Deeds, they have come to create Trouble in Paris. Camped in Alleyways, Cemeteries, and under our Bridges, these Vagrants seek to Destroy the Rights of Parisians.*

"*Vagrants?*" fumed Odette. "Are we not all Parisians here?"

> *Therefore, under this Most Recent Decree, the dwellings of such Vagrants will be Removed, beginning with those under the Bridges, but especially those Defiling the Pont Neuf.*

Stunned, Camille said, "They're going to take your house away? But why?"

Odette's eyes blazed. "They think we're no better than rats! Les misérables, outcast and reviled. They'd like it better if we Lost Girls didn't exist. They'd rather have a fake city where everything is shiny and grand, rather than a real city with real people in it living their lives. They have got the idea of revolution all wrong," she added bitterly.

Margot nodded. "Yesterday a policeman hammered a notice to the house saying we're to be evicted in ten days' time."

*So soon?* "They cannot do this—"

"Ah, but they will," Odette said. "They have the power, and those with power do as they like. They bend everything to their desire."

"*I* won't be bent by them," said the pickpocket, Héloïse, as she drew her shawl close around her daringly cut dress. "We must find a way, if only for Céline."

"Our littlest," explained Giselle with a fond smile. "She's playing outside."

Eagerly the girls told her how they'd found Céline when she was tiny, climbing a pile of rubbish. And how, when she saw Héloïse in her fancy dress, she held out her arms and cried, "La Belle! Pick me up, Beauty!" They hadn't been able to resist her and had taken her home with them.

"She reads better than most girls of six," Henriette said proudly. "And she's been safe with us, until now."

"She's our heart and our hope." Anxiously, Giselle said, "But without a place to live . . ."

Anger flared through Camille. The newspapers were full of articles about changes that were coming, all the problems that the National Assembly would address. Thousands upon thousands of words, but not a single one about these girls. But surely anyone who might read about their lives—for Camille was certain that every girl there had a story to tell that would harrow readers' bones and wring their hearts—would be able to see that something must be done to save their house?

As she thought of their stories, she felt a sudden flicker of hope. "I know of something that might help—"

"Tell us, because if we have to live in the streets," Giselle said, "it will be terrible. People in Paris are hanging tinkers, beating up vagrants. Why, they would have killed me for refusing to sell my body to that nobleman if I hadn't escaped! And then there are magicians setting traps for children—"

*Even these girls believed that?*

"Those magicians are naught but rumor," Margot said airily. "I know what a sorcerer looks like, and I haven't seen one in Paris yet."

Camille exhaled. "But if you told your stories in a newspaper, people would see that you aren't vagrants and that you should stay in the home you've made." Wasn't that what she'd wanted herself, when her brother had taken everything and their landlady had threatened them with eviction? A place of safety that was her own.

Claudine crossed her arms. "How?"

"You'd tell your stories, people would read them—"

"Who'd we tell our stories to?" Héloïse asked. "Who's going to listen to us?"

"A newspaperman—"

Adamant, Giselle shook her head. "I've had enough of men to last me quite a while."

"Just listen," she pleaded. "There are newspapers that print three thousand copies—*Le Père Duchesne* prints eighty thousand. Imagine if fifty thousand people could read what was happening to you—"

Giselle's face pinched with doubt. "What if those fifty thousand decided we don't deserve anything? We aren't saints. Then we'd be worse off than before."

Perhaps. It would depend on how the stories were told. But she didn't have time to say that before Odette spoke up. "I know how these people are. It's too dangerous to reveal ourselves like that. They might arrest us all. And that would be worse by far than losing the house."

Camille's heart constricted. How would she convince them now? Odette had given voice to their fears, and murmurs of assent filled the room.

"Don't take it too hard," Giselle said. "It was nice of you to try to help."

She understood their fear that whatever they had was better than what was coming, because in their lives things never got better, only worse. Why ever would they trust her, a stranger? As she knew only too well, the cost of trust was high, and that of hope even higher.

There was nothing to do but go, and as quickly as possible. Trying to hide her disappointment, she could only nod at the girls, open the door, and take refuge in the riverbank's hazy gloom.

# 9

*victed*. Camille stormed along the shore, kicking at stones. The city had no right to throw them out of their home! Had the person who'd made this decision even given a thought to what would happen to the girls? Where they would live instead?

Without realizing it, Camille had reached up to trace the scar above her collarbone. She hadn't forgotten the shock of it, the hot spill of blood when Alain—*her own brother*—had cut her. She still remembered the snap of her head when he'd hit her, the endless drop of her fall. She'd had no choice but to use magic to save herself and Sophie: first la magie domestique, and then the more dangerous glamoire. These girls could steal and cheat to try to stay alive. But it wouldn't be enough.

Her jaw clenched. What was it Papa had always said? *Words are their own magic. Words make thoughts visible.* She thought of the press waiting in the dark—*what if?*—and then, like a punch, the bookseller's disdain and dismissal.

"Mademoiselle?" said a little girl's voice.

Camille stopped.

Holding out a hair ribbon to her was a little girl, her clothes neat but pretty, her toffee-colored hair carefully braided. "Did you drop this?"

"I did." Camille stooped until she was eye level with the girl. "But you may keep it, Céline."

"I didn't think you needed it, being as you look like a princess with your dress anyway," the girl confided. She spun it over her head so it fluttered in the wind. "I'm pretending it's a dragon that will set the Seine on fire."

"It must be a very powerful dragon!"

"A mademoiselle dragon," Céline said sagely.

"Of course it is." She couldn't walk away, not now. "Céline, I must speak to—"

"My sisters?" She held out her hand to Camille. As they walked, Céline described how the fire would be—*très belle, but no one would be hurt, because it would only be the river that was aflame and not the people nor the dragon*—until they reached Flotsam House and Giselle stepped out, a narrow silhouette in the lamp light. "Camille? Is something wrong with Céline?"

She had to try one last time. "I have an idea."

"Tiens, they don't want more ideas. We've decided to fight the eviction and if necessary, be taken away by force."

They would lose that fight. "Let me try, Giselle."

She sighed and opened the door. "You are persistent."

Back in the tiny cottage, the girls falling once more into mistrustful silence, Camille knew what she must do, even if in the end they rejected her. "Does anyone have a piece of paper? A pencil?"

"Why?" Margot asked.

"Just give it to her," Giselle said, irritated.

Margot reached up under her skirts and pulled out several sheets of paper. "What?" she said as the other girls laughed. "I get cold, standing in the arcade with my iced fruits!" The sheets were posters—one shouted

*WHO STEALS OUR GRAIN?* while the other complained *THE KING DOES NOTHING.* Their backs were blank. She handed them to Camille. "Because you're Giselle's friend."

Henriette said, "I've got something to write with, if that's what you need." In her ink-splotched fingers, the forger reluctantly held out a quill. "But ink's precious to me. Tell us what it's for."

Camille knew she couldn't get their trust for free. Coins couldn't be transformed from scraps of metal to heavy gold louis just by wishing. To work magic, one needed the power of sorrow.

"I wasn't always as you see me now. A *princess*, like Céline called me." Some of them smirked. Others frowned, suspicious. "Once, I was almost where you are." It was a part of her life she wished to put in a box and never open again. But she remembered Papa's words—*to try is to be brave*—and pressed on.

"My parents died of smallpox, and my little sister almost did, too. After that, my older brother couldn't stop drinking. He started gambling, and then he couldn't stop that, either." One of the girls swore under her breath. "Whatever my sister and I managed to save, he'd take. I wasn't afraid of him. Like you, I was afraid of losing our home and living on the streets. But it didn't matter how hard I worked, the cards stayed stacked against me."

She had felt so alone, working small magic and needing everything to change. Into that life had stepped Lazare—and also, a much more dangerous magic.

A few girls turned her way, listening.

Encouraged, Camille pressed on. "I was afraid of having to get money in ways I didn't like. I was afraid that if I died, my sister would be defenseless against him. To my brother we'd become *things*, something to trade away. He tried to erase me," she said bitterly. "He wanted me to stay silent. But you don't have to."

Odette picked up the newspaper and stabbed the air with it. "We don't want to talk to reporters."

"I could write your stories myself. I can't print eighty thousand copies. But I would do my best. Together we might change Parisians' minds." Ignoring Odette's wary scowl, she promised, "It would be done only with your consent. I'd write the first one and print it. After we saw how people reacted to it, if you didn't like it or felt it made things worse, that would be the end of it."

The room was still, the only sounds the snap of the fire and the idle lap of the river beyond the walls. The minutes dragged by and no one spoke. It was another resounding *no*. Behind her back, Camille clasped her empty hands to keep them from shaking.

"Giselle, you know where I live, if you change your minds." Heavy-hearted, she squared her shoulders and once more turned to leave.

"Wait." Giselle stepped forward. "I believe in you. You *saw* me. Everyone else at Sainte-Chapelle looked through me as if I was invisible. But *you* spoke up."

"And now you trust her with your life?" Margot asked, hurt coloring her voice.

Angrily Giselle said, "Camille stood up for me the way that you stand up for me. We're out of options, and I'm betting she can help us keep the house. Let me go first."

"Giselle," Odette warned. "You're not thinking this through—"

"I already have." She faced Camille then, full of fire and certainty. "I'll tell you what happened."

# 10

It was late by the time Camille returned to the forbidding Hôtel Séguin. As the door closed behind her, the housemaid Adèle came into the entry hall. Her eyes were saucer-sized. "Your shoes, Madame!"

What had once been a pretty pair of boots were now unrecognizable lumps thick with mud. Above them, Camille's stockings and petticoats were stained a vile, creeping brown, as if she'd been wading through a sewer.

"It doesn't matter," Camille said quickly. "Please don't go to any trouble." She hated the thought of someone cleaning them for her. And worse, with each moment that passed, Giselle's words threatened to slip away.

"Your sister has been worried—she wanted to send the young men to search for you through all of Paris!"

Guilt pricked at her. "But they didn't, did they?"

"Monsieur Mellais convinced her to let you go." Adèle flushed. "He said it was very important to you."

*My heart.* "He's right. And my sister—will you tell her I'm home?" Camille would have to apologize later. Wrenching off her shoes, she headed for the elegant doors that led to the dining room, where the printing press waited.

Adèle followed. "Madame, do you not wish to bathe? It's late to be working now, and in such a condition. You will most certainly become ill!"

Camille bit her lip. "There are girls living under the Pont Neuf who will be evicted if we do not help them."

"Under the Pont Neuf?" Adèle recoiled. "You will have contracted a terrible disease—"

"Adele, if you'd spoken with them, you'd say the same as I do, I am certain of it."

Mollified, Adèle curtsied. "If it's important to Madame, it is important to all of us at the Hôtel Séguin."

"I'm grateful for your support." Camille spun on her heel and set out once more to the printing room.

"Madame?" Adèle asked, trailing after her. "Is there anything I can do to help those girls?"

"May I have some coffee, please?" Camille opened the dining room doors and inhaled the dry scent of paper, the exhilarating wet bite of ink. How could she have thought she would give this up? Already her mind was shaping the words she would use to tell Giselle's story. "It would be a great help, for I have much work to do."


Pacing the length of the printing room, she reread the notes she'd taken when Giselle had told her story. A few of the girls had refused to listen. Others had crowded close, intrigued by the spectacle of Camille scribbling on a poster's back as Giselle's story unspooled to the tune of the wind humming along the seams of the patched-together house.

She'd felt so much while she'd listened to her story, but the notes turned out to be only the vaguest outline of what had happened. Journalistic facts she'd thought she needed to record. They didn't do justice to Giselle's pain and defiance and strength. But she didn't want to be sensational. Reality was bad enough. She would tell the truth, nothing more—but nothing less.

Leaning over the table, she scribbled a description of the house under the bridge, how it felt to be there, the city close yet a world away. But as she looked over what she'd written, she realized it was what *she* had seen. What *she* had thought. If their plan to convince readers that the girls deserved to live in Flotsam House was going to work, the pamphlet couldn't be made up of Camille's thoughts. Giselle herself had to speak.

Reaching into the upper case, she took out the type for the words that marched through her mind. Deftly, she set them into the tray, beginning at the upper right and facing them backward, working toward the left.

## THE LOST GIRLS SPEAK
## THE FLOWER SELLER

The skin on the back of her neck prickled and once again she had the disquieting feeling that the house was shifting itself to peer at what she did. She didn't know if metal type and ink and paper could convey the heartbreak of Giselle's words. But she would try.

### YOU MIGHT THINK
I was forced to make my living under the bridge.
I was not.  I  C H O S E  this place.

Camille stood back, surveyed the bold capitals. The short lines and the simple words felt right. They felt the way Giselle had spoken: not pitying or sentimental. None of the philosophical phrases Papa had woven through his writings, no references to long-dead authors or revolutionaries. Instead, it was simply *true*.

Now that she'd begun, her fingers couldn't set the words fast enough to keep pace with the stream of words she knew she needed to print.

My mother could not feed us all so handed us
away to those who could. My sister and I were given
as servants to the woman who ran the gambling den
nearby. We were but ten and eleven, what did we
know? We had no rights. No protection. Maman
thought she did well. But though we worked, we
never got paid. We were always hungry.

Camille wanted to leave a space there, for the long, angry pause Giselle
had taken before continuing.

It would be an extravagant use of paper, but what else was it good for?
She skipped three rows, enough to let her readers reflect—on Giselle, on
how they were lucky they were to live as they did—and began again.

The neighbor locked us in our rooms at night,
made us slaves in all but name. Anything we needed,
like a new chemise or hairpins, she sold it to us,
against the money we earned by selling flowers and
fruits to the patrons who came to gamble. We saw
quick enough we might die having never walked
outside again.

My sister and I promised each other we would flee
if we saw the chance. We vowed that if the chance
came, we wouldn't wait to tell the other one, but to
run and know we would be reunited on the outside.
Our meeting place would be the steps of Sainte-
Chapelle.

One morning I woke up and she was gone.

Giselle had been so strong, restrained, even, but when she'd told this
part of her story, she'd pressed the heels of her hands to her eyes, her mouth
a twist of pain. Then she'd set her narrow shoulders back and started again.

Dieu, how happy I was to know she had fled!
Two days later I too escaped, and the Lost Girls took
me in. We have our own home and the money I get
is mine to keep. Bien sûr, there are men who don't
understand a flower seller sells flowers, not herself,
but most days I manage.

For a long time I waited for my sister to find me.

Each day I walk around the high walls of Sainte-
Chapelle, searching for her, but she's never come.

I used to fear she died in that house, her body taken
out on a board in the night when I couldn't have seen
it. For how else would I not know my sister had gone?

But now I believe she did escape and she found a
better place. Even if it means she cannot come to me,
I'm happy as long as

SHE LIVES FREE

The tiny hairs on Camille's arms rose as she reread the last line. Any
other time, she would wait until morning to check the type, and then print
under natural light to make sure it was right. For candle glow could play
tricks on the eye.

But the eviction notice was a relentless clock, and the story was a fever,
burning in her hands. She couldn't wait. She blackened the type until it
gleamed and carefully set a sheet of paper down over Giselle's words.

"Please be right," she said out loud to the empty room. "Be perfect. Persuasive." Pulling hard, she brought the lever down to press the paper into
the inked type—and winced. The edge of the metal plate had caught her
hand. It was hardly worth noting, more of a pinch than anything. There was
only a thin red line of blood.

But in the room, something shifted. The way a cat's ears prick at a scratch in the wall. The way someone bends close to listen. In the tray, the blackened letters glistened as if alive. As if they might peel off the press and wing away.

She was getting tired, she knew. Should she leave it for tomorrow? Sophie would say to rest. But Lazare had stood up for her. She wanted to prove he'd been right.

Besides, she didn't know if she *could* stop. She felt compelled.

She stepped back and held up the sheet. Even in the weak light she could see there was blood on it. Her cut had started bleeding again. *Merde!* Binding her hand with a clean rag, she was about to toss the bloodied page on the fire when, out of the corner of her eye, the words on the paper *wavered*.

Shadows slid like spilled ink across the page.

The letters swam, gleaming like fish surfacing in the Seine. And as the shadows ran, she saw in them images, like oil on water. Now the old Pont Neuf, now the running-away river, the carved-out hollows in all the girls' cheeks. But also glimmers of hope: the gold light of the stove the girls gathered around, little Céline with her ribbon at the water's edge, Giselle's trust in Camille. They were so real she reached out to touch them—before they vanished as if they'd never been.

The room flared back into being. There was the fire, throwing off smoke, making the room smell of ash and cinder. She'd only imagined the pictures, she told herself. It had only felt like magic.

She hung the wet sheet on a line. It swayed there for a moment, and though she was her harshest critic Camille could see it was perfect. Beautiful, clear, and compelling. But would it be enough to be noticed in the deluge of pamphlets and newspapers flooding Paris? Enough to persuade the public to help the girls stay?

It *must* be.

It was past midnight now, and she still had so much to do.

All night Camille worked by candlelight. When she finally left the dining room, the tapers had dwindled to stumps and only a few hours remained before dawn. Unsteady with fatigue, she paused in the gloomy hall and rested her forehead against the doorway. The cat Fantôme appeared in the gloom and pressed against her skirts. Around her the house settled and creaked and whispered its ancient magic, and it bothered her less than it had before. She imagined there was something approving in it, the way it seemed to amplify what she was doing. For it was almost as if she could hear the ink drying, the sheets of paper rustling in their impatience to make their way into the streets.

At her escritoire, Camille scribbled a note to Adèle, asking her to make certain the pamphlets were taken to the bookseller Lasalle in the morning. It was a risk. He hadn't exactly asked for more pamphlets, but he was the only one who'd offered anything like encouragement. And then she stumbled up to her room, tore off her filthy dress, and collapsed into sleep, more tired than if she'd been gambling through the night at Versailles.

# 11

Begrudgingly, Lasalle promised to try selling the pamphlets. But the note he'd sent to Camille had been curt, offering no guarantees.

It was so hard to wait. It made no sense to print more, since she didn't know if they would sell, and when, later that morning, Adèle announced that Monsieur Mellais was in the hall, she rushed down the grand staircase to greet him. As it happened, he was on his way to meet with Lafayette and had only stopped in to make certain she was well after her adventures last night. She told him what had happened and asked if he hadn't been worried.

"I, worried?" he replied nonchalantly, though Camille thought she detected a shadow of concern in his face. "You are a wonder, mon âme. This pamphlet will be the one that does it," he said before he kissed her hand good-bye. "I know it."

But as she watched him go, his long strides eating up the distance to the street, she wasn't at all certain.

The next day delivered no note from Lasalle. To stay busy, she went with Sophie to Le Sucre. Sitting in the pink-and-white room that had once been a sweet shop, she listened to gossip while she pleated blue, white, and red ribbons for the revolutionary corsages that were so in demand that Sophie and her seamstresses could hardly keep up. In the afternoon, when Sophie went to the workshop to help Rosier with the puppet costumes, a secret smile on her lips, Camille hurried home to rifle through the letters in the silver salver.

Rien.

Failure gnawed at her. Just as relentlessly, she pushed it away.

On the morning of the third day, there was still no news. Determined not to think of it, she wrote a note to Lazare, inviting him for a drive in the Bois de Boulogne. As she dropped sealing wax onto the folded paper, the afternoon unfurled dreamily in her mind: she and Lazare in an open carriage, a picnic basket tucked at their feet, the sun dancing in a lapis sky. Just the two of them together, shoulder to shoulder, nothing to interrupt or pull them apart. And later, beneath a willow whose trailing branches curtained them off from the rest of the world, there would be a blanket spread on the grass, food and drink almost forgotten as everywhere thrummed the drowsy hum of late-summer bees, Lazare stretched out beside her, leaning on his elbow, laughing, his amber-flecked eyes so close, so close she might almost—

But a note came back with his regrets.

He was preparing for the aeronauts' training that afternoon and could not get away. He wrote: *Forgive me. Another time, mon âme. As soon as we can—for where you are concerned, I am loath to wait.* She bit back her disappointment. Unsettled, unable even to sit by the courtyard fountain with her new gothic novel, she printed off another five pamphlets, the ink liquid and darkly enticing. Not that there was a need for more. For all she knew, the entire stack of pamphlets was being used to light candles at Lasalle's.

She had just finished another set when Adèle appeared at the door, carrying a letter. "Madame? This arrived for you."

Apologetically, Camille held up her ink-stained hands. "Could you tell me who it's from so I know if I should read it now?"

"Oh! It's from the bookseller," she said eagerly. "Madame, is it about the girls?"

"I hope so." Quickly Camille wiped her hands on her apron. Across the letter marched Lasalle's firm handwriting. Taking a deep breath, she cracked the seal and unfolded the paper. Despite the large sheet, the note was surprisingly short.

>  *Early sales promising; send more.*
>  *–Lasalle*

She smiled so broadly that Adèle couldn't help asking, "Good news, I hope?"

"Incroyable! He wants more of the pamphlets—can you believe it?" She'd have been happy to know he had sold a few. That strange fever that had come over her when she was working . . . it must have been the feeling that things were coming right. She'd believed the pamphlet was good, but this? The news was dazzling, like wishing for a ten of spades and having it dealt right into her hand.

Adèle beamed. "But that's wonderful! Shall I send Daumier with the new ones?"

She nearly said yes. "I'll go. But there's something else you might do."

Just as she was heading into the courtyard with a basket of food Adèle had packed and a bundle of pamphlets snug under her arm, Camille collided with Rosier.

"My apologies!" he exclaimed, flustered. He swept off his hat with a bow. He had abandoned his odd, flopping hat for a smart tricorne, and carried his pipe in one hand and in the other, a swoop of pink cabbage roses. "Are you all right?"

"Of course," Camille assured him. "I'm quick on my feet."

He regarded her carefully. "Going out?"

She patted the basket. "I was about to take these pamphlets to the book-seller."

"I am well aware of your latest and most extraordinary pamphlet—Sophie has already told me about it! Which is why I came to show you this—take a look." Giving her the roses to hold, he extracted from his pocket a rolled-up newspaper and unrolled it with a snap. "See? Your pamphlet is quoted here."

"But it's only been a few days." She stared at the tiny print. It was a very small mention in a rectangular box at the bottom of the page. Taking the paper from him, Camille read it aloud. "'Camille Durbonne—'"

"How daring you are to use your real name!" Rosier remarked. "Why not sign yourself Anonymous like so many other pamphleteers?"

She'd had enough of disguises and pretending. "Jean-Paul Marat uses his own name. And Giselle was willing to say so much. If they are brave enough to reveal themselves, then so must I be."

Rosier raised an approving eyebrow. "Continue."

"'Madame Durbonne,'" she began again, "'has done Something Extraordinary.'" Her breath caught. "Oh, Rosier!"

He beamed. "Read on, read on."

She wanted to rush through, inhaling it, but she made herself read slowly. "'She has given us a True and Authentic Insight to a Girl of the Streets, as if We were sitting just opposite Her, such that any Reader might understand the Sadness and Pain of a Girl's Plight and how she came to be Where She Is, through No Fault of her Own.'" *Through no fault of her own*—that was exactly what she'd hoped to show. "'Told in Plain and Moving Words, the Flower Seller's story would Convince Anyone that Something Must be Done. Who are We if the Sorriest Among Us receives no Aid?'" Camille frowned at the last line. "'The sorriest among us' goes too far. Don't you think? The girls are so clever and determined."

"My thoughts exactly. But don't stop, the final sentence awaits."

Finding her place, she read, "We anticipate the Next Story, and Hope that the Intrepid Writer will succeed in Convincing the People of Paris to Prevent the Razing of the Lost Girls' home. WE are Convinced."

"There!" exclaimed Rosier. "Good, non?"

It was so good she could hardly believe it. It was the kind of good that made the sky seem bigger. "Can you imagine if we managed to change the tide, Rosier? The girls might keep their house and their independence. And then—who knows what else could happen!"

"Brava! Keep going. You will be a star in the firmament of literary Paris, I know it."

Seriously, she said, "It is the girls' stories that matter, Rosier."

He waved his pipe at the idea. "Of course, of course. But some small credit must be due to the one who does the writing, non? I have always sensed it—first, Jeanne d'Arc of the Air! And now—Jeanne d'Arc of the Seine?"

"More like Jeanne d'Arc of the Mud," she said, remembering her ruined shoes, "but thank you, Rosier." She looked at him more carefully: smartly tied cravat, clean suit, on his coat an elegant tricolor rosette just like the ones Sophie made—there was a new brightness about him. "You haven't said why you've come."

"To deliver the newspaper to you, naturellement, and the flowers to your sister before we go to her shop. She has preliminary costumes for Les Merveilleux to show me and claims they're much better than what I'd come up with. There is no doubt about that."

"I think I heard her upstairs—shall I let her know you're here?"

"Not at all! Beauty takes its time. But I'll relieve you of the flowers."

Before handing them to him, Camille brought them to her nose, inhaling scents of jasmine and clove. "She will love them."

"Will she?" Rosier mused. "Or will she stick them in a vase with bouquets from all her other admirers?"

It had taken only one ride, two weeks ago, among the jostling, peacocking crowds at Longchamp before the invitations piled up for Sophie. Last week alone her presence had been requested at an English tea, a midnight dance, a card party: every hostess in town wanted to display this pretty mademoiselle who'd sprung up from nowhere to live at the mysterious Hôtel Séguin. "They think us wealthy," Camille had said in Sophie's ear one night. "And what of it?" her sister had said with a toss of her head. "Is anyone who they really are? I for one wish to enjoy it."

To Sophie's credit, she didn't repeat the error she'd made with Séguin. Shrewdly she saw through the dull, rich suitors as well as the handsome ones who had nothing more than charming manners to their names. The Marquis d'Auvernay, as she'd said to Lazare, was wealthy in every way, for he had youth, money, looks, and intelligence. But he hadn't yet asked for Sophie's hand.

"No one's proposed, if that's what you mean."

Rosier's eyes lit. "Just what I wished to know! Bien sûr, I know I am a long shot. But as long as there's a chance, I will keep trying."

Camille hoped he would. After her visit with Rosier yesterday, Sophie seemed happier than she had in a long time. "Bonne chance, dear Rosier. I will be cheering you on."

Once she'd left most of the pamphlets with Lasalle—who had *bowed* to her, who had no pamphlets remaining, who had all sorts of questions about what she might write next—she made her way to the river. It was midday and a few of the girls were sitting on a bench tucked close to the wall of the little cottage.

"It's our Printing Princess!" exclaimed the fruit seller, Margot, as she rose to usher Camille inside. "Has she brought something for us, Céline?"

"Come see!" Camille set the basket down on a worn table in the center of the room. The girls crowded around, lifting up the linen and pulling out bread and pastries, lemonade and cider. Giselle was quick to hand the prettiest pastry to Céline, who had to stand on her toes to peer inside the basket.

"Thank you, princess," said Céline with her sweet lisp after she took a bite.

"You are all very welcome to it," Camille said. She didn't even care if they called her princess, she could hardly keep the smile from her face. "Do you know what's happened? The pamphlets are selling so well the bookseller has asked for more!"

"Giselle's pamphlet?" asked Claudine the lock picker, dressed as before in pants and a boy's coat.

"Voilà." Camille held up a copy. "Giselle's story."

The flower seller stared as if Camille had suddenly produced an elephant. "Truly? May I see?"

"I'll read it for you," said red-haired Odette, rising from her chair. Taking the pamphlet from Camille in her ink-splotched hands, she examined it carefully, then raised it to her nose. "Freshly printed."

"Odette's our writer," tiny Henriette the forger said proudly. "Always thinking."

"What do you write?" Camille asked, but Odette was already climbing onto a stool. Outside a river barge sailed by, sounding a horn. Odette waited for silence before she began. In her rich, commanding voice, the story unfolded, tragic but shining with Giselle's love for her sister, and her hope.

As Giselle listened to Odette read, powerful emotions crossed her face. Though it was her own story, she looked as if she were hearing it for the first time. As if a play had been made of her life, and she was watching it.

Camille's throat ached with happiness. It was powerful to be seen.

When Odette finished, no one said anything. The noises of the city and the plash of the river felt very far away. "Well, what do you think?" Camille asked Giselle.

Giselle considered. "Until you asked me to tell it, I didn't think I had a story. Or a *life*, the way people say. What happened to me was only a jumble of things, all of them bad, and people who did cruel things. But hearing it written out in my own words," she said, her voice catching, "I see it wasn't my fault what had happened to me. And despite what they did, I *survived*."

*Survive* was a word with edges, rough and strong and powerful. Tiny Henriette began to clap, and when the others joined in, Giselle took a little curtsey.

"You too, princess!" Céline demanded.

Camille obliged. "There's something else."

"Will wonders never cease?" Odette asked.

Her sharp questions hurt. Camille doubted Odette would ever accept her, but she told herself it didn't matter. She unfolded the newspaper and pointed to the column that praised the pamphlet. "People are already becoming convinced it would be wrong to evict you."

"Truly?" Giselle said. "How quickly it's happening!"

It was happening almost too fast, like dry wood catching fire. Like magic. But she would not let it worry her. "Imagine this. If we printed a few more stories and made it a series, it would be like a chorus. Many voices are more powerful than one. And since the first one is selling so well, people might pay in advance for a subscription to the rest to make sure they got the next one as soon as it was printed. The money would be yours." She paused, remembered again the uncanny certainty she'd felt as she'd printed the first one. This could work, but she needed them to believe. "Is there anyone else who might—"

"Me." The forger Henriette, with her cloud of pale hair, stepped out from behind Odette. "I'm next."

# 12

That night the doors to the printing room yawned open, as if waiting for her.

Inside it reeked of ash, stronger than before. Pamphlets telling Giselle's story hung from lines running crisscross along the ceiling, more than she had remembered printing. It was no mystery why they were selling. The design—the striking way the letters were laid out, the amount of breathing room—was part of it. But there was something else in them, even beyond Giselle's story. A kind of dark allure.

A few nights ago, she'd blamed what she'd seen on her fatigue. That the fire smoked. That she'd been imagining things. Now the worry she'd buried when talking with the girls returned: there was something unnatural about what was happening.

The old house was woven through with magic, but whatever was happening in the printing room was new. Only when she'd printed the story about Giselle had she felt it: a shift, like the air crackling before a storm. There had been the blood from her hand on the paper. And, she remembered, with a creeping horror, she'd made a wish: that the pamphlets be entrancingly perfect.

Magic, she knew, compelled. It was one of the first lessons she'd learned: how magic, worked with sorrow's fuel, made things irresistible. The more time she'd spent at Versailles, the more the courtiers had fêted her, the palace's hundred doors welcoming her to parties and games. Even the magic Chandon had used to cheat at cards had a persuasive glamour to it: he nearly always won, yet everyone still clamored for the privileging of losing money at his table.

*No,* she told herself, *it wasn't like that.* Magic was no longer something she did.

But as she began to set the type for Henriette's story, the strange fever rose despite her intentions. This time she resisted, imagining that she pushed away the scorching tide. Sweat pricked on her forehead and her upper lip. Her fingernails dug into the wood of the press as she tried to resist the fever's pull.

"Get away," she said out loud. But it only came on stronger, racing along her skin, hot and cold at once, urging her on. Once she began to work, the type seemed to leap between her fingers.

*Too fast. Too easy.*

She hesitated again, a handful of type clenched in her fist. As her arms trembled from the strain of holding back, she wondered: *Too fast for what?*

Too fast to save the girls from the streets? Too easy, when what they and others like them faced was violence and misunderstanding? They stood to lose so much.

But what if she was working the pamphlets with magic? No matter how she sometimes secretly yearned for it, for magic to fill the hunger it had once carved into her, she would not return to it—blood and craving and destruction.

The voice in her head whispered: *Does it truly matter? You could do so much good.*

She thought of Rosier and his marvels, his dream to bring hope to the people of Paris. What she was doing wasn't that different, she told herself. But what would Sophie think, who'd always hated magic? And Lazare, who reviled it?

If she had learned anything from what had happened in the spring, it was that magic brought unforeseen consequences. Whatever she did now—used this strange new power or turned away from it—would change the path she stood on.

She did not know how to make the choice.

Sharp pain made her nearly drop the handful of type. Tiny marks showed red where the type had bitten into her flesh. For an unsettling, dizzying moment, she imagined turned coins gleaming in her palm.

For the thousandth time, she regretted how little she knew about magic. Maman, either reluctant or afraid to tell her any more than she absolutely needed to know, had left her in the dark, and Chandon, who knew so much, was unreachable at his estate. His magic had always seemed dazzling but ordinary, used mostly for cards. But who else could she ask? She'd write to him for help.

But that could take a week. And the girls didn't have a week.

It would be perilous to wait.

Magic or not, whatever would follow, she must set the type into the frame and tell these stories. They would be bricks in a wall to shelter the girls. It was what she'd so desperately wanted.

Just because the type burned like embers in her hand didn't mean she had to stop.

# THE LOST GIRLS SPEAK
# THE FORGER

## I WAS THREE YEARS OLD WHEN
## MY TALENT WAS DISCOVERED

Forgery was not what I thought I was doing when
papers were laid before me and I was told to copy
them. At first, it was P L A Y. Then I began to think
myself very fine. An A R T I S T. For wasn't I doing
what all artists did? Copying nature or copying a
letter, what was the difference? When I was seven
I would sit on a high stool in the apartment of my
father's distant cousin, who I discovered, later, was
a forger himself. By twelve I was better than he was.
I was like an apple tree to him, something he could
pluck for its fruit. He planned to marry me, though it
would be more accurate to say B U Y M E, and keep
me working for him.

My hard work, stolen.

I don't blame my parents. We were all so hungry.
They believed I would be taken care of by the man
who had taught me everything I knew. Almost
everything. But I was only twelve years old. Two
days before the wedding, I despaired. I walked into
the river with stones in my apron.

The Lost Girls who live under the bridge stopped
me. Instead of dying, they said, I might pretend I

was dead. So when a corpse washed up on the banks of the Seine, its hair like mine and its face half-gone, we dressed it in my clothes and filled the apron with stones again, in case he came looking. And then we pushed that copy of me into the water.

IT SANK. I ROSE.

# 13

While Camille was caught up in the strange magic of telling the girls' stories, Les Merveilleux had become decidedly more marvelous.

If Camille mistakenly called it a circus, she got a scowl from Sophie and a lecture from Rosier. Jabbing the air with his unlit pipe, he implored: "S'il te plaît, don't say circus! Say instead: An Amazement! A Spectacle!" In only a week, it had transformed from something like a puppet show put on by street urchins hoping to earn a few sous to something resembling a dream. A fairy tale, all glitter and beauty, but with darkness underneath. At first, Sophie had insisted that the costumes all be red. But Rosier felt it was too bloody. "Is there not already too much gruesomeness in Paris?"

Only the most radical of revolutionaries would disagree.

Yesterday a frightened Adèle had told Camille a vagrant had broken into a house two streets over. A mob then dragged him into the street. When the police arrived, nothing was left but an arm torn off at the shoulder, its sleeve slick with gore. The girls too might be called vagrants, and it set Camille's heart uneasily racing. After she'd comforted Adèle, she wrote to Lasalle, demanding to know if he'd heard anything about the girls' eviction. There were only a few days left before they'd be out on the street. *People do care*, he wrote back. *The pamphlets are a wonder. Send more stories. Subscriptions growing. Speaking to a friend in the mayor's office tomorrow. News when I have it.*

And so the red costumes had been sent back to Le Sucre to be reused in tricolor sashes and something new had been invented. Today they'd gathered at the workshop for its unveiling.

The puppet theater had grown, as had the height of the curtains. As they slowly parted, light snow made from tiny pieces of silver paper began to fall. The puppets came out, one by one, seeming to float in their white costumes. They too were taller, nearly the height of human beings. Behind the two lovers—or so Camille thought of them—lumbered a bear puppet, its large head swaying from side to side, snow sparkling in his fur. It was enchanting. And slightly spooky, which was just the effect, Sophie declared, she'd intended.

"They are beautiful," Camille said. "The girl reminds me of a swan."

"Hopeful as a blank slate?" Rosier said as he admired one of the puppet's feathered wings. "A vision of the future?"

"Exactement," Sophie said, pleased.

"And the story?" Lazare asked.

"Too abstract!" Rosier consulted his notebook. "We are rewriting it."

"We're moving the story to the forest, in winter. Do you remember, Camille, the masquerade at Versailles? That woodland feeling," Sophie said dreamily, "is what I hope to achieve. A feeling of being transported to a place that's familiar, but more beautiful."

"What's next for Les Merveilleux?" Lazare wondered.

"We perform at the Palais-Royal very soon," Rosier informed them. "Imagine the audience we will enrapture there! Huge crowds! People from all walks of life! The word of mouth alone will be extraordinary."

Camille glanced at Lazare. Perhaps she could tear him away from his balloons to attend? "When will it be?"

"When it's ready." Rosier winked at her. "I am usually all for rushing, but not in this case."

Outside the workshop, the sky had darkened. Ragged edges of pewter clouds gathered behind church towers and spires, threatening rain. A cool wind smelling of moss and stone buffeted the russet chestnut leaves strewn along the rue Saint-Antoine. Camille tucked her arm around Lazare's elbow, using the excuse of the sudden chill to draw closer to him. He walked with his hands in his coat pockets, a pensive turn to his mouth.

"What's wrong?" Camille asked. "Do you not find Les Merveilleux as marvelous as the lovebirds do?"

"Lovebirds?" he said, surprised.

Rosier and Sophie strolled up ahead, their heads angled toward each other.

"Something's changed," Camille said conspiratorially. "She hasn't been out with her suitor, the Marquis d'Auvernay, in at least a week, and this morning she told me she's letting her seamstresses make the revolutionary trims so she can have more time to work on the costumes. She loves designing them. Perhaps that will lead to something?"

Up ahead, Sophie laughed, sweet and bright.

He gave her a swift look. "What's to say it hasn't already?"

"Touché," she acknowledged as a large orange leaf sailed by her shoulder. "Tell me—are the balloons ready for the launch?"

"Just as I was about to ask you about the Lost Girls! I won't be diverted, you know."

"You must promise to tell me about the balloons after. It's been going very well, and Lasalle has promised to take up their cause with a friend in the mayor's office. Though he needs to hurry." She explained that it was becoming a series, and he listened intently as she recounted the details of Henriette's forger life. "Like Sophie with her costumes," Camille said, "Henriette is a true artist. Can you imagine if she had a chance to do something more—portraits, perhaps, like Vigée Le Brun, who paints the queen?"

"Why not? Aren't these revolutionary times, when who knows what doors might open? What you are doing is extraordinary, mon âme." He reached out and gently tucked a wayward curl beneath her hat. "*You* are extraordinary."

Heat warmed the place where his finger had grazed her skin. "It's the least I can do, with what I have," she said modestly, but secretly she was pleased. Seeing herself in his eyes was intoxicating. Not simply because it was Lazare—his burning touch, the promises she sensed behind his words—but because in his eyes she was who she wished to be. Not a starving girl who'd used destructive magic to survive. Not a girl feverishly printing pamphlets in a magic-filled, malevolent house, avoiding thinking about the consequences.

"Now you must tell me what's happening with the balloon corps."

He kicked at the fallen leaves so they sailed into the air. "Do you remember what Lafayette said at the salon?"

"He proposed to make military use of the balloons. I also remember how you reacted."

"Hotheadedly, I bet," he said in an off-hand way. "He came to the training for the new pilots I held the other day."

Overhead, the chill wind rattled through the trees. "He doesn't mean to send you to war—"

"In a balloon?" Lazare frowned. "I doubt it. He worries about unrest. Here in Paris, of course, but also at the borders. As the king hesitates, calculating how to respond to the Assembly's demands, other countries think of invading or plotting to help the king and queen flee. Austria might do it."

"You'd said the balloons would be used for surveilling. Does that now mean . . . spying?" She could not put her finger on it, but there was something unsettling about the whole affair, like the nap on a jacket brushed the wrong way.

"Gathering information," he corrected. "Which reminds me." He smiled then and it was as if the sun had come out. "He's promised every team will take measurements when they go up."

*That sounded more promising.* "What kind?"

"Barometric, atmospheric . . . it's the clouds that interest me. Do you remember them in the distance when we went up together the first time? Or the way they were when the balloon plummeted to the ground, only to be saved at the last minute by a brave and lovely girl?"

"Storm clouds," she answered. She would never forget their speed, nor the drenching rain that fell.

"They intrigue me because they're always changing. One day, who knows? We might have the ability to predict the weather. Imagine how it would help the farmers and sailors—all of us. My theory is that clouds are like the play of emotions across a face"—his gaze went to her cheeks, then dropped to her mouth—"and can tell us what forces are behind changes in the sky."

Camille flushed. "Are you saying I am easy to read?"

"Not at all." Some shadowy emotion moved over Lazare's face and was gone.

She smiled up at him, though her thoughts circled back to Lafayette's plans. "But if the balloons *were* used for spying at the border, where there was unrest, you would not have to go, would you?"

"I'm pleased to see that doesn't make you happy." He tucked her hand tighter around his arm. "I will stay in Paris. Firmly on the ground."

It made her glad, though a knowing voice inside whispered: *feet on the ground does not sound at all like Lazare.*

"A few more training sessions and then Lafayette hopes to demonstrate the balloons on the Champ de Mars. He wants it to be a success. Rosier will be pleased. We'll finally have the big balloon spectacle he's always wished for."

"But that's wonderful—"

"It is." But he did not look at her.

"I was wondering," she said lightly, "your father's friendship with Lafayette—"

"Camille!" Sophie was racing toward them, her hand clamped to her hat to keep it from blowing off. Behind her loomed the open space of the Place de Grève, half-full with a jostling crowd. "It's the king!" she shouted. "Hurry, you two! They are saying he will make a speech!"

# 14

"Vive le Roi!" someone shouted.

Louis XVI, king of France, shuffled toward the front of the stage. At Versailles, courtiers snidely said that when he wasn't wearing court finery, Louis could be mistaken for a gardener. But today he had dressed the part. Across his creamy gray suit was wrapped a wide blue sash, the Cordon Bleu. Lace fluttered at his thick throat and pinned to his coat, next to a silver star, was a tricolor cockade just like the ones sold at Le Sucre. His hair was tied with a plain black ribbon, as if he were a man of the people. But everyone knew he ate two chickens for breakfast and gorged on delicacies starving Parisians could only dream of.

Shouts rippled through the crowd as Marie Antoinette appeared behind him. She wore a saffron silk gown à la française, embroidered with sprays of tiny white flowers. Simple, but costly. Her hair was gray, but not from powder, and the radiance of her skin, which had been the envy of the court when she was a girl, had faded. Séguin had kept her looking young with his magic, but now that he was dead, it was as if all of the sorcery he'd lavished on her had vanished. She now seemed no different than anyone else.

"The queen is much changed," Camille remarked. "I can't understand why she would have come."

Lazare wondered, "And of all the squares in Paris to choose the Place de Grève, with its terrible history?"

"I can't think it an accident," Rosier remarked as someone onstage called for the people's attention. "In any case, we are about to find out."

From the stage, the king blinked at the crowd. A tall, pale-faced man, dressed in black and wearing a red cloak that billowed behind him, handed the king a piece of paper. The wind snatched at it, threatening to tear it away.

"Our people!" he read. "How happy we are to be in Paris with you! We have been too long separated."

Applause and jeers jangled in the square. "Send your wife back where she came from, the Austrian whore!" someone yelled.

"As the National Assembly does its crucial work," the king intoned, "we have come to Paris, in our duty as the father of our people, to warn you of a great danger." Camille could feel the crowd's attention sharpen. The king must have felt it too, for as if overcome with emotion, he pressed a heavy hand covered with rings against the rich fabric of his coat. "My people, listen! There are dangerous, traitorous magicians who dwell in our midst."

The crowd rumbled, low and ominous.

The king's words echoed in her ears. What could he mean?

"For centuries France has lived with this plague of magicians. Our great-grandfather, Louis XIV, was the first of our family to fight them." The king puffed out his chest. "He could not bear that they preyed on the blood of honest and hardworking French people, worse than any feudal lord or aristocrat."

A wave of revulsion rolled over Camille. Chandon had told her that magicians—perhaps even her own ancestors—had tortured the poor to gain their sorrow. Just like Séguin, they'd done it to lessen magic's toll on themselves while maintaining their well-being and power through others' suffering. It horrified her.

But Louis XIV was no crusader. He had *brought* the magicians to Versailles to ward his palace with spells that would entice the nobility, and so keep them under his thumb. But when the magicians' status at court had begun to rival his own, he'd turned on them, executing those who didn't flee in time. In killing them, Louis XIV hadn't wanted to help the people. He'd only helped himself hold on to power.

In the face of revolution, his great-grandson was doing the same thing.

"Down with the magicians!" someone shouted. "Bloodsuckers!"

"Regardez!" The king gestured theatrically to Marie Antoinette, who stood behind him. "Even her majesty the queen was a victim of an unscrupulous magician!"

The queen—a *victim*? It was for the queen's sake Séguin had tried to enslave both her and Chandon by making them his sorrow-wells!

Around her, people grew restless. It was just the same as it'd been with the flower seller: one word could ignite them. The people were hungry for something more. Someone else to blame. Something *worse*.

"Magic," Louis continued, "is against our new Republic. It makes a mockery of freedom, of brotherhood, of the happiness of the French people." A crooked, big-lipped smile. "Our great-grandfather made the magicians stand trial, even though many were his noble courtiers. He did not flinch when the guilty were executed. The first step toward freedom from magic is putting our intentions into law. Therefore we, in our sacred duty to protect the people of France, do hereby decree: magic is henceforth outlawed." He raised the paper in his hand to peer at it, his diamonds glittering. "On pain of death."

Silence, a held breath. Beneath the shadow of her hat, Marie Antoinette smiled.

The people roared. As the crowd shoved forward, Camille lost her footing. She thought for a moment she would be crushed and then she felt Lazare's strong arm under her elbow, keeping her standing. "Are you all right?"

"Lost my balance, that's all."

"I see his game now," Rosier said grimly. "A masterful—terrible!—stroke of genius to lay everything at the feet of magicians."

"How dare he tell that false story!" Camille exclaimed. "Especially when his own wife was complicit—"

"Hush!" Sophie glanced at the people around them. "You mustn't—"

But she could not stop. "He blames magicians when *he* and the queen are the ones who have caused all this suffering!"

The crimson-cloaked man who'd given the king the paper came forward. His face was stern, his bearing that of a military man who would ride for weeks to hunt a criminal and bring him to justice. An executioner. On his cloak was embroidered a hand surrounded by yellow flames, in its center a black C and M intertwined. He raised his arm for silence, and waited until it came.

"His Royal Majesty Louis XVI does hereby proclaim that anyone possessing magical objects or practicing magic will be arrested by the newly formed Comité des Récherches Magiques. He will be charged as a traitor to France. He will be tried as any other traitor and given no special privileges, no matter his class or rank."

Camille curled her hand tighter around Lazare's arm. *No one must see my fear,* she thought. *No one can know.*

At that the crowd erupted into applause, chanting "Mort aux magiciens! Death to magicians!" Then one lone voice rose above the others: "À la lanterne, les magiciens!" and the crowd roared even louder in response.

"Magicians don't exist!" a burly man growled. He stood only an arm's length from Camille, wearing a workman's trousers and clogs, his fair hair gritty with stone dust. Shaking his fists at the king, he cried, "It is the king who is at fault!"

"Liar! Shut up!" A man in a dingy butcher's apron shoved him so hard the workman stumbled back. His coarse mouth twisted with fury. "It's the magicians that bewitch our wives and lay curses on our children!"

Another man tried to pull him back. "Come away, Paul. You'll make things worse—"

The mason strode toward him, fists raised, shouting: "You defend the king? Can't you see he takes no responsibility for what he's done?" Wild-eyed, he spat at the butcher. "You are a traitor to the revolution!"

In the butcher's hand was suddenly a long knife.

"Stop him!" Rosier shouted.

Arms reaching, the crowd closed around the butcher—but not before he managed to force his knife into the mason's side. The stricken man collapsed to his knees. Blood bloomed across his shirt, thick and fast.

Camille could not move.

"Call the police!" a woman screamed. "Fetch a surgeon!"

Bracing his foot on the mason's shoulder, the butcher yanked his knife loose. Gore welled from the wound. The crowd fell back, muttering and afraid.

"This frightens you, does it, cowards?" The butcher raised the red blade above his head. "You want revolution? You must get used to the sight of death! Magicians and the traitors who support them will be the first to die!"

"Paul!" his friend shouted. "Come away!"

On the stage, the scarlet-cloaked man from the Comité signaled to one of his guards, who threaded his way toward the stabbed man. The butcher grinned as he wiped his knife on his apron. "He's coming to congratulate me, I don't doubt! Any other magician-lovers I can take care of?"

*They had to get away.*

Under Camille's feet, the ground rippled nauseatingly. The skirt and bodice of her dress were splattered with blood. A dark red river covered the cobbles and soaked the toe of her shoe. Her stocking was wet with it. *Soon,* she thought dimly, *his blood will fill it entirely.*

"Camille?" Lazare said urgently. His face was very close, his cheek hazed with crimson spots. She tried to meet his eyes but could not: instead of seeing comfort there, she saw only his fear. She tried to take a deep breath, to steady herself, but her stays were too tight. Black pinpricks swarmed at the edges of her vision, closing in, and she felt herself falling backward—

"Camille!" Sophie cried.

"She's feeling faint!" Lazare said to the bystanders. He had his arm around her, holding her up. "I'll take her home."

Camille clutched at his coat as if it might keep her afloat. "Walk with me," he said in her ear. "Pretend it is nothing, pretend—"

*Pretend what?*

Pretend she did not live in a magician's mansion where magic seeped from the walls? Pretend that every object and room in the house was not suddenly a death sentence? What of the pamphlets that sold better than any pamphlets had a right to do? The fever that came upon her when she printed them? She knew she'd felt it before. It was as familiar to her as the beating of her own heart.

"It was the blood," she said, though it sounded unconvincing even to her. "That's all it was."

"Please, tell me," he said urgently. "You have given it up, haven't you?"

She had tried. For everyone's sake.

But instead she'd somehow unloosed it. And the consequences had been good—things he'd admired her for. Now what? How could she explain it to him? She could not say, *Something happened when I printed the first pamphlet. A fever came on me, and I couldn't stop.* How could magic compel someone to purchase a pamphlet, or a newspaper the story was printed in? It made no sense.

But magic, she knew, had its own logic.

*You are extraordinary, mon âme.*

She had seen the admiration in his deep brown gaze. But in the tension in his shoulders, the vague wariness in the line of his lips, was there not something else? Judgment? Revulsion, or fear? What would he think of her pamphlets if he knew that magic might be involved?

She knew: she would be extraordinary no more.

"Of course." As if by saying it she could make it true, she added, "Magic is nothing to me."

# 15

She could not wash the blood away. Though they had fled the mob, running back to the Hôtel Séguin, she had not been able to leave it behind. Adèle had thrown away Camille's shoes and whisked her dress away to be cleaned, but the blood's dark, iron scent clung to her skin. Lazare had washed his face, but when she looked at him, she still saw the tiny pinpricks of gore on his cheeks.

The boys stayed for dinner, and as the salt was passed and the soup served, Camille pretended she was not afraid. That what had happened in the square was nothing for *her* to fear. She pretended to eat her food. She pretended not to see the worried looks that Sophie and Lazare gave each other when they thought she didn't see. She pretended not to hear as they discussed what the new law might mean. As Camille flinched, Rosier claimed magicians were an easy target and wondered who would be next—foreigners? Jews? Under the hum of their conversation and the clink of glasses and silver, she could hear the relentless rustling of paper, like leaves before a storm.

It pulled at her like a tide.

Once the boys had gone home, Lazare kissing her on the forehead and telling her to rest, and everyone in the house had gone to bed, she stole downstairs, down the long hall to the printing room. She set her ear against the door. On the other side, the murmuring grew. The tiny hairs on her arms rose.

*Magic.*

For a terrifying moment, she thought she could hear words in it. *Names.* She thought of the burned box in which the enchanted dress had once been kept, the way it had seemed to call to her. She could pretend and pretend it did not exist, that she was somehow finished with it, but it was a lie. As long as this magic was here, as long as it wound its way into the pamphlets she printed, the officers of the Comité in their bloodred capes could arrest her for working la magie.

What would Lazare think of her if the pamphlets failed and the girls were evicted? What would he think of her if she pretended to be someone to whom magic didn't matter? When he'd told her to pretend, had he meant something *more*?

Who would she then betray?

Lazare?

The girls?

Herself?

*You are extraordinary, mon âme.*

The choices felt impossible.

Crouching stone-still, listening to the sighing of the pamphlets and the restless creaking house around her, she felt like a mouse trapped in its hole. The weight of the Hôtel Séguin's magic so heavy it would crush her. Whatever was happening, she had no idea how to control it. Why had Maman not taught her more about magic? Had she thought to protect Camille from magic through ignorance?

The oil paintings in the hall shimmered, the clouds in their landscapes darkening. The faces in the portraits grew watchful, alert. The walls and the floor and the ceiling seemed to draw closer, as if the house wished to hold her in the palm of its hand. Too tired to resist, she gave in to the mesh of magic drifting around her.

Faintly, a memory tapped against the window of her mind.

Late at night, cold slinking along the colder floor, tears in her mother's voice. Firelight wavering. An angry shout.

What was it that had happened?

She closed her eyes and the memory fluttered free.

She was small, and had woken to voices.

Insistent, arguing. They were coming from the little salon in their apartment. Sliding quietly from bed so as not to disturb Sophie, she crept down the hall. The door to the salon stood open, and Camille wedged herself behind it so she might peer through the long vertical opening between the hinges.

Illuminated by a sinking fire, her parents faced each other on the carpet, stiff as soldiers. Papa's usually gentle face was ferocious, unrecognizable. His hand was out in front of him, palm up. Waiting. Opposite, Maman's blue eyes blazed. Clutched to her chest was a small book, clad in green leather and decorated with a silver pattern. To Camille it resembled a forest, all leaves and branches. She'd learned her letters that winter, but she couldn't read the book's title. It slid away from her like water.

"Give it to me, Anne-Louise," Papa said.

"So you can throw it on the fire? Absolutely not."

Her parents always told her: books are precious. Why did Papa want to destroy this one?

"You wish to keep a book of magic in this house? After the way your mother treated you—your mother the *magician*?"

"You know I renounced her." Maman's voice was both angry and sad. "I renounced that entire life for you. For all of us." She looked so sorrowful then that Camille wanted to run to her, clasp her small hands around her mother's waist and hold her tight. "You dream of raising up the downtrodden but cannot see we magicians were also persecuted. I don't deny some magicians have done terrible things. But we are also people, and to be burned, beheaded—"

"My darling." Papa took a step toward her. "I'm sorry—"

"Let me finish." She was a stern statue, an angel in church with a burning sword. "We will be persecuted again, and you cannot tell me otherwise."

"The revolution will bring good times for all of us, Anne-Louise."

"*If* we magicians hide, like we are hiding now." She gestured at the walls of the apartment, and Camille shrunk back into shadow. "But what if those good times do not come? Or if they come, they don't come for us?"

"Anne-Louise, I beg of you—"

She tucked the book protectively to her chest. "I am annotating it for Camille."

Papa growled, "Do not insist on this."

"She cannot be left ignorant about her heritage. Let her choose, later, if she wishes. Because I left my family to be with you, my education was cut short. There is too much about magic that I don't know! Perhaps this book might even save us, if your revolution fails. Had you thought of that? Magic need not be wrong." In a choked voice, she said, "Didier, am *I* wrong? Am I evil?"

Papa's face crumpled. "Never."

"But you won't accept that I do magic?"

"It is against everything I believe." Papa's voice was flat. "Everything I work for. Doesn't our Camille deserve more than . . . magic?"

"More?" Maman stared at the fire, and Camille could no longer see her face. "Perhaps I'll never have to teach her. Perhaps this beautiful new world you believe in will come true."

Papa wrapped his arms around her, and she dropped her golden head on his shoulder. Camille could no longer see the green book. Maman's back shook with sobs. She did not want to hear Maman cry.

Back in her room, the bed was still warm. Her eyelids were closing when her mother knelt beside her. "Bonne nuit, mon trèsor," she whispered, brushing her lips to Camille's forehead. "It was just a bad dream."

Even then, she knew it wasn't.

Camille blinked. She was still kneeling on the cold floor outside the printing room.

Maman *had* wanted her to know more about magic. It was Papa who had not.

She hadn't known what "annotated" meant then, but she knew now: Maman had made notes in the margins for Camille to read. She'd wanted her to know what was written inside. Camille's throat constricted at the thought of that green book lost. A book like that might have instructions for how to manage her feverish magic. But it was gone.

The fire of revolution had taken it.

*Wait.*

There could not have been only one copy in all of France. There had to be others. She got to her feet.

All around her the rustling continued. Louder, more insistent. In it were new voices, as faint and dry as husks. They were coming from the library, the room where the house's magic was the strongest, the place she'd steadfastly avoided.

Until now.

# 16

Candle in hand, Camille climbed the marble stairs toward the wing where the library waited. When she'd passed it before, the bitter burn of magic leaking from under the door had sent her hurrying past.

Now she stood in front of its carved wooden door, inhaling those same acrid fumes. In the skull-shaped keyhole sat a great brass key. She turned it and the door swung back silently into the dark. Holding her candle high, in case—*in case of what?*—she stepped over the threshold.

*In case something is there,* a small voice inside her replied.

A shutter had blown open and vague moonlight filtered into the room. Adèle had told her the entire library had been pried loose piece by piece from some ancient castle and reinstalled at the Hôtel Séguin. Blackened oak panels ran from floor to ceiling, many of them carved with words in a scrolling language she did not know. She sensed they were wards to keep the books safe. Halfway up the walls, a narrow balcony ran like a ribbon around the room to give access to the books stored there, protected by filigreed metal gates. She squinted at their titles, but the words seem to rush away from her. The silvered spine of Maman's green book had behaved in the same way. Imagine if she were to find a copy here—

But first she would close the shutter. She wound her way past a desk, a long table covered with papers, a taxidermized deer. Reaching into the windy night air, she caught hold of the shutter, and pulled it closed.

On the wall beside the window hung a large portrait of Séguin. In it, he sat beside a table, a crystal globe in his hand. His clothes were doubly gold: pale golden silk fretted with gold embroidery, and his stare was that of a raptor: proud and secretive, handsome and unnervingly cold. At the corner of his eye was painted a tear. His fingers were blackened, as if with soot. *Strange.* And in the corner of the portrait was a gilt circle with an *M* inside it, surrounded by five tiny stars. There was something captivating about the stars, and as she leaned in to see better, her hand brushed the portrait's frame.

It *burned.*

She tried to pull away, but couldn't. Unwillingly, her hand gripped the frame as a stream of anguished memories rushed through her. Fear, as someone—Séguin? A person he loved?—was carried away by a river. The cloying rose scent of the queen's perfume. More slowly, other images came. A dried leaf, an empty room, a pitiless expanse of ice, and an aching despair at no longer being able to work magic.

And then, in a candlelit room, in a whirl of laughter and color, there was a girl in a blue-gray dress who seemed to shine brighter than anyone else. She was cheating at cards. He spoke to her and, as if his wishes were coming true, she held out her hand so he might read her palm. A hunger rose up in him when he touched her, the jump of magic from her hand to his like fire in his veins. How he wanted what she had. The urge to *take take take* was so strong he nearly sank to his knees in front of her. *She is what will save me.* But the agony it caused him, to resist, to *wait*—

Camille yanked her hand away so hard that she stumbled backward. The girl in the blue-gray dress, the girl full of magic, had been her. Séguin's desire for her had been for her magic, that she knew. That he had needed it so badly that he'd do anything to get it, she hadn't guessed. But that was what magic did.

Pressing her scorched hand to her lips, she went up the staircase to the little balcony that ran around the library walls. As she held up her candle, the lettering on the spines shifted like smoke. Tentatively, she reached out to touch one. For a moment, the swirling stilled. *Alchemical History*. Another one, bound in pale blue: *Essays on the Magical Life*. She tried to pull it out but it refused to budge.

For an hour, she searched the shelves, running her fingers along the spines of the bespelled books. She found several green books—each one set her heart hammering—but none were a copy of the one she was looking for. Or if it was, it was so well hidden by magic that she'd never find it on her own.

She recalled the scarlet-caped leader of the Comité, standing beside the king. The grim set of his jaw, the cold disgust of his stare. And that badge upon his cloak: a hand surrounded by flame. Its fingers blackened, like in Séguin's portrait. She did not think it a coincidence.

Before, her ignorance had been an embarrassment, something to feel ashamed of when someone like Chandon knew so much about magic and its history. But now her ignorance was a danger. Not just to herself and the girls who were counting on her to help them, but also to Sophie and Lazare. She needed answers, and she needed them soon.

She would go downstairs and write to Chandon.

As she stepped into the hall, ready to close the door behind her, she glanced back into the library's gloom. She could have sworn the portrait had wanted to show her something. To *remind* her of something.

But what?

WHAT IS MAGIC

BUT

A TOOL

TO CHEAT AND STEAL

AND

MURDER?

⁌———————⁍

PATRIOTS

IN THE NAME OF FRANCE

STAND UP!

*ERADICATE*

THIS
PLAGUE
OF MAGICIANS

# 17

Two days later she had printed enough pamphlets to bring to Lasalle's, and all the way there, she felt as if she were being watched. Though she could not see anyone following her, she still felt exposed, and pulled the collar of her cloak up around her neck. On the lips of passersby she heard the word *magician*, spat like a curse; on an old wall, freshly printed posters denouncing magic spread like vines. She itched to uproot them with her hands.

In the bookshop, on the large table where Lasalle displayed pamphlets and posters for sale, she noticed one that compared magicians to a plague. It was long, the entire back of the sheet covered, and unsigned. The type seemed familiar, as did the printer's mark. "Who writes these, monsieur?"

"I don't know. As you see, the writer is anonymous. But they sell well."

"Why is that?"

"Straightforward and to the point. Exciting. People feel safe when they hang them up. My great-grandmother hung garlic, tied with red thread, on her front door. This is . . . a more modern approach."

She gritted her teeth. Magicians were now evil spirits to be guarded against? How could people be so simple as to believe this? With a few well-chosen words, Louis XVI had made things much, much worse. "Do *you* think magicians are like vampires?"

"Can a magician slip through a keyhole? Down a chimney? Rumor has them everywhere in Paris. I doubt they even exist. They are the monster under the bed the king uses to make the people behave." His mouth twitched. "Now! Madame, do you see this?" He pointed to a small metal box with a lock. "Donations for your girls."

"Truly?" she gasped.

He gave it a brisk tap. "Customers have learned of their plight and given money in case it might be useful."

"Thank you, monsieur!" The girls could use this, she knew. But more than money they needed their home. "Has your friend at the mayor's office had any luck?"

Sagely, Lasalle nodded. "I believe it will happen. The mayor fears an outcry if he doesn't stop the eviction."

"That's fantastic!" She wanted to throw her arms around Lasalle. "Can I tell them it's over? That they can stay?"

He held up his hand. "Another few days. It's the mayor's decision."

"But I can give them hope?"

"That you can do."

The past few days had been dark and difficult, but now a tide of happiness welled up in her. Revolution was ever spinning, like a many-sided die tossed out in a game—you never knew which side might face up. Now the girls' luck, at least, had changed. Even Lasalle had been changed, and the thought made her bold. "I have a business idea to propose."

"Oh?" He began to fill a purse with coins from the box.

"A subscription, for a series called 'The Lost Girls Speak.' I've written two so far—why not keep going? If the girls get money ahead of time, they'll

be eager to continue. And might not a subscription bring in even more readers to the shop?"

"Clever!" Lasalle declared. "Indeed it might. I'll let people know. You
keep interviewing. Keep writing. And don't send your pamphlets anywhere
else, I beg you."

"I promise," she said as she took the heavy purse from him. It had the
reassuring solidity of a hard-won victory. She and the girls had changed
public sentiment. There was no turning back now: she must tell their stories
a while longer.

And somehow learn to manage her magic.

After she left Lasalle's shop, trying to forget the anti-magician pamphlet
she'd seen there, she crossed the busy street of the old rue du Temple without looking. Out of nowhere a young man roughly plowed into her. Scrambling on the damp cobbles, she nearly lost her footing.

"Have a care, citizen!" Camille cried.

He wheeled around. With the carved head of his cane—an ivory dog
with a jewel for an eye—he tipped up his hat. His was a handsome face, with
high color in the cheeks and a wide, square jaw. Under his tricorne hat, his
wavy, walnut-colored hair was free of powder, tied back with a blue ribbon.
But the hazel eyes she knew so well were not full of merriment, not this time.
Instead they were very grave.

"Chandon!" She could hardly believe he stood in front of her. "I've been
thinking about you! What are you doing in Paris?"

"Hush!" he hissed. "Keep yelling at me!"

"What?" she said, bewildered.

He raised his voice. "It was you who crashed into me!" And he gave the
tiniest tilt of his head to the right. Under the brim of her hat, she looked in
that direction. In the crowded street, she saw a closed carriage drawn by a
sweat-darkened horse, an empty vegetable cart. Nothing out of the ordinary.
She was about to turn back when she saw: two streets away, a Comité guard
under an awning. His black-hatted head was bent over a newspaper, but she
could have sworn he wasn't reading it. Instead, like a raven, he was waiting.

Watching.

*Pretend*, she told herself. "Hardly, monsieur! You are at fault and owe me for dirtying my skirts!"

"Foolish girl!" he shouted. "Take it up with my lawyer if you must—here is his address." He pressed a piece of paper into her hand. "I myself am finished with you!" And with that he pulled his hat down low and strode off into the crowds, his coattails flapping in his wake.

She did not dare study the card he'd given her until she'd returned to the Hôtel Séguin. In the red salon, she closed the door quietly behind her. The tapestry knight's lance dripped crimson; the windows rattled a kind of ghostly welcome. When she was certain that no one was coming, she opened her fist. What she'd believed to be a card was only a piece of white paper. It was folded in a complicated way, though when she pulled at one of the corners it undid itself. From it rose the faintest hint of smoke.

> *A Meeting*
> *8 o'clock, tomorrow night*
> *The cemetery of Saint-Julien-le-Pauvre*

She frowned at the paper. Perhaps there was a kind of double meaning with the address, because as surprising as some of the parties she'd attended at Versailles had been, a meeting in a graveyard on an autumn night would top them all. *Somehow*, she thought as she ran her thumb over the ink-black words, *it did not seem like that kind of invitation.*

Camille flipped it over to see if there was an explanation, but the back was completely blank. Disappointed, she was about to set it down when a single line of text appeared where there had been nothing before.

> *Tell no one.*

The back of her neck prickled.

*Magic.*

She sensed it thread into her, insistent as hunger. Irresistible as the warm tang of bread when she was hungry, the cool relief of water when she was thirsty. In themselves, the words that had appeared on the paper were not persuasive. Or even ominous. They could mean the dinner was a secret. But something about the gleaming blackness of the letters unnerved her. She decided then, almost without realizing it, that she would in fact tell no one. Not Sophie, nor Lazare. It would be *her* secret.

As she stared at the invitation, the paper began to gray around the corners. Then cracks appeared in it, and before she could even think to let go, the note was nothing more than a pile of ash cupped in the palm of her hand.

# 18

The graveyard behind Saint-Julien-le-Pauvre was shabby with overgrown grass. Parishioners still used the weathered church, but its burying ground had long been abandoned. A grove of cypress trees made gloomy shapes under the evening sky and in a few places, roses grew among the graves. With no one to tend to them, they'd run wild, their bare, thorny canes covering the graves like shrouds.

As she walked hesitantly between the tilting stones, searching for anything that resembled a door, a figure stepped into the light cast by a lamppost at the cemetery's edge. He wore a heavy monk's habit that dragged the ground, a hood shadowing his face.

Camille stiffened. "Who are you?" she said with more bravery than she felt.

He inclined his head. "A servant of the Marquis de Chandon, who awaits you inside. Come, you must not linger here where eyes may see you."

She followed him through damp grass and past funerary urns to where an ancient chapel stood. Beside it crouched a marble sarcophagus. On its lid perched an angel, its wings veined with lichen. The man grasped hold of the statue, and pushed.

The enormous lid pivoted away to reveal stairs descending into nothing. From the opening came a cold wind heavy with the scent of rot. It made Camille gag.

"Après-vous," he said.

There was nothing she wished less to do than to follow this unknown person down through a tomb into a—a crypt? "Chandon is down there?"

"He gave me this token to show you." In his palm lay a tiny jeweled box, decorated with a silvery pearl. It was the snuffbox Chandon had won from her when they first met at Versailles.

Camille squared her shoulders. "You first."

He went down a few steps and held the lantern high so that she might find her way. Carefully she placed her feet on the moss-slicked stones, one after another, as they descended into the ground. Chandon would never go to these lengths for a lark. His dream of happiness was strolling the apple orchards with his beloved Foudriard in Normandie. For him to be in Paris, asking her to come in secret—*here*—meant something was terribly wrong.

The tunnel she found herself in filled her with foreboding. It was no wider than her outstretched arms, and only a hand's width higher than the top of her head. Its sides curved slightly, and in the wavering light of the servant's lantern she saw they were bricked with bones. Wedged between them were skulls with sightless eyes. And everywhere the cold smell of decay.

She swallowed. "What is this place?"

"A private catacomb. Very old."

*Only bones*, she told herself, and pressed the edge of her cloak over her nose and mouth. For several minutes they walked in silence, the lantern light bobbing, the bones gleaming close and white and then sinking into shadow. When she felt she could stand it no more, she choked out, "How much farther?"

"Nearly there."

It was true that the tunnel seemed finally to be widening. Ahead, she thought she heard faint voices, though it could have been the strange breeze shifting among the bones.

And then the man—and the lantern—disappeared.

"Where are you?" she cried. She took a step forward and bumped into him.

He shouted, "Open up!"

A door creaked wide. Dim light illuminated a set of dry stone steps. "Straight up, through the gallery—you'll see him there."

She found herself in a long room, both its walls and floor made of pale gray stone. Above her, the wooden ceiling was covered with painted diamonds in greens and faded reds. Here and there, still-bright silver stars shone out, and in the corners, carved wooden angels, their paint long gone, peered down at her.

In the air hung the heavy fug of magic.

A bolt slid back and a door opened in the hall's far end. And there was Chandon, striding toward her, his heels clacking on the ancient floor. His face was serious, as if he'd just been told something he did not wish to hear.

"I'm dreadfully sorry about the bones," he called to her. "They can feel extraordinarily grabby. And forgive me for our encounter in the street. How rude I must have seemed! You saw how they watch me—I did not want to come to your house and endanger you further."

"It doesn't matter now," she said warmly. "I'm so happy to see you!" She would never have predicted it, but simply being with her friend reassured her. It had been true even during their time at Versailles, when he'd been, of necessity, very secretive. Only now did she understand why: around him she did not have to pretend magic was nothing. "Tell me, what is this place?"

"Pardon! The king's announcement has so rattled me I've forgotten whatever manners I might once have had. Besides, without my invitation you won't be able to pass through the wards." He threw open his arms.

"Bienvenue à Bellefleur, my ancestral home! The oldest part of it was once a monastic house associated with the church of Saint-Julien. This room was the refectory. Imagine if you will long tables, hooded monks bent over their gruel . . . how terribly medieval it must have been!" He raised an amused eyebrow. "My ancestors pulled down the monastery and used the stones to build our house. But the refectory remained standing because of the tunnel. It makes a helpful entrance or exit when kings are persecuting magicians." Any momentary mirth vanished from Chandon's face. "As kings are wont to do."

"Then why have you come back to Paris?" she wondered. "When you might have stayed away?"

"My parents *were* reluctant to let me come. They fear we will be blamed for everything. A house burns because the thatched roof is too dry? Magicians. A well goes foul? Magicians. A child dies?" His hazel eyes were grave. "But I said to them: must we give up and hide until this is . . . over?"

Hiding seemed less risky than speaking out. "Why, what do you have in mind?"

"We must plot, bien sûr! I invited all the magicians I know but most were too afraid to come. One had his house set on fire, so naturally he declined. The rest prefer to hide behind their moats rather than come to Paris to help find a cure."

She imagined an inoculation, like for smallpox. "For what?"

"Revolution." He chuckled at her startled expression. "A jest, nothing more! Come, let's join the others." A hand on her elbow, he steered her through a stone archway into a long, dimly lit gallery, part of the house proper. On the gallery's walls hung portrait after portrait. Some were painted on wooden boards, clearly hundreds of years old. Men in costly cloaks and hats, ringed hands resting on the pommels of their swords. Women in velvet and brocade, their jewels gleaming. Their proud faces gave nothing away.

Chandon brushed a speck of dust off a portrait's frame. "My ancestors are all handsome and clever-looking, don't you think? Except for a few who worked magic for ungrateful kings"—he gestured at a man in armor, his helm tucked under his arm—"most of them probably never did anything more horrible than order dinner. They worked small magic if they had to and tried to avoid beheadings."

How matter-of-fact he was! She wondered what it must have been like to grow up in a family where magic was so much a part of everyday life, where no one had to renounce their magical ancestors but instead displayed them casually in the hall, where their faces could be seen to resemble one's own. If Camille had grown up like this, she might know what was happening with the pamphlets. She might even know how to control it.

*And*, said a tiny voice deep inside, *perhaps you wouldn't be so ashamed of what you are.*

As they walked on, Camille's eye snagged on a portrait of a young man. His long dark hair coiled over his shoulders, his mouth defiant. Set into the forest green of the background was a small seal, no bigger than a coin: a gilt circle with an *M* inside it, surrounded by five tiny stars. From the corner of his eye dangled a lapis-colored tear. His fingertips were black, as if ink-stained.

"At the house there's a portrait of Séguin"—Chandon flinched—"painted just like this."

"It's a kind of iconography." With his ringed finger, Chandon pointed out the unusual features. "The tears indicate the sorrow the magician uses to work his magic. The blackened hands represent the burned smell of magic, and how it scorches to use it. The stars are a bit bold, I admit—they mean the person is a magician. This style was fashionable until the purges under Louis XIV. After that, these kinds of portraits were hidden in back halls like this one, warded against non-magicians who might start shouting for inquisitions. The style is known as à la merveille. I find it quite beautiful."

*In the style of marvels.* But spells and wards could fade, couldn't they, like the glamoire worked on Versailles? A portrait like this would be an admission of guilt, and yet, here they were. "You're not afraid to have them hanging here."

"Where else would they hang?" he asked, genuinely curious. "The house protects its magicians." A shadow shifted across his features. "Or did you mean I was afraid of what they'd done? I'm not my ancestors—not at all!—but I am rather pleased with who I am. Not even a king has the power to make me hate myself."

Again that little voice whispered: *Can you say the same of yourself?*

She pushed it from her mind as they came to a pair of carved wooden doors. "Here we are," he said. "Are you ready?"

"Ready for what? I thought we were here simply to listen to your plan."

"I'm afraid it may be a bit more complicated than that." He took her arm. "Shall we go in?"

# 19

Chandon flung open the double doors. Beyond was a room of candlelight and shadow. Where she had expected at least a handful of people, there was only one frowning young man, elbow on the mantelpiece. Wearing a foppish high collar and extravagantly tight clothes, he raised a monocle to his eye and glared.

"Come in!" Chandon said, practically pulling her along. As she hurried toward the fireplace, she took in the heavy oak furniture, long rows of black bookcases, tapestries so fine they could have come from the Gobelins. Beneath her feet lay a fantastical carpet crowded with curvetting dragons.

"Ignore every stick of the furniture," he said under his breath. "It was Maman's idea to have medieval things to match the house. I won't answer for it. Roland!" he called to the magician by the fire. "Our final guest has arrived. May I introduce Camille Durbonne, the Vicomtesse de Séguin?"

"Vicomtesse," the young man said. "The Comte de Roland, your servant." He was a little older than she and Chandon and slight, with a sharp, arrogant nose and wavy mahogany-brown hair. He wore a haughty smirk, and the small bow he gave Camille was, according to any standard of etiquette, a certain snub.

But he was not the only one in the room. Another young man in a military uniform was kneeling by the fire. As he rose to greet her, the Baron de Foudriard, Chandon's lover, was as fiercely handsome as ever. Dark-haired and possessed of a lion's grace, he looked as if he could spring into action at a moment's notice. The scar on his cheek curved white against his newly sun-browned skin, and his smile was wide and kind.

"Foudriard!" she exclaimed happily. "When Chandon said 'magicians,' I didn't expect to find you here."

"Not a magician, merely a steadfast supporter," he said with a bow. "Baroness—I mean, Vicomtesse—it is a pleasure. Chandon would have been devastated had you not come. There is, as I'm certain he's told you, much work to be done."

"Foudriard will not let me rest for even a minute," Chandon said affectionately. "But he is right—we face great dangers as a result of this new anti-magic law and must work hard to protect ourselves. The first step is—"

"Chandon, do not be ridiculous!" Roland laughed. "*We* have nothing to worry about."

"There you are wrong, monsieur." The quiet authority in Foudriard's face brooked no argument. "Among the people, the fear of magicians grows, and the king has just shown us he intends to wield that fear as a weapon. For many, what magicians *do* matters less than what they're believed to be *capable* of doing. The more afraid and distrustful everyone becomes, the more people will cheer the king and his Comité."

In her mind's eye, Camille saw again the fight in the Place de Grève, the blood welling dark around the butcher's knife, the reverberating screams of the mob as it called for death to all magicians. Imagine if they had known the magic she'd loosed to write the pamphlets? It would have been her in a lake of her own blood. The hatred was ancient, but not extinguished. It had taken only a spark to rekindle it.

"To make things worse, France's borders may soon tighten," Foudriard predicted. "Even when émigrés fled France after the fall of the Bastille, there was talk of restricting aristocrats' movements and seizing their assets so they could not raise armies for a counterrevolution. It's only a matter of time before they do the same for magicians."

"Magicians will then be trapped in France with no escape," Camille said. "Jailed, murdered, or forced to stop working magic . . ." What would she do if it came to that?

"Exactly," Chandon agreed. "We magicians will need a way to protect ourselves. And a way out. The Comité is confiscating books on magic and reading them. If we do not stay one step ahead, they will devise ways to catch us." He raised an eyebrow at Roland, as if to say: *Understood?* "But before I tell you what I believe we must do, there's one more magician I wish you to meet. I've searched everywhere for someone with his knowledge. He is a bookseller on the Île de la Cité. Delouvet?"

From behind the bookcases stepped another young man. He was thin and as narrow as the spine of a book. Every piece of clothing he wore was fashioned in shades of white and cream: elegant, with not a spot of dust on them. His skin was so pale it was nearly translucent; violet shadows fanned out under his light brown eyes. Even his hair was so fair that it was nearly white. Among the medieval furnishings of the room, he resembled nothing more than a fashionable ghost.

He blinked slowly at all of them, as if emerging from a dream, and bowed. "Blaise Delouvet, your obedient servant, et cetera, et cetera."

Roland scrutinized him through his monocle and seemed to find him wanting. "How can a bookseller do anything?"

"Roland, you try my patience," Chandon warned. "Do you remember the protection I spoke of half a minute ago? You are looking at it."

"I bring you a solution from the past," Blaise Delouvet replied. "All you need to do, Marquis, is listen." From a nearby table, he picked up a small book bound in mahogany-colored leather. Tiny gold suns surrounded the title: *Journal of the Burning Years, 1678–1682* and beneath was written: *Laurent de Parte.* "Monsieur de Parte, the Marquis de Saint-Clair, lived during the Affair of the Poisons. Then it was Louis XIV who purged magicians and tried them in a special court, the Chambre Ardente—the terrifying Burning Court that gives his memoir its name. A time unfortunately like our own." With a genteel cough, he cleared his throat and began to read.

> *Château de Puymartin*
> *December 2, 1679*
>
> *Having fled Versailles after the king's arrests, I have now returned home. For one week, I have been closed up in my library, determined to find something that will keep us safe from the king's infernal magic hunters.*
>
> *My reasoning thus far . . .*
>
> *Premise the first: In order to save their own lives, magicians must be able to work a magic of invisibility. It is well known that the king's men have devices that can detect the presence of magic, therefore, it is not enough for a magician to discontinue working it.*

"They do?" Camille asked.
Blaise shrugged. "They did. They are trying to do it again."

> *Premise the second: In order to work this invisibility, a magician will require an enormous amount of magic.*
>
> *Premise the third: The greatest source of magic is a sorrowful memory.*

*Problem! Memories fade over time, becoming less powerful*
*and therefore less useful as a means for working magic.*

*Premise the fourth: An externally preserved memory*
*is the strongest because it is not dulled by reliving it or*
*attempting to master it. This preservation may be achieved*
*by collecting the magician's tears and working the magic*
*commonly known as "Tempus Fugit."*

Chandon frowned. "I've never heard of it—what is 'Time Flies'?"

"I can't say. I've gone through all the books in my shop and have only seen it referred to, never explained. I worry it was once such an everyday working that no one bothered to write it down."

Roland muttered something derisive under his breath.

*Premise the fifth: When needed, the preserved memory is*
*consumed in the form of the magicked tears. The memory*
*of that sorrowful event would be so powerful that while*
*the magician reexperienced it, he would be "there"—and*
*therefore invisible "here." In this way a magician would be*
*veiled by the power of his own most terrifying memories. I*
*propose, therefore, to name this new magic the Veil.*

"I've also heard it called the 'blur.'" Blaise looked up. His violet circles seemed to have darkened. For a moment, no one said anything.

"A magic of tears? But it is grotesque!" Roland said, appalled. "No magician would do such a thing!"

*Not true*, Camille thought. There was one who had.

In his luxurious rooms at Versailles, Séguin had tortured her with threats of what he would do to Sophie and Lazare in order to get the sorrow he needed from her. When she finally broke down and wept, he'd licked the tears from her cheek, claiming that the tears of a magician were too valuable to waste.

She could still feel the scrape of his teeth against her skin. "Did Séguin ever collect your tears, Chandon?"

"In a vial of the finest Venetian glass," he replied with a shiver. "It was fitted with a fragment of cork, topped with silver. It was more terrifying than any tool of torture. When I first met Blaise, I told him that Séguin had bragged he'd figured out a way to make himself invisible. So you see," he said to Roland, who stared disbelievingly at him, "it can be done."

"But did you see him become invisible?" Roland demanded.

"I did," Camille said. "The night of Aurélie's birthday party, when you were so ill, Chandon. He was only half there, like smoke. No one else seemed to see him." For a minute or two, Séguin had been more like a breath or smoke than a person made of flesh and bone. Could he have been working this magic? Was that why he had needed both her and Chandon's sorrow—because he needed so much pain to fuel it?

"All the better to sneak around and work at our destruction," Chandon said with a sigh. "But how?"

"Collect the tears in a vial, and you're done, isn't that what Monsieur Delouvet said?" Roland asked.

"Call me Blaise, s'il vous plaît." The bookseller gave a faint sigh. "There is the matter of working the transformation via the . . . tempus fugit. And the small matter of the *dangers*. You see," he said, flipping forward a few pages in the journal, "there are consequences to this magic."

*Château de Puymartin*
*February 5, 1680*

*After conducting a series of experiments, everything that I hypothesized two months ago has proved correct. Though horrifying, the magic of the veil of tears does work. There are, however, two more points I must add:*

*First point: By collecting his tears and the sorrow, a magician separates the memory from himself. Well and*

*good! The sorrow's power is contained elsewhere and no
longer troubles the magician.*

What if, she wondered, by working this veil of tears she could somehow
hide her magic? From everyone?

"And now," Blaise said, "what makes it such a dangerous magic."

> *Second point: While this frees the magician from sorrow's
> negative effects, each time he uses the veil the magician
> lives less and less in this world, retreating further and
> further into his memories. It is a grave danger I do not
> know how to prevent. Nevertheless I believe this damage
> would take years to occur. And, to be blunt, when one's life
> is at stake, it may not matter.*

"Bien!" said Roland, shaking out his cuffs as if everything were resolved.
"We make the veil, have invisibility when we need it, and then there's no
need to stop working magic or even leave France. Problem solved! Though
I'd normally be loath to admit it, you are a genius, Chandon."

"I wish I could agree," Chandon said, "but we have no idea how to work
the tempus fugit."

Roland stared expectantly at Blaise. "You seem to know everything.
Surely you must have a book somewhere—"

"The books we need," Blaise said, "are being burned. Have you not seen
the pyres on the river? You might mistake them for ordinary fires, but they
are not. Barges, piled high with magical objects. Paintings igniting as oil and
canvas feed the inferno. Books," he choked, "their pages flapping open . . ."
He cradled the *Journal of the Burning Years* to his chest.

"This is the work of the Comité?" Foudriard asked.

"And of the people," Blaise added. "Why hold on to magic when it may
bring the Comité to your house in the middle of the night and land you
in prison?" He must have seen something in Camille's face for he added,
kindly, "For now, at least, prison is but a rumor."

It was hardly a comfort.

"But this crisis is also an opportunity," Blaise said. "Because I am known, in certain circles, to be interested in magic, people have been coming to my shop to sell me magical objects. I buy mostly books, naturally, but if they have some . . . vials . . . or other curiosities, I buy those, too."

"And have you found a vial of this esteemed blur?" Roland challenged.

As if he had been waiting for this moment, Blaise took from a pocket in his waistcoat a tiny glass cylinder, no longer than his little finger. It looked very much like the one Chandon had described Séguin using. Holding the glittering vial up to the light, he tilted it slowly from side to side. Inside, a tiny amount of viscous jade-colored liquid shifted hypnotically back and forth.

Roland held out his hand. "May I see?"

"Certainly, just please be careful—" But before Blaise could give it to him, he snatched the vial out of his grip and pried loose the cork.

Blaise lunged for the vial. "This is a dangerous magic!"

"Oh là là! What is the worst that could happen?" With a flick of his wrist, Roland tipped the bottle into his open mouth. Two pale green drops fell onto his tongue. Wonderingly, he said, "Horrendously bitter."

Blaise's mouth worked, but he said nothing.

"You are a fool, Roland," Chandon snapped. "But now that you've taken it, you can at least tell us what's happening."

"It feels like sticks snapping against my skin. But *inside* my skin. Not nice." For a few long minutes, Roland said nothing. He did not fade, but his eyes narrowed, as if he were watching something they could not see. Pain spasmed across his face, and then his shoulders bent into a protective hunch. A wrenching sob tore from his mouth. It was a ghastly, haunting sound. "All her memories! Poor child. So much suffering—"

And then Roland *dimmed*.

"Where is he?" Foudriard asked, bewildered. "Did he leave?"

"Look!" Chandon pointed at the fire. "He's over there, very faint now."

By the fire was a shadow without a person, a figure made of smoke. Roland kept silent, and only once, as he moved around, did he make a noise loud enough to draw attention to him.

"Incroyable," Chandon said with a low whistle. Then he took out his watch and waited. Five minutes passed before Roland began to reappear, but slowly, and not all at once. Camille was able to first see him out of the corner of her eye, then full on.

His eyes were red with tears.

"Well?" Blaise's curiosity seemed to have overcome his anger.

"The worst thing I've ever experienced. I lived through a girl's sorrows. Broken dolls. A dead pet bird. A cruel best friend. And then a stepfather who tried to"—his voice broke—"have his way with her. A marriage with a duc who beat her and took her money. Mon Dieu! How do we allow these things to happen?"

They all stared.

"Alors," demanded Chandon, "could you see us?"

"As through a haze. All the while I struggled mightily to stay here. It was like falling into a river. I was almost carried away." Pouring himself some wine, he hastily threw back a glass. "I could have lost my mind completely!"

A cold finger of misgiving ran down Camille's spine. The magic that overtook her when she was printing was *already* too much for her to control. If a magician like the Comte de Roland had nearly been carried away— what would that mean for her? She felt already too susceptible. Would it mean she would never be able to use this magic?

Foudriard said, "We have learned something, but now it seems we are missing a bottle of the very substance we need."

"Stop!" Roland sank into a chair. He had the gray, worn-thin look Camille knew all too well. "I regret it!"

"In any case, it wouldn't have been enough for all the magicians I hope we can help," Chandon said. "Our task remains: we must find a book that tells us how to work this tempus fugit and so, the blur. As an act of penance, you must scavenge your libraries, Roland."

"Fine."

"Why not come to the Hôtel Séguin? The library has hundreds of books," she said to Blaise, who gave her a look of gratitude. "Séguin once told me the queen gave him access to ancient grimoires from a secret library at Versailles . . . perhaps they're in the collection. There's only one thing I ask." She hesitated. It was hard to say it aloud. "I don't wish anyone to know of it." *My sister. Or Lazare.*

"It will not be a problem," Blaise replied, but there was something melancholy about the way he said it, as if he understood what she was asking more than she did herself.

"We will come in secret," Chandon promised. "Until we have the blur, we must not give the Comité any reason to suspect us." He studied them all carefully. "*Unexpected* as Roland's experiment was, we now know it works. And its effects, as it were. But before I make a toast to the success of our search, I would like to give you a gift—a useful one—that Monsieur Delouvet has prepared for us."

From a table nearby, Blaise picked up a short stack of papers. They were blank, with a silvery sheen, and cut into palm-sized squares, which he divided among the magicians. "These are message papers of my own invention. I will demonstrate." He took one of the sheets, crumpled it, and placed it in his hand. "Bringing up sorrow, and thinking of what I wish to communicate, I will ignite it, and send it into the sky."

"We are inside," Roland pointed out.

"Do you trust magic, monsieur?"

Cowed, Roland shut his mouth. Blaise held out his hand, the crumpled, silvery paper lying on it. Briefly, he closed his eyes. His mouth twisted mournfully, his forehead furrowed with lines. Camille's heart ached for him. She had never liked for anyone to see her working magic, especially the glamoire's blood magic. It had seemed too raw and revealing. But Blaise worked his magic unflinchingly in front of them all.

The paper caught fire.

It rose from his hand, hovering above their heads. As if hesitating, or *thinking.* And then it drifted to the fireplace and with a swoop, disappeared up the chimney.

"Right now," Blaise observed, "it is burning above Paris. But also, I suspect, somewhere else?"

Camille's ears tingled. "I feel it on my skin. And I feel—your wish for us is to find answers to lead us to the blur."

"Just so. You are all bound in this magic," he said to the group. "If one of us needs help, send up a paper. If the others do not happen to see it in the sky, they will feel it. And then you will know to come here to Bellefleur as soon as possible."

"Well." The Comte de Roland sniffed, impressed.

Blaise smiled enigmatically. "As the poet said, there are more things in heaven and Earth than are dreamed of in your philosophy."

He was right, Camille thought.

One summer in Paris the weather had been so dry that the leaves hung lifeless on the trees. The water in the Seine had sunk so low that a rowboat crossing the river had struck a large object. *Nothing but a scuttled ship*, Papa guessed, *nothing to see*. And Camille thought nothing of it until one afternoon he burst into the apartment, panting, "Come, mes enfants! They are bringing it up!" From the banks they watched as a snarling dragon's head broke the water's skin. It was ancient, darkened by water and time, torrents pouring from the holes that once were its eyes. *A Norse raider's ship*, Papa whispered, *from when they sacked Paris*. She remembered her awe, tinged by the fear that it might roar to life. How the air itself seemed to change, as if the boat had brought with it a breath from a thousand years ago.

Sometimes, under the surface, there was treasure.

She could not turn away from it now.

"On that note," Chandon said as he uncorked a bottle of ancient, amber-colored wine and filled five glasses. He raised his goblet high, a determined smile on his face. "To the tears of magicians—may we find a way to survive this coming world."

# THE LOST GIRLS SPEAK
# THE FRUIT SELLER

## I CAME WITH MY MOTHER AND
## MY BROTHER TO PARIS ON A BARGE

Before that, it was a clipper across the gray
A T L A N T I C. We left our island of Saint-
Domingue, where the sun danced on the waves
and touched my skin like a kiss, to come here, all
three of us. A better education for my brother
was the reason. But Jean-Pierre wished to start a
revolution in Saint-Domingue, not go to school
in Paris. And when we arrived here, there was
already one underway.

A revolution, but not for us.

People who see me—brown skinned, curly
haired—assume I am a slave.

But I have always been free, in body and heart.
People do not understand that there is no freedom
they can give me through the laws they plan to make.
It already belongs to me.

By saying they can give it, as if it belongs to them,
they try to take it away.

Why then, you ask, do I sell oranges and
strawberries on the streets?

When we came to France, I believed I would, like my brother, have something more. I believed my mother would let me step into this new way of life easily. New ideas, new hopes. But she only saw fears and danger in this cold foreign place. And when I came home with a new friend, he was nothing but a threat.

I WAS GIVEN A CHOICE:
HER AND THE OLD WAYS & COMFORTS
OR
HIM AND THE NEW
I chose
*FREEDOM*
BUT
FREEDOM IS NOT FREE
IT
HAS
A
COST

# 20

In a precise line on a grassy field, five tethered balloons trembled in the wind.

For the last few days, while Camille had been printing Margot's story and trying not to hope for too much from the magicians' visit to the Hôtel Séguin—for wasn't it possible Blaise might find what she'd searched for in vain in the library?—Lazare had been busy with preparations for the launch.

Though they'd made plans to see the first public performance of Les Merveilleux at the Palais-Royal, Camille hadn't seen Lazare except for one late dinner at a restaurant on the fashionable Left Bank. In the room, candles had glowed among pools of dark. Lazare had proposed champagne—*we must celebrate being together, when the world conspires to keep us apart*—and between courses they held hands across the tablecloth, her small pale one clasped in his long-fingered brown one as they dreamed about what they might do, together. After his work with the balloon corps was finished, after she'd made sure the girls were free to stay in their home. They might take a balloon voyage over the Alps, combining pleasure with cloud studies. Talking and laughing late into the night, they had a thousand ideas, each one more entrancing than the next. As their faces flushed with the restaurant's warmth and their own excitement, the possibilities seemed endless.

Over dessert, surrounded by the wealthy of Paris in their costly silks, both of them had wondered how the diners could live as if nothing had changed. They wore fur stoles and ate the choicest meat, their wineglasses never empty, gossiping about parties and card games and masquerades—in sharp contrast, Camille said, to the girls' plight. For while Lasalle was selling subscriptions, and the people of Paris were voicing their support, the mayor's office had not yet revoked the eviction. Yesterday Camille had gone back to Flotsam House to show the girls the latest pamphlets.

As she'd written and printed them, she'd had the blur's dangerous magic at the back of her mind and she had wondered: What would happen if, instead of holding back, she let the magic race through her? *An experiment,* she'd told herself. Giving in had felt dangerously good, though, the fever running hot and wild along her skin.

But here on the Champ de Mars, the early morning wind was cool on her cheeks.

Each balloon was tied to the ground with stakes, ropes radiating starlike from them. Inside the wicker gondolas, fires burned in braziers and looped along the edges of each basket was tricolor bunting, tied at the corners into rosettes. In contrast to the tricolor's bright hues, the silk of the balloons paled: dull blue, stippled with flecks of gray. Not balloons embroidered with romantic names, but balloons designed for stealth. For disappearing. Lazare had told her and Rosier that for this first balloon trial, there was no room for error—not if the corps were to continue.

"Do you see him?" Camille stood on her toes, searching over the heads of the people waiting, a mix of military men and all sorts of Parisians, including a small group of boys who peered awestruck at the swirl of activity ahead of the launch.

Rosier pointed. "There!"

Lazare was kneeling by the far balloon, testing the knot around the stake. He wore a vivid azure-blue suit she had not seen before. A gentle wind played with the end of his cravat, disheveling his hair. But he did not notice; all his concentration was on the rope.

Could her heart leap such a distance? She willed him to turn and see them.

"Lazare Mellais!" Rosier called out, waving.

Lazare stood, his face lit with a broad smile. He came toward them, almost running. On his coat was pinned a sky-blue badge with a red balloon embroidered on it, golden rays behind it. "Well? What do you think?"

"It's impressive to see them all like this," Camille said. "You're ready?"

"Another minute or so and we'll let them all go at once." He saw the question in Camille's face and said, "You're right, it's risky, but Lafayette . . . he is as fond of the grand gesture as you are, Rosier."

"I assume the bunting and the fantastic badges are one of your touches, Mellais?" Rosier said innocently.

"Me? I had no control over those things. It was . . . almost as if someone else had suggested it."

"A genius hat designer, no doubt," Rosier replied.

"Bunting or not, the balloons are beautiful, Lazare," Camille said. "Like rain."

"Or clouds," he said. "Best of all they are fully kitted out with barometers and altimeters and every measuring device I could think of. I was allowed to assign two cadets to watch each balloon as it takes off. Not only to assess the aeronauts' flying skills, but they will record a flight path for each one, for me to read against the five separate sets of measurements I'll have at the end." He narrowed his eyes at the row of waiting balloons. "Assuming nothing goes wrong."

"Not on a day like today!" Rosier exclaimed. "So many people have come to watch! Really, Lazare, we might have had a very small military band to play a jaunty tune."

"The size of the crowd—should I thank you for that, too?"

"Naturellement."

"Soon," he said, "you'll even take credit for my parents."

*His parents?*

"They're here?" Camille regretted not choosing something more expensive to wear. That they had tried to arrange a marriage for Lazare to a ludicrously wealthy girl still rankled.

Lazare gestured toward the last balloon, where he'd been standing when they arrived. His parents waited at the very front, his father serious, his proud stepmother's diamonds washed out in the sunlight. They were speaking animatedly with the Marquis de Lafayette, elegant in his blue-and-white uniform. Though handsome, with a long straight nose and bright color in his cheeks, there was also a kind of severity to his face, as if he were assessing something in the distance and finding it lacking.

They were a tightly knit group, and she understood now the pressure Lazare had been under. "I'm sure they'll be proud to see your project take its first flight into the world."

Lazare tugged at his perfectly tied cravat. "As long as everything goes well. Lafayette has made it clear that if the balloons can't do the surveillance he wants, he will put money into something more reliable."

There was a weighted silence, into which no one said anything until Rosier observed, "Still, it's good of your parents to come—they haven't always been enthusiastic about balloons."

"An understatement if there ever was one, Rosier. But they changed their minds," Lazare replied carefully, "once Lafayette was involved."

Rosier's head snapped up. "Speak of the devil—here comes the man himself."

As Lafayette approached, everything about Lazare seemed to tighten. He crossed his arms over his chest, then uncrossed them and set his shoulders back. In the line of balloons, the pilots were making final adjustments to their loads. A few cast glances in his direction.

"Which balloon is yours?" she asked.

"None. I'm not going up."

"What?" she gasped. "I thought you were going to lead them in the air!"

A muscle ticked in his jaw. "I'm sorry if I gave you that impression—"

Camille turned to Rosier for confirmation and saw that Lafayette now stood beside them. The marquis clamped a hand on Lazare's shoulder. "Sablebois is too valuable to send up into the air. Not simply because of his expertise, but because he is the future of France."

Rosier blinked. "Is he?"

Lafayette's voice was smooth and rich. "He is a young man of science. He is a nobleman but also of the people's cause, as am I. A foot in both worlds, one might say. Revolution is a delicate balance, especially if we wish to avoid war." Lafayette released Lazare from his grip. "Your friend was born for this great task. He is, as you said at Madame de Staël's salon, our hope. And you two are patriotic in your support of him." He bowed slightly to Camille. "As his commander, I appreciate your understanding."

Lafayette wished them to say nothing. He had wrapped it in tricolor ribbons, but his demand was clear: be silent and complicit and keep Lazare doing what Lafayette wished, not what Lazare wanted to do. It made her furious. "But can't Lazare also—"

Lazare didn't look at her. "Is it not time for launch, monsieur?"

"Indeed," Lafayette said. And with a curt nod to Camille and Rosier, he steered Lazare toward the small stage that had been erected in front of the line of balloons.

Camille's heart sank. "Rosier, what's happening?"

"I hardly know. Whatever it is, our friend is not happy about it."

A bright bugle rang out, and the crowd swayed forward. Anticipating.

With Lazare beside him, Lafayette addressed the crowd. His voice carried easily over the parade grounds. "Mesdames, messieurs—welcome to the inaugural launch of the National Aeronautical Corps! You will now witness an expression of France's unsurpassed military strength and innovation." Indicating that Lazare should stand by the balloons, he said: "Monsieur Mellais, our head aeronaut and leader of this unit, has helped make this possible. Please, a round of applause."

Lazare made a modest bow.

"Now, messieurs," Lafayette cried to the aeronauts, "prepare for departure!"

A gun fired a shot, and the cadets released the first balloon. It rose smoothly into the air, one aeronaut at attention, the other filling the brazier with fuel. Another shot rang out and the second balloon took flight. The balloons rose gracefully into the air, one after another, without any difficulties, until the last one was released. As the crowd gasped, the balloons sailed higher and higher, until they were no bigger than birds in the sky. The pilots would be cold now, she remembered from her time in the air, putting on extra coats and dampening the fires once they reached the correct altitude.

And Lazare?

While she'd been watching the balloons rise, he'd rejoined his parents. As he listened to something his father was saying, his face was a careful blank.

"Grace à Dieu, it went so well," Rosier muttered. "He would have been devastated had anything gone wrong. This is rather more of a high-stakes game than I had thought."

She thought of Lafayette's hand on Lazare's shoulder. "Because Lafayette is calling the shots?"

"That," he mused, "and his parents. It didn't strike you as strange that Lafayette showed up at the Sablebois estate, balloon proposal in hand? Why not wait until Lazare returned to Paris?" He took a thoughtful drag on his unlit pipe. "Though, as Lazare said, perhaps he was in a rush, worrying about Austria at the borders."

Camille watched as Lafayette pointed to the balloons, explaining something to Lazare's parents. His father, who had seemed so stiff and formal when Camille had last seen him, had become jubilant, his gaze never leaving Lazare. "Do you trust Lafayette?"

"He has the face of a good gambler. Working all the odds. Though what he believes in, I can't say."

It was true—no great emotion altered his features, only small ones: a smile, a circumspect frown, a careful nod. Instead, he seemed to be thinking several moves ahead, as in a game of chess.

"I'd guess he believes in France, the way my papa believed in the People and the journalist Marat believes in Change. But because of that," she said, as the memory of her parents' argument about magic and revolution came back to her, "they forget the big ideas are actually made up of people."

Rosier raised an impressed eyebrow. "Well said, pamphleteer."

She gave Rosier a sidelong glance. "Do you think Lazare always knew he wasn't going up?"

He shook his head. "I'd wager it was a new development. Why not tell us, otherwise?"

*Why not indeed?*

They both turned to watch him.

By the launch line, Lazare was greeting the spectators, one after another. In return he was clapped on the shoulder. Commended. Saluted. Each time someone congratulated him, he seemed almost to flinch. Anyone who *didn't* know him would have said he was smiling. But Lazare's smiles were nothing like those narrow grins. Anyone who did know him could see Lazare longed to be away from the crowd and whatever burden Lafayette had placed on him, and instead, up in the air.

Overhead, the gray balloons had almost disappeared. Only the bunting on their baskets blazed against the sky. Soon that too would be invisible.

*Next time*, she wished. Next time, he would be in the air. For surely Lafayette couldn't keep him grounded forever?

# THE LOST GIRLS SPEAK
## THE PICKPOCKET

### I HAVE BEEN PICKING POCKETS
### AT THE PALAIS-ROYAL
### SINCE I WAS FIFTEEN
### AND NO ONE HAS EVER SEEN ME

My eldest sister was beautiful. My mother married her off first, to a butcher in St Germain. Once our favorite sister was gone, Maman got busy with the rest of us. One fine gown for the bigger girls, one fine gown for the smaller ones. False diamonds and wigs, satin slippers and tight corsets were what we wore when men came to call. All of us upstairs, a nest of waiting mice, listening for what the man would say.

Sometimes he would ask for a song on the piano, or something to be sung. Or a dance. And if the dance was not to his liking, another sister would go down to try, but only after the first one had come up and, full of joy from having freed herself, thrown off the gown for the another sister to put on.

For the moment

SAFE

We could all dance and play the fortepiano and smile as if we meant it. We could talk and flatter and blush.

I believed marriage would free me from this never-ending show and so I went with the first man who brought me flowers and a ring. Yet there was no grand carriage waiting outside as I had supposed. Instead we walked to his house. It was far, and the buildings were no nicer than ours. It was not what had been promised.

I might have endured it, though, and continued to pretend at Happiness for at least I was rid of Maman, but for one thing he did, which I took as a Sign.

He did not offer me his arm, as I had been taught a rich gentleman should. Instead he held me by the wrist, his hand hard as a manacle. I was not free, but chained. As luck would have it, a carriage nearly ran into us, and when he fled the horses' hooves, I fled him.

I could do my pretending elsewhere and make my own living by it.

I never steal from the poor.
Because the
POCKETS OF THE RICH
are
FULL

# 21

Tonight, she decided, was only for marvels.

Though she hadn't been there in months, the Palais-Royal remained the dizzying carnival it had always been. Under lanterns in the gardens, people were dancing; beneath the arcades, shoppers peered through gleaming windows at fine books and lace and jewels. From political cafés erupted shouts and loud conversation, and sometimes, fistfights. There were flower sellers and fruit sellers, and Camille wondered if Margot in her bright clothes were there tonight, her oranges kept cool with ice. Or Héloïse, dancing in one of the rooms in the palace, her dangerous smile on her partner while her hands relieved him of his purse. Though she searched the crowd, none of the girls she spotted at the Palais-Royal were ones she knew. She refused the leaflets handed out all

over, even when they were pressed into her hands. She smiled and continued on, her hand tucked instead around Lazare's arm.

If he didn't wish to speak about Lafayette and what had happened at
the launch, she would not pry. Perhaps she'd misread him, for there was
nothing about the way he was behaving now that suggested he'd been angry or disappointed. Perhaps he had accepted his position and what it
entailed.

She decided to believe it. Tonight nothing would get in their way.

"Can you see where Les Merveilleux will perform?" she asked.

"Not yet." Lazare wore a new suit, beautifully cut to flatter, over an
elegant waistcoat embroidered with tiny hot-air balloons, a gift from his
stepmother. The unsettled, evasive mood of the balloon launch had vanished, replaced by a kind of electricity that made it hard for Camille to look
anywhere else but at him.

"Will they be under the trees, do you think, or in the arcade?"

Lazare craned his neck to see over the crowd. "Toward the back of this
courtyard, I'm sure of it."

By the time they found the painted sign proclaiming LES MERVEILLEUX,
TONIGHT!, an eager audience was already gathering, drawn in by a violinist
playing a sweetly melancholy tune. Between two chestnut trees red curtains
hung like twinned waterfalls. On either side of them, torches illuminated
the waiting stage.

"It seems so much more real, somehow, than before," Camille observed.

"Rosier promised we would be amazed at the transformation."

The curtains rippled as Sophie stepped out from behind them and came
to stand alongside Camille. Her pleased smile gleamed in the dark. "Just
you wait."

In the evening air, the lilting music floated into the trees. As Camille
listened, the buzz and chaos of the Palais-Royal, the criers and the pamphleteers, the arguing café patrons and the intoxicated gamblers faded, until the noise was no louder than wind rustling through dry leaves and all
that existed was this glowing space of dreams.

The curtains drew apart. Beside her, Sophie tensed.

On the stage were two puppets—tall as humans, but otherworldly.

Long-limbed and elegant, they wore flowing white costumes, touched here and there with golden stars. Behind them stood two puppeteers dressed in black, holding the sticks that made the puppets move.

"Well?" Sophie asked confidentially. "Do you like the new puppets?"

"They are so large, Sophie! Almost like people . . . or beautiful spirits. Or is that wrong to say?"

"Not at all." Sophie's face shone as if Camille had given her a gift. "That is perfect."

One of the puppets was a princess, wearing a gold crown. She surveyed the skies, her arms outstretched like wings, then she bent low, nearly gliding along the ground.

"A snake!" someone called out.

Sophie frowned. "*That* is not perfect."

As the princess searched, the young man watched from the eaves of a forest. He wore a beard, a tall hat, and a gold earring that glinted in the torchlight. A pirate? As the princess ran through the dark forest of firs behind them, one of his feet tapped impatiently on the stage.

"How lifelike it is!" Lazare said in her ear. "Their movements are so human—"

They *did* seem human, and yet they were not. There was something about them that was like magic—enchanted objects brought to life? But there was no sorrow in it that she could see. Watching Sophie gazing eagerly at the stage, Camille knew it was mostly love.

From behind his back, the young man produced a single red rose.

"Oh!" someone exclaimed, and was hushed.

The princess stopped searching, finally seeing him. He gave the rose to her; she planted its stem in the ground. As the violin played faster, the flower began to grow.

"Regardez!" cried a little girl. "Look, Maman!"

Camille couldn't tell how they had done it, but the rose grew and grew until it had become a tree full of red roses. The princess plucked one of the blooms and pricked her finger. A handful of petals were tossed out into the audience as great white wings unfurled from her shoulders. As the crowd gasped, the princess lifted into the air. When the young man examined his own back and found nothing there, the crowd demanded, "Give him wings!"

"Just as we hoped," Sophie murmured.

The princess had landed on a wire, like in Astley's circus. She teetered one way, then the other, before she reached down and pulled him up. Together they stood on the wire in perfect balance before flying away. Paper snow glittered over them, though where it came from no one could tell. When the curtains swayed closed, the circle of watchers were silent and awed before bursting into applause.

"Fantastique, Sophie!" Camille exclaimed.

"Truly marvelous," Lazare added. "You are to be congratulated on the costumes."

"I did more than that," Sophie said archly. But Camille could see she was thrilled. She had not seen Sophie this happy in a long time. "I must find Rosier before he gives the puppeteers their notes. The princess cannot be mistaken for a snake! And I really do think we need to bring back the bear." Blowing them a kiss, she hurried through the crowd to the back of the stage. From behind the red curtain, Rosier emerged, pipe in one hand, notebook in the other, as Sophie led him away behind the chestnut trees. The only emotion on their faces was joy.

"Shall we walk a little?" Lazare offered her his arm, and they strolled away from the torches and gaiety of the puppet theater. Among the walkways, criers shouted the latest news from the Assembly at Versailles, and she and Lazare slowed to listen. It seemed the nobles and the clergy—some of them, at least—were renouncing the hereditary rights that hurt their tenants. "The revolution continues!" the crier said. Nearby a man had set up a table with a metal machine on it, as tall as the top of his head. On the placard it said: EQUAL IN LIFE, EQUAL IN DEATH! A FREE DEMONSTRATION OF DR GUILLOTIN'S EXECUTION MACHINE! As passersby clustered close to watch, the man operating the machine stuck a carrot in the base of it, then let the mechanism go. With dizzying speed, the blade screeched from the top to slice the carrot in half.

Camille blanched. It felt like death was everywhere. "Have you heard of this machine?"

"In the Assembly, Dr. Guillotin has vowed there shall be no more hangings," Lazare said. "All criminals will die as efficiently as aristocrats have been privileged to do, by the sword. I can't help but wonder, though, if there aren't more pressing issues."

"Like voting rights for women."

He nodded. "And freedom for French slaves in the West Indies."

They left the guillotine behind just as a commotion broke out. The door of a jewelry shop hung brokenly on its hinges. Shouts rang out from inside as two red-cloaked Comité guards dragged the jeweler into the arcade, stopping in front of a young woman with a tricolor sash around her waist.

Camille's heart began to race. This close, the guards were huge, towering over the jeweler. Their dogs growled, showing their teeth.

The woman waved a pamphlet in the jeweler's face. Camille caught the first few words:

MAGICIANS

TRAITORS

TREASON

A knot of fear tightened inside of her.

"I am innocent!" the jeweler cried. His costly jacket had been torn at the shoulder and his wig was dirty, as if it'd been stepped on. "She has no evidence! Put my diamonds to any test and you will see that they are authentic."

"Authentic?" hissed the woman. "What I bought from you is no longer diamonds but dust! You are a magician!"

Camille froze in horror.

One of the guards reached out a calming hand to the woman. "Do not trouble yourself any longer, madame. You've done the people's work. We will take over now." Inside the shop, a pale-faced assistant was locking the door.

"Camille?" Lazare asked, worried. "Is it the Comité?"

She kept her voice low, smoothing the terror from it. It was not something she wished Lazare to see. "That woman said the jeweler had cheated her, that the gems she'd bought had turned to dust . . . but what proof did she show? With this new law, anyone can be accused!"

The woman's tale had the ring of truth. For wasn't that how magic worked, forever fading? But it was also the kind of thing that was printed in pamphlets or on posters like the one the woman carried. Camille didn't know what frightened her more, that it was true—or that it was not.

"King Mob will soon rule Paris," Lazare said, his voice flat, as the guards shoved the jeweler along. "And what will become of our city then? Besides, why would a magician run a jewelry shop?"

"I don't know." But she could guess. Desperate to stop talking about magic, wanting to keep this night a night apart from these troubles, she cast around for something else to do, another place to go. She had no interest in card games anymore, but there was something else: the magic lantern show, where pictures came to life. She'd always longed to step inside the darkened room where a blazing lantern illuminated painted slides of faraway places. It was, Papa had told her, like traveling without setting foot in a carriage. Impulsively, she asked, "Have you ever seen the magic lantern?"

That lazy smile. "I haven't, but I would go with you."

Heat flushed along her throat. "It's on our way out," she said as she steered him away from the difficult things and toward what she'd hoped the night would be, to the gaudy sign advertising the magic lantern show.

"When did you last come to the Palais-Royal?" he asked.

"A few hours after we first met, as it happens." How desperate she had been then, gambling to win back what Alain had taken. "I came to find my brother, who had stolen our best dresses. He'd gambled them away and gotten drunk on the proceeds before I'd had a chance to follow him."

Anger thinned Lazare's lips. "And?"

Proudly, she said, "I played cards with the girls who'd won the dresses. They cheated, but I beat them anyway." It wasn't the whole story.

"And the magic lantern?"

"I only caught a glimpse before the barker shooed me away. I didn't have money for a ticket."

Ahead of them, the mesmerizing light of the lantern beckoned from the doorway, just as it had that night in the spring. On the glass window was written in Latin, in curving gold letters: LANTERNA MAGICA. Beneath it was a smaller sign indicating tonight's show: ALL AROUND THE WORLD.

As they went in, the same barker who'd once waved Camille off now happily took the coins she gave him before gesturing for her and Lazare to find their seats. The chamber was dark and smelled of the whale oil used in the special lamp—as strong as ten candles together—that lit the slides. A smoky haze hung under the low ceiling. Taking her by the hand, Lazare led her to a small sofa. They squeezed together, Lazare trying to make room for her skirts. "Close enough?" he asked, laughing.

Was there a close-enough where Lazare was concerned? She didn't think so. "Perfect."

"Silence!" intoned a voice from behind them. "Regard the screen! Your journey around the world begins now!"

A hush came over the room as the first image flared to life. Ruined buildings, woolly sheep wandering through the weeds. "Rome, cradle of civilization, brought low by greed and corruption!"

The slide shifted—a blink of night—and then a new picture appeared. Pyramids in a desert. Strange, horse-like creatures standing in front of them.

"What are they?" Camille whispered.

"I think they must be camels."

And so their journey through space and time continued. The lazy canals of Venice, a building with a circle cut out of its domed roof through which rain fell, a wide wall that ran away to a mountainous horizon. A small family standing by a river, their slender boat loaded with pelts. And arching over them, enormous trees. Camille recognized it at once. "A family of Indians," the barker announced, "preparing to sell their furs to the French on la Rivière Hudson."

Lazare shifted next to her. "Not Indians."

In the froth of her skirts, Camille sought his hand and interwove her fingers among his. "This," she said softly, "was the slide I saw that night, when I looked in. How beautiful they are, this little family, n'est-ce pas? See how the trees protect them! When I first saw it, I didn't hear how the man described it. I imagined—" Suddenly she felt incredibly silly. Why was she telling him this?

Lazare turned slightly toward her, the light from the projection setting his eyes aflame. "Tell me. What did you imagine?"

"That they were going on a grand adventure. Somewhere far away. How I envied them!" Her life had become much bigger since then, but the longing remained. "I still do."

"I did once promise you a great adventure."

They'd talked about many over dinner last week, but there was one above all she wished for. "Over the Alps."

She felt his smile against her cheek. "Why not? Or perhaps we might settle into that little boat and paddle it into the unknown. Would you run away with me, Camille Durbonne? So very far?"

In that moment of velvet darkness when the slide had vanished and before the next picture appeared, she leaned daringly close. He smelled of vetiver cologne, leather and wood smoke, the heat of his skin. He was adventure and possibility, risk and daring and desire. It intoxicated her, and she said into the curve of his ear: "Yes."

"Then we must do it."

The next slide, a crimson fort ornamented with cupolas and minarets, filled the room with a reddish glow, and out of the corner of her eye, she saw Lazare's face light with wonder. "This one I know from books," he said. "We would have to go very far, all the way to India."

"I cannot wait."

As the next slide slipped into place and Lazare whispered hot in her ear, his breath making her shiver as he told her what he knew of that place, she knew she'd gotten her wish: tonight *was* an evening of marvels, all darkness forgotten.

*BEWARE*

the

TREASON

of

MAGICIANS

RISE UP

*AGAINST THE TRAITORS IN OUR MIDST*

⤜ ⤛

CITIZENS!

BE A PATRIOT

BE THE EARS & EYES

THAT CATCH THESE DEVILS

REPORT THEM TO THE COMITÉ

LIBERTÉ

ÉGALITÉ

FRATERNITÉ

OU

LA MORT

# 22

Soon strange notes began to appear at the Hôtel Séguin. At first Camille found them tucked among the everyday letters and bills, though the way they behaved was anything but ordinary. Some notes disintegrated to ash. Others lifted into the air, as if carried by an undetectable wind, and dissolved when they brushed against the ceiling. And there were those that melted in her hands like a marzipan flower held too long.

Despite the sheer number of notes, the news wasn't good. Blaise reported he hadn't yet found a book that revealed the secrets of making the blur, and now that he and Chandon had scoured most of Paris's bookstores and personal libraries, they would come to the Hôtel Séguin. *Let us know when it is safe*, he wrote. As the ink faded from the paper and she thought of what she'd witnessed at the Palais-Royal, she wondered: What did he mean by *safe?*

Late at night she'd wander the hallways of the old mansion, and as she passed the printing room, hear the pamphlets sighing beyond the double doors. It was obvious even to those who knew little about magic that they were . . . unusual. Arrestingly beautiful and, as reviewers never forgot to mention, exceptionally persuasive. They had brought fame and money to the girls, and that had saved Flotsam House.

They themselves had told Camille the story of how it happened.

Only a couple of days ago, a police officer had arrived at the cottage with a letter. Henriette the forger had read it aloud. By order of the mayor, the letter announced, the house would not be destroyed and the girls would have the right to remain in it as long as it remained standing. When she finished reading, the girls whooped with joy, Héloïse embracing the shocked (but not entirely reluctant) officer.

Camille tried to convince them to speak in public, to show people with influence in Paris that more help was needed, but they weren't interested. "They will want to change us, and we are happy as we are," Henriette said. A copy of the first pamphlet, *The Flower Seller*, was preserved in a curlicued frame that hung from a nail in Flotsam House. "It is," Giselle observed, "the piece of paper that changed our lives." Odette and Margot had grumbled that Giselle put too much weight such a small thing when so much had changed for them—all of Paris was improving because of the revolution— but Giselle, her enormous eyes fixed on Camille, had squeezed her hand and whispered: "Merci mille fois, mon amie."

And if magic, however unwilling she was to have it, had made that happen, how could she stop? Wasn't it worth it, even if the fevered printing felt wrong but also . . . uneasily right? What she needed, she told herself, was to control her uncontrollable magic. There had to be a way. More than ever, it could not seep out and be discovered.

Magic must stay hidden.

For after what she'd seen at the Palais-Royal, the Comité had crept into her dreams. In cloaks dyed red they followed her, their snarling mouths packed with yellow teeth. Once they sniffed out her magic, they tore off her fingers, one by one, and swallowed them whole. Outside her dreams the Comité was everywhere—even the seamstresses at Le Sucre complained to Sophie that red fabric was hard to come by, now that the long capes of the Comité guards required so many lengths of it. And, they said in a hush, the reason they wore red was so that they when they caught evil magicians in the act of whatever . . . abomination they practiced . . . any blood spilled wouldn't show. Sophie had laughed it off, telling them they were being silly, but she told Camille it made her nervous.

"Don't worry, it cannot touch us," she said to Sophie.

But her nightmares said the opposite. She needed a way forward, and soon.

Meanwhile, at the Hôtel Séguin, invitations to parties and salons and events celebrating the revolution and Camille's part in the change arrived like a blizzard of early snow. Unlike the vanishing magical notes, these accumulated in drifts on salvers, on the mantelpiece, and on the escritoire, where they threatened to overwhelm it. Sophie teased Camille that she needed to hire a private secretary to manage her correspondence.

At first she accepted them all. It was intoxicating to listen to speeches by the wild-eyed Jean-Paul Marat, scientist and writer, who'd started his own newspaper, L'Ami du Peuple, and burned with an almost religious fire. His belief that the poorest of the French deserved the most resonated with her own. There was also the passionate lawyer Georges Danton, who stood like a hero on the chairs at the Café Procope and encouraged the audience to rise up. "What else is there?" he shouted. "You must dare to change!"

Then one day an invitation arrived for both her and Lazare, several tricolor ribbons stuck to it with red wax. They were to be honored at a dinner for the rising figures of the Revolution, the young Parisians who had already made a great contribution: Camille for her pamphlets on the Lost Girls, Lazare for the balloon corps.

"Why do they want us?" Lazare had wondered. "Surely there are more deserving people in Paris."

"I imagine they'll be there, too. But think what this might do for the girls—and the corps! Surely there'll be someone there who can see that balloons can be more than military machines. And, I promise, if it gets dreary, we'll slip out."

"In that case, I'll be hoping for the dullest, dreariest night I can imagine," he said, though there was something in the way he said it that made her think he wasn't convinced they should go at all.

It turned out he was right.

There were speeches between the dinner's many courses. During dessert, men stood up one after another, puffed and proud, speaking loudly to be heard. Camille and Lazare, among others, were asked to stand as their contributions were described to resounding applause. Boys placed laurel crowns on their heads and tricolor corsages on their shoulders. The men in attendance wore plain suits, when at court they'd peacocked in pastel silks along with the nobility. The women dressed in white, with sashes of blue, white, and red draped over their shoulders. The jewels they'd once worn to court adorned their necks and ears only so that they could be tossed into a basket to raise money for the revolutionary cause, the women who made these donations wildly applauded to cries of "Vive la Nation!"

There was something about it that felt wrong.

Sitting at a large table littered with half-empty plates and glasses as yet another speaker rose to list the virtues of the revolution, Camille turned to Lazare. "Does it unsettle you?"

Lazare's eyebrows drew together sharply. "Do they believe what they're saying? Or did they just change to suit the times?" He'd finished eating and was folding his napkin into intricate shapes. "Eventually they'll want to change us, too. Would you do that? Be more . . . whatever it is they want?"

She had changed already. Not long ago she'd vowed never to use magic again, and already she had. Not for her own benefit, she told herself, but for the girls. Though as she remembered the applause that had greeted her short speech about the plight of the poor, and the pleasure she'd had at their cheers, what exactly was for the girls and for the Revolution and for herself was more tangled than she'd thought.

She took a bite of a too-sweet dessert. "If it were the right change?"

Lazare's napkin now resembled a listing balloon. "And how do we know if it's the right change?"

"If it's for the good. If I have to put on a white gown with a tricolor sash, what of it? If I come here and show my face and they toast me, and it helps Paris's poor children, why not? I am not so very proud." But as she said the words, she felt less certain. Was it possible to change too much? Or in the wrong direction, so that the changes you made took you to some place other than you'd intended?

"Your motives at least are good," Lazare said, softening.

Rebellion sparked in her. "Not always."

His dark gaze traveled to her mouth, and for a moment she thought about finally telling him what she was doing with magic, how she couldn't control it. And that sometimes she didn't even want to.

It would be a relief to finally be honest. For though she basked in his praise, it was beginning to feel like a costly and beloved jacket that had grown too tight. If she told him, would he say she was right to do it? That magic was nothing to him? That he trusted her?

She had no way to tell. And when he was looking at her like this—so intensely her heart began to race—she didn't want to find out.

"*You* are true," he said finally, "while others are only playing parts. Take the duc." Nearby a tall man lounged at a crowded table, surrounded by eager hangers-on. "He calls himself Philippe Égalité, but no one forgets he's still the powerful Duc d'Orléans, cousin to King Louis. Or that he himself wouldn't mind being king if things changed. When it's convenient for the cause, his name and title will be used against him. What's to say they're not using you and me in the same way—to put on a good show?" He crumpled his napkin into a ball. "They're pretenders, all of them. And I hate the feeling of their hands on my soul."

The strangeness at the balloon launch came back to her. "Has something happened, Lazare?"

He shook his head. "I wish I didn't have to pretend right along with them."

While the toasts rang out in the warm, well-lit room, outside in the streets, the people of Paris still starved. Suspected magicians were dragged from their shops. Bakers who ran out of bread were strung up from lampposts. Only yesterday Sophie had confided she'd heard about a list with the names of antirevolutionary nobles written on it in blood. But Camille had said nothing about these things in her speech. Instead, she'd said what the organizers had wanted her to say.

Was that pretending, too?

There was a sudden commotion in the hall as one of the double doors swung open. A young man appeared, dressed in the uniform of the National Guard. The room stilled, heads pivoting toward him. "Monsieur Mellais?" he called out over the assembled guests. "Monsieur Mellais?"

Lazare rose from his chair, the music fading as everyone stared.

When the guard reached the table, he handed Lazare a letter. He cracked the seal and quickly read through the note. He gave instructions to the messenger, who retreated back through the hall and out the door.

Lazare seemed suddenly very far away.

"What is it?" she asked urgently.

"There's been an incident, mon âme." The paper shook in his hand. "The corps had been planning to go eventually to Lille, near the border with the Austrian Netherlands. Lafayette wants a garrison there, with one or two balloons, to gather information at the border. But the time line has been moved up. An Austrian man was caught distributing antirevolutionary pamphlets near there, and Lafayette is sending us now."

"But why you? I thought he wanted you on the ground." *Safe.*

"The pilots don't have the experience. No one expected an incident so early, not while they were still in training. If I go with them, and we fly together, I can guide them."

*All the way to Lille?* "When?"

He tore the letter in half. "Lafayette wants us to leave tomorrow, if the weather holds. It will reassure the people, he says."

Something else gnawed at him, she could tell. She saw it in his restless movements, the way he raked his hand through his hair. "What is it, Lazare?"

"For it to work, we must fly together . . . I do not know if they will listen to me."

Puzzled, Camille said, "The other aeronauts? But they must—"

"What if they don't consider me their leader?" He tore the letter in half again. "I am an amateur and not military trained. I got my position through . . . connections. They mistrust me because of the way Lafayette treats me—we are both of equal rank, after all. And there is, as always," he said bitterly, "the color of my skin."

At the launch, she'd seen the pilots' sharp looks. "This cannot be tolerated—"

"No? I am well used to it." His voice was grim. "And if it isn't my Indian blood, it's my title and my wealth. Caught in between, neither one thing or the other, I cannot win." He managed to tear torn paper in half again. "To them I am *different*, and that's what matters. They haven't disobeyed one of my orders yet, but how can I trust them when I hear the things they say? Their suspicious stares? And yet"—he ripped the letter into tinier and tinier pieces—"I must. For Lafayette, for France, for the Revolution." He let the shreds of the letter fall onto his plate.

"Look at me." Slowly, he turned his beautiful face toward her. She loved the scar that sliced through his eyebrow for what it said about his fearlessness, the inky tilt of his lashes that framed the worlds in his eyes. "You are better than ten thousand of those pilots. Fifty thousand! Lafayette knows you alone have the knowledge to guide this flight. That's why he came to you. There's no one else in France who can do it. Everything you are goes into what you do. And they are fools if they don't realize it."

He glanced helplessly around the noisy, crowded ballroom. "Do you ever wish that there was a place where it wasn't like this? Where things were different? Where we might simply *be*?"

Her throat tightened. "All the time."

"Remind me of it when I return," he said sorrowfully, "for now I must take my leave."

"But I'll see you at the Champ de Mars—did Lafayette say what time the launch will be?"

"He says it's military only." He took her hand and pressed his mouth to her knuckles. It was suddenly unbearable that she would not be allowed to see him off.

"Why would he care if I were there? Wasn't I once an aeronaut?" she added.

Faintly, he smiled. "I would rather have you with me than anyone. But you will help me most by following his orders."

"I can at least walk you out."

He shook his head. "Please stay. I can't be responsible for you not finishing your cake. À bientôt, mon âme."

He made his way out of the room, avoiding questions as best as he could, making for the doors. This was his occupation now, she told herself. This is what he did. She too did what she must. Still, fury crackled through her when she thought of the men who refused to see him as their leader because of the color of his skin. So far the revolution had not delivered equality.

The room fading around her, she saw in her mind the best version of the launch, as if she could work magic to turn a tarnished event into gold. No military band, no fluttering flags, no proudly worn badges. Instead there would be a serene sky, a flurry of efficient activity as the balloons were prepared for the journey. Various members of the corps running back and forth, carts arriving with more straw and cut wood. No suspicion or disrespect on their part. She and Lazare would kiss before he ran to his balloon and vaulted inside. The ropes would be untied as the brazier fires flared, and slowly, majestically, the balloons would rise. The crew on the ground would cheer. And she, the only bystander, would applaud as the balloons rose into the morning sky.

Watching a balloon rise always filled her with hope. A thing of the earth—a silk sack, a wicker gondola—transformed into a thing of the air. It was one of the most beautiful things she knew.

At the ornate double doors, Lazare paused to survey the crowded room. When he spotted her, he smiled that crooked, one-sided smile she adored, full of promise and determination.

It would be a flight of great uncertainty.

It was nothing new, but it still was hard. She waved adieu and, though he was too far away to hear, she softly entreated, "Please come back to me."

# 23

It was past ten when she left the revolutionary party. At the door, guests eager to be seen with the pamphleteer offered her a ride in their carriages, but she told them she needed fresh air. Lazare's words tinted her thoughts, so that in each of their smiles she saw only the glint of want: she was a means to an end for them, nothing more.

Outside, Camille inhaled: the air was brisk, sharp with wood smoke. Far above the stars were faint as pinpricks. Passing through pools of darkness and pools of yellow lamplight on her short walk home, she was deep in her thoughts about Lazare and his disdain of pretending as she crossed the Place des Vosges. But when she turned onto her own street, she was jolted out of her reveries.

At the iron gate to the Hôtel Séguin stood five guards of the Comité.

They were like fragments of gloom: long cloaks, muttered words like curses rising into the night. And straining on the end of a lead, a giant dog built like a bull. It shoved its massive head against the gate as it sniffed the air.

She pressed her back to the Hôtel Séguin's stone wall, flattening herself away from the street lamp. In her ears, the blood pounded so hard she strained to hear what they were saying. Keeping to the shadows, she crept closer.

Accidently she kicked a pebble and the dog raised his head, ears swiveling. The man who held the lead spun in her direction. Under the brim of his hat, the grim line of his mouth was an angry slash.

"What is it?" one of them said.

The dog gave a low, harsh growl. "Puissant heard something."

For several heartbeats she waited. Not daring to breathe. If she'd had that vial of blur, she thought desperately, she could have snuck around to the stables. But now she was trapped.

Puissant lowered his head, snuffled again at the gate. "A rat, no doubt."

In the light that fell from the gate's lantern, the men loomed monstrous. Already bigger than ordinary men, their high-crowned hats made them even taller, as did the long cloaks that twitched at the slightest movement. On their shoulders glowed the badge of the Comité: a white hand, fingertips blackened, surrounded by flames. Magic burning. One of them held a branch that gleamed dull silver in his hand.

The biggest one grabbed the gate and shook it so it rattled. "Open up! We have a search warrant!"

On the second floor of her house, a window suddenly brightened. Someone was there, watching. Adèle? Sophie? Soon they'd discover she wasn't home. Perhaps they already knew, perhaps they were waiting for her. Either way they'd be frantic with worry. Her pulse ticked faster. Their fear for her might make them open the door. Cross the courtyard to see if she was in trouble—

The gatehouse door opened and ancient Timbault stepped out, a determined scowl on his face. "It's late, messieurs. Go to bed. Warrant or not, you're not coming in."

The dog barked. Saliva dripped from its long yellow teeth. "We are here by order of the Comité. King's business."

Through the glowing window's thin curtain, Sophie stared out, statue-still. Camille wished she could signal to her somehow. What if the guards came to the door? Came inside? Sophie was strong, Camille knew. But they might take her as a witness, or use her to get to Camille. It was an old familiar fear, growing new tentacles.

The burly guard shook a length of chain at Timbault. "We will pull this gate down if we have to."

Timbault shrugged. "Try it."

They conferred, and then one of the smaller guards said, "Warded, is it?"

Timbault said nothing. The dog raised its head and howled, the frustrated call of a predator denied what it wanted.

"These old houses," the burly one spat. "Centuries of magic to tear down. But it's possible."

Long minutes went by as they argued. More windows were illuminated in the Hôtel Séguin, and the lawyer who lived across the street came out to stand in his doorway, holding his own growling mastiff by the collar. Anything the Comité tried would wake the neighborhood, and for now, at least, they wished to seem lawful, more like the police than the mob.

As Camille waited—like an owl, she thought, staring into the night— something shifted.

"We'll be back, traitor," one of the guards threatened. "You won't keep us out forever." And with one last shove at the gate, the red-cloaked figures and their dog melted into the night.

Camille sank back against the wall. Waited until she had heard every last footstep diminish into silence. And then she slunk to the gate, not daring to step into the light of Timbault's lantern.

But he'd already seen her. "Madame," he hissed. "Get inside now!" The bolt was shot, the key turning in the lock, and she was inside. "To the house," he ordered her, "before they return!"

She fled across the court and up the stairs, where Daumier was waiting to let her in.

"Mon Dieu!" Instantly Sophie had her arms around Camille. "I can't believe you were out there with them!"

"This night of all nights I decide to walk home alone!" Camille sagged onto the marble bench as Adèle, Sophie, and silent Daumier, who stood with his back against the closed doors, regarded her worriedly. "Everything is all right. They've gone."

"All right?" Sophie squeaked. "The Comité was at our door!"

"At the *gate*, and we survived." She tucked her hands under her skirts to keep them from shaking. "Timbault and the house protected us."

"It is warded," Adele agreed. "Every magician who owned this house worked magic to keep it and its people safe. But if they come inside—"

"That will not happen," Camille said briskly.

"We do have to go outside," Sophie snapped. "Occasionally."

Daumier tried to diffuse their worry. "It's not you they want. It's what's in the house."

The bleeding tapestries. The bespelled artifacts. The documents covered in invisible ink, the oils of magical landscapes, the mirrors that reflected other rooms than their own. The floors, the chandeliers, the enchanted locks, the armaments. The snuffboxes and the curios and everything in the attics she'd not yet dared to examine. Her dress. The books. They would burn it all.

*Or would they use it as evidence to try a magician?*

"Daumier," she said, "are you familiar with weapons in the armory?"

He inclined his head.

"Please outfit yourself, Timbault, and everyone in the house who wants one with a weapon. What would you give Timbault? A musket?"

"Consider it done." With a bow, Daumier disappeared down the hall toward the room where the ancient weapons could sometimes be heard, muttering like knives being sharpened.

That night she wrote an urgent letter.

There was no time to waste, now that she'd learned the Hôtel Séguin—and possibly she herself—were in the Comité's sights.

As she waited for the ink to dry, she listened to the house rattle and clink. It sounded as if it were being fitted with armor, metal scales creeping over its windows and doors. But there would always be a chink in it.

If she knew anything, it was that there was always a way in.

# 24

A worried response to her letter arrived from Chandon early the next the day, informing Camille that he and Blaise would arrive by noon. Now that the house's clocks were striking twelve, she felt the ancient house waiting. Biding its time. If she were forced to say what it was waiting for, she would say: more magicians. More magic.

As if there wasn't already enough.

In the front salon, she pulled aside the curtain. The street was empty but for a few pigeons pecking at manure. No sign of the Comité. Or the boys. She was so intent on watching that she startled when Adèle came up behind her to say a gardener had come to the stable door, inquiring about a position.

"But we already have a gardener."

Adèle faltered. "He says you have been expecting him?"

"I'll come and speak to him." Adèle led her to the kitchen entrance at the back of the house. Camille stepped down into the kitchen, where a scullery maid scrubbing carrots was glancing nervously at the gardener. Obscuring his face was a felt toque covered with bits of straw and mud, as if it had been dropped in a particularly dirty street.

*Chandon.*

And behind him, so pale he could only ever belong indoors, was Blaise, looking uncomfortable and furtive in a straw hat.

"I know them," she said to the startled staff. "If you'll come with me, mes amis?"

Once they were out of the kitchen, Chandon grasped her arm. "Why the urgent letter—has something happened to the books? You haven't found something about tempus fugit, have you?"

She shook her head. "The Comité was here last night."

"Merde!" Chandon swore. As the boys huddled close, she told them what had happened. When she'd finished her story, their faces were drawn and white with shock.

"And you, outside, unprotected by the wards!" Blaise muttered. "I do not envy you that."

"But how did the Comité know to come here?"

"That pale branch you saw them carrying—during the Affair of the Poisons, it was believed to be useful in locating magicians, like a dowsing rod finds water. Or the dogs smell something. But really, I wonder if they have maps," Blaise said thoughtfully, "of magic houses in Paris."

Such things existed? "Is Bellefleur on it, too?"

"Hence the bone entrance," Chandon replied.

How could they both be so calm—as if this was nothing? "Won't they keep coming back until they get in?"

"Unless you let them in, the house's magic will keep them out," Blaise said. "It would take a siege engine to break its walls, and by then, I assume, you would have escaped."

It was hardly reassuring.

He peered down the hall. "Is the library that way?"

As they walked, Chandon asked, apprehensively, "Have you seen the latest anti-magician pamphlets? The worst ones—cowardly anonymous ones—have a bird for a printer's mark. All over Paris they are calling for our deaths. Or at the very least, demanding that people turn us in." That night at Bellefleur, he'd put on a good show for them all—courageous, determined. But it was even getting to him.

"It's already happening," Camille said. "They dragged a jeweler from his shop at the Palais-Royal. A woman had accused him of using magic to cheat customers. She was so pleased to see him brought low."

"The Comité," Chandon fumed, "has no scruples. And they give those who hate an excuse. The guards carry signed warrants with a blank space to fill in whatever name is needed on the spot—they have carte blanche. Truly we have no time to waste."

"Blaise," Camille asked, "you haven't come across any leads in your shop?"

"Yes and no. I've bought crates and crates of books these past weeks. It takes time to go through them but as to the blur . . . so far, nothing."

The house was still and quiet as they climbed the stairs. *Too quiet*, Camille thought. But not for long, because as they stepped onto the second-floor landing, a door in the far wing of the house slammed closed.

"Interesting." Blaise seemed utterly unperturbed, as if he did this kind of thing every day. Perhaps he did, handling the magical texts and grimoires that came through his shop. Old texts, reeking magic and *stirring* under his hands as he paged through them. Chandon, however, had gone quite gray.

Matter-of-fact, Blaise asked, "How many books are in the library?"

What had she glimpsed the last time she was in the dim, shuttered room? Shelves packed with books like lice on strands of hair. Paintings. A statue of a deer. Strange papers. "I don't recall, exactly—perhaps a hundred?"

"You haven't examined them?" Blaise asked, mild astonishment in his voice.

She glanced at Chandon. "I was frightened. And they resisted me."

"Bespelled," Blaise said, hurrying. "It's close now, isn't it? I can hear the books."

Soon they stood in front of the library's heavy oak doors. Medieval carvings crawled across them: snakes coiling through bare-limbed trees; men and women with gaunt torsos that ended in flipping fish tails; staring skulls on stakes, planted among poppies. Where the doors met was a large silver ring, tarnished. The air seeping through the skull-shaped keyhole smelled of smoke and sounded like rustling paper.

"Think this is it, Delouvet?" Chandon gave a low laugh. "Could there be anything in the world that reeks more of magic?"

"I would clarify it smells mostly like *books* of magic." He blinked benevolently at Camille. "Shall we go in?"

She slipped the key from her sleeve and set it in the keyhole. "You're certain you wish to do this?"

Chandon raised an eyebrow. "The most daring gambler at Versailles has a case of the nerves?"

"You would if you knew what was in there! Apart from the books that are gnashing their teeth so loudly we can hear them, there's also a portrait"— she swallowed—"that conveys memories if you touch it."

"It sounds like magie bibelot," Blaise said cheerfully. "The books are growing impatient, so if you don't mind . . ."

She didn't want to be the person who was too afraid and stayed out in the hall, even though there was a part of her that wished to do just that. Camille turned the key in the lock and the door swung open.

Blaise slipped inside, and flashing Camille a devil-may-care grin, Chandon followed. Camille fished the key from the lock—she had a sudden horror of being locked *in* if she left it in the keyhole—and joined them. By the time she'd lit the candles, Blaise had already found the set of tiny keys for the metal grilles that covered the books and was making his way up the spiral stairs to the second-floor gallery. As he approached, the books quieted. Deftly, he unlocked the first set of grilles and, starting at the top, ran his fingers over the spines of the volumes, just as Camille had. But when he touched them, each one seemed to brighten, a candle flickering to life. Blaise's eyes were closed, his pale lashes trembling.

Worried, she cried out, "Blai—"

"Hush! He's reading now," Chandon said in Camille's ear. "We mustn't speak to him, or interrupt if we can possibly help it. He may be seized by a fit elsewise. Let's explore instead. Who knows what we may discover? I find my curiosity has overpowered my earlier repulsion."

The room seemed to have grown since she was last there. Had there been a divan in it before? But the shadows in the corners were just as thick, the portrait's golden-eyed stare just as ominous. Chandon grasped her wrist and pulled her along. Together, they peered into a large glass cabinet where pinned insects jostled with the skeletons of tiny animals she did not recognize. Chandon pronounced them dreadfully gruesome and they hastened away. There was a pair of waist-high Chinese vases that echoed faintly with voices if they put their ears to them, a silk carpet that dampened their steps completely, a large table covered with papers and books. Idly, Chandon stirred the papers, and they rose up off the table, hovering before fluttering back to the polished wood.

"Like butterflies," Camille said, wonder in her voice. How could a magician as terrible as Séguin have fashioned something so beautiful?

"Aha! You will come to love magic yet, I'll wager on it."

"If there is a good kind, perhaps, that will not kill me—"

"What's this?" Chandon gestured to an oil painting, small enough to tuck under an arm. It showed a man in a black suit, standing by the head of a black horse. The horse's head was small, his eye wild. Beyond them lay a green carpet of grass, and at its end, a stone house.

Nowhere was there a signature or a name that would indicate what the house was, so Camille took the painting off the wall. "Maybe there's something written on the back?"

Before she'd even turned it over, she felt its creeping magic. A deed had been sewn to the back of the canvas, though the stitches did not show on the front. And below it, under a dense cocoon of red thread, lay an iron key. There was something repulsive about it, like a sleeping insect.

"Quite a ferocious warding, isn't it?"

"Is that what feels so sickening?"

"How would you get the key out?" She was loath to even to touch it.

"Silver scissors." He yawned. "Let's check on Delouvet."

"But, Chandon, don't you see? *This* is the kind of magic that repulses me."

"That's like saying you don't like a particular cane, because the person who owns it hits you with it. Magic is but a tool, as my tutor always said!" Then he grew serious, and said, "You know that feeling of being watched you have in this house?"

She nodded.

"Mon amie, it's nothing but magic!"

"Séguin's dark magic," she insisted. "The magic of his ancestors—"

Chandon shook his head. "You're the magician that matters now. If you let it, the house will warn you. Even take care of you. But you mustn't turn away from it."

"But how? I don't . . . feel at ease with magic, not the way you do."

"That's just the kind of person I am. A simple boy with simple dreams." He smiled so that his dimple showed. "In all seriousness, the magic matches the magician. Only you can find the way to be at home with yours."

Before she could demand Chandon explain, Blaise slowly came down the iron stairs, a few books clutched to his chest. "There's not much here that has anything to do with the blur, I'm afraid." He was gripping the railing so hard his knuckles were white.

Hurriedly, Camille pulled out a chair for him. "Do sit, Blaise!"

He waved her off. "It will pass. Unfortunately so much of what these books are is arcane ramblings about alchemy by magicians who had too much time on their hands. There's very little that is practical."

"Another dead end," Chandon said, irritated.

Blaise was looking up at the rows of books in the gallery, many of which were still twitching and glowing with whatever magic he'd used to read them. He was exhausted, but his eyes were full of awe.

"How do you know so much about magical books, Blaise?"

"I grew up alone," he said quietly. "They were my best companions. My only ones, really. People—have always been difficult. Books are much easier."

Her heart twisted at the thought of him alone with his books. "Is that why you have your bookshop?"

"The first books of magic I ever read belonged to a kind parish priest, who took pity on a lonely and misunderstood boy. Les Mots Volants is my feeble attempt to reconstruct his astounding library."

"But you're doing it in secret."

He gave an infinitesimal shrug. "We magicians have been in danger for a long time. I don't believe magicians are blameless for the cruelty they inflicted on the powerless. But if we are to change ourselves, we have to preserve the records of magic both good and ill. It's important to remember what really happened."

Chandon wandered over to the window and opened the shutter.

"I never read any books of magic in our house," Camille said, "though I remember my mother had one: green and stamped with silver. Though it could be bound in any color, couldn't it?"

"Not that one. It is always bound like that."

"You know it?" she said eagerly. "Do you have a copy?"

He shook his head. "I'm sorry."

Only a moment ago she'd had the feeling of something big rising to the surface, something that might help her understand what was happening to her. And now it had frustratingly sunk beneath the surface once more.

"Will you let me know if you come across anything about it?"

"It's called *The Silver Leaf*," Chandon said from the window.

"*You* know about this book, too?"

"It's a primer most magicians study as part of their education," Blaise explained—somewhat sadly, she thought.

"Chandon?"

"Did I study the dreaded *Silver Leaf*? My mother warned me I'd never amount to anything in life if I ignored it. I read it, and look at me now."

Chandon didn't realize how lucky he was. "What kind of things were in it?"

"I can't possibly remember. It's more like a recipe book than a novel or a history, always there to refer to in case you forget." He twisted his rings, thinking. "How to bring forth sorrow, of course; lives of the great magicians; types of transformative magic; warnings about using magic for ill. Which Séguin and many other magicians over the centuries clearly ignored. And much, much more. The type was painfully small."

"Was there anything about tempus fugit, the magic needed to work the veil?"

Blaise blinked. "I hadn't thought of it being in there! But you are right, Camille—the Marquis de Saint-Clair says it is a common magic, therefore, it should be in a basic text. Hiding in plain sight! You may have brought us one step closer."

Closer wasn't close enough. "So you will keep an eye out for a copy?"

"Certainly." Blaise waited serenely.

"You wish to know why *I* want it. Apart from the blur." The way he talked about lost libraries as if he longed for something he hadn't been allowed to have echoed how she felt. He seemed to understand her own tangled feelings about magic.

"Honestly, I'm afraid! My magic overtakes me like a fever. And I don't know whether I should force it away—if I even can—or somehow accept it. I worry that the pamphlets I've written are infected with magic, and that's why they've been successful. And now the Comité has me in its sights . . ." Miserably, she turned away and caught Séguin's portrait watching her. "Can't I put it in a vial and keep it there until I need it, even if I'm not trying to make a blur? Wouldn't that be one way to control it?" *And keep myself and those I love safe?*

"You did not call it by wishing or feeling?"

The Lost Girls had felt trapped, just as she had. Longing for a way out, always working so hard but despite it, everything slipping through her fingers . . . "Perhaps I did. But what can I do? I cannot stop feeling."

"Some magicians do. That was one of the dangers Saint-Clair warned of with the blur—that by making it we separate ourselves from magic." *That was what she'd seen in Séguin's portrait. It was what he'd wanted, but without feeling, he was no longer the magician he'd once been.*

"And then the magic is so powerful," Camille said, remembering what had happened to the Comte de Roland and how it felt so much like the way the fever-magic consumed her, "that it threatens to vanish you. How then are we to survive?"

"These things are manipulations of magic," Blaise said. "They're not the way magic *is.*"

Frustrated, Camille clenched her fists in the fabric of her skirts. Why did they only go round and round and not get anywhere? "If we aren't able to hide our magic, the Comité will hunt us down. And the books we need are nowhere to be found. Why isn't there a list, or a map for them—"

Blaise's other eyebrow rose. From the stack he'd collected, he pulled a slender green-bound volume. It had no silvery leaves on it but it was nevertheless so familiar that she reached for it.

"It's only an index. Made by some industrious student, I suppose, to help her learn *The Silver Leaf* better."

"Do you see?" Chandon interrupted from his perch by the window. "How ominous the clouds are becoming—as if it might rain for weeks."

*Lazare.* Balloons were not made for rain. If it rained for days, would he have to stay longer in Lille?

Under her fingertips, the book's magic hummed.

"Copies of *The Silver Leaf* were so common," Blaise said as he peered over her shoulder. "No one took care of them because they could easily get another. Ephemera, we book collectors call them. And now they are being destroyed in fires."

But Camille was hardly listening. Instead she paged quickly to B.

*Blood Magic.*

*-Glamoire, 256*

Camille stared in wonderment. "Really?"

"That is why I was surprised you hadn't read it. Chandon said you had worked such a compelling glamoire."

It shouldn't have pleased her, but it did. "Thank you," she said, and raced through the other subcategories for *Blood Magic.*

*-Irresponsible use in fortune telling, 378*

*-To bring back lost memories, 325*

*-To bond a sorrow-well, 524*

Her fingers tightened around the book's spine. Was it always like this with magic, teetering between beautiful and horrible? "How many entries there are under blood magic!"

"Too often misused, I'm afraid."

She ran her finger down the column of B-words. There was no entry for

—

*Blur.* Perhaps the working for the blur was under its other name, the veil? Hurrying, she paged past *Control of magic,* 37; *Illness,* 57; *Spells for love,* 392; and *Spells for enemies,* 401 until she reached the very end of the index: *V.*

*Value of magic,* 10

*Vanishing letters,* 258

*Veil,* 613.

"It *is* in *The Silver Leaf!*" she cried out. Next to the entry for *Veil* was a star. Séguin must have marked it—proof he'd been working on the veil, as they'd guessed.

But most the most important would be under *T,* and it was:

*Tempus Fugit,* 13.

Nevertheless they were hardly closer than before, because this was only the index. She gripped the book in frustration. All these books, and still no answers!

"I promise you, I will keep trying," Blaise said.

She closed the index and handed it to him. As soon as it left her hand, she missed the warmth of it and wanted it back.

"They're funny like that," he said with a fond smile as he patted the books on the table. "Magic compels." The clock in the library began to chime the hour. "I must go—I hate to leave the bookshop unattended for too long."

"Please be careful, Blaise," Camille said. "With the Comité looking for books, will they not come to Les Mots Volants?"

"It is warded," he replied. "I am safe enough for now. Nothing without risk is worth doing." He produced a calling card and gave it to her. "But, Camille—"

"Yes?"

"I know it is not easy. But please, do not be afraid of answers. They may come to you in strange ways. This ancient house," he said, gently smiling at the grim, magic-laced library, "has secrets to tell. You must find a way to listen."

# 25

B ut Camille wasn't certain she wished to listen. After the magicians had said their adieux and slipped back out the kitchen door, Adèle came to tell Camille that a wagon load of furniture had arrived from Versailles.

Perplexed, she asked, "For whom?"

"It's the old master's things, collected from the apartment he kept there. You don't wish to go over them?"

She wanted nothing to do with them. The unicorn tapestry that had watched while Séguin had drugged her, the glasses that had held the poisoned wine, the embroidered chair he'd shoved her against, trapped and weeping—no. She wished to see none of it again. "If you could . . . ?"

"Of course," Adèle said. "Mademoiselle Sophie is waiting for you in the courtyard."

Sophie almost never went into the courtyard. *Too enclosed*, she said. *It makes me feel trapped.* "She's returned from Le Sucre so early? Is she not well?"

Adèle considered. "She seems—distraught."

Through the wavy glass of the doors, Camille saw her sister pacing back and forth by the espaliered pear trees, heavy with yellow fruit. In her hand, she gripped a fallen branch. Each time she hit it against the wall, a piece of it broke off and fell to the grass. Not promising.

"What are you doing outside?" Camille asked as she hurried down the path toward her. Overhead, iron-gray clouds loomed. "It's going to rain any minute."

"Why can't I be out here?" She thwacked the wall. "Can't I change my mind sometimes? Or behave differently?"

Something was definitely wrong. "Has something happened to you? Rosier?"

"Why should anything happen to Rosier? And if it did, why would it concern me?"

"I just thought you might have been together—working on Les Merveilleux."

Sophie smacked the wall again, hard. Camille's heart constricted. Had Rosier hurt her, somehow? At the back of the garden, near the roses, a fountain purled. As if she were trying to calm a nervous cat, Camille asked, "Would you tell me about your day? We might sit on the bench by the fountain."

"There's no need to sit, as it will not take long to tell it." Sophie pressed the branch against the wall until it snapped. "I've received a marriage proposal."

Bewildered, Camille asked, "Are congratulations in order?"

"I don't know!" Sophie said, flinging herself down on the bench after all.

Camille sat beside her. As mildly as she could, she asked, "Who proposed?"

"As if I have thousands of suitors! I have only one, and it was he who asked me."

"Rosier?" she guessed.

"He is hardly a suitor! It was the Marquis d'Auvernay."

"Oh!" She looked more closely at Sophie. Were her eyes red? "What did you say?"

"I told him I required time to consider the proposal with which he had so honored me." She glared at Camille. "Isn't that what a girl is supposed to say? Besides, I am far too young to marry."

Only a few months ago Sophie had insisted she was of marrying age. "If you wished, you might have a long engagement. Or do you not like d'Auvernay enough?"

"What is enough? D'Auvernay is everything a man is supposed to be. Everything I wanted."

"But?"

Sophie sighed. "Then I think of you and Lazare, how you are together."

How they had been, once. Now she fretted about Lazare, cynical at the revolutionary dinner. Talking about pretending in a way that made her worry he knew she was pretending not to have anything to do with magic. Uneasy that she might never be able to tell the truth. "You overestimate us, I think."

"Oh?" Sophie said, suddenly interested. "Has something happened?"

"I fear—" In her mind she saw a road with a fork in it, the one path dividing into two, each of which ran away from the another. Like the branches of the carefully tended pear tree, growing apart. "I fear we will go our separate ways."

"You, part? You are made for each another!" A V of worry appeared between Sophie's pale brows. "Aren't you?"

"What happens when people don't tell each other things, because they're afraid the other person won't like them anymore? Or because they fear they're becoming a different person, one the person won't like—"

"Hush! You always fret when he's away and imagine awful things. You *are* prone to imagining, you know. When Lazare looks at you, it's as if his whole being looks at you. And when you look at him, I see that you love him." Sophie poked at the gravel with what was left of the stick. "I know d'Auvernay cares for me."

"Which is not the same as you loving him, is it?"

Sophie shook her head.

"And Rosier?" To hide whatever her face might reveal, Camille bent and plucked a dandelion growing up through the stones.

"He's not the kind of young man I planned to marry."

"And what kind was that?"

"Someone like d'Auvernay, of course."

"But why? I understand you felt that way when we were poor, and trying to keep our apartment, and we needed a way out. Now you have your own business—"

"What if that's not enough?" Sophie's voice wobbled. "What if something comes to take it away? If you heard the rumors the seamstresses and the customers tell . . . sometimes I wake in the night, alone in my bed, and I am so afraid, Camille."

She clasped her sister's small hand. "Tell me."

"My fingers are ice, my heart beating hard in my chest, and all I can think is that I will never be truly safe. That the hunger and the uncertainty will come back. And whatever my heart says, my head says d'Auvernay is safe."

Safety was both blessing and curse. "Perhaps there is no *safe*, not any longer." Camille plucked a yellow petal from the flower and let it drift away in the cool wind. "What if we have to learn to live with the feeling that the walls around us could crumble at any time, the rug whisked out from beneath our shoes? What if we cannot find safety in another person, but in ourselves?"

Sophie gave her a canny look. "But you feel safe with Lazare, don't you? That is what I want."

Did she feel safe with him? As she pulled off another petal, she wondered: What if the paths they were taking didn't curve back to meet again, but like the pear tree's branches, grew apart forever, never crossing? What if the plans they'd hatched in the restaurant's dreamy glow could never come true, because each choice they made was taking them farther away from each other—but unlike the gardener who pruned the tree, they did not know it?

It chilled her to think of it.

"And d'Auvernay will give you safety?"

Sophie made an impatient sound. "More than Rosier will!"

"Are you certain? What about everything you've done together on the circus—"

"It's not a circus."

"Les Merveilleux," Camille said, exasperated. "I thought it made you happy. Not just the costumes, and the performance itself, but being with—"

"No!" Sophie stood up. "I've no wish to talk about it any longer. I should have guessed you would take his side, since he is your friend and Lazare's. If he wished to marry me, he would have asked!"

All the hope and joy had gone out of Sophie's face. She *did* love Rosier. But for whatever reason, he had not proposed. "Oh, Sophie! I do think he loves you—if that is what you want. You are under no obligation. You must know," she said impulsively, "that he made Les Merveilleux for you."

Sophie flinched, as if she'd been slapped. Her lower lip trembled, though with anger or some other emotion, Camille could not tell. "Rosier is too unpredictable and foolish with his games and enthusiasms! Whatever kind of life would that be?" she said before turning on her heel and running down the gravel path into the house.

"A marvelous one," Camille called out as the glass doors banged open.

But Sophie did not hear. She was already gone, and it had started to rain.

# THE LOST GIRLS SPEAK
## THE LOCK PICKER

### MY FATHER ALWAYS WISHED FOR A BOY

My mother had lost two babies, both boys. But
Papa wanted a son to follow him in his trade so he
taught me to make locks, and keys, the things that
protect the valuable and mysterious in our lives. He
always said

### A LOCK WAS LIKE A PERSON:

complicated, but something you could figure out
if you listened hard.

### NO ONE EVER WAS SO KIND TO ME
### NO ONE EVER SO UNDERSTOOD ME

We were happy until my mother died in
childbirth. That little brother lived but two days,
though we did all we could to keep him. But when at
last he slipped through our fingers and was laid in the
coffin in the crook of Maman's arm, it was as if Papa
too stepped into that grave and buried himself with
them.

Four months I worked on the unfinished orders
in the shop. No new ones came. Customers saw Papa
wandering the square, gaping in people's windows
for where my mother might be, and they wanted

nothing to do with me, who was too little to be
anything like a true locksmith.

When they put Papa in the madhouse, I was sent
to the orphanage.

There I discovered I could pick any lock they
tried to put on me. And so I fled to Paris, city of ten
thousand locks, where I could practice the only trade
I have ever mastered.

THERE IS NO LOCK
that can
KEEP ITS SECRETS
from
ME

# 26

The rain Chandon predicted continued for three long days. Despite the fires in every room, damp filled the house. In the streets, rain collected in dank puddles that soaked boots and stockings. It raised the level of the Seine and ferried branches and debris from upriver, floating dangerously below the surface. Like mushrooms encouraged by the wet, pamphlets and posters covered Paris, claiming the flooding was the work of magicians.

She heard nothing from Lazare.

Perhaps he hadn't left Lille before the rains began and was now stranded at the border. If that was the case, surely he could travel by coach? But perhaps the corps kept him there. It was impossible to know. Restless, she wandered the house, frowning at the enchanted objects and even the servants—so much so that Sophie told her to rest.

At least Camille could escape by reading. Settling into bed one dreary afternoon, she opened the gothic romance, *The Castles of Athlin and Dunbayne* by Mrs. Radcliffe, where she had left off. As she read, the author's description of the Scottish Highlands, with its vast gloomy moors unmarked by paths and its torrential waterfalls, began to merge with the storm outside. She could hardly keep track of where she was, and soon her head sank back against the pillow. As she slept, she dreamed of crossing through fields of heather, searching the sky for Lazare.

When she woke it was to the slap of rain against the windows.

*It's getting worse*, she thought, and rolled onto her other side. Why was the rain so loud? Was the window open? Unable to sleep, she sat up. The fire in the hearth had shrunk to glowing embers. She held her breath, listening hard. There it was again. Scattered tapping, almost like rain.

No rain pounded that hard.

Pulling her silk dressing gown over her cotton chemise, she crossed the room and opened the shutter. Beyond the glass, the deluge continued. The street lamp remained lit, its circle of light reflected in puddles. At the edge of the light stood a figure. Tall, lean, his arms crossed and his head tipped down, the rain pouring off his tricorne hat. There was a weary slant to his shoulders that made her heart ache.

She fumbled with the shutters, threw open the windows. "Lazare!"

He raised his head, searching for her. When he found her, his expression changed. Brightening. "I'm coming up."

"What?" she said as she saw him take hold of the drainpipe that ran up the house's facade. "Come to the front door!"

"Too late," he called up, and it was true—he was climbing quickly. Halfway up his foot slipped. The drainpipe creaked ominously, and her heart was in her throat, but he found a foothold in the roots of the ivy that covered the upper story and kept going.

When he was nearly there, she took his hand—wet, slippery—and pulled him toward her. Then he was climbing over the sill and pulling off his hat, his eyes never leaving her. "You ignored the pebbles I was throwing for a very long time."

"I was sleeping! There is a front door, you know."

"I was in no mood for maids and footmen," he said. "Not when I only wished to see you." He ran his hand through his hair; water streamed down his wrists and into the sleeves of his coat.

"What has happened?"

"Lafayette offered to send me by coach tomorrow, but I could not wait. So I rode in the back of a cart all the way from Pontoise. Dieu, I'm exhausted."

"And very wet."

Smiling ruefully, he shook his head so that tiny droplets of water spattered everywhere.

"Stop!" But she didn't mind.

He peeled off his dripping coat and draped it over a painted Chinese screen that stood near the fire. The rain had soaked even his waistcoat and chemise. "I'm afraid I'm too wet to even sit down. Mind if I—?" He gestured at his waistcoat.

Camille shook her head and he quickly unbuttoned his wet garments and hung them on the screen. She was having some difficulty speaking. The fine fabric of his chemise had become translucent and clung to his skin, revealing the planes of his shoulders, arms, chest. Tenderly, she pushed back a lock of his inky hair so she could see his face. Fatigue had painted shadows in the hollows of his face, and his warm brown skin had gone dull and worn.

But what mattered was that he was safe. She touched him along the muscled slant of his neck, where his shirt had fallen open.

"I cannot tell if you are real, or something I dreamed."

"Do appearances so deceive?" He looped his arm around her waist and pulled her close. "Why don't you find out for yourself?"

She rose on her toes. "You *seem* real," she said. "But in my experience, appearances *can* be deceiving."

For a long moment, neither of them spoke. Around them, in the almost dark, the old house creaked and shifted. Outside, the rain fell restlessly. Camille thought of the spring, when they had kept so many secrets from each other, pretending at being someone else, trying to stay safe. But now she wondered if they'd been trying to protect each other.

"Camille," he murmured into her hair. "I'm sorry about the things I said at the dinner. I felt like everything was slipping away. Nothing seemed right, especially *me*. All the time I was gone I thought of you, wishing I had been different, said something different." His brows drew together in a regretful line. "I'm a fool."

"You are not."

"I am. But we are all fools in love, n'est-ce pas?"

*Perhaps*, she thought, gently wiping a few drops of water from his cheekbone. "Besides, can we not withstand a little separation if our paths take us away?" She wanted so much for it to be true.

Reassuringly, he said, "Love is what matters. All the rest of it is—"

"It's important, though, isn't it? The work we do?" Once again, she felt on the verge of telling him about the magic in the pamphlets.

Outside, thunder rumbled.

He raised a curving eyebrow. "The rest does not feel important when I am with you."

She felt it then, a rising certainty, that this was true. Her worries about them growing apart and their different paths—*this* was what mattered, that they wished to be together. "And now," she said, "you are with me."

The floor dropped out from under her as he kissed her.

It felt new, different now. His mouth on hers, his hands at her waist, bringing her close. He kissed her throat, lingering at the spot beneath her collarbone where her dressing gown had fallen open. She hadn't known she could feel like this, the edges of her self dissolving until there was only the press of his body against hers. She caught his lower lip between her teeth, and he groaned. Slowly, his hot kisses drove her backward and it was as if she were walking through honey, deliriously sweet and treacherous—until she felt the solid bulk of the bed behind her.

"Camille," he murmured. His eyes were luminous, deeper than the night outside, framed by the sweep of his wet eyelashes. He took her hand in his. With agonizing slowness, he pressed burning kisses along the inside of her wrist. His hair, cool and wet, caressed her skin. "What do you want?"

"You," she breathed. "I want you."

There was a sound in the corridor, and both of them froze.

Footsteps, and, under the door, the trembling light of a candle.

"Camille?" Sophie called, urgent. "I heard a noise—are you well?"

Instinctively, Camille pulled her dressing gown closed. Lazare grinned at her, and she had no idea what to do. He had erased her mind with his kisses. *Help*, she mouthed, but he only bit playfully at her earlobe.

"Yes?" she stammered.

"You're worrying me—can I come in?"

Teasingly, intoxicatingly, he kissed the hollow of her throat. Any more of this and she would cease to exist. "I'm trying to sleep," she called out weakly. "I'll see you in the morning."

A long pause. "If you say so." Sophie's shadow disappeared from under the door, and soon the flickering candlelight faded away.

Lazare laughed, and she tried to clamp her hand over his mouth. "Quiet!"

"You were nearly found out!"

"I?" She choked back laughter. "What about *you*?"

"I don't count—I'm only something you dreamed, remember?"

"But you're not, are you?"

He shook his head. His brown eyes were gone to black, his pupils wide with desire. "I'm not a dream."

"Prove it," she whispered.

As his body met hers, she tilted her head to meet his mouth. She knew there were no dreams like this, no dreams so alive and full of wanting. It was nothing she had ever felt before, but now it was everything she wanted. Her fingers fumbled at the neck of his shirt, pulled the damp linen over his head. Tentatively, her hands explored the line of his collarbone, dropping to the smooth slope of his chest.

"Mon âme," he murmured as he slid her dressing gown off, letting it fall to the floor. She pulled at the ribbons on her chemise so that it slipped off her shoulder. "How beautiful you are." His mouth on her skin scorched, setting her on fire.

Where once had been edges, boundaries, and borders now was ash.

Why had she worried about diverging paths and pretending? In their fierce, suddenly desperate touch was sweet oblivion. Whatever she'd feared stood between them was gone. In this torrent of fire, there was nothing to hold on to except each other.

And outside, the rain rushed down ceaseless until dawn, thrumming its sweet tattoo.

# 27

In the morning, she woke to Lazare. He lay stretched out on the sofa, lazily toasting a piece of bread over the fire. When she stirred, he smiled devilishly. "I may have frightened the maid," he said, twirling the poker he'd put the bread on, "for which I am truly sorry. On the other hand, she returned with breakfast for two."

Camille was famished. She had woken in the gray hours before dawn, while he still slept. The rain had finally stopped, and the world felt remade. Lying on her side, resting her cheek against her arm, she had lain in the half-light, drinking him in. His black hair spilled like ink across the pillow, his long eyelashes resting against his cheeks. Under his ear his pulse beat slowly, steadily. His chest rose and fell, and she wondered what it might be like to kiss him while he slept. Would her kiss become a part of his dream, the way the rain had been in hers, last night? Or would he wake?

And what then?

Her breath caught as she remembered the fierce press of their bodies, as if they could eliminate every space between them, the tender but hungry exploration, the feeling that she was entirely herself and yet completely blown apart. What if last night could begin again?

It would be delicious to find out.

Bending, she kissed him gently on the corner of his mouth, the one that curled irresistibly when he teased or jested. His eyelashes fluttered, and his lips parted as if he might say something, but he didn't wake.

Should she kiss him again? It was barely dawn, and he'd traveled so far last night. She would let him sleep. He would be there when she woke. *Believing* this—not simply hoping for it—had been a new and delicious joy.

A little shyly, she said, "Salut."

His gaze smoldered. "Getting out of bed wasn't easy. You were so warm, and I imagined—" He stopped himself. "You were even in my dreams."

Flushing at the memory of her stolen kiss, Camille slipped on her dressing gown and joined him on the sofa, tucking her legs up underneath her. Faint city sounds of fishmongers and knife sharpers amid the din of horses' hooves drifted into the room and those everyday sounds made what had happened between them seem very real.

As she settled down next to him, he tucked a stray strand of her hair behind her ear. "What will happen if I can't stop staring at you?"

"We won't be able to leave this room," she said, surprising herself with her daring. "Not that I would mind."

On the low table sat a large oval tray, crowded with plates of sliced bread, rich butter, a crystal pot of the pear jam Madame Hortense made from the trees in the courtyard, rich and summer sweet. There were also a few small apples in a silver bowl, a pot of hot chocolate and another of coffee, steam drifting from its spout. Tucked under the tray were the latest newspapers.

"How did you get her to bring so much food? The most I ever get is coffee and a crust," she said. "And I am hungry this morning."

"I must have certain powers of persuasion," he teased. He removed the poker from the fire, checked the bread, and slid the perfectly browned piece of toast onto a china plate. "Here's a bigger crust for you, my sweet."

He certainly did have powers of persuasion. As she busied herself over the breakfast tray, pouring herself a cup of coffee and spreading butter and jam on her toast in the English way, she felt happiness like sunlight radiate through her. Lazare, here, in her room, was a joy. The flex of muscles in his neck and chest as he held out the poker, the careless ease of him lounging on her sofa . . . was he watching her as much as she was watching him?

"Alors," she said, trying to ignore the heat rising in her cheeks. She must at least attempt to behave like a normal person, a person who could think of something other than *that*. "Tell me everything about your trip. You traveled first to Lille?"

He nodded. "Lille is pretty city on a river; from what I could tell, they hardly think of themselves as French and don't care much for the revolution. It was a relief, in a way, not to have so much attention on us. One day we made a flight west, toward the coast." His face went dreamy and far away. "The landscape wide and open, as if it could never end. Then there was the Channel at the horizon, bigger than I could have imagined."

She'd seen etchings in Papa's books of the narrow arm of the Atlantic that separated France and England. She imagined something like the Seine, but broader somehow. "Tell me about it?"

He sat forward. "Camille, it was like nothing I've ever seen. The sea was wide and gray, cut with thousands of tiny waves. Stretching out in every direction, like the sky. And beneath the surface, it's said, are deep caverns and valleys, like we have here on land, but they are full of fish and . . . sea monsters."

She laughed, and gave him a little push with her foot. "Not those!"

"Oh yes, those. Though I can't promise they'll be there when we fly over."

*We?* "Is that a promise?"

He smiled, the heat of it dazzling. "Soon, I hope. You would love it. With my long glass, I could see dolphins racing alongside a schooner's bow. They were . . . so free."

She sniffed the air. "Is something burning?"

He turned suddenly to the hearth, where the toast was charred. "Merde!" He pried it off the poker and tossed it in the flames. He watched as the pieces crisped to black, then crumpled, the center caving in. He was silent for a long time.

"Lazare? What's wrong? Was it the flight? It sounded so beautiful, but—"

"What if we went to London?"

"You're feeling restless?" She thought of Paris's crowded streets, its tilting buildings and grand houses. London was larger, a vast and sprawling city, completely unfamiliar. "Have you tired of our city?"

"I love it because it's where you are," he said simply.

First the magic lantern show, then the trip to Lille, now London . . . she tried to be brave. "But Paris is full of ideas and balloons—"

There was a discreet knock on the door, and Camille tensed.

"You think it's Sophie again?" he said low.

"She would have barged right in, especially if she knew you were here."

From the hallway came Adèle's voice. "Madame? An urgent letter for you, by messenger."

"I suppose I must." Camille called out, "Come!"

A bit nervously, Adèle entered holding the letter tray; as soon as Camille had taken the note from her, she curtsied and fled. "I think she's smitten with you," Camille said as she broke the seal. It was from the bookseller, Lasalle. As she read, her heart began to pound.

"What is it?"

Wide-eyed, she said, "The chance of a lifetime! Lazare, we must go to Versailles!" She leaped from the sofa and ran to the screen where a few dresses hung on hooks beside his coat. She stepped into a flouncing set of petticoats, then slipped into her stays, snugging them tight around her ribs. Apart from his coat, Lazare's clothes lay strewn about the room. She picked up his cravat and tossed it at him.

"But why?"

"Women from Paris are marching to demand bread from the king!

They're going all the way to Versailles." Quickly, she twisted up her hair and pinned it. "If we leave now, I could be the first to write about it." She glanced at the paper again. "There are already several thousand women marching, and they are bringing in people from the shops and markets to join them!"

She imagined the women arm in arm, sauntering down the streets. Other Parisians joining in, seeing how necessary it was to support the woman who had the least and the most to fight for. Realizing that they shared a common cause. It would be glorious. That alone would persuade the king. It would be nothing like the storming of the Bastille. This would be a peaceful affirmation of the revolution's ideals.

"The revolution continues," he said darkly. "After that dinner, I'd had enough to last me a while."

"But women standing up to the powerful is what revolution *should* be." Camille tugged on the dress she'd chosen, a simple gown in celadon green. "Will you lace me up?"

Lazare rose and came to stand behind her. Slowly but firmly he tugged the laces that ran up the back of her dress. His breath on the nape of her neck made her tremble.

"You think these market women are any different than the revolutionaries at that dinner?" he asked.

"What reason would they have to pretend? They are hungry and angry and want justice."

"I'm sure you're right." He did not sound convinced.

She desperately wanted him to come with her. "What is it that's bothering you, if it's not the women?"

Carefully, he tightened her lacings. "When we were at Lille . . . all Lafayette could talk about was war." He dropped his voice in a perfect imitation of Lafayette's. "Of course," he said in English before shifting back to French, "it is what they would do in America!"

"But going to war would be a disaster!" It would only increase the suffering of the poor, diverting food to the army and attention away from their plight. And the revolution would become splintered, a battle fought on at least two fronts.

"He does what he believes is best for France." He gave her laces a final, definitive pull. "I wish I'd never become involved with it. But there was such pressure to say yes."

"Because you needed the measurements for your cloud studies?" she guessed.

"In part."

"Is it the pilots?" She was almost afraid to ask. "Do they still not respect your command?"

His hands lingered on her waist. "That's been resolved."

She wished he would tell her what was wrong, what troubled him— what secrets he was keeping. Instead she said, "Come with me, Lazare."

"You don't need me with you, fretting over how the revolution is losing its way."

"Listen, my love." Camille cradled his face in her hands. "You doubt the revolution. I don't blame you. It doesn't sit entirely well with me, either." If he only knew how the revolution threatened her. "But please—come with me today. See for yourself. It won't be about Lafayette's strategy or courtiers who change with the wind. Instead it will be the hardworking women of Paris demanding bread from their king. This peaceful march will be the *people* standing up."

His eyes did not leave hers. What did he see there? Her hope—or her fear? "You truly wish me to go with you?"

"There's nothing I wish more." She would show him that the revolution was more than spying at the Austrian border. It was more than speeches or raising money or wearing tricolor cockades in your hat. The revolution was what was happening with the girls and these women, France's downtrodden. It was about change for the people who most needed it.

And then, she wondered, the hope as thin as a wisp of smoke, once the king did the right thing for his people and they were well fed and had the freedoms they deserved, might not they forget about their hatred of magicians? Might she not have to choose which version of herself to be? Women were marching on Versailles and suddenly anything—anything at all— seemed possible. And she could not let Lazare turn away from it.

"You believe in it?" he asked.

"I do. *This* will be the moment when the revolution becomes what it is destined to be, when everything changes."

His face softened. "Do you remember what I said, when we went up in the balloon the last time?"

She would never forget it. "Tell me again?"

"I said that I didn't know what was going to happen, but whatever it was, I wanted to go through it with you."

Her pulse quickened. "Then you'll come?"

His broad smile was a yes, and she flung her arms around his neck and kissed him, emphatically. "You won't regret it."

He raised a dark eyebrow. "A bold claim."

"I'll be the judge of that." On a nearby table sat a little silver bell. She was about to set it ringing when his hand closed over hers. Playfully, his long fingers eased the bell's handle from her grip.

"What are you doing?" she asked.

"Stopping you from ringing it." He brought her hand to his lips.

Desire threaded through her, rich and compelling. "Lazare—"

"Let me take you by balloon."

Bewildered, she asked, "But how? Isn't your balloon still at the border?"

"A benefit of Lafayette's scheme is that we now have access to a whole fleet of them. One could be ready in an hour. It won't be the trip over the Alps I promised you." He raised a dark eyebrow, the one with the scar in it. "But I will try to make it as thrilling as I can."

Camille flushed. "I have no doubt you will make it quite thrilling indeed."

# 28

As they approached Versailles, Camille looked out over the palace and gardens and for a dizzy, unsettling moment, she thought: *home*. Below lay the familiar road she'd traveled so many times: going to court with the glamoire glittering under her skin or trundling back to Paris at dawn, her pockets heavy, her body aching as the magic left it, her mind spinning over what she'd seen and done.

The great palace's pale stone shone in the vague, rainy light. There lay the court where she'd first arrived, unsure but determined, stepping down from her hired carriage in her glamoired dress and her dreams. Behind lay the unending gardens, their gravel paths radiating from the long mirror of the Grand Canal. There she had played late-night games in the dark and fragrant greenery. There she'd heard nightingales sing in the towering yews and peacocks scream from the roofs.

"Do you think we can drop a little lower?"

Lazare nodded. "I'll release some air."

Slowly, the balloon lost altitude.

Below, crowds swarmed into the courtyard. Guards from the palace were moving among the people, who were carrying—*weapons?* Uneasy, she took the long glass from Lazare's pocket and held it to her eye.

As if he sensed her worry, he came to stand beside her. "What do you see?"

She spun the rings to focus. "Women. Hundreds of them. They have shovels in their hands, rakes." The weak sunlight glinted on a curve of metal, and her stomach lurched. "And scythes! Oh, Lazare, I fear they have come to fight."

Someone, somewhere, was beating a drum. Its rhythm was a wild heartbeat. The night the Bastille fell, the people of Paris had beat drums like that too, and she'd run stumbling through the city's dark alleys to the safety—or so she'd thought—of the Hôtel Théron. She reached out to Lazare, who took her hand in his.

"There are thousands of people here," he observed. "If they want to go into the palace, nothing will stop them. They are armed to the teeth."

"Lasalle said they were protesting for bread." Camille moved her glass to the line that snaked away, dark as a river, from the palace. A group of women had taken a cannon—*from where?*—and were hauling it along the road. There were wagons used as roadblocks. A forest of blades held high. And members of Lafayette's National Guard, so many of them in their blue uniforms. Had they come to put a stop to it—or to join the women?

The balloon sank lower.

Guardsmen were inside in palace gates too, as were members of the king's personal guard. The guards of the people faced the guards loyal to the royal family. At the courtyard's far end, where a cart had been overturned to make a platform for speeches, protestors congregated. A tall woman with cropped hair and burly arms jumped down from the cart—and Camille saw she was not a woman, but a man, dressed in women's clothing. Someone offered him a bottle of wine. He wandered off as the spectators turned to a young woman clad in a tall black hat and black dress, sitting astride a black horse. A sword swung from a red sash around her waist and a brace of pistols wrapped her hips.

"Lazare, look there—it's Odette! One of the Lost Girls!"

Gathered around Odette were a few of the others: Claudine with a tricorne over her short hair, Margot the fruit seller in a bright green dress, little Henriette the forger with her pale cloud of curls streaming loose. All of them were watching Odette. The wind unfurled her red hair, blowing it behind her like a banner. Her face was fierce, determined. There was something about her that made people pay attention. And when she had their attention, her speech set them on fire. Though Camille could only hear snatches of what she said, the hot blaze of those words was reflected in the faces of everyone who was listening.

The balloon drifted down.

Closer.

Odette pulled a pistol from her belt and held it over her head. So loud Camille could hear it, she shouted, "Vive la révolution!" and fired her weapon in the air. Odette's horse reared as the gun's crack reverberated over the rooftops. People cheered, reaching up to grab her, but Odette kept her seat, smiling. Hands yanked at the horse's reins and he crow-hopped, shoving people in the crowd. "She needs to get out of there," Camille worried. "The horse is ready to bolt."

Odette swung her mount around, and the people fell back. A path opened up. She kicked him forward, the plume in her hat dancing. The crowd in the courtyard had grown denser, but to the side, where Odette had ridden out, a clear space was forming. It widened as people edged away.

In the clearing a man hoisted a pike high in the air. It was heavy, and it wobbled as he tried to raise it. When he finally did, the crowd erupted into wild screams. On its point was a severed head. A woman grabbed it from him and raised it higher. "Vive la révolution!" she shouted. "Vive la France!"

Behind her surged the crowd, hoisting high their scythes and pitchforks. From several of them hung effigies, clothes stuffed with straw. The king and queen in their fine clothes, their crowns tipped drunkenly on top of horsehair wigs. And behind those, there were more: painted faces, blackened fingers. *Magicians.* Swaying from scythes as if they were real bodies, hanging from lampposts.

Camille's hands shook so violently she feared she'd drop the spyglass. Instead she swung it away. In the middle of the courtyard lay a little boy. His jacket had come off, and lay beside him, like a blanket he'd tossed off while sleeping. His legs were bent. And his head with its brown curls was covered in blood and dirt. Her stomach heaved. On the boy's shirt was the dark print of a shoe. Someone had stepped on his broken body.

Camille clenched the edge of the basket as another wave of horror crested over her.

"Camille?" Lazare slipped the glass from her hands. "What is it?"

"A little boy," she choked. A boy like the ones who had stabled her horses when she'd come to Versailles, running up alongside the carriage and opening the gates. Boys sent on errands, boys called to help with anything in a pinch. Always underfoot, ready to do something for a few coins. Quick, clever, brimming with laughter. Always running.

Long glass to his eye, Lazare looked out at the court, as if he might see something to redeem this terrible loss. "They have lost their minds."

Then the air boomed.

A sudden whistle—Camille and Lazare stumbled backward as a cannon-ball shot past the balloon's gondola. It passed so close that the basket shook. Camille gripped Lazare's arm, trying to steady herself. The ball that had almost destroyed the basket plunged to earth. It was large and lethal—the hole it could make in the basket would destroy it. If it didn't kill them first.

Camille leaned over the gondola's edge. Below, a plume of smoke drifted from a cannon mired in the mud. Shaking their fists at the balloon, the women surrounding the cannon loaded it again.

"They mean to shoot us down," Camille screamed. "We must rise!"

Lazare was already kneeling by the brazier, stuffing it with straw to raise the temperature of the air in the balloon. "More fuel!" he shouted. Scrambling on her knees, Camille gathered as much as she could from where it was stacked around the edges of the gondola and pushed it into Lazare's hands. *More more more*: the fire roared.

"Higher!" she shouted.

Another cracking boom echoed below them, followed by the scream of the cannonball. The gondola shuddered as the ball passed beneath it. Shouts erupted as steadily, the balloon rose.

The noise of the crowd grew dim. The smoke of the cannon faded. But her fear did not.

Camille sank to floor. She thought she might be sick. Had they been hit and plummeted to the earth, that alone would have ended their lives. But if by some miracle they'd survived the fall, they'd have their heads hacked off. Paraded around on pikes.

For a long time, neither of them spoke. Over Versailles, storm clouds gathered, and the wind that accompanied them blew the balloon east, toward Paris. Camille felt as if she were a dead leaf, a nothing, floating over the countryside. Her thoughts eddied and swirled. How could the people do this? Of course, they were hungry, their rights trampled underfoot for centuries, but to kill children? Shove heads on pikes? Is this what the revolution had become, a lust for blood?

Revolution had always meant change. But did it have to mean death?

She saw his legs again, bent as if running. "That little boy."

"I know, mon âme." Lazare pulled her close and she tucked her face against his chest. Under his coat, his heart beat slow and steady. "It is a terrible tragedy. I wish I could undo it. When I think of what he must have felt—" Gently, he ran his hand over her hair, tucking the loose strands back. "But you are safe now."

It did not feel that way.


It was past midnight when they returned to Paris.

When they'd run out of fuel, they'd made a soft landing on the rain-slicked lawns of the palace of Saint-Cloud, on the Seine's western banks. A gardener had found them a driver and a wagon to take them into the city.

When the cart rolled to a stop in front of the Hôtel Séguin, she said to Lazare, "I cannot say how sorry I am. I wish we had never gone."

"Sorry for what? That we saw the truth of what's happening?"

"If the truth is that people are being killed—the boy and the guards and perhaps others—I suppose I am glad I saw it. If that is what the revolution has become."

"It is the old question," Lazare mused. "Do the ends justify the means?"

Nothing could justify their deaths. "There can be no number of lives lost that is acceptable—can there?" Or was there some kind of dismal calculation that made that make sense?

He shook his head. "It would seem a hollow victory."

"Am I doing enough?" she wondered aloud. "What should I do?"

"You'll do what's right," he said as he helped her down from the wagon. In the midnight city's gloom, the only light the lamp at the side of the gate, he turned to her. "Shall I stay with you?"

Everything in her wanted to say yes.

She imagined lying next to him in her bed, the curtains closed around them, shutting out the world. Listening to the even rise and fall of his breath until it lulled her to sleep where she would be safe from her thoughts. But she saw how exhaustion pulled at him and she remembered, with a stab of guilt, that he hadn't been home since he'd returned from Lille. "I fear your parents will be worried."

He frowned, as if he'd forgotten them, too. "I'll come soon. Send a note, and I'll come before that."

It felt like hope, and she reached for it. "Come as soon as you can."

He stooped and kissed her tenderly. "Until then."


In the red salon, Sophie was pacing, anxiously waiting for her. After hearing Camille's account—Sophie gripping the arm of the sofa so hard her knuckles went white—she told Camille the news that had come back to Paris ahead of them. The queen had been chased from her chambers by women and men intent on killing her, but had found the king in time. Lafayette, trying to control his National Guard that had insisted on marching in solidarity with the women, had cleverly saved the day by convincing the king and queen to speak to the crowd. And then, the king seeing no other way to save his life and that of his family, gave in to their demands and returned to Paris. Accompanying the king, the throng—sixty thousand strong—sang songs and drank wine, riding home on cannons or sitting in front of the guardsmen on their horses: victors at last.

Numbly, Camille stared as Sophie finished telling what she'd heard from her customers at the shop. "The crowd *forced* the royal family to come to Paris?"

"A customer had it from one of the queen's ladies-in-waiting. They saw no way out. Once the king had agreed in principle to sign the constitution, it was either return to Paris, or die."

"And where are they now?"

"In the old palace, the Tuileries. Under the watchful eye of the people of Paris."

Agitated, Camille stood. Her mind was a storm of thoughts.

Sophie regarded her carefully. "Are you going to bed?"

She shook her head. "I'm going to print."

"Shouldn't you rest? You look awful, Camille."

"I cannot," she said, deathly quiet. "If I let my eyes close for a moment, I see that little boy. Murdered! His body broken. Legs bent as if he were trying to run, trampled upon as if he were grass!" She exhaled. "Tomorrow there will be a deluge of writing about this march and soon after, one story will come to dominate. And what if it doesn't mention that boy?"

With a weary nod, Sophie gave up trying to convince her. After she went upstairs, Camille made her way to the printing room. As she opened its doors, she inhaled the sharp bite of ink and the soft, warm scent of paper that lingered in the air. Comforting and familiar. She lit another candelabra and the room flickered into being: an antidote to darkness.

But when she stood in front of the press, she hesitated. Her fingers hovered over the cases of type. Before her she saw again the swaying pike, the gruesome head, its long hair clotted with blood. And worse—if anything could be worse—the cheering, baying crowd. Thrilled. Ecstatic.

She'd loved their righteous anger. But she did not love the violence, nor the way it spread, like a wave, crushing everything in its path. She was a writer, a pamphleteer for the revolution. And yet she didn't know what to do. How to write about what she'd seen.

Thousands of women had marched six hours or more in the rain, all the way from Paris to Versailles, to demand bread from their sovereign. Women and girls who had taken life in their fists and shaken it, who'd said, *"I will not lie down and die. I will fight! I will make change happen, no matter what it takes!"*

All of that was what she'd hoped.

But not the deaths.

What mattered, and how? How would she put what she'd seen into words? She could describe it—this happened, and then this—but it wouldn't be what she had *felt*. In her ear, she heard Papa's ghost whisper:

*Be clear and simple with the words you use. The goal of any pamphlet is to persuade.*

But what simple words could convey what she had seen?

And persuade her readers of what? That had never been a question before. The girls' lives had been riddled with pain, sorrow, crime, and abuse, but she'd known it was right to tell their stories. To tell them *true*. But this?

What was this truth?

She gripped the wooden beams of the press. The smooth oak was warm under her touch. It steadied her. The fever—the magic—ran along her skin like its own fire. Feeding her, strengthening her. And as she set the letters for the first sentence, her magic rose.

## VIVE LA RÉVOLUTION

Papa had lived—and died—for this idea. Freedom and justice, equality between men. He'd given up their family's livelihood because of his beliefs.

She gritted her teeth. *That little boy.*

Angry tears scorched in the corners of her eyes. Picking up a tiny piece of type, she held it up to the light.

It was a question mark.

In the wavering candlelight, it curved like a snake. A river. A scythe.

Magic, hot and wild, slithered along the back of her neck, igniting her mind and racing down her arms into her fingers as the words gathered in her. Sentences unspooling, words laid out in rows like marching soldiers.

She had to tell the truth. Messy, disordered, and not easy. She would show the right *and* the wrong, and try not to flinch.

And if she had to use magic to do it justice, she would.

WOMEN MARCH ON VERSAILLES
TO DEMAND BREAD FROM THE KING
WHAT
ONE
WITNESS
SAW

Six thousand women marched from Paris.
They marched with sickles and pikes, swords and crowbars, scythes and
pitchforks,
HOPE and RIGHTEOUS ANGER
that they could not feed their families
They were joined by twenty thousand members of the National Guard,
accompanied by Lafayette—threatened by hanging à la lanterne—who
demanded the King approve the decrees of the National Assembly and
the Declaration of the Rights of Man and return to Paris.
The King agreed.

IN THE MIDST OF OUR VICTORY
WHAT HAPPENED NEXT?
Fear
Murder
Terror
Children killed
Guards slain
Heads paraded on pikes
Demonstrators bathing in the blood of those murdered

WHO ARE WE
WHEN WE MURDER
OUR OWN?

WHEN WE LET HATE
NOT REASON
FUEL
OUR ACTIONS?
There has been much rejoicing
But consider, P A T R I O T S, the cost!

# VIVE LA RÉVOLUTION

?

# 29

When Camille came downstairs to check on the pamphlets she had printed last night, she wasn't sure what she'd find hanging from the lines. She half expected them all to have changed in the early dawn hours, like turned coins losing their magic, becoming the ravings of a girl who'd seen terrible things.

Outside the printing room doors waited the footman Daumier in his dark blue livery coat and white wig, his massive arms crossed over his chest. He smiled impassively when he saw her.

"Bonjour, Daumier."

"Bonjour, Madame," he replied. "Mademoiselle Adèle told me you were printing last night. Do you need anything taken to the bookseller?"

"I do have something to go to the *printer's*—I need more copies than I can make myself. Would you ask them to set it just as I did and print three hundred copies?"

He bowed. "I'll wait until it's ready."

She went in, pulled back the curtains, and threw open one of the windows. Cold air and the soft patter of rain blew into the room. Was it raining too at Versailles, washing the cobbles clean of blood? The thought unnerved her. Taking down one of the pamphlets, which, despite her fears, was just as it should be, she passed by the open window.

Hunched against one of the courtyard's yews was a small, dark shape.

In the rain it was hard to tell, but it could be an animal. Or a wet, bedraggled child. The hair on the back of her neck rose as she thought of the little boy.

"Daumier," she said, trying to keep her voice even, "before you go, look out this window, won't you? What do you see?"

Obligingly, Daumier did as she asked. "A child, or a small woman about your height, madame."

Relief washed over her. Not a ghost. "But that's hardly the place—"

"It is not." Daumier headed toward the entry, the pamphlet in his hand. "I'll speak to her. Tell her to move on."

"Wait! She can shelter here until the rain is over, in the—"

"In the stables?" Daumier suggested.

"That's perfect, thank you."

She had just finished taking down the rest of the pamphlets when Daumier appeared in the doorway.

"Madame, the person in the courtyard says she knows you."

*Who could it be?* "Then why did she not come to the house?"

"Ashamed, I should say, madame. She is waiting in the foyer if you have time to speak to her."

Standing by the door, dripping rain onto the marble tiles, was Odette. She still wore the black clothes Camille had seen her in yesterday at Versailles, but they were now so full of rain and mud that they sagged shapelessly to the floor. Mud coated her shoes, and when she raised her head, a trickle of water poured off the back of her hat. Its dancing plume was crushed.

"Odette!" she said, astonished.

"I am sorry to trouble you—"

"What's happened? I saw you at Versailles. On the black horse, giving a speech. Everyone was enraptured and then—"

Odette pushed her lank hair from her face. "The horse tried to bolt, but I got him out of the crowd. I'd only borrowed him, of course, but his master made a fuss. He accused me of stealing the horse and pulled me off into the mud." She showed the side of her face to Camille. An angry red welt, surrounded by an indigo bruise, spread across her cheekbone.

"They hurt you? How dare they—"

"It's nothing." Odette looked down, her voice getting smaller. "Worse is that they said they would come after me and I didn't want to lead them to Flotsam House. Who knows what they would have done to the girls. I wandered until I knew they were not following me and then came here."

Giselle must have told her where she lived. "You walked all the way from Versailles?"

Her shoulders sagged. "I didn't know what else to do."

"You did right. Borrow some of my clothes while these are cleaned, and whatever else you need. A bandage—"

Odette continued to stare at her shoes. "Might I stay a few nights? Until it's safe?"

"Of course!" Hot shame seared through her. Here was a girl who had nothing, who needed shelter just as she once had. Anyone else would have offered her help immediately. What was wrong with her? "I should have offered—"

"Madame?" Adèle stood at the back of the entry, near the tapestry. Beside her was Sophie, an unconvincing smile pasted on her face.

"Sophie, Adèle—this is our guest, Mademoiselle Odette Leblanc."

Adèle revealed nothing of what she felt, and the discreet nod she gave in Odette's direction was very correct, but Camille could tell she wasn't pleased. "You may of course call on any of the maids," Adèle said, "but if there is anything I may help you with, don't hesitate."

"Merci, Adèle," Odette said with a winning smile. "I'm sure everything will be wonderful." Her sharp gaze ranged over all the things in the entry, the staircase, the rooms and rooms beyond this one. "Such a grand house, and so very ancient." She inhaled deeply, and sighed. "It smells like home."

Upstairs, a window rattled in its frame.

"You must have lived in an old house, then," Sophie observed. "You're not afraid of ghosts?"

Odette flinched. "Why? Are there any?"

"Not that I've seen," Camille cut in. She glared at Sophie, who finally came forward.

"Welcome, Odette," she said. "I'm Sophie, Camille's sister. I've heard so much about you and the girls at Flotsam House."

How insincere Sophie sounded! "Why doesn't Adèle show you your room, Odette? I'll be up to see you have everything you need."

Closely following Adèle, Odette climbed the stairs to the second floor. Her head swiveled from side to side, as eager as a bird's, as she took in the paintings, the rich tapestries, the velvety curtains, the Chinese vases, much as Camille had on her first visit to Versailles. When Adèle reached the landing, she waited for Odette to stop staring at the furniture and catch up. Then, side by side, they disappeared down the hallway.

"Camille!" Sophie grasped Camille's arm, and pinched. Hard.

"That hurts!" Camille rubbed at her arm. "Why—"

"Good," Sophie snapped. "How could you have invited her in without asking me? I live here, too."

"She was hiding in the courtyard, wet, hurt, frightened—"

"I doubt she is ever frightened." Sophie cheeks blazed with angry color, grimly determined. "Did you see how she coveted everything? She cannot stay here."

Camille lowered her voice. "She ran into trouble at Versailles and didn't wish to bring it with her to Flotsam House. Where else is she to go?"

"Rent rooms somewhere for her."

Camille remembered how solid and impenetrable she had thought the iron gates at Madame Théron's, how the gate and the gatekeeper would keep her and Sophie safe. But trouble had come to them anyway. "Don't you think whoever did this to her won't come after her?"

"My point exactly," Sophie huffed. "What if they come here?"

"We'll protect her. Timbault has a musket, remember?"

"But *why?* She's just a girl—"

*A girl like me. Like the girl I once was, when I was trapped and we had no money, and barely any hope.* "I have to help her."

"I know you care for the girls, which is only right and good, but this is too much. You already helped them keep their house. After all, how well do you know her?"

"Is it because she's poor? Or a revolutionary?"

"*We* were poor. *Papa* was a revolutionary. As are you, in your way," she added, almost reluctantly. "But I don't worry you'll run off with my best jewelry."

"She won't." How would she make Sophie understand? "It's like what happened to us with Alain, except Odette has no one else to help her. I was lucky enough to have you." *And magic.*

"We were lucky to have each other."

"Please? It's only a few days."

"Fine," she conceded. "But if she steals anything, I'll blame you."

"*Fine,*" Camille laughed. "I promise she'll keep her hands to herself. I'm going up to see our guest settled."

"*Your* guest," Sophie clarified as Camille ran up the steps. "Don't forget!"

Odette's room was a pretty one, intended as a guest room for a noblewoman. All the furniture was delicate, the bed hangings as well as the carpet a moonlit, silvery blue. Odette stood by the window, looking out. "The room faces the garden."

Camille frowned. "I thought—that's what you would prefer. Isn't it more restful? With the fountain?"

"I like to watch the street."

*Odd.* "We can switch it, if you like."

"It's not necessary," Odette said. "I won't stay long."

"Let me know if you change your mind. It's no trouble, truly." A chambermaid came in with a basket of wood and a candle, and proceeded to lay a fire in the grate. Odette followed her every movement. As if . . . making sure it was done the way she wished? But surely Odette had never lived like this, a maid to wait on her.

*It smells like home.* What had she meant?

"I'll let you settle in," she said finally. "We have dinner at eight. If you want anything, just ring the bell."

"Merci." Odette's gray eyes met Camille's. "I didn't want to say anything when I saw you with the girls, when Giselle first brought you to Flotsam House. But I remembered you right away, from the streets. When I was running."

She felt the shame of it like scalding water. Camille had been too frightened for her own safety to say, *Step into this alleyway. I'll divert the constable, you run. Here are the last coins I have—spend them quick.*

As if Odette could read her thoughts, she said, "I could tell you wished to help. That mattered. Though I didn't know where you were, or who, I knew I had a sister out there. At least there was one person in Paris who cared."

Again she was struck by how different this Odette was from the one she'd encountered in that darkening street. "I wish I had done more."

Odette held up her hand. "It's water under the bridge." She glanced around the cozy room. "Would it be possible to bathe?"

*Would it be possible to bathe?*

There it was again: a refined turn of phrase. The other girls didn't speak like that. "Of course. I'll let Adèle know."

Odette seemed barely to be listening. Instead, she drifted over to a low chair by the fire, kicked off her dirty shoes, and wiggled her stockinged toes into the deep plush of the carpet. Even though her stockings were riddled with holes, there was something charming about it: the fiery revolutionary, who seemed never to think of her own ease and enjoyment, relishing the creature comforts provided by centuries of magic.

Her reddish eyebrows were drawn sharply together, her wide mouth determined, as she stared into the fire. The hardness in her gray eyes was like steel, like that of a general about to send his soldiers into a battle. Camille pulled the door closed, not wishing to disturb her.

As she went downstairs, she wondered again over Odette's strange phrasing. It reminded her of when an enchanted coin lost its magic. The in-between moment, when she saw what it still was but also what it'd once been. What *had* Odette been doing when Camille first saw her, running from the constable? What had happened between that time, when their paths had first crossed, and now?

Perhaps there *was* one more Lost Girl story to tell.

But would Odette tell her the truth?

# 30

The next day Sophie and Odette avoided each other, like planets in different orbits. They were polite and considerate, but watching them was like watching two wary lionesses in Astley's circus. Already Sophie had complained that Odette was rude to the servants. "Give her a day or two to adjust," Camille advised.

Sophie frowned, irritated. "I thought she was leaving in a day or two."

But she did not. Instead Odette wandered the house, peering in every room that let her in.

Meanwhile Camille dreamed her hands were painted black and she could not wash the color away, no matter how hard she scrubbed. When she was awake she thought she saw, in the tail of her eye, the ghost of the murdered boy. Trees in the garden became the poles from which effigies swung. It was a waking horror she could not blink away.

Only in printing did she find refuge. She lost herself in it, the dark rush of bitter magic engulfing her like a river. Against the helplessness she'd felt in the balloon, the magic gave her power—and she relished it. Though most of her pamphlets were now printed by Arduin Frères, twin brothers who had several presses and apprentices, she still made a few print runs especially for Lasalle. They were signed, and commanded a high price. She printed another twenty of each of the Lost Girl pamphlets for Lasalle. And another fifty of her pamphlets on the women's march on Versailles.

Later that day, as Camille was finishing the last of a set of pamphlets, Odette wandered into the room. She trailed her fingers over piles of paper and picked up books to inspect their spines before setting them down as if they weren't what she wanted. Idly, as if she were only making conversation, she pointed to the curving iron lever raised in its top position.

"Some insist women aren't strong enough to pull the lever, and so they can't be printers."

"Rubbish," Camille said with a smile.

Thoughtfully, Odette ran her hand along the lever's curve. "So much power. And so much responsibility."

The longing Camille caught on Odette's face as she touched the press reminded Camille of a reflection she'd once seen of her own face in the window of a printer's shop after Papa had died. "Did you want to work on something while you're here? I could—"

"What I write is different." Odette unpinned a sheet from the line and began to read the pamphlet. When she came to the end, her mouth crimped with dissatisfaction. "Something new? It's quite bold. Different than the girls' stories."

"It's not about the girls. Well, not directly. It's meant to be different."

Odette's eyes narrowed. "Are you *criticizing* the march?"

"I'm still trying to understand it. It was . . . more complicated than I thought it would be. There was so much blood, so much killing—"

"You are against spilling blood?"

Camille stared. "Aren't you?"

"What needs to be done will be done." She shrugged her narrow shoulders. "Sometimes things happen. It's not the fault of the revolution."

"Whose fault is it, then?" Camille snapped. "It wasn't *lightning* that killed that boy."

"Have you never seen a farmer harrow his field to get it ready for planting?" Odette said scornfully. "There may be weeds growing there, but he uproots them so that new seeds can grow."

Anger crackled along her skin, fever-hot. "The boy was a *weed?*"

"I didn't say that." Odette tapped the pamphlet. "I wonder why didn't you write about the magician effigies?"

Uneasy dread sifted through her. To write about them would have been to draw attention to them. "I saw only the effigies of the king and queen."

"Didn't you hear the chants from your balloon? 'Vive le Roi!' the people cried. 'Mort aux magiciens!' You must tell the truth about what happened."

The tiny hairs on the back of Camille's neck rose. What Odette was saying was no different than what hundreds of pamphlets and posters slapped up all over Paris had been saying since the king's speech. But hearing it in her own house made her feel terribly exposed.

*Steady,* she told herself. Slowly, she raised the lever and removed the last pamphlet from the press. The black letters coiled and gleamed. It gave her some dark comfort. Over her shoulder, she said, "I didn't see them clearly enough."

"How could you not? They were swaying from poles! Black-fingered, tears running down their faces." She chuckled, a rough sound, as if she wasn't used to making it. "It's probably the only thing the king and the people agree on. Include the effigies in your next one. I bet you'll sell a lot."

Camille's jaw clenched. She noticed that Odette was wearing a black Kashmiri shawl, embroidered in cream silk, that showed off her pale skin and red hair. It was one of Camille's favorites. "Are you going out?"

"I plan to visit a few of the cafés in the Palais-Royal. Last I heard, the talk was of aristocrats fleeing France. Imagine if we had a net to catch them in? Those émigrés are traitors and cowards fleeing the problems they helped create. Perhaps we shall devise a plan." Gesturing to a stack of the new pamphlets, she asked, "May I take a few with me? I know some people who would be very interested to see a different point of view."

"Please do." Camille wiped her fingers on her apron, and laid a blank sheet of paper in the press as Odette gathered up the pamphlets. When she was at the door, Camille said, "Wait, Odette."

"Yes?"

Did Odette really believe that blood had to be spilled for change to happen? That some people, maybe the boy or maybe the magicians, had to be sacrificed for the revolution? And if she did, *why*? Was there something in her story that would explain it?

"After what happened at Versailles," Camille said, "I was hoping you might tell your story along with the other girls'. Yours would be the final one. Would you be willing?"

Some strong emotion passed over Odette's face and then, like a storm cloud, was gone. "I'll tell you everything."


Instead of sending the pamphlets with Daumier, she went to see Lasalle herself. The bookseller and his friends—the priest and the butcher—were drinking wine and laughing when he rose to greet her.

"More of your exclusives, très bien!" Taking them from her, he placed them reverently on a table. Glancing at the title, he said, "We could sell a hundred more of these, you know. Everyone who wasn't there wants to know what happened."

"If I did, they wouldn't be exclusives, would they?"

"Touché!" Lasalle acknowledged. "Is there something you're looking for?"

"There is . . . do you have any engravings about the women's march?"

"Bien sûr!" He took her to a table covered with sheets of densely printed paper: newspapers and pamphlets and posters; slim, cheaply bound books that could be read and discarded as you would a newspaper; engravings in stark black-and-white. A few were about the march. In one engraving, the women marched with shovels and scythes over their shoulders. In another the women—along with what were clearly supposed to be men in women's clothes—streamed into Versailles. And there was Odette: a young woman standing on the back of a horse, her arms flung out to embrace the crowd, giving a speech. Powerful and certain. A figure for the revolution.

Sifting through the engravings, she eventually discovered a drawing of the scene at the gates: the press of people, the boy's crumpled body, the effigies on their poles. And there—magicians painted with tears, their hands black with soot. Suddenly light-headed, she steadied herself on the table. She didn't know what was worse, that people wanted magicians dead—or that she hadn't been brave enough write about it.

"Sickens the stomach, does it not?" Lasalle said pleasantly. "Anything else?"

She picked up the engraving that showed Odette on the horse. "I'll take this."

"That's a fine one—such power in that girl!"

"If it *was* a girl," the butcher said. "Many were men dressed as women. Can't imagine a girl on a horse like that."

If Camille could have scorched them with her glare, she would have. "As it happens, I know her. Her story will be the next one I write."

"Pardon, madame!" said the butcher. "It is just that there are so many rumors, one never knows what is true or not these days—"

"How much do I owe you for the print?" she asked Lasalle.

"It's on the house. Bring me the story of that girl on the horse and I will sell every copy of it."

Odette had told the truth about the effigies, and Camille had been shown to be the liar. Then why couldn't Camille shake the feeling Odette was keeping a secret?

# THE LOST GIRLS SPEAK
# THE REVOLUTIONARY

## I STARTED LIFE AS THE DAUGHTER
## OF A RICH MAN

I remember the unending food, the servants, the feeling of S A F E T Y, that nothing could ever be too much or too difficult. Until it was, on the day my father left.

My mother wept for she could not live without him. He was a man of many moods, some of them dark, that we had both suffered under. But now? She called him her rock, her savior, and he was gone! Though I did my best to comfort her, she could not stop weeping.

Two weeks later, I woke to an empty house. My mother had gone to join him and left me behind. She took everything, even her last year's dresses, but she left me. I was worth less to her than her clothes.

As long as I could, I lived in the costly apartment, but soon I was pushed into the streets. There I saw how the people of Paris lived: some like kings, like my father, and some like rats, like me. A flame sparked inside of me to speak out against injustice.

I spoke on the street corners. I spoke in the parks and at the Palais-Royal. At first people laughed to hear a little girl with such a big voice, but then they listened and threw coins in my cap. One person who heard me was a girl who said I needed a home. A new family.

Did I D A R E to trust again? Was there someone there who would C A R E?

There was.
They did.

Poor girls with little of their own were the ones who saved me.
They gave me the strength to stand.
Now I stand and speak for all of those who are left behind.
Now I speak out, to remind the people of their duty.
We cannot hope for others to save us.

WE MUST INSTEAD LIGHT A FIRE

# 31

The next day the weather was gray, the chill of autumn in the air. Above Paris, the clouds stretched into wisps. She wondered what Lazare would make of them. What weather did they foretell? A change to sunny skies? Worsening into storms?

As promised, he'd come to the house yesterday, but she had been at Lasalle's. The note she'd sent back had narrowly missed him, her messenger said as he showed her his empty hands. She guessed Lazare had gone out with his parents, or perhaps on an errand for the balloon corps. But she ached to be with him, her need for him a hunger, no different than food or warmth or shelter.

A brisk wind rattled the branches of the trees, and she tugged the warm collar of her coat higher around her neck. She'd been up late, trying to lose herself in her work, and had taken the last exclusives to Lasalle herself, despite the magie-weariness deep in her bones. They were in demand, he told her. Could she write more?

She had said yes.

But if she was to keep writing and printing, she'd have to find a way to manage the magic. If it was true what Odette had said, and effigies at Versailles were not the work of a few but were instead showing how all of Paris felt about magicians, each new pamphlet she printed with magic put her in danger.

Though she waited for one of the magical notes to arrive, telling her of a discovery, nothing had come from Blaise or Chandon since they'd searched the library. She thought of the bonfires, the Comité's hounds, scenting the air for magical things—for hadn't it looked as if that was what the dog was doing? What if the books they desperately needed were lost, burned, and there would be no knowledge for her, no way out for them—

"Madame!" At the edge of the park, her apron flashing white, stood Adèle.

Worry gripped Camille as she hurried toward her. "What is it? Is Sophie not well?"

"Nothing so bad as that, madame! Monsieur Mellais is at the house, and he says he wishes to speak to you before he goes."

Disquiet spilled through her, cold as ink. "Goes? Goes where?"

"I wish I knew, madame. He said only he couldn't wait long."

But when Camille rushed into the sitting room, her heart hammering beneath her stays, Lazare stood at ease by the fireplace, his elbow on the mantelpiece. His hair was loose, his cravat hastily tied. He straightened when he saw her. "My love."

At the sight of him the events of Versailles flooded over her, dark and devastating. Her whole being longed to throw itself into his arms—to take refuge there—but she held back. He was leaving Paris, Adèle had said. The longer she stood there, her dirty shoes on the thick carpet, her hat and gloves still on, she was certain that there was something wrong, a stiffness in his shoulders, a tightness around his mouth that set a warning ringing in her.

He bowed, and then, taking her hands, drew off her gloves. How could she still take pleasure in it, the flood of heat through her body, when she knew he was leaving her? But she did. Slowly he kissed her fingers, as if he were trying to impress them on his memory. When he looked at her, his eyes were deep, unreadable.

"Your mantel clock has stopped, did you know?"

She felt close to tears. How could he speak about the clock as if nothing were happening? "Is that why you've come, to fix the clock—before you leave?"

He flinched. "She told you?"

"She fetched me from the square, thinking it urgent. Is it?"

He didn't answer, but rapped at the glass with his knuckles, listened, then unhooked the clasp on the case and opened the curved glass. "It just needs winding. Do you have—ah, I see it." The clock's key lay on the bottom of the case.

"Lazare, what is it? Your parents? The balloon corps?"

"I came yesterday to tell you." His hand shook a little as he fitted the key into its hole and began to wind. "It started two nights ago, the night we returned from Versailles. A family was walking back and forth near my house. A grandmother, her daughter, and a little boy. In the morning I asked my parents if anyone had moved in nearby, but no one had." He turned the key again. "Then yesterday, as I was going to oversee repairs on one of the balloons, the family appeared again. The older woman stopped me and asked, 'Are you not the Marquis de Sablebois?' She told me she was the Duchesse de Cazalès and that she needed my help."

Already Camille dreaded the answer to her question. "For what?"

He swallowed. "Her son had been wrongfully imprisoned at La Force prison but through some scheme had escaped before his execution. It was clear she feared nothing for her own life, only for her son's wife and child. Already they'd been warned not to leave Paris before the police could question them about the son's disappearance. She'd heard there was a nobleman in the balloon corps. It was not difficult to discover my name or where I lived."

"And?"

"She asked me to fly them to England."

Surprise—and sudden fear—startled in her chest. "How could she ask that of a stranger?"

"She believed in our common bond as aristocrats, I suppose." Carefully, he turned the key a little more. "I met her grandson and his mother. She'd let out her stays—she's having another child."

"Does she know how dangerous it is to fly over the sea?"

"They are desperate. They tried to give me a diamond necklace as payment! What do you think the boy said?"

Numbly, she shook her head.

"'It's the least we can do, Sablebois. We will not take charity.' With his father gone, he's been forced to grow up too soon. I replied that we had a very serious problem, since I'd take nothing for the journey."

*The journey?* "Lazare, this is madness—"

He held up his hand. To Camille it felt like a slap. "The Cazalès could be us in a week. A month. Tomorrow." Carefully, he laid the key back in the case. "After what happened at Versailles, I see what the revolution has become. A poison poured in the wells of all of Paris."

It was hard to argue with that. "Why must *you* go?"

"Because of you," he said solemnly. "You are my inspiration."

Bewildered, she said, "For this flight across the Channel? I would never do it—it is too dangerous!"

"I saw what you did for the girls. You saved their lives. And what was I doing? Giving my hard-won experience and knowledge to Lafayette so he might make balloons into war machines."

"Surely they are only watching the border—"

"They are not." He closed the clock's case so hard the glass trembled. "Lille, the revolutionary dinner, Versailles: each one was a hole in the defensive wall I'd built to protect me from the reality of what I was doing. What you'd done so selflessly for the girls showed me where I'd gone wrong. You showed me what revolution could be. *True* rebellion. I can't live with myself if I don't take the Cazalès."

On a pedestal beside her stood a bust of a long-dead magician. Gripping the corner of its cold marble base, she tried to steady herself. *She* had done this? Wishing so hard to be admirable, *she* had set his feet upon this path that would take him away from her? She felt untethered, the room tilting around her. There had to be another way.

"Can they not go by boat?" she asked.

"They're already wanted by the police. Someone, somewhere has their names on a list of possible traitors. They wouldn't get past the Paris gates."

The rumors Sophie had heard were true after all. There were people in Paris keeping score, keeping the tally card of rights and wrongs, and the list would only keep growing. It was frightening, but the terror of him taking this journey was worse.

What could she say to convince him? "But the balloon corps, they need you—"

"Lafayette wishes to add guns to the balloons. That's what I learned when I was called to 'oversee repairs' on the balloons." He raked his hand through his hair. "And *I* gave them this weapon. I showed them how to build it, how to fly it. And for what?"

*Clouds*, she thought wildly. "Science. Progress—the things you believe in."

"That's what I told myself, too. Convenient lies. You know another lie? I never told you that it was my father who invited Lafayette to Sablebois. My parents had lured me to the country just for that purpose, though I didn't know it. My father was so pleased Lafayette could provide me with a way to use the balloons that made sense to him, in the way my experiments never had. You know what he said?"

Camille tightened her grip on the statue.

"'*You could use your balloons for a real purpose.*' That's all it took for me to agree. My father's approval was the price of my soul. And I was too ashamed to tell you. That alone should have warned me." His mouth worked, as if the words were bitter to speak. "But even saying I did it for my father is one more lie. I did it for myself."

*Oh, Lazare.* "Do you remember how hard I tried to sell my father's pamphlets? I thought that was what I was supposed to do. That what my father thought was best. He wasn't even alive, Lazare, and still I wished to please him." But the girls' desperate need had changed that.

*Magic* had changed it.

"So you understand why I must go?" Hope softened the desperate lines of his face. "I don't want to be the person my father believes me to be. Someone who cares nothing for science but dreams of a medal on his shirt. A clap on the back that makes him feel secure in knowing his place."

"But this is too dangerous," she pleaded. "Not just the journey over the Channel, which you know aeronauts have died attempting. You'll be harboring people wanted by the police. They will come for you!"

"They will not know anything about it," he said quietly. "Who would tell them? No one knows but you, me, and the Cazalès." He reached out a hand to her. "If I don't take them, who would I be to you? You say you want me to stay, but if I did you would slowly begin to despise me. You are too noble—"

"Too noble?" she heard herself say. "You don't know who I am if you think that."

In the silence she heard the clock ticking, fast as wings.

"Camille? Say something." He seemed stricken, as if he might weep. "What do you mean? Who do you think you are?"

*Who was she?* She no longer knew. She was becoming . . . something else. Someone else. Magic was an acrid seed, like the gnarled pip of an orange planted deep inside her long before she'd known it was there. She had watered it with her sorrows, and now whatever this tree would be had threaded its stems and branches through her. It had produced words and pamphlets and changes in opinion. What other fruit would it bear?

She didn't know.

It was frightening not to know. But neither could she pull it out.

What if she told him the truth?

He might see the wrongness of what he was doing. It would not, she knew, make him love her more. It would make him despise her. But if it kept him alive, did it matter? She let go of the statue's pedestal, took a step toward him.

"All those *successful* pamphlets? I printed them with magic! It was with magic that they convinced all of Paris. It was magic—magic I once hated—that raised me up and gave me a voice! You wish to sacrifice yourself by flying the Cazalès over the sea so you can be *worthy* of me? Whatever Rosier says, I'm not a saint. I am, if anything, the opposite." The little voice she heard in her head—the voice of that magical seed—whispered: *You know what you are.*

The room was so quiet she could hear him breathing.

He did not look at her. He only said flatly, "I believed you when you said it was nothing to you."

*It is in me, too deep to unroot.* "Lazare, it's like a fever. I don't know how to manage it—yet."

"Yet?" He took a step toward her. "What are you waiting for? You've put yourself in terrible danger. If someone were to find out—"

"No one will find out. We are searching for a way to control it."

There was a shell on the mantel, beside the clock, and he clenched it in his hand. "Who is helping you?"

"Chandon and another magician." She knew how bad it sounded. How secret. "They're searching for a book—"

"A book? A book?" For several long minutes, he looked at the shell as if he would smash it. "Tell me, if I asked you to come with me to England, to escape this place, you would say no?"

Bewildered, she asked, "That is what you've come to ask me?"

He inclined his head. Beneath his lashes, his beautiful eyes were like dark moons, impossible, unreachable.

"I can't leave them without finding the answers. And you see how terrible things are for magicians. They need a way out before the borders close, we are close to finding it, I hope. Besides, I cannot leave Sophie—"

His face shuttered. "Of course not. I was wrong to dream of it."

He turned as if to go, and Camille grabbed his coat sleeve. "Lazare, please listen. What if magic isn't wrong? I used it to help the girls"—she remembered her mother, clutching *The Silver Leaf* to her chest—"perhaps it might save me, too."

"It will get you killed." He shook his sleeve free. "You chose it, long before you chose me. I could never compete with it. I was a fool to try."

"How am I not choosing you?" she said, bewildered. "I wish for you to *stay*. To not risk your life."

"You have chosen to stay for the sake of magic and the magicians." But his dark gaze said: *You are breaking my heart.*

"It's not just for them that I stay."

"What, then? Why remain in this country that wants neither of us?"

She did not want to be pushed out. She wanted, for once, to stop running. "For me."

"What do you mean?"

"I did stop working it, you know. But it came back, just the same." Servants stirred outside the door, murmuring in the hall. "What if magic is not something I do, but something I *am?*"

"It cannot be." Lazare looked as if he were trying to pick up the pieces of something that had broken. "You said there might be a way to get rid of it."

"Yes—no."

"You might continue to use it? To *be* a magician?"

Sorrow rose like a tide beneath her skin and suddenly she despaired of making him understand. Tears coursed down her cheeks—tears of sadness and fury and regret so mixed she could not tell them apart. What if, in the end, magic was all she had?

"I never had a true teacher, not even my mother. I did it alone. Mocked and used by my brother. Lost, hating myself and what I had to do to survive. But no more."

She yearned for him to embrace her and say he loved her. But he did not even reach out his hand.

Instead he said, "It's rich that you warned me of the danger of taking this suffering family to England. Knowing all the while that *you* have been putting yourself in danger every day. Pretending to be a printer."

"*Pretending?*"

"Apparently you have not lost your taste for it," he said. "How could you do it again?"

She took an uncertain step back. "And you? Have you not been pretending?"

"I had been," he said sorrowfully, "but not anymore."

Camille took another step away. "Is that what you object to? My keeping this from you?"

"I don't know if it is the magic, or the secret. Nor am I certain I wish to know."

His voice was so cold. She had misjudged him, tallied everything up wrong. "Tell me, Lazare: What is magic to you?"

As if it were very clear, he said, "The thing that will forever keep us apart."

She tipped up her chin, defiant. "And if this is the thing that makes me unlovable, unworthy, then you are finished with me?"

"No." He unfroze, and with one step he closed the gap between them. He cupped her face between his warm hands, ran his thumb along the slope of her cheek. Anguish contorted his beautiful face. "I love you, Camille."

"But you wish—"

"And am I wrong to wish for it? Isn't it what you wish for, too?" He sighed as if he were in terrible pain. "I do not want to be second best in your heart."

In his dark pupils, she saw herself reflected: insubstantial as a moth. What place did she have in *his* heart?

The clock on the mantel began to chime. She could think of nothing more to say.

"I must leave. If anyone asks," he pleaded, "tell them I've gone to Sable-bois. Promise me."

Her voice caught on a sob, but she managed to say it. "I promise."

"Dieu, this is not the meeting I'd hoped for." From his pocket he produced a small object, wrapped in faded red fabric. "One favor, if you'll grant it? Please keep this for me. It's my father's and I don't dare take it up in the balloon."

As she tucked it into her sleeve, he stepped close against her skirts, until their bodies were nearly touching. What if there was a kiss that would undo it all, a wave of feeling and desire that could sweep away the words they had said and the pain they had caused? She pressed her mouth to his, desperate and hard and fierce. His answering kiss was angry, desolate, lost. Roughly their hands tugged at one another's clothes, clutching at collars and lacings as if those were the barriers that kept them apart.

With a groan, he pulled away. His chest was heaving, and he ran a shaking hand over his face. "How can we be together if there is this thing between us?"

Something broke inside her then. A shivering crack, as of splintering glass. It was all wrong. Maybe once she'd thought she could stop working magic. But not now. She would not be that moth, insubstantial and too easily torn.

"If you can't love me without wanting me to be something other than I am," she said, "then yes—this *thing* will keep us apart."

Before he could see her hot tears spill, she strode to the farthest window and put her back to him. Though there was only the space of a room between them, it was vast as a chasm. This is who she was: a magician. Cursed, or gifted, she did not know. He could leave her—but she would not let herself feel small.

"Camille!"

She would not go to him. She could not say how long they stood there, the house clattering and shifting unhappily around them, but finally he left. Nauseated, she listened to the rapid click of his shoes as he descended the stairs, his polite murmured exchange with Daumier, the doors closing behind him. In the hall, Adèle and Odette were calling her name.

From the window, she watched him cross diagonally across the street, heedless of the carriages, his hair flying about his shoulders. His beautiful hands, the ones that had just held her, were clenched in fists at his sides.

She might never see him again.

Someone might be trailing the Cazalès family. He might be caught before he left France. If not, the balloon could crash anywhere between Paris and Calais. It could tumble into the ice-cold sea. And then—nothing.

He had reached the park.

Every movement, every gesture he made as he crossed the faded grass of the Place des Vosges she wished to commit to memory. Like an important date, a name, a spell she could use to conjure him again.

She could not let him go like this.

Grabbing her skirts, she raced from the room. Past the startled servants, down the stairs, across the street, she ran, her breath ragged, until she reached the Place des Vosges, where she startled a cloud of pigeons into flight.

But Lazare was gone. All that was left were the trees in the square with their bare black branches, the fallen leaves tarnished like brass.

# 32

In the Place des Vosges, she waited for Lazare until her hands were stiff with cold, hoping he'd turn around and come back. Maybe then there would have been a way to erase what they'd said—what they'd done—and begin anew, the way embroidery could be unpicked from a sleeve.

But what had happened between them couldn't be undone. There was no way to unpick it and make it as if it had never happened. It *had*. She hated how small and powerless she had felt, and she did not wish to feel that way ever again. If it meant being without him, then she would have to find a way.

She was running lightly up the grand marble stairs of the Hôtel Séguin when she heard, eerily clear, the sound of someone crying.

It couldn't be Sophie, could it? Camille searched the house until she found her in her dressing room, holding a gown under her chin. She startled when she saw Camille.

"Dieu, what's happened to you? You look terrible!"

"Lazare has left Paris. But I can't talk about it now."

The fabric slid from Sophie's grasp. "Why ever not?"

"Can't you hear the crying?"

Bewildered, Sophie said, "Hear *what*?"

What was it Blaise had said? That she needed to find a way to listen to the house?

The heart-wrenching sobs continued. It seemed as if they were coming from the mansion's older wing. She hoped they weren't coming from the library, for she didn't want to go back inside with the rustling books and the enchanted portrait. She followed the sobbing down the long and gloomy hall until she came to a particularly ornate door. The weeping emanated from Séguin's bedroom.

Gritting her teeth, she went in.

It had been emptied of anything personal and might have been anyone's room but for a gold-and-black lacquered Chinese cabinet that seemed vaguely familiar. She opened a set of drawers and listened, feeling like a fool. Rien. She peered inside a towering armoire: nothing. And then she looked more carefully at the lacquerware cabinet. The knobs on its doors had been bound with red string.

Her first thought was that it was a kind of magical protection. Then she realized they'd been tied together to keep them from flapping open—the cabinet was one of the things that been sent back from Versailles when Séguin's rooms had been cleared out. She hadn't wanted to look inside. Her memories of his apartment in the palace, what he had done there . . .

She grabbed a letter opener from the desk and sliced the string. The doors creaked open as the sharp smell of magic filled the room. The sobbing grew louder. Clothes were piled in the bottom, coats and robes heavy with embroidery. Underneath them lay something hard and smooth. With an effort, she dislodged it. Pulling it out, she fell back on her heels. In her hands was a rectangular object.

It was a valise, covered in worn maroon leather.

The sound of crying was coming from inside.

There was a lock on it, and she thought of the key ring downstairs and how many she'd have to try to find the right one. But the house, both Chandon and Blaise had said, cared for her. Maybe it would open if she tried.

She put her hands on the lid and the top lifted free.

Lined with worn rose-colored silk, the box held a small wooden rack. In it were rows of crystal vials, each labeled with the words *Larmes de . . .* followed by a name. It was a collection of tears. Hands shaking, she found one labeled *Larmes de Jean-Marc Étienne de Bellan, Marquis de Chandon.* There were a few more, the bottles dusty and discolored by age.

Gooseflesh rose on her arms.

She ran her fingers along them, touching them, reading the names aloud, and somehow this soothed the magic in the box, because eventually the crying quieted. The vials were in no particular order, though the labels on some seemed newer. The one with the cleanest label rested in the bottom rack. *His last victim.* Plucking it out of the case, she held it up to see.

In Séguin's spidery script was written: *Larmes de Camille Durbonne, Vicomtesse de Séguin.*

He had taken her tears after all.

She held the tiny vessel to the light. The liquid inside was tinged pale blue and slightly thick, as if it had been condensed. Tipping the bottle, she watched the substance that had been her tears slide slowly from one side of the vial to the other. Had she cried while she slept? Had he scraped up the tears that laced her cheeks after he'd trapped her?

She wondered what sorrows lay inside.

The vial had a miniature cork stopper, covered with a thin layer of silver decorated with a pattern of tears. Prying it loose with her fingers, she brought the bottle to her nose and inhaled. A familiar powdery smell, like dried roses. The liquid scent of ink. Cold water in a well, dark and deep and quiet. Muffled cries.

They were her own, caught in the tears like flies in amber. When she covered the mouth of the vial with her thumb, they quieted. When she removed it, they rose up to her. Around her, the room thinned, becoming transparent. She sensed herself, very small, a child hiding under a table, a sob choking—

She shoved the cork back in.

The memories were so potent they had nearly crawled out of the vial.

Shaking, she unlatched the window. The sharp autumn air helped clear her head. The cries faded, as did the memory they'd contained. A childhood hurt that still felt raw and humiliating. Something nestled so deep inside her that she no longer remembered the wound. But it had power, she had sensed *that*.

Saint-Clair had been right.

She shut the valise's lid before setting it safe into the wardrobe and pocketing the crystal vial. It wasn't the book they needed, but the valise was still a treasure. She knew it was dangerous to use others' tears, but in an emergency? Even if the magicians never found the secret of the tempus fugit, there was enough blur to get them past the gate, past a checkpoint or out of France.

As she closed the door behind her, a loud bang echoed downstairs. It was unlike any of the maids or footman to let the glass doors slam shut. Instead it sounded as if the Hôtel Séguin were trying to get her attention. Summoning her courage, for the first time she let down her guard. *Here I am.* She let herself truly feel the house around her, its changing corridors and unexpected rooms, its enchanted objects, the life and history webbed into its nearly sentient stones. *Show me*, she thought. *Tell me.*

And then, from deep inside the walls of the house, came a single, rushing susurration: *Hurry.*

# 33

When Camille reached Odette's room, the door swung back silently on its hinges.

The window stood slightly open, a breeze ruffling the curtains. The room was empty, the bed made. In the wardrobe hung the dress Odette had worn during the women's march, when she came to the Hôtel Séguin. It had been laundered and pressed. The bloodstain that had run along the collar was gone. On the desk sat the breakfast tray. The dishes that had been sent up to her, heaped with bread and chocolate and butter and the apple tarts were clean, shining. Not a crumb left behind, as if Odette had licked her finger and run it over the plate until she'd caught every last speck.

Otherwise there was no sign of her but for a small, worn satchel. Camille went closer. She had almost put her hand inside when the curtain twitched.

*The house will warn you.*

There, in the park, under the trees—Odette. She wore the coat Camille had lent her, as well as one of Sophie's broad-brimmed hats. As if she could feel Camille watching her, she hesitated and looked back over her shoulder. Under the swoop of the hat, her face was angry and determined.

Camille's pulse hammered in her throat. Odette was going somewhere, and didn't wish to be seen by someone in the house. But where?

*Hurry.*

For ten minutes, Camille followed her.

She could hardly believe she was doing it. Was it because she'd heard a voice in the house—that the house had warned her? Stranger things had happened. After all, the house had denied entrance to the Comité's guards. But it was more than the Hôtel Séguin. It was the prickle on the back of her neck when Odette had mentioned the effigies of magicians. The way she had run her fingers along the press's iron lever, like a caress. The suspicion that Odette's story had, at its heart, a missing piece.

A secret.

She'd kept well back, making certain there were people between her and Odette. It was easy to keep track of her, her red hair like a flare. Odette knew Paris well, taking the shortcuts Camille also knew, as she walked briskly toward the river. When she reached the Pont Neuf, she did not cross but headed down the bank, under the arch.

Flotsam House.

By the scrim of trees, Camille paused. Candles were already lit in the cottage. She imagined the girls by the fire, toasting bread and talking. The subscriptions Lasalle sold had brought in more and more, and she sent it all to the girls. There was no reason Odette shouldn't go there, too.

But she trusted the voice inside her that whispered something was wrong.

Slowly, deliberately, she edged down the bank. The door of the house opened, and Odette stepped inside. She could hear the girls exclaiming, and the hubbub of voices gave her cover to come closer. Poised outside, wondering once again what she was doing and why, she heard someone say her name. "Really? Camille?"

And then Odette's response, fierce and angry: "She will betray you all."

Camille stopped, held her breath.

Someone—undaunted Claudine—challenged her to explain.

"It's simple," Odette said, "unless we stop her, she will hurt the revolution! And you will suffer because of it! You have no idea what she's capable of."

Camille's heart ticked faster. Was this because of what she'd written in the pamphlet on the women's march? She'd made one criticism, and suddenly she was a counterrevolutionary? A tumult of voices broke out from inside the house and little Céline came outside to play, away from the arguments. Camille pressed herself against the wall and Céline passed her without noticing. She wished she were inside, a listening spider hidden in her web.

Then she realized she could be.

From her pocket she pulled the tiny crystal vial. There was not much in it—three or four drops—but she guessed she didn't have to use them all. When the Comte de Roland took the blur, it had faded fast. She would have to get in and out quickly before the magic wore off.

Inside the tears glittered like rain. She twisted loose the stopper. The scent of cold water, sharp ink, and lavender drifted toward her.

She didn't know if she could do it.

Even the *scent* of the blur had carried with it a terrible memory. What would it be like to swallow it? To have that despair bloom inside of her? She already feared she might lose herself in magic. This would be worse. She had seen it with Roland—not only had his body vanished, but also his mind. He had disappeared into that girl's memories.

She was not certain she wanted to return to hers.

The portraits at Bellefleur came back to her, the long line of ancestors in that darkened hall. The way they looked as if they were about to speak and tell her their stories. She had wondered: if she had grown up with her magician past around her, might she be less ashamed of what she was?

Might she also understand who she was?

The blur was a memory from the past. Perhaps it was also a key.

She let a single pale-blue drop land on her tongue.

It was bitter as sorrow.

In a storm, sensations overtook her. They had the dim feel of stories long forgotten. Lost, or never meant to be retrieved. An achingly sunny day, bright with promise. A scatter of sharp furniture tacks on the floor. A child trying to keep quiet as sobs stuck in her throat.

The magic was consuming her. Memories, trapped in tears, unleashed.

Camille rubbed at her eyes, trying to see in *this* world, *this* time. She made her way to the cottage's half-open door. From inside came angry, hushed voices. She was nearly inside when the blur took hold once more.

The sound of weeping. Thin, muffled. Somewhere, a child was crying.

Around her, the river and the buildings of Paris receded until she only dimly sensed them, as if from behind a pane of dirty glass. Instead, there was a bright, quiet room. High in a house. Ferns of frost etched the windows. A pitcher of water, cracked ice on top. And the weeping?

It was coming from herself. A red-haired little girl sitting on the floor.

She was hugging her knees tight. Maman squeezed her shoulder, reassuring, as waves of sadness rolled through her. "Try now," Maman encouraged. "You are strong enough."

Picking up a black tack, Camille rolled it between her childish fingers. It pricked her, and she squeezed her finger to see the bright jewel of blood. She let the sadness stream through her, wishing the tack smooth. Soon its point dulled and the tack collapsed until it was nothing but a small, iron disk.

"Better?" Her voice was very small.

"Very good," Maman said in Camille's ear. In the haze of the blur, her mother was close, so close. *I love you*, she wanted to say. *Do not leave me yet.*

"Camille?"

Who had called her? Was it someone there—or here?

With that sharp, panicky question in her mind her childhood vanished, and in its place was the cottage's warmth, the watery rush of the Seine, the splash of firelight on the girls' tense faces.

Odette glanced over her shoulder, right at where Camille stood—*as if she could see her*—and Camille flattened back against the wall. If her luck held, for a few more minutes, she was invisible.

Giselle took a step toward Odette, then faltered. "Why are you wearing her clothes?"

Odette tossed her head, making the plume in Camille's hat dance. "I'm staying at her house."

Giselle's chin wobbled. "Why?"

"I needed to spy on her to find out what she truly is."

"And that is?"

Her smile gleamed like a knife. "I promise I'll tell you later, once I have proof. But trust me, once you know . . . you'll wish you never knew her."

Tiny Henriette, the forger with the cloud of blond hair, jabbed a finger at Odette. "You know she helped us keep this house. Those subscriptions keep us in food and clothes. You're telling us to throw that away?"

Sly, Odette asked, "Haven't you wondered if she's using you?"

Suddenly the little room wavered as Maman's perfume and her comforting warmth flooded back. Softly she murmured, *Remember, mon trésor. Some will say magic is a terrible thing. A lie, a parlor trick, cheating. But they are seeing it wrong.*

Camille the child hadn't tried to understand what her mother had said. It had been too grown-up and far from her own wants and fears. But now she wanted say to her mother, *Tell me! What is the right thing to do? Who should I be?*

The fire crackled, and she was back in the warm cottage, the girls shouting among themselves, Giselle scowling at Odette.

"It isn't true!" Margot said.

Worried, Claudine said, "But what if it is?"

"You could help me prove it. See it for yourself." Odette's eyes gleamed with persuasive cunning. "There are rooms in her house that are locked, that I cannot get into. I need evidence. Come with me, Claudine, pick the locks and I will show you—"

*Prove what?* And the terrifying question, its slow dark tug like an ebb tide: *Who have I let into my house?*

Camille backed out the door.

*Hurry.*

The girls were still arguing. "And even if it was true," Giselle interrupted, "what of it? She has been good to us!"

"It's nothing but pretend," Odette sneered. "When you learn what she has done, come to me. I'll still be here. I'll still be your friend."

And then, like a cold intake of breath, the last of the blur dissolved and the hard edges of her own world came into sharp focus once more. Fatigue crept into her lead-heavy limbs. Her skin crawled as if a thousand pins pricked her. The magie-sickness was coming, and she had to get away.

Odette pulled Camille's cloak close around her and swept out of the cottage and up the bank. Camille watched her go. If she could return to the Hôtel Séguin before Odette, she could lock her out. The house would protect her and Sophie.

A barge clanged its bell, and the girls paused to listen.

*Now.*

Forcing her unsteady legs to carry her, she moved as fast as she could along the muddy shore. The ache, the disorientation, all of it was worse than what she'd felt when she'd worked the glamoire. Each heavy step took an eternity. Finally, she reached a chestnut tree by the riverbank. She clung to it, gasping as her breath rattled in her throat. Above her, the branches of the tree made a heavy shadow. She wondered if she could nestle beneath it, like the time she'd played cache-cache in the gardens of Versailles. A yew hedge like cut velvet under the distant stars. Lazare emerging from the trees to catch her. His smile, gleaming in the dark. What had she done, letting him leave her? She had broken everything.

She was so weary. Another step, and she would hide until she was well enough to get home.

But she never reached it.

# 34

Camille stood on a high bluff. Below was a silver-tongued sea, storm clouds above. The air crackled with thunder. Lightning split, revealing high white cliffs and a balloon, sailing across the water.

It was losing altitude.

Closer and closer it came to the water that roiled with the tentacles of sea monsters. Distantly she saw Lazare putting on a cork vest as the balloon plunged into the waves. Could he not see the creatures?

Around her hips hung a brace of pistols. She unbuckled them and tossed them out over the sea: *Catch them!* They sailed out—so far, so impossibly far—before plunging into the water just out of Lazare's reach. A sickly white tentacle slithered into the gondola. Lazare didn't see it as he reached for the sinking guns.

Why hadn't *she* shot the sea creatures instead of throwing the pistols?

"What's happening?" asked a soft voice.

Hands held her, and she struggled against them. "He's fallen into the sea!"

"What sea?"

"Tell him to stay in Dover, or else he will be lost!"

"Hush," said the voice. "You're only dreaming."

Slowly, painfully, she opened her eyes. Giselle's worried face hovered over her. The tense conversation by the fire came back to her, and she scrambled to her elbows. Her head swam. She did not feel wholly *there*. "Where is Odette?"

"You were outside?" Giselle gasped. "You heard what she said?"

The blur's fog still hung at the edge of her mind. It was hard to remember. "She believes I'm hurting the revolution. Hurting *you*."

"I hate her," Giselle said fiercely. "We don't believe her. At least, I don't—"

It didn't matter, not now. "Help pull me up," she said, and together, they stood. The river tilted uneasily behind her. "I must go home."

"Should I walk with you? You don't seem at all like yourself, Camille—"

"It's nothing, mon amie. It will pass." *I hope.* She was grateful for Giselle's kindness, but she had to hurry, to prevent Odette from getting inside the house. "Thank you for believing in me." And then she was in the street, stumbling at first but slowly finding her feet *here*, on the Quai des Ormes, and not *there*, in the cold room where her mother told her she was strong, running until the steady rhythm of her pumping legs carried her home.


As she burst into the entry, Camille surprised Adèle, who was changing the flowers in a vase. "Madame! Are you hurt?"

"Is there someone here?"

"Yes—"

Too late. Camille steadied herself against the wall, trying to shake away the wisps of memory that clung to her and the magic-weariness that came with it. "When did she arrive? Is she upstairs?" *The vials.* "She mustn't get into Séguin's room—"

Her eyebrows at her hairline, Adèle said, "Who do you mean?"

"Odette."

"Oh! *She* has not returned."

Camille exhaled shakily. "Grâce à Dieu! Lock the door on her if necessary. Get Daumier to help you if you need it."

"Of course." Adèle seemed to relish the thought of it. "And your other visitors?"

She blinked. "Who are they?"

"The Marquis de Chandon and Monsieur Delouvet. They wished to wait in a room without windows, so I showed them to the butler's pantry. It is hardly the place for such magicians, but I did not know what else to do."

They were afraid. "You did well, Adèle."

"You know you can count on us, madame. The old master kept us here by force. But you do it with your kindness."

Adèle didn't have to say it, and Camille was grateful. "Thank you."

"Now, madame, your dress—"

But Camille was already striding toward the butler's pantry. It was more like a short corridor than ran between the kitchens and the dining room than an actual room. When she reached the door, she said low, "It's me, Camille."

The key clicked in the lock, and the door inched open.

Chandon and Blaise were squeezed together in the narrow space. On the long counter that ran the length of the room, a candle guttered. It cast wavering shadows, its light barely reaching to the highest shelves and cabinets where glasses and platters were stored. At the very back of the room was the pantry's second door, also locked, which led to the dining room. Chandon had found a bottle of wine—or perhaps he'd convinced Adèle to give him one—and he and Blaise each had a glass in hand.

"Fancy meeting you here," Chandon said brightly. "Your housemaid had no idea when you'd return. But, I will say, your staff are proper magician's staff, accustomed to strange whims! She knew exactly where to bring us." The boys pressed against the cabinets to make room for her.

"What's happened?" she asked urgently.

"What's happened to you?" Chandon sniffed. "You smell like the Seine."

She noticed that Blaise in his spotless cream-colored clothes had taken a good step backward. "I was spying on my houseguest. And then, because I didn't know how to do it without being seen, I took some of the blur."

Blaise's calm evaporated. "*What* blur?"

"I found it here, in the house, an hour ago! Vials of blur Séguin had made. It was as if the house . . . led me to them. You were right, Blaise—I think it's been trying to warn me for a long time." She was giddy with the promise of it. "It's upstairs, shall we go?"

Both of them stared at her wide-eyed. Chandon threw back a gulp of wine. "How much is there?"

"I didn't stop to count. Perhaps five or six?"

"And you simply tried one?"

Sharp blue drops on her tongue. The wrenching pain of her memory. "It did have my name on it." Gently, she added, "There's one with your tears, too."

"I'm not surprised," Chandon said. "Though, I must say, this might be the first good thing ever to come of that brute Séguin!"

"Tell us," Blaise asked seriously, "what was it like?"

It still lingered, cold and watery at the edges of her mind. "I fell into the past. I was very small. A moment I hadn't remembered. It was just as the Marquis de Saint-Clair said in his journal: the blur had contained and preserved it, almost as if it had been extracted from my mind." And she explained how it'd felt, the power of the sorrowful memories flooding into her mind as if a lock in a dam had been opened. How she'd struggled to be both in this world and in that one.

"Just as I do with the magic I feel when I print, I felt the blur would consume me. It really did make me disappear. Apart from seeing my mother in the memory, it was awful. I hope to never have to use it again."

Both magicians looked grim. "But it might be one of the only ways to protect ourselves," Blaise said. "That is, when we can make our own."

Now it was Camille's turn to stare. "What?"

A faint, gratified smile. "I found a book," Blaise said.

Far away, in the foyer, a door slammed shut. Around them, the house creaked, and in the pantry cupboards, the wineglasses clinked together. *Odette.* She had to trust Adèle and Daumier would take care of her.

"Tell me!" she urged. "Where is it?"

He tapped his temple. "Somewhere safe."

"You've committed it to memory?"

"Not yet," Blaise said. "It's only a small blue book written by an obscure magician, but he explains the process of a magic he calls, in a very offhand way, 'tempus fugit.' He even mentions something to relieve the magie-sickness that comes afterward, though he mentions nothing about the effect lingering, as you experienced."

"Where's the Comte de Roland?"

"Tours. I've already sent word. As soon as he arrives, we can use tempus fugit to transform our tears."

"We must make as much as we can," Camille said. "It lasts such a short time, we'll need several doses for each of us."

Chandon gave a fretful sigh. "I fear it will be a very dreary evening."

"Because we will have to make ourselves sad," Camille said, "to collect our own tears."

Did a shadow pass over Blaise's white face? "It's a bit more complicated than that," he said. "But in essence, yes. The tears Camille found should function as our reserve. Hers are fairly new—but what if the others have become too old? Off, like bad wine? Or what if the memories are too terrible to endure? That might have been the case with the ones Roland took. Even if our memories are difficult, at least they're our own."

*But even that didn't make them easy to relive.* The difference was, she thought, that what she relived might help her understand what she hadn't before. Maman's love and her belief in Camille's strength.

"I'll bring the vials to the meeting and we can divide them among us," Camille decided. "You'll send a flare when you've determined on the time?"

"As soon as Roland returns," Chandon said. "Foudriard warns of borders tightening. The city is papered with pamphlets and advertisements calling for our deaths, offering rewards for any information at all about magicians. The Comité's already been to the Hôtel Séguin and I've seen them outside

Bellefleur, too. We must be careful. Whatever warding magic protects our houses cannot last forever."

"Chandon is right," Blaise said. "There have also been strange goings-on at Les Mots Volants. Suspicious customers, wandering in and never speaking to me. It's hard to find a warded book if you don't know what you're looking for. So what *are* they looking for? I fear we are running out of time."

"We shall not delay, mon ami." Chandon set his wineglass down and embraced them both. "Damn their persecution! We *will* be free. All that time I spent gambling and using my magic on card tricks, I never thought much of my life. But now there's a chance to do something good, I fear I might lose it."

"You did do something at Versailles," Camille reminded him. "You protected Foudriard."

"Ah!" Chandon brightened. "I'd forgotten I nearly gave my life for him."

"True love," Blaise said, a sad smile on his lips. "And now I think we should go our separate ways."

His caution unsettled her. Blaise didn't exaggerate. "How did you come in?"

"By the kitchen, as before."

"One of you can go out through the kitchen, the other down the passageway to the right, all the way to the end. There's an odd servants' hall that opens onto the stableyard. The groom will let you out the back gate."

The plan that they'd worked toward for so long was becoming real. They would make the blur, and they, as well as all the magicians of France—once the magic was written up and shared—would be able to hide themselves if they needed to. No journey would be completely free of peril, but being able to evade the Comité would make it less so.

"À bientôt, then," Blaise said. "Be on your guard, both of you."

Slowly, Chandon opened the door and peered out into the passageway. "All clear. I'll go out by the stables." He blew her a kiss and was gone with a clatter of heels on stone. Blaise headed toward the kitchen, floating along like a pale strand of moonlight in the gloom.

Above her head were rows and rows of ghostly vessels. Glass from Venice, thin as mist: crystal decanters glittering with shards of diamonds and dozens of ballooning wineglasses, etched with the Séguin family seal. She wondered if she'd ever be able to drink from them all.

Suddenly they tinkled, as if someone were walking nearby.

She tiptoed to the other end of the pantry. Beyond the door, in the printing room, she heard the quiet hush of a leather sole on a parquet floor. The faint crinkle of skirts held close to stop them from rustling.

"Sophie?" she called. "Are you eavesdropping? I have something to tell you!"

And then she flung open the door.

# 35

"Surprise!" Odette smiled broadly at Camille.

She could only stare. How had Odette slipped past Adèle?

"Quelle coincidence!" Camille said, finally. "What are you doing here?"

"I thought I was living here," Odette said, a tinge of hurt coloring her voice. "Or have you forgotten about me so quickly?"

Disquiet threaded through her. Even though she'd heard Odette disparaging her at Flotsam House, now that she was here, standing in front of her? Odette was someone else entirely. Someone to be wary of.

"Not at all!" Camille exclaimed. "I meant only to ask why you were standing here, outside the door. I could have hurt you as I came out."

"I was trying to find a servant to make me some tea."

"You can always ring for one of the housemaids." Odette knew this; she'd not been shy in setting the servants running to fulfill her wishes. It was clearly an excuse.

"But I didn't see anyone, so I thought I'd look for you in the printing room. Where you often are." Her eyes gleamed like a cat's in the night. "Instead, I found you in the pantry."

A warning bell clanged in her mind. "You were listening."

"All I heard was mumbling voices. The doors in this house are rather thick. Sorry to have troubled you—I'll fetch the tea myself." Odette spun on her heel and headed toward the door.

In two steps Camille had her by the arm. "You didn't hear what we said?"

Odette shrugged her off. "I'm your friend, remember? Not a *spy*." Even if Odette had heard nothing, there was something about the way her face sharpened when she said the word *spy* that made Camille wonder if Odette had somehow seen her using the blur at Flotsam House. But how? It made no sense, unless the magic was much quicker to fade than she'd thought.

The debilitating haziness of the blur made it difficult to remember. She struggled to recall what Odette had said about finding out who Camille was. Perhaps that was why she had crept into the printing room—to see what pamphlets Camille was printing? Something antirevolutionary to use against her? She'd wanted Claudine to come with her to the Hôtel Séguin, to pick the locks. To break in. Find the secret rooms and the evidence. But evidence of what?

Once, when she and Sophie and Alain had had nothing, Camille had gone to a distant neighborhood to buy meat with her last turned coins. At home, she'd unwrapped the piece of mutton, and, as her stomach churned with anticipation for the meal, discovered the meat writhed with worms. It had looked good from the outside.

"Get out," she spat.

Odette blinked, the picture of innocence. "To the kitchen?"

"I said, get out of my house." Behind Odette, the edge of the carpet began to curl, rolling itself closer and closer to where she stood. Overhead the pamphlets muttered on their lines. The temperature in the house was rising.

Odette clenched her hand around the doorjamb. "Because I happened to come in here? I thought you cared about us girls."

"I do. And I'm certain the girls will take you in for a few nights, now that you're back on your feet." *Quiet*, she thought at the house. *Settle.* The carpet uncurled but the wind remained, yawning through the rooms. It snagged at the ends of Odette's hair and in her cloak's tasseled trim like a warning.

She narrowed her eyes. "I don't wish to leave yet."

Odette had been against Camille writing the pamphlets from the beginning. She'd never fully embraced what the pamphlets had brought the girls. She'd cared nothing for the subscriptions that kept the girls in money every week. Then there had been her strange comments about the effigies she had seen at Versailles, at the march. And worst, what she'd said to the girls and her attempt to bring Claudine to the house to pick its secrets.

But why?

It reminded her of how Chandon had shuffled playing cards through the dazzling nights in the gaming rooms at Versailles, his hands setting the pips to spinning, the cards flashing like falling snow. It was misdirection, a distraction so no one would look at what he was really doing.

"Daumier!" Camille called. The house sent her voice out as an echo through its hallways and rooms.

Odette frowned as sturdy footsteps came closer. When the footman came into view, Odette crossed her arms, bracing. "I demand you leave me alone."

"I only take orders from the mistress of the house."

Just as Adèle had said, staunch and loyal. "Daumier, would you please escort Mademoiselle Leblanc while she packs her things. She has decided to leave."

"How dare you?" Odette spat. "Everything you did for the girls—for us—was a lie! You only *pretended* to care!"

"You know that's not true," she said coldly. "But if it makes you feel better, by all means, believe it."

Odette took a step closer. The floorboard creaked menacingly beneath her feet. "You will regret making us enemies."

"You've done that all on your own. Adieu, Odette."

Daumier grasped her arm under the elbow. "I'll show you the way, mademoiselle."

"Let go of me! I can walk myself. I have no wish to stay here any longer."

But Daumier held firm, as if he were taking her out onto a ballroom floor for a minuet, and led her away.

Once they were gone, Camille rested her forehead against the glass cabinet. It was cool, and soothing, and slowed her pounding heart. It had been awful, but it was over. The minutes ticked away as she waited for Odette to leave. Far away, the front door shut, solid and reassuring. The house creaked and sighed, as if it too were relieved, tucking itself to sleep the way Fantôme the cat did.

She should have felt safe. But as she left the butler's pantry, she couldn't shake the feeling that that was not the last she'd see of Odette. That on the great pile of wood a new piece of kindling had been lit and was beginning to smoke.

# 36

"Sophie?"

After Odette had been escorted out, Camille wandered the house, searching for her sister. As each room turned out to be empty—the red salon, the kitchen, Sophie's bedroom and sitting room—she considered the day's events. The bright hope of the valise of tears, with its tiny vials of magic, the book Blaise had finally found, and their plan to make enough blur to use if an escape became necessary. Against all of that weighed Odette's betrayal.

But again and again, she came back to the fight with Lazare. It felt as if they'd stripped away the grease paint smiles they'd worn for a performance and now, with them gone, neither of them recognized the other. Had their paths taken them so far apart that they couldn't be brought together again?

The thought of it was a stone inside her. *I will not cry*, she told herself. If that was who Lazare was—someone who could never accept magic—there was no future for them. No final act, no encore.

Camille finally found Sophie kneeling by one of her mannequins, surrounded by heaps of white feathers and lengths of white organza. In the middle of one pile slept the black cat Fantôme. From pegs on the wall hung several puppet costumes—fox, bear, fawn, and others—mysterious and beautiful. The mannequin wore one of the princess's white costumes, the plainer one she wore before wings transformed her into a bird. Around its chest was wrapped a bright tricolor sash, which Sophie was tying into a bow.

"What's happening with the costumes?" Camille asked.

Sophie didn't turn around, but continued to fuss with the knot. "I am *fixing* them."

"With revolutionary ribbons?"

"Rosier didn't tell you?" She sat back on her heels, studying the effect. "A *patriot* complained about our second performance at the Palais-Royal. He called it antirevolutionary. 'There was a princess! Magic!' Now we must change it so that it's *realistic*. In line with revolutionary values."

Camille hated the weariness in her sister's voice. "How can they care so much about a puppet show?"

Sophie got to her feet and fluffed the ribbon. "We had an enormous audience. Rosier had advertised and has sold tickets already for the next one. But apparently puppets are dangerous."

"Need you go this far with the trims?"

"I should, but I won't!" She yanked the tricolor ribbon off and crushed it in her fist. "Revolution, revolution! I am well tired of it, Camille. I could have designed costumes for the opera. Or the Comédie-Française. But it will never happen."

"Surely you still could—"

Angry spots flamed in Sophie's cheeks. "All over Paris possibilities are shrinking. Soon we'll only be allowed to wear the tricolor and plain hats and dresses. Soon there will be no play or opera that doesn't praise the government or the revolution. The characters will shout out patriotic slogans instead of declarations of love or funny jests. 'Vive la Nation! Vive la Révolution!' As if there were nothing else in the world than *this*." She threw the crumpled ribbon on the floor in disgust. "There will be no more paintings but those horribly stiff ones by Jacques-Louis David. And the worst of it? If I may be selfish?" A stifled sob strained her voice. "It's happening just as I've discovered what it is I love to do. Now fantasy and beauty and fairy tales are forbidden."

"Magic, too," Camille said.

Sophie seemed to see her then. Her hand went to her mouth. "Dieu, what has happened? You said Lazare left but—"

Camille bit her lip. "Rien, truly."

"Nothing?"

Her throat constricted. "I promised not to tell anyone."

"*Anyone* does not include your sister. Especially when you look like you might cry."

Camille sank to the fabric-covered floor. It took too much strength to stay standing. "He has left the balloon corps and is—against the law, and really, against all reason—flying an émigré family to England." As Sophie listened intently, Camille told her about the Cazalès' plight and Lazare's plan. "And do not dare tell me it's romantic! He might be killed."

Sophie restrained herself. "He's a very good aeronaut. If anyone can do it, he can. But that's not all, is it?"

"He wished for me to go with him."

"To emigrate?"

"I won't leave." She blinked, hard. "He said he was taking them because I'd inspired him with my work with the Lost Girls. His father had got him the commission for the balloon corps, and he hadn't wanted to tell me because I had such high standards, I would despise him for it!"

Sophie gasped, incredulous.

"It was utter madness. I didn't want him to fly over the sea, in the cold, so I thought if I told him . . . please don't be angry."

Sophie cocked her head, considering. "I can't promise I won't be. But I will still love you."

Gathering her courage, she explained to Sophie about the pamphlets, and the uncontrollable magic in them. Sophie's eyes grew wide with shock, but to her credit, she did not criticize Camille for what she had done.

"If he knew," Camille said, "I thought he'd realize how foolish he was being and stay here. If I wasn't a saint, he needn't be one, either." She dropped her head into her hands. "It did not have that effect at all."

"Oh, Camille." Sophie squeezed her hand tight. "You gave away your secret and he did not care."

Bitterly, she said, "Oh, he cared, but not in the way I'd hoped. He called me a pretender. He said he loves me but wishes I were not a magician. But what if I can't purge it from myself, or even contain it? What if it is who I am? If he loves me, how can he ask me to be someone else?" She wiped at the tears running down her cheeks. "When he was leaving, we kissed, but Sophie! He pulled away and I felt so small. I have been making the same mistakes, over and over, like the girl in the tale who spins straw into gold, but it doesn't help her at all. I should have told him earlier! I should have told *you* earlier."

Sophie sifted through the piles of fabric for a scrap that would make a suitable handkerchief and gave it to Camille. Kindly, she asked, "Why is this magic so bad?"

She couldn't believe Sophie was asking this question: Sophie, who hated magic. "Because it's a lie, a trick. Pretending." She heard Lazare's voice saying the words, incredulous hurt closing him down. "Because magic almost killed me—and Maman. Because it's against the revolution—"

"Is it? You sound like Papa." Sophie found a half-sewn white organza rose and began to shape the fabric into petals. "To me it seems the opposite of that."

"What do you mean?"

"You told the girls' truth. How is that pretending? Working the glamoire and using a fake name at Versailles is pretending." Her needle flashed as she sewed. "Remember when you'd turn the metal scraps into coins? When they lost their magic, they'd slowly start looking like what they really were underneath the magic. This is the *opposite*." She took another stitch and petals bloomed in her hand. "*Other* people pretended the girls were not worth helping. They pretended the girls didn't deserve the house they built with their own hands, because they were thieves or flower sellers or wore low-cut dresses or were somehow not deserving. But your pamphlets scraped that away, like the tarnish it was!" She set the fabric rose down. "Who can say if magic made your pamphlets compelling. Maybe yes, maybe no. Or perhaps it was just you."

"You're defending magic?" she said, incredulous.

Sophie shrugged. "Mostly I'm defending you. I am proud of you, you know. And I have become much fonder of magical things of late."

Slowly, inside her, Camille felt a tide changing. It was true that Papa had raised her to think magic was wrong. She had only to think back to her memory of the fight over *The Silver Leaf*. But as she'd done with the pamphlets, she'd confused his beliefs for her own. And she'd done it because magic was hard and big and unpredictable. "But this magic—it's like a terrible fever."

"Like love?"

"Don't tease, Sophie." But perhaps it *was* like that. "I'm so angry at what he said, but at the same time, I cannot lose him."

"You won't. Both of you feel so much. Naturally you will have strong opinions and get confused."

Camille smoothed the scrap of white silk. "I fear it may be more than a confusion this time."

"Wherever there is love, there is a way forward."

"You are a hopeless romantic."

"An absolutely correct romantic," Sophie countered.

"When did you become so wise?" Camille asked, wonder in her voice. "Why did I not come to you first?"

"That," Sophie said, "I have no answer for." She got to her feet and pulled Camille up with her. Around her ankles, white feathers drifted and banked.

"Please tell me you're not going to stop the performances," Camille said.

"Never. Rosier hasn't given up hope, and neither have I. We will do *something*." Thoughtfully, she tucked the organza rose she'd made into the collar of the princess's gown. "Are you feeling a little better now?"

"I am, thank you."

"Then you must tell me what is happening with Odette!" she exclaimed. "Adèle was here moments before you arrived, brimming with gossip but very few details."

Camille worried at the edge of her fingernail. She'd always tried to keep worrisome things from Sophie, but she realized now that there was no need: Sophie understood. In a rush, Camille told her almost everything: about the magic blur they'd been searching for, the valise of tears and how she'd used the blur to spy on Odette, who had tried to rally the girls against her, and that Blaise had found the book the magicians needed. "She even spied on us! It was very satisfying to have Daumier throw her out."

She left out that she still had no answers to her own magic—and that because Odette had been thrown out of the house didn't mean she was *gone*.

Sophie clapped her hands. "But that's fantastic! I hated the way she snuck about the house, peering at every object as if she were thinking of buying it. This is shaping up to be a fantastic day. Minus the part about Lazare, of course."

"You're even pleased about these magical things?"

"It's true, I never used to be. But this means your friends will be safe. And so will you." Her lips twitched. "Besides, there are other exciting things afoot."

"Such as?"

A laugh bubbled merrily out of Sophie before she could clap her hand over her mouth.

"What is it? Won't you tell me, even to cheer me up?"

"I am sworn to secrecy."

"Come, have you changed your mind about d'Auvernay? Or is it something to do with Les Merveilleux?"

Sophie shook her head so that her earrings danced. "Hélas, I cannot say! I'm going to have to leave you now or you will have it out of me and then I shall be in terrible trouble."

"But when?"

"Tonight," she promised. "Let's go out and celebrate the discovery of the magic book, Odette being gone, and even those gruesome vials, if you wish—and then I will tell you."


In the last few days, it had grown unusually cold. Fronds of frost etched the windowpanes, and tonight, as the sun sank and the shadows came on, the air tasted of snow. Camille was to meet Sophie in less than an hour at a little restaurant they liked on the Île de la Cité called Aux Deux Sœurs. It wasn't one of the revolutionary cafés electric with conversation and arguments, but instead a quiet cozy place with good food and lanterns in the shape of stars.

In her dressing room, she searched for a warmer cloak. As she was rifling through a particularly deep drawer, her fingers brushed against a bundle wrapped in thin paper.

It was a worn cloak that had once belonged to her mother.

She raised it to her nose and inhaled. Even two years after her mother's death, it still held her perfume. Faint, like a memory. What would it say, if it could? What would Maman tell her, now? A wind traveled like fingers along Camille's cheek. In it, she imagined her mother's voice, close and loving, but also always urging her forward: *Mon trèsor, there are mysteries ahead of you. I know you are not one to take the easy way out.*

Maman would want her to find *The Silver Leaf.* In it there would be answers to her questions about who she might be and what she needed to do with her magic.

Tucked into the frame of her mirror was Blaise's card. Les Mots Volants was only a few streets away from the café where she was to meet Sophie. She flipped the card over to read the words that had appeared there days after he'd given it to her. *Come any time.*

She would ask him. Perhaps there was even something helpful in the new book he'd found? In the rush of today, she'd forgotten to ask. Carefully, she tucked the cloak away. From her wardrobe she took a midnight-blue pelisse, trimmed in beaver fur, and shrugged it on over her blue-and-gray striped dress. Then she left the house, taking the stairs two at a time.

Outside, the sky was gray, a few bright snowflakes twirling down.

Everything was changing. She could feel it.

WHAT
IS A
MAGICIAN?

ONE WHO PRETENDS
TO BE A FRIEND TO FRANCE

WHILE HE EXULTS IN
ILL-BEGOTTEN WEALTH
&
DRINKS THE
BLOOD OF CITIZENS

# PATRIOTS!

*A MAGICIAN IS A MASTER OF DISGUISES*

AVERT YOUR OWN

DESTRUCTION

BE VIGILANT

ALERT THE COMITÉ

DEFEND FRANCE

*BY WHATEVER MEANS NECESSARY*

# 37

Between two ancient cross-timbered buildings was squeezed a narrow shop. A row of elongated windows ran along the front, their casings painted white, books stacked against them. On top of one pile slept a white cat, its rounded, furry back pressed flat against the glass. The sign on the door hung crookedly: LES MOTS VOLANTS. Before she had a chance to open the door, it swung open of its own accord.

Inside there was hardly room to turn around. Bookshelves covered the walls from the floor to the high ceiling, which was painted to resemble a summer sky. Instead of birds soaring among the clouds, there were books, their pages like wings. Books were stuffed between the arms of several tattered armchairs and teetered in rows along the seat of a sofa. The counter at which Blaise presumably sat was covered with a blizzard of papers. As she watched, one sheet loosened from the others and floated to the floor. Clocks—hidden behind books—ticked cheerfully into the silence. Hanging in the air like incense was the faint char of magic.

On a ledger sat a small white plate, a fork, a half-eaten apple pastry. She stood on her toes to see over the maze of books. "Blaise?"

For a moment, there was no sound but the ticking of the clocks—followed by a shuddering thump, as of books falling to the floor. "J'arrive!" he called.

Slowly, a shelf of books separated from the wall, creaking open like a door. As Blaise came out, dressed in white, Camille glimpsed the room he'd come from: pale walls, a cream-colored carpet on the floor, white roses in a vase. And many more shelves filled with books, their spines illegible. Bespelled.

"I worried something had happened to you," she said. "Pinned down by a stack of books?"

"It isn't out of the question," he said seriously. "But what brings you here? Something that couldn't wait until our meeting?"

"That makes it sound so dire." Though it did feel that way. Blaise set down the books he'd been carrying. A handkerchief was wrapped around his hand, its white fabric was splotched red with blood. "You're hurt!"

"It's nothing. I cut myself on purpose." He regarded her calmly. "I thought I would do a little reading."

"But you didn't use blood to read books at the Hôtel Séguin—"

"Some books require it." He cleared a space on a table and set down one of the larger volumes he'd been carrying. "Would you like to see?"

The book was covered in a deep burgundy leather, almost black, and thin for its size. Already she could feel Blaise's intention gathering over it, like clouds before a storm. The air sharpening. "You need the blood because of the warding?" she asked.

"Exactly." He opened it and flipped forward a few pages. There was a single image of a hand. It was life-size and decorated with running lines and the kinds of small rectangles, stars, and triangles fortune tellers pointed to, picked out in gold paint. "Here, I'll show you." He unwound the handkerchief: a thin red line ran across his palm. He stretched his fingers and it began to bleed again. As the blood welled up, he placed his palm within the thick black outline of the hand and pressed.

The space around them tightened. The pages in the book began to flutter.

"Now we can read it," he said, serenely. "Not much to it. Magie bibelot." He fished a clean handkerchief from his pocket and tied it around his hand. As he paged through it, maps bloomed on the pages. A city on the water, run through with canals. Certain buildings picked out in gold. An island she recognized as the kingdom of Sicily, pricked with gold circles. A map of Paris, dotted with gold circles.

"What are the dots?"

"Safe houses. For magicians."

He flipped forward, the pages crackling and loosening as he did so. "Voilà—here's yours."

The picture showed a large castle, almost like a fortress, nothing like the elegant mansion it appeared to be from the outside. Instead there were barred windows, the narrow loopholes for arrows, a massive portcullis. It felt familiar, though it wasn't. Suddenly she understood. "The outside of the house is glamoired."

"It changes with the times, I imagine. Magicians have always built these kinds of protective houses, for we are often misunderstood." The pages of the book curled. "Bien sûr, there are always bad magicians. But this is because they are bad people, not necessarily because they are magicians."

"It's what I want to believe."

"Still," Blaise continued, "the fear of magicians has always outweighed the threat some of us might pose. It is simpler to think in black-and-white, instead of gray. Which is why books like this, which would be so valuable to the Comité and others like them, have to be warded with blood. But that is not why you came here, is it?"

Why was it so hard to speak about this thing? To admit that there was something about herself she didn't understand? Something she might not want—or worse, something she might?

"You know so much about books, and magic—I thought you might know." She took a breath and shakily exhaled. "When you came to the house, I told you about the magic that comes on me like a fever. You're right that I'm somehow working it, by wishing—or wanting. But, Blaise, it frightens me. I need it to print anything convincing, but it's too powerful. I can feel it in me all the time now. I fear . . . I'll be swept away by it. That it might reveal me somehow to the Comité. That it will destroy me."

Blaise waited as if he had all the time in the world.

"I know a memory can be kept in tears. Preserved, like a fly in amber. Couldn't I keep the sorrow that fuels this fever inside a vial, too? As a way to keep it separate from me." Even as she said it, though, it felt wrong.

His pale eyelashes fluttered. "There's something, but it may not be what you wish to hear."

"Tell me, whatever it is. I've spent my whole life knowing too little about magic."

"Sorrow," he said, "once caught in tears, can be kept in a bottle. Though it may *seem* that the sorrowful memory is gone, my theory is that what Saint-Clair wrote in his journal isn't exactly right."

Disappointing, but not a surprise. She had felt it herself when she'd taken the blur. Like the dried pea in the fairy tale, hidden under a thousand mattresses, the sorrow remained. "It's still inside."

He nodded, and ran his thumb down the edge of the pages until he found one that was folded and pressed it smooth. "You simply don't feel it as much."

"But we are in danger! Comité is arresting magicians!" She twisted the broad ribbon of her cloak.

"Camille," he said kindly, "everything I have read says magic cannot be truly separated from the magician. You cannot cut it out like a tumor or bleed it out, for magic is not in the blood. But you *can* decide what to do with it."

Was *that* what she was trying to do—cut it out? Was that what Lazare had wanted from her? The thought filled her with a kind of horror. "But now more than ever, magic feels like doom hanging over me."

"The Comité?"

"Not just them." She hesitated. "Someone I love doesn't understand."

"I remember when you said you didn't want them to know," he said quietly. "But please understand: magic is only a curse if you think it so. Think of the two sides of one coin. Or a mountain: shadow on one side, sun on the other. What would happen if you took away the shadow?"

A person wasn't a mountain, she wanted to argue. A person did not need darkness. "That person would be full of light," she said stubbornly.

"That person would not exist."

"Magicians love riddles."

Blaise's mouth twitched. "Some things are best understood that way. We try to keep secrets safe in our own heads. But heads can be dangerous places. Full of anguish and sinkholes and tempests that make us feel lost. A riddle is a way to get it out, *and* keep it safe."

It was true that her head was full of storms. She wanted to be her true self, but she didn't know what that was. She relished the power of her magic, but it frightened her too—a dark and creeping shadow forever bound to her. But also, she thought, a strength. Uncontrollable it might be, but it was still power.

Frustrated, she picked up a square tome that lay open on the seat of an armchair. Its pages were covered with a dense mirror-writing. "What's this one, Blaise?"

"A history of magic."

"Is that what you're working on?"

He propped his chin in his hand. "There is no one history. Still, I hope to trace a line, like in a family tree, to the beginnings of magic, and find what lies at its root. The problem is that histories are simply stories," he added, "stories we tell ourselves about what we believe. Or what we *want* to believe. It makes my task harder."

One thin page of book rolled slowly inward; absently, she smoothed it flat. "Are you saying what we know about magic isn't all true? That it might have a . . . secret history?"

"Just so. For example, in the oldest books of magic, like the medieval *Le Livre d'Eau*, there's no mention of sorrow as a catalyst for magic."

"What?" Camille struggled to understand. Wasn't sorrow the way all magic was worked? "But what would they have used instead—"

Beyond the shuttered windows, in the nighttime street, footsteps echoed. The scuff of a heel on cobblestone as someone halted outside the door.

The doorknob rattled violently.

Blaise slid off his chair and crouched down behind the counter, making himself very small. His panicked eyes met Camille's as he mouthed: *Warded.* Slowly, she too sank to her knees. The door wrenched in its frame, but it held. Still as prey they waited, until the noises outside the shop faded away.

"Blaise," she hissed, "what was that?"

"You must go. Strange people keep coming into the shop. Not the Comité. But whoever they are, they are looking for magic. Sniffing, as if they might smell it." Agitated, he said, "Trust me, please. We need to move faster to make the blur, even if it means starting tomorrow, before the Comte de Roland arrives."

She could feel it, a snare drawing tight.

He glanced once more at the door. "Go now, please. I would blame myself if anything were to hurt you."

She hated to leave him alone when he was so afraid. One of the clocks in the shop had already begun to chime nine o'clock. "Please, Blaise—won't you join us for dinner at Les Deux Sœurs? It'll only be my sister and our friend Rosier."

"A collector has made an appointment with me tonight."

"So late?"

"He doesn't wish to be seen in daylight, bringing magic books to sell. He says he has a wagonful—I will buy them all. Perhaps there will be answers there. And even if not, I couldn't resist them." The corners of his mouth quirked up in a rueful smile. "It can't be helped, can it? We are who we are, n'est-ce pas?"

*Are we?* That was precisely what she needed to know, and she hardly felt closer to an answer than she had before. "Come meet us afterward, please? But if not, I'll see you very soon at Bellefleur."

Promising to stop at the restaurant after he was finished, he waved her into his apartment behind the secret bookcase door—a small white room, quiet as a held breath, books everywhere, a single bed neatly made—and then out into the alleyway behind the shop. "It's safer this way. À bientôt."

As she waved good-bye to him, so still in his ghostly clothes, she felt more at a loss than when she had come. She craved answers, and it seemed that in all of Paris, there were none to be had. And time, Blaise had said, was running out.

# 38

Snow had begun to fall, thinly, as if it could not make up its mind.

With Blaise's unease like a chill wind at her back, she made her way toward Aux Deux Sœurs. The restaurant lay close by, and when she found the street and saw the star lanterns beckoning in its windows, she walked even faster toward its warmth. Inside, candlelight flickered on faces and the hum of conversation and laughter filled the room. The tables were crowded with diners drinking wine or tucking into the café's famous roasted meats. At the back of the room, snug against the paneled wall, sat Sophie and Rosier. When Sophie saw Camille, she waved happily.

The way they were sitting suggested that a fresh proposal from d'Auvernay was probably not what Sophie wanted to tell Camille about. She guessed it was something momentous about Les Merveilleux—or, she thought, as she embraced them and noticed there was already champagne on the table, perhaps it was something else entirely.

"So kind of you to come, Camille!" Rosier held up the bottle. "Some wine?"

"S'il te plaît!" She set an empty glass in front of him. "Tell me, what are we celebrating?"

"I wish Lazare could be here," Sophie said, wistful.

"I'm certain he wishes he could be, too." Camille gave her a warning look. "Now tell me what's happening!"

"You must have already guessed." Sophie reached across the table and took Camille's hand. "We're to be married!"

Her eyes brimmed with sudden tears. "I hoped, but I didn't dare believe it!" she said as she threw herself out of her seat and kissed them both, several times. "I am so happy for you!"

"Merci, ma sœur!" Sophie swept away a few tears of her own. "Merci for everything."

"What did I do?"

"You went along with my plan!" Rosier said. "Of course, I revealed everything to Sophie before I asked for her hand—not that she didn't already know! And, Camille, you helped us hope."

"There was that time we talked in the courtyard, when I was ready to throw it all away," Sophie said seriously, "and you reminded me of what was important, and of who I truly am. Just like Charles Rosier did."

He took Sophie's little hand and kissed it reverently. "I am the luckiest boy in the world."

"And I," said Camille, "am so happy in your happiness." As she took a sip of wine, felt the bubbles rise, she felt her heart lighten. There was so much wrong, but so much right. One magical book had been found and surely, despite Blaise's worries, others could be, too. Answers were coming. They had the vials of blur, Odette was gone . . . and now there was this promise between two people she loved. It made her wonder if she and Lazare might mend also what they had broken. Was it so much in pieces? Couldn't *feeling* bring things back together?

Each of these thoughts was a candle to wish on, a flame to drive out fear and darkness. It felt as though, crowded around this tiny table, they had a chandelier's worth of possibilities. "Have you set a date?"

"As soon as possible?" Sophie said, and Rosier laughed.

"We expect Lazare back any day, non?" he asked. "We would not do it without him."

"I cannot say when he will return. Besides, you did promise you would have a long engagement."

"I reserve the right to change my mind! And who knows?" Sophie said slyly. "I have always dreamed of a double wedding—"

Just then the door to the restaurant swung wide open. Snow swirled in and hung suspended in the candlelight. Into the room stepped a rough man in a tricorne hat, gesturing wildly at the patrons at their tables. Conversation faltered. The air hummed with waiting, and then the man shouted, "Stand and follow me, you who are patriots! A mob seeks justice!"

Chairs squealed as people got to their feet, some crowding together inside, others pushing to get out. Camille, Rosier, and Sophie stared at one another in horror. "What shall we do?" Sophie cried.

Camille clasped Sophie's hand. She thought of Giselle, how the crowd had formed and then dispersed. "Perhaps we can help? But we must stay together."

They pushed their way past overturned chairs and half-empty glasses of cider to reach the door. Once out in the street, they saw several customers hurrying away, heads down.

"What's happening?" Sophie said, a catch in her voice.

Suddenly they heard it: angry voices echoing down the island's narrow streets. Shouting, the pounding of feet. The clash of metal. A sharp, jagged tune, played on a horn. The door of the café burst open again and several men excitedly shoved their way outside. "Let's go! It is the Comité!"

"Rosier?" She pushed back the fear that threatened to crush her. The Comité abroad at midnight could not be good. "What's happening?"

"Citoyens," Rosier called to the men, "tell me, what is underway?"

But the men raced away, kicking up a fine spray of snow. "To the tree!"

"What tree?" Sophie demanded.

The tree at the end of the island.

The tree where she'd waited for Giselle to give her the tray. The tree with the list of names nailed to its trunk, shining like the palm of a white hand. "The old oak, by the well!"

In the direction she pointed, the invisible crowd roared. Screams rose above the rooftops. "We have him now!" a man's voice shouted. Stuttering to a halt, the horn released a triumphant shriek. Then someone cried, "À la lanterne! String him up! Death to the magician!"

*Magician.*

Dread, icy and black, rushed through Camille. The crowd had come from the direction of Les Mots Volants.

"Blaise!" she choked out. Grabbing her skirts, she ran. Underfoot the snow was slick, treacherous.

"Camille, wait!" Sophie called.

"Hurry!" she shouted over her shoulder. "We must stop them!"

She didn't wait to see what they would do. Her legs were nightmare slow, her heart a frantic timpani, but still she ran. Toward the torches, and the terror.

# 39

Down the narrow streets, toward the river, toward the tree. Running until she thought her heart would explode. Soon they caught the tail of the crowd, pushed their way through. It was a gruesome carnival of laughter and terror and anger. Torches that made faces into masks with vacant holes for eyes. Deep in the crowd, the crimson flare of Comité cloaks. The baying of hounds. And all the while, like a drumbeat, the restless chant: "À la lanterne, magician!"

She didn't know what she would do if she found him.

How she would get to him, how to take him away from these people—*his neighbors*—who wanted to kill him. Shoulders bumped hers, boots crushed her feet. Not tall enough to see over the heads of the crowd, she'd lost sight of Sophie and Rosier.

And she had not seen Blaise at all.

"Let me through!" She tried to elbow past the people, but they shoved her back. Their hands grabbed at her, pulling her hair, mauling scraping stamping—not as separate people, but as one thing. A monster with one mind, bent on destruction. "Stop this!" she cried.

The crowd's roar was thunder. "Magicians deserve to die!"

*Where is he?*

"Traitors!" another shrieked. "We will see his limbs ripped from his body, like traitors of old!"

*Blaise!*

"Enough!" shouted Rosier, suddenly behind her. He had a stick in one hand and brandished a sharp, short knife—*where had it come from?*—in the other. "Let us through!"

The people saw the knife and fell back. A space cleared around them. At the end of it spiked the forked shape of the tree, another crowd chanting and screaming beneath it. Rosier forged ahead, swinging his stick. They were close now.

"Blaise!" she shouted. "We're coming!"

The lamp in the square shone through the tree's spreading fingers, shining on something that hung from one of the oak's low-growing branches. It spun, very slowly, as if eddying in a wind.

A ghost.

Camille was running, sliding, shoving her way through the jeering crowd milling around the trunk. It could not be. Let it not be. Her head and heart were a storm of *no*.

Behind her, Rosier cried out, "Don't!"

But she had already seen.

A body hung from the tree. Pale suit rumpled, brightened by the mob's swarming torches. Slowly, it swung toward her. Blood clotted the ends of white-blond hair—

Black spots teemed in her vision. She grasped at Rosier to steady herself. Around her shoulders, a supporting arm: Sophie was there, too. Pupils wide with fear, her lower lip trembling.

"It's Blaise!" Camille heard herself scream, stumbling toward the tree.

"Quickly! Help me!" She grasped Blaise's body at the waist to ease the awful tension on the rope around his neck.

"We're going to cut him down," she heard Rosier say.

"Foolish girl!" said the owner of the café. "He's already dead, and what's worse, he's a magician. You don't want to get caught up in this—"

"He is a human being!" Camille spat.

With his knife, Rosier sawed at the rope. When it finally unraveled, she staggered under Blaise's weight, sinking to the ground with him in her arms. His head lolled like a broken puppet's. "Wake up!" she cried. "Please hear me, Blaise!" *Wake up!*

Her scream echoed back to her from the walls of an empty room, a younger self shouting these words at Papa as he lay doll-eyed in his bed, his skin blistered with weeping pox, the cords in his neck tight as wires. She had chafed his hands and patted his face and sobbed, but even the hot tears falling on his face had done nothing to revive him. He was gone, the spirit emptied from his eyes like water trickles from a cupped palm.

Camille's tears made tiny useless spots where they fell on Blaise's silk suit. How had magicians believed tears had any power? What good were they if they could not bring those they loved back to life?

"Why would they do this?" she raged. "He was so kind and gentle—he never harmed anyone!"

Policeman were yelling all around them, breaking up the crowd. Rosier kneeled beside her. Very gently, first one, then the other, he closed Blaise's eyelids with his thumb. "What's this on his hands?"

They were ebony from fingertip to wrist. She touched his palm and her finger came away black with soot. "To show he was killed for being a magician."

With his handkerchief, he wiped away her tears. "We must go, Camille. I'll take you both home. The police have come; they will take his body to the morgue. And"—he said in her ear—"Sophie told me. It's not safe for you here. The Comité's arrival is imminent."

She let herself be lifted to her feet. It was then that she noticed the spot of white on the oak's gray bark.

A piece of paper, nailed to the tree. She ripped it loose.

It was another list of names.

Ten, twenty . . . her vision stuttered, she could not tell how many there were. Most but not all were aristocrats, and a few had a new designation after their names.

*Eugène de Tolland, Comte de Roland. Magician.*

A cry of anguish tore at Camille's throat when she saw, several names below, *Étienne Bellan, Marquis de Chandon. Magician.* She raced through the others, dreading to see her name, but not finding it.

At the very bottom was written: *Blaise Delouvet. Magician.*

His name was run through with a ragged line, and underneath was scrawled a single word: *MORT.*

# 40

It was well past midnight when they returned home.

The vast house was still and silent, as if it knew what had happened.

Rosier promised to stay in a guest bedroom, to be close by if he was needed, and with Adèle's encouragement and aid, he gave Sophie a sleeping draught. She lay terrifyingly still in his arms as he carried her upstairs. Watching them go up together, Camille longed for Lazare. She wanted to disappear in him, for him to enfold her in his arms so that she might press her ear to his chest and listen to his steady heartbeat instead of her broken one.

But there was no one to comfort her. So while the servants readied Rosier's room, Camille went alone to the attic.

There in a towering wardrobe, under lock and key, hung the enchanted court dress.

In the wavering gleam of her candle, the fabric glowed as if with an inner light. When she took it off its hook, it rustled and slithered into her arms. It still smelled of magic: burned wood and bitter ash, sorrow and fear—and power. Once she'd not been able to abide its scent and had dabbed it away with cologne. But now, for a reason she could only dimly fathom, she inhaled deeply. The smoky scent eased the ache within her.

In her arms it had the weight and shape of a body.

She knew the servants would think it strange when she came down the attic stairs, the dress's train trailing after her, leaking magic. But she was past caring. "Madame?" Adèle called after her. "May I—"

Camille shut her bedroom door behind her with a click. There she shrugged off her ruined fur-lined pelisse. Tearing off the striped dress, she shoved it behind the Chinese screen. She wished never to see it again.

Outside, snow sighed against the shutters.

Once she'd promised herself she would never wear the enchanted dress again, but now that promise felt as if it had been made by someone else. Inside she felt frighteningly empty, as if at any moment she might drift away. Like a husk, a dried leaf. And so she slipped on the heavy court dress.

Under her palms, its ancient silk was smooth and cool. Gently she traced the embroidered ferns that spiraled between crystal-studded flowers. How desperate she'd once been to don this dangerous dress and work the blood magic it required. And though she'd been afraid, she had done it. They had gone into battle together: determined but hopeful.

She had been such a fool.

She'd believed that, though anti-magic pamphlets and posters had inflamed the people of Paris, underneath they were good at heart. That they all wanted the same things. After all, hadn't the people of Paris helped the girls? Didn't they all believe in freedom and brotherhood?

This night had shown her otherwise. She thought back to the other time she remembered it snowing, when she'd walked out onto the ice of the Seine and it had cracked. It had seemed solid, but it was thin. And underneath was always that black water.

She had been wrong not to see it.

Kicking off her shoes, she crept onto the high bed and lay down on her side, pulling her knees up tight. Around her the dress's skirts fanned out like great wings. *Oh Lazare*, she thought as she hugged the pillow close. There was no trace of his scent there. *Have I lost you too to magic?*

As her tears fell onto the sleeve of the dress tucked under her cheek, its threads began to stir. Not hungry, as it'd been so often before. But resolute and calm, as it had been that dreadful day of her marriage to Séguin and during the duel, when she had been so hopeless. It had helped her when no one—not even Lazare—could. It had believed in her when she had not believed in herself.

In her grief, she tucked herself tighter into its shell.

In return the dress fit protectively around her. She closed her eyes and the memories it held of Camille shimmered through her in a blur: the hushed glide of a gondola through the Grand Canal's mirrored water, cool dew on grass, the thwack of a paille-maille ball scudding over the lawn, the daring crush of Lazare's embrace. Then, endless as the sea, her ancestress's memories, held so long in the dress, followed after in waves. As they swept over her, they were like a veil that hung between her and her sorrow and rage, so that she might finally sleep.

Her hand loosened its grip on the list and it fell, crumpled, to the floor.

The house creaked and fretted.

And outside the snow fell steadily until Paris was shrouded in white.

# 41

Two days passed in grief. Slow and heavy, curtains closed over windows. In the library, the books could be heard to weep, and the weapons in the armory clanged against the door, wanting out. The house closed off rooms and hallways it had opened before. Its wind keened through the rooms, overturning vases and tilting paintings. Its melancholy was its own, and also Camille's.

When Sophie recovered, she tiptoed into Camille's room to sit on the bed, but Camille didn't wish to talk.

She needed to think.

Her mind went back to the things Blaise had said, things she should have paid more attention to. He'd been worried about leaving Les Mots Volants unattended for too long. Strange people had come into the shop, peering at the books. Someone had tried to force his way inside the night Blaise was murdered. The doorknob's violent rattling haunted her. But he'd also told her the shop was warded. Who then could have got in and pulled him out into the street?

"Camille," Sophie said, "what do you think about selling off the magical things in the house? In case the Comité comes? Or simply get rid of them?"

"What shall go first—the dress? The tapestries? Why not the entire house?"

Calmly, infuriatingly patient, Sophie persisted. "You must see that any hint of magic is more dangerous than it's ever been. I saw Blaise . . ." She laid her blond head on Camille's shoulder. "Whether magic is good or bad, why not finally be free of the magical objects? Know that you are safe?"

It was a safety that reeked of coffins and locked boxes.

From her bed Camille could look out over the inner courtyard and the garden. Beyond it, the stable roof, the walls, in the corners where shadows collected: Was someone there, watching? Waiting? How long would it be before someone came forward, saying they'd seen her at Les Mots Volants? How long before the Comité stepped out of the night again, the signed warrant a sheet of doom in their hands?

How had her Paris become *this* Paris? Lazare, with his dreams of traveling, his talk about London, had already lost faith in it. Sophie, too. And her own Paris had become a shadowy, sinister place where being a magician was a death warrant. It was as if the darkness in the alleyways and broken courts of the city had risen, drawn together, and like a great hand, was closing around her throat.

Worry pinched at the edges of Sophie's blue eyes. "What are you thinking about, Camille?"

"Blaise. And Paris."

"You are not going to write about this."

Anger tensed her neck, her jaw. *Steady,* she told herself. "Am I not?"

"We need to think of how to protect you and the other magicians, not draw more attention—"

"Does not this *murder* draw attention to magic?" Despite herself, her frustration grew. "What is the point of living—in believing in something—if

I do nothing? If I hide in this house, afraid? I could have saved his life, Sophie!"

"Don't be reckless," she pleaded. "You will put yourself in danger!"

Camille's fingers clenched the coverlet bunched in her hands. "If I wait, and keep quiet, what will happen? Who will I be?" What was it Lazare had said? *I can't live with myself if I don't take the Cazalès.* Now she felt the power of that conviction burning within herself.

Tears stood in Sophie's eyes. "I know you loved your friend. At least wait a few days, until things calm down—"

"That will never happen unless we *do* something." She flung back the bedclothes. "I can say I loved him, but what is love without action? Hollow, empty words! Talk is dirt-cheap, and it sickens me. Love must be proved."

"But you'll only make things worse!" Sophie insisted. "Unsafe!"

"There is nothing safe anymore," she said grimly as she set her feet on the floor. "And I will not remain silent."


Time was running out for magic. But with Blaise gone, how would they make the blur? There were barely enough vials in the valise to get them out of Paris, let alone all the way to England or Austria. She thought of setting a paper flare but wasn't ready to call all the magicians together. Then she wrote a note to Chandon, only to tear it up.

Well past midnight, when every person in the house—but not the house itself—was asleep, she went down to the printing room. As she opened the double doors, a breeze, like a chill breath, caressed the side of her face.

"Blaise?"

She stilled, remembering how, after her parents had died, she thought she sensed them in any darkened room. That they were not so far away. There were many times she'd whispered their names into the gloom, and waited, not wanting to spark a light and chase them away.

One more heartbeat. Two.

Nothing but the wind.

From embers in the hearth, she lit the sconces and the many-branched candelabras. Taper by taper, the room came awake: the squared-off shape of the press, the long tables with their rustling papers, the ropes running along the ceiling like paths on a map. It was all hers. She had never thought of it like that before.

What was it Blaise had said?

*You cannot bleed it out or cut it out . . . but you can decide what to do with it.*

Not so long ago she'd believed that magic was something she could lock up in a box or a bottle and ignore. A part that could be separated from the rest. But it couldn't. She thought of lace, or a web—pulling away one part destroys the whole.

*Magic is only a curse if you think it so.*

She'd feared that the magic had crawled inside of her and taken up residence in her body, like sickly poison thickening in her veins. Taking her over, making her into something she did not wish to be. How had she forgotten that there was power—rich and dangerous—in it? In herself?

The power had always been a part of her. Like her freckles, the red of her hair. Perhaps the magic that glittered through her had given life to the house, steeped as it was with enchantments. As she had slept in its rooms and printed her pamphlets and eaten food cooked in its kitchen, keeping it alive, the house had—perhaps—also given her something.

Before Blaise was murdered, she'd been afraid of being exposed. *It could have almost as easily been me.* But she was finished with being small. With being safe. Now she was going to strike back.

Pulling the case toward her, she picked out a few letters. They were warm in her hand. *Good.* Along her neck, down her arms, the fever began to rise, burning and powerful.

*Not a fever,* she told herself as she set the type. *My magic.*

## MES AMIS

When the magician was seized upon by a mob and hanged
from the great white oak,
did you laugh?
Cheer?
Turn away?
Or say, loudly or in a whisper: he deserved it?

Had he done something to deserve this fate—

or was it because he was a magician?

The people and their king have agreed that there is nothing lower

than a magician. Nothing worse to be feared, no snake sooner to be

stepped on. After all, for centuries they tormented us—

don't they deserve what they get? How dare they?

We shrug. Perhaps they do deserve it.

OR

HAVE WE ONLY CREATED

A NEW

TYRANNY?


A French revolutionary said:

SOMEONE MUST DIE, IF WE ARE TO LIVE

Some must be

SACRIFICED for the GREATER GOOD

FOR

OUR

PROGRESS

What progress is worth the sacrifice of another human being?

FOR THAT IS WHAT A MAGICIAN IS

What if the person who died were YOU?

In your heart, ask yourself:

ARE YOU READY TO DIE FOR AN IDEA?

ARE YOU CERTAIN

IT IS THE RIGHT ONE?


It took one long day, but then they were finished.

Across Paris, in the soft morning hours before dawn, the pamphlets went
out. They were tied and knotted with rough twine and bundled into wagons
while half-sleeping horses waited drowsily, one leg cocked. They were swung
into doorways. Piled and stacked. Knives slipped under twine to shear it off
so that the pamphlets could be settled onto shelves or counters or folded into
bags for selling on the street.

To be read, consumed.

Sheets of paper, like feathers from a burst pillow, lofted into the city's tangle of streets. Floating away on the slightest breeze, landing in stores and squares and cafés. Paper passed from hand to hand to hand. A stream of words, wending its way through the city's heart and out through all its arteries, until Camille's defense of Blaise and of magic was on everyone's lips.

And then came the response. Swift, unambiguous.

Clothing stuffed with straw, heads shaped from a pillowcases or sacks. Features painted on, bright crimson lips. A ruff of dried leaves for a cravat. On every face were blue tears, spilling from hastily drawn eyes. Tears, fat and heavy like rain. Some effigies had hands made of gloves, the fingertips blackened with tar.

They were shaped out of hatred, hatred itself fashioned from the fabric of fear.

And all of them, strung up like pheasants, were effigies of magicians.

# 42

"You were right to stand up for magic," Adèle said the next morning, when she brought Camille a breakfast tray.

She rubbed at her aching temples. "All night the Comité threatened me in my dreams. I can only imagine what is happening in the city."

"It had to be said. And besides," she said, a note of pride in her voice, "they cannot get in here." She handed her a small cup of coffee and set the letter tray beside her chair.

A small package lay on it. It was dirty, as if it had passed through many hands. Brown paper enfolded it, bound with red string. The careful handwriting was only vaguely familiar. As she untied the string, the wrapping fell open. There seemed to be nothing in it except for a card that tumbled out onto the coverlet.

On it was written:

*A scant five minutes after you left the bookstore, I came*
*across a copy of the book you are looking for. I nearly sent*
*it but changed my mind. Instead I've set it aside for you.*
*Come to the store as soon as you can. If I am not here,*
*take it with you.*

*And as to what is enclosed, consider it a gift from*
*someone who struggled with his heritage just as you*
*have.*

*Ton ami,*
*Blaise Delouvet*

Beneath he'd sketched a mountain. One side was shaded with inky hatch marks, the other side illuminated by a sun.

He had done this for her. He hadn't been afraid when she'd told him what she suspected about herself. He hadn't reminded her that magic was wrong, or treated her like a fool who clung to something that was forbidden by law, a magic that could kill you in more ways than one. He'd reassured her that magic itself was not bad. That it might even be good, necessary.

She imagined him opening one of the crates of books and seeing the flash of green and silver, setting the book aside for her. Writing this note. And then letting the customer in, through the store's wards. Soon after the mob broke down the door—or were allowed in. Did his books scream like the ones in the Hôtel Séguin as they dragged him away?

A tear slipped from her eye and landed on the word *here.*

Where it had fallen, the blue ink blurred. Its edges dissolved and the space around the words trembled. Had he hidden something in this letter? She blinked and the words ran together, nothing more than a smudge.

But then they sharpened.

*I did not dare send the three things at once, lest they be*
*intercepted by the people who are watching the shop. Come*
*soon, and please be careful.*

He'd found the book she'd been looking for: *The Silver Leaf.* What were the other two things?

Hastily, she reread the lines as they started to fade. In a minute, they were gone, as if they'd never been. As she began to fold the brown paper up, her fingers came across something hard. An object, caught in the wrapper's folds.

It was a tiny vial. She knew what the narrow label wrapped around its neck would say before she picked it up. *Blaise Delouvet.* He'd already worked the magic of tempus fugit from the book he'd found and made the blur. These were his tears.

She held it up to the light: pale green liquid filled a quarter of the crystal vial. Between her fingers, the glass radiated a small heat, like the flame of a candle. But why her? Why did he want her to have them—did he really think they would help her, in case he himself was gone? Without him there was no blur to be made.

Unless.

*Three things,* he'd written. The vial of his tears. *The Silver Leaf.* Was the third thing the book that explained how to make the blur?

But it wasn't at all clear from his letter where that book was. He might have already sent it to her, and it hadn't yet arrived. But she didn't think so. *Come soon,* he had written. Perhaps it wasn't *The Silver Leaf* that was at the shop after all. Perhaps it was the book explaining how to make the blur, the one he'd disguised with a blue binding. The one he'd told her he'd kept in a safe place. It had to be at the shop. Somewhere.

Carefully, she slipped the vial into the secret pocket sewn into the seam of her skirt. It felt both light and heavy at the same time.

On the silver salver lay another letter, facedown. She flipped it over. The dashing, impatient letters spelling out her name set her heart to running. Hands shaking, she unfolded it and pressed it flat.

*Mon âme—*
*I send these lines to you in haste. Two days ago I said my*
*adieux to the Cazalès family. The grandmother is brave*
*but frail, and when she requested I accompany the family*
*by coach to London, where she has a cousin, I could not*
*refuse, though it kept me from Paris longer.*

*London is a city of marvels—I wish you had been with me*
*to see it.*

She imagined a crowded street, Lazare watching the unfamiliar passersby not with displeasure or annoyance but instead with his intense, consuming gaze. The signs in foreign English, the conversations a babble of
unintelligible words. For a terrifying moment she thought he meant to stay.
She skipped to the end.

*I am already in France. The farmer who drove us from*
*Saint-Cloud has taken me in. Tomorrow morning, as early*
*as I can, I land at the Champ de Mars. Please ask Rosier*
*to bring a wagon.*

And then, underlined twice:

*I regret everything.*

He did not ask for anything. Not for her to be there, not to forgive him.
There was only regret and longing.

While he'd been gone, her friend had been murdered, and she had published a pamphlet defending magicians. Even if she had wanted to, there
was no way to be rid of her magic now, nor even to contain it. How big was
his regret?

*As always, I am yours, body and soul—*
*Lazare*

She surprised herself by bringing the paper his hands had touched to her mouth and kissing the place where he had written his name.

He was safe, and he was coming home to her. Perhaps not everything was lost. Perhaps there was some way to mend what was broken. Throwing open the door to her room, she ran down the hall, letter in hand. When she reached the grand staircase, she leaned over the banister and shouted: "Sophie? Rosier? Lazare is nearly home!"

# 43

It was nearly dawn. Soon Lazare's balloon would appear over the horizon. The rising sun would glimmer on its silk as it descended over the frost-tipped grass of the Champ de Mars. And Rosier would be there to embrace him.

She would be here, in the Hôtel Séguin.

It was safer this way. No one would be searching for Rosier, not the way they'd be searching for her. It was also safer for her wounded heart.

On the table beside her lay the small, wrapped package Lazare had entrusted to her.

She shook it gently, but it made no sound. Tomorrow would be soon enough to give it to him. Until then, she did not wish to part with it.

Dropping it into the hidden pocket, its weight was like a talisman. A wish for good luck and a safe landing.

Almost imperceptibly, the sky beyond her window lightened.

She took another sip of coffee. As she did so, her fingers brushed against a piece of paper, lying on the cup's saucer. Where had it come from? It was a ragged scrap, densely printed with words. A piece of rubbish? In the corner was written 345; clearly, it'd been torn from a book. *Strange.* She rose, intending to toss it on the fire, when a prickling on the back of her neck made her turn it over. On the reverse—page 346—in the margin, was scribbled:

*Balloon*
*Champ de Mars*

She frowned. What did it mean? And who had written it? She didn't recognize the handwriting. Could it have been one of the servants? She hadn't told them about Lazare's journey—he had asked her not to say anything, and she had told no one but Sophie, and last night, Rosier. Besides, why would one of the servants care?

Then she remembered.

After she and Lazare had argued, and she'd rushed from the room to try to stop him in the park, the servants had been outside in the hall, flattening themselves against the wall as she ran past. Adèle had called after her to know if Camille were well, if there was something she might do. But there had been others—she tried to recall. The late-afternoon hall, the dust motes suspended in the wash of light through the circular window. Adèle, Daumier, a housemaid. Odette.

Odette, in the printing room, furious at the nobles leaving France. *Those émigrés are traitors and cowards.* Odette, warning Camille that she had made an enemy of her.

Down the hall she raced. She threw open the door to the room where Odette had slept. It had been cleaned, the bed stripped and covered, the moonlight-blue curtains drawn. Nothing out of place, as if Odette had never existed. Camille opened the garderobe doors: empty. The drawers in the bureau, one after another: nothing. Odette had taken everything with her when Camille had asked her to leave. *Except*, she realized, a book lying on the small table by the bed.

It was the gothic romance Camille had been reading when Lazare was in Lille, *The Castles of Athlin and Dunbayne*. She picked it up, and opened it—her own name stared up at her from the flyleaf. But what else had she expected to see?

*Something*, she thought. *A sign.*

From the hall came the faintest sound, the feathery brush of a moth's wing: *Hurry.*

Roughly she felt along the tops of the pages. She flipped to the page where her bookmark lay, thinking maybe Odette had placed it there it to mark some important passage. That it might be a thread, a clue to guide her, but the bookmark lay exactly where she had left it. *It was the evening before they reached the castle—*

The font. It was the same as on the scrap she'd found. Quickly she paged forward: 300, 342—345. Along the margin was scrawled: *Tell the police to watch for him.*

The bottom corner was torn away.

What had Odette said to her next? *Imagine if we had a net to catch them in.*

Lazare was in terrible danger.

Racing into the hall, she rang the bell that hung there. The sound echoed through the house until the ringing tolled like a summons. "Daumier!" she shouted as she raced down the stairs. "I need the carriage immediately!"

# 44

When the horses pulled to a stop at the Champ des Mars, the sun had not yet risen over its flat expanse. In the vague dawn light, the wide band of river gleamed like tarnished silver. Arcing over the marching ground, the sky was the palest blue, almost gray, the only clouds low and inconsequential along the horizon.

On the enormous empty field there was no sign of a balloon. Or, thankfully, any solider or police. Just a low wagon, its one shaggy horse dozing, its driver watching the sky. Shakily, she exhaled. If she had to be wrong about something, she was glad to be wrong about this.

"You came after all!" Rosier exclaimed. "You have changed your mind about Lazare?"

"I had a sudden fear that something had gone wrong. But all is as it should be?"

Rosier nodded, and checked his pocket watch. "Ten minutes."

"Really? Can you be so precise?"

"One can hope! Who knows what marvels await us?" Tucking his watch back under his coat, he said, "It doesn't matter to me if he arrives on time or not—such a long journey!—but that he arrives."

To the west the sky revealed nothing, and she no longer knew what to think about the torn paper. She felt certain Odette had scribbled the notes. But perhaps she hadn't known what to do with them after? Would the police have believed her? "Still, I worry, Rosier—"

"Do not—Lazare is the hero of this story, and you, its heroine!" His clever eyes sought hers. "Your friend's death was a great tragedy. As is the threat to magicians and to the revolution itself. But your story ends happily nevertheless, I know it—we are waiting only for the final scene. An apology, perhaps, as the boy descends in his balloon from the theater's fly loft. A kiss! Then the curtains swing closed and the play is done. Fin!"

She wanted so much to believe his version of the story. *Was* there only one last scene to be performed before the play ended: danger averted, lovers reunited, the curtains closing, applause reverberating in her chest? Why then did it feel as if she were instead blundering in the dark behind the stage, trapped between props and scenery, her arms outstretched, fingertips searching but touching nothing?

She'd thought she'd stayed just far enough ahead of the wave of violence to be safe. But no matter how fast she ran, the red tide poured after her. She could no longer say she was outpacing the tide. It had filled her shoes and bloodied the hem of her skirts.

"I am worried about the ending." She held out her hand and Rosier clasped it, tight.

He scanned the sky. "Worry is for smaller souls than yours." Suddenly he pointed. "Look! He must have been blown off course—he's coming from the south!"

The balloon was very close, and dropping. This one was the blue of a night sky, the silk painted with stars, as if the music box he'd given her had come to life. It had to be a sign, she thought. A sign that good things were finally coming.

Lazare stood at the basket's railing, spyglass in hand. She remembered the first time she saw him, when his balloon had been hurtling toward the ground. Now he waved happily as he worked the release valve, smoothly, easily, lowering the balloon until it settled gently on the ground.

"Fantastique!" Rosier shouted. "What a landing!"

She could not look away from Lazare. His smile gleamed wide against the dusky bronze of his skin, worry—over her?—tightening the lines of his handsome face. She had imagined they would talk, she would wait for his explanations, examine them for flaws, all the while protecting herself from more hurt . . . but she could already see the apology in the tense lines of his shoulders.

*My heart.*

She picked up her skirts and ran. Lazare leaped lightly over the side of the basket and raced toward her. When they reached one another, he swung her off her feet.

Clutching her to him, he said, "I thought you would not come. I don't think I have ever been happier to see anyone."

She kissed him, hard and fierce, and he laughed.

"I feel the same." She ran her hands down his neck, along the breadth of his shoulders, down his strong arms to his elegant, capable hands. *He is here. Whole, and unhurt.* "I wish we had not parted like that, in anger—"

"I thought of nothing else when I was away. What I said—" His gaze went to the line of trees by the river.

"What is it?"

He squinted in the direction of the rising sun. Under her palm, his heart beat.

"Attention!" Rosier shouted. There was high note of panic in his voice. "Riders!"

Lazare's body stiffened against hers. "Don't turn around, my love."

She tried to, but he held her tightly against him. "Is it the police?" His heart beat fast, fast, faster. "Tell me!"

"Somehow they must have found out I took the Cazalès—"

*Odette had found a way.*

Had Camille not let her in, this would not have happened. She had undone the wards without even knowing she had imperiled him. "You must go," she urged. "Take my carriage and get away!" She put both hands flat on his chest and pushed, but he didn't move. "If you won't go home, at least get back in the balloon!"

"I won't run, Camille."

Out of the corner of her eye she saw the police: four silhouettes against the dawn sky, the dangerous, dull shine of pistols in their hands. The thumping of their horses' hooves, their shouts . . . all at once, the night of Blaise's murder came roaring back. His blood black in the torchlight, his broken neck, everything gone, gone, gone.

Lazare's brown eyes shone with tears. "I may never have another chance to tell you."

"But *I* cannot bear it if they take you. You have only just come home," she sobbed as she pummeled him on the shoulder. "Go away, Lazare!"

He dropped his head, his breath ragged against her ear. "I cannot leave you. Camille, I was wrong in what I said—forgive me."

"Please go!" she wept. "They are nearly upon us!"

She could *feel* the soldiers now. The pounding of hooves on the grass. Thundering side by side, almost there.

*Think!* She and Lazare could escape to the Hôtel Séguin. Blaise had promised it would protect her. But she couldn't go there, where Odette would know to find her. *Where else, where else?*

There was another safe house.

"Quick, Lazare, to the carriage!" She pulled him with her. "If you love me, run!"

The black-and gold carriage waited, very close. From his perch at the top, the coachman saw them coming and steadied the horses. The police changed course, veering to cut them off. Stampeding closer, they shouted for them to stop in the name of the law.

Ten strides. Five. Four.

They were almost there. Over her shoulder, Camille shouted to Rosier, "Go to Sophie!" and was gratified to see him race to the waiting wagon.

Three. Two. One—and Lazare was wrenching open the carriage door, Camille leaping inside. The far horse whinnied, half rearing, as the coachman cracked his whip. Gathering themselves, the horses plunged forward before Camille and Lazare had even closed the door. They fell back against the seat as the carriage tore off across the field. Clods of dirt kicked up against the windows as the Champ de Mars rushed away.

"Dieu," Lazare said, stunned. "Where now?"

"Somewhere safe." She pulled down the glass of the window. "Hold me, will you?"

Once she felt Lazare's firm grip on the back of her coat, she called to the coachman, "The graveyard of Saint-Julien-le-Pauvre!"

His answer was a crack of the whip. The horses galloped even harder toward the secret boneyard entrance to Chandon's house, Bellefleur. With one hand, she gripped the window frame. With the other, she reached into her dress's secret pocket. From it she pulled a piece of paper. She crumpled it, placed it in her hand, her fingers cupped gently around it, willing it not to blow away. Then she made her urgent wish.

Sudden heat burned her palm and she released the flare. The fiery paper rose straight up into the sky, impossibly high, where it glittered like the morning star.

*Help us.*

# 45

Flickering with lantern glow, a rectangle of darkness yawned below them.

Apprehension in his voice, Lazare asked, "What is this place?"

"A crypt, and a tunnel to Bellefleur. We must hurry—we can't be seen going in."

They had been lucky enough to lose the police in the fog that rose from the river, but she didn't dare linger and risk them catching up. Pushing away her unease, Camille stepped into the sarcophagus. Lazare followed, pulling the lid closed behind them. Ahead, lanterns lit the way. Quickly they left behind the walls of bones and the dank of moldering earth. Soon they were running past the portraits of magicians, who observed their progress with the knowing smiles of those who had seen this before, and then pushing open the doors of Bellefleur's great room.

For the space of a breath, she saw Blaise's pale outline standing by the black wood bookcases. Then she blinked and there was only one magician there, pacing in front of the fireplace, purple smudges of fatigue under his eyes. Chandon's chemise was rumpled, as if he'd slept in it, and instead of a coat, he wore a silk dressing gown figured with winged dragons. "Dieu, is that you, Sablebois?" He rushed to embrace them both. "You have been flying, I take it? I could feel the fear in the flare you sent, Camille. Tell me, what has happened?"

"I did not know where else to go," she said. "It's a long story. But the short of it is that we must go to Les Mots Volants tonight. I believe the book that Blaise found, the one that will teach us to make the blur, is there, but may not be for long. But before I tell you more, if there is perhaps a desk where I could write a note to my sister—Roland isn't here, is he?"

"Not yet, that lazy eel! But he will be soon. And to even imagine that in all of this enormous medieval pile there's not a desk for you? Come with me."

Leaving the great hall behind, they went down a wood-paneled corridor with doors on both sides. One he pushed open. Beyond it waited a small sitting room, a low chair by the fireplace, and a desk beneath the many-paned oriel window. On the walls hung lifelike paintings of flowers: bright blooms, green stems, and reaching, webby roots. "Voilà—my mother's study. Have a seat at the desk, Camille. I'll send someone in with some wine." He held up his hand when she started to protest. "Don't you dare say no. I can tell you've had a terrible fright."

"Thank you, Chandon," Lazare said. "You are very kind."

Chandon bowed, and set off down the hall, his heels snapping on the ancient floor. Soon afterward a maid came in, carrying a tray with wine and water in crystal glasses, a plate with bread and sliced hard sausage. Camille asked her to wait while she wrote to Sophie.

The desk was tidy, unlike her own, with plenty of thick paper engraved with a single poppy. In her letter, she wrote that she and Lazare were safe at Bellefleur and, describing to Sophie where she could find the valise, asked her to send it to them by messenger as soon as possible.

The letter written, Camille flung herself into the chair by the fire while they waited for Chandon to return. That was the first step accomplished. There were not many vials in the little box. Enough, if they were lucky, to slip past a guard, but they would need much more. And for that, they needed the book.

Lazare stood by the fire, leaning against the wall with his forehead pressed against it, as if it was the only way he could stay standing.

"Lazare?" she said softly. "Tell me how it went with the Cazalès."

He came toward her carefully, as if not wanting to step on something fragile. Sitting down on the carpet, he rested wearily on the arm of her chair. "They are well. When they arrived at the inn at Dover, a letter was waiting for them from her son, the marquis. He is safely arrived in London. They are reunited now, I imagine." The way he said it made her acutely aware of how cast apart and unsafe they were here.

"And the journey?"

Wryly, he said, "Harrowing at best. There were too many of us in the balloon." His hand hovered over hers. Hesitating. "But that is nothing, mon âme, not compared to what happened here when I was gone."

"My friend Blaise was murdered for being a magician." There were other things she wished to say about him, and what had happened, but they caught in her throat like tiny, sharp bones. Her voice flat, she said, "I was betrayed. I threw a spy out of my house. I published a pamphlet that made things worse for magicians. I was frightened over so many things. I felt so alone."

He held out his hand to her; childishly, she put hers under her skirts. She hated the hurt that flared in his dark eyes. But he was not deterred.

"Mon trèsor, I wish it had been different. I thought I did right by taking the Cazalès." Lazare exhaled, frustrated. "I *did* do right. I saved their lives. And I made some small amends for what I allowed to happen with the balloon corps."

The fire crackled in the grate. "Your sense of honor is restored."

"Is it? The kind of honor my father taught me to live by feels like a relic from another time." Was it the flicker of flame on his face, or did he truly seem haunted by what had happened?

"I'm sorry. It was wrong to say that—"

"It was right to take the Cazalès and it was wrong for me to leave you. Both are true. But the thought that haunted me during that trip across France, over the stormy waters of La Manche, as I walked the streets of Dover . . ." His hands tightened on the arm of the chair.

She was trying to stay strong. Even if it would be easier, she could not settle by simply returning to the way things were before. She reminded herself of how she'd felt when they parted: *so small*. If they were to be together again, it had to be in a new way. *Remade*. "What was it?"

"Over and over in my mind's eye, I imagined landing in the Champ de Mars and not seeing you there." In the firelit room, his eyes had gone black with despair. "A magic lantern slide I never wished to see. It was worse than the sea at night—an endless expanse of nothing."

An ember jumped out from the fire and landed on the hearth. She extinguished it with her shoe. "But you needed to go. Not just for them, but because that's who you are: kind, caring, noble—in the right way. All the things I try to be."

His voice dropped, rich and teasing. "You try?" He moved nearer, until he pressed against her leg. "You *are*."

"Don't distract me by sitting so close," she said, allowing herself a small smile. "If I'd tried to make you stay? I would hate myself for forcing you to be someone for *me*. Instead of being someone for yourself. All my life people have wanted me to be something for them. But you—"

Lazare was very still. Waiting.

"You did not." She blinked to keep the sudden tears at bay. "Until the time when you said you wished I was not a magician."

He clasped her knee. "Camille, please—"

She held up her hand. "I could have told you about the pamphlets. How there was some force of magic in me that I couldn't control and that I didn't understand. But I was ashamed. I'd determined to leave magic behind after I killed Séguin." A log tumbled in the fireplace, the fire crackled. "So many times I intended to tell you. But when you said how extraordinary the pamphlets were—how extraordinary *I* was—I couldn't."

"Merde," he swore. "What an ass I was!"

Despite herself, she laughed. "I was in love with your vision of me as hardworking and talented and magic-*less*. It was as if I were living in a hall of mirrors, wanting to believe that what I saw was true."

"My love," he said, his voice rough with emotion, "the day of the king's speech, I wondered. But I didn't want to believe it. I abetted you in your silence, when I could have made it easier for you to talk to me about it."

"You are already forgiven, for you've forgiven me." She picked up an iron poker and jostled the logs in the fire, sending up sparks that rose vanishing into the chimney's mouth. "I used to think about the adventures we'd have, the voyages we'd go on by balloon. But the revolution has taken our dreams from us."

"The places we saw in the magic lantern . . . our flight over the Alps . . . those dreams will never die," he said softly. "They are my dream of a life with you. The dream of us."

He took her hand. In the fathomless deep of his eyes, she saw love and heartbreak. "Let me help you with whatever it is that you are planning. Whatever it takes, whatever magic is in it."

She brought his hand to her mouth and kissed it. The scent of him, the warmth of his skin, the callouses on his palm and the pale scars across the knuckles of his fingers—all of him was precious to her. "You may help me, Lazare Mellais, under one condition. Please, be careful of my heart. I cannot lose you again."

"I promise." Gently he drew her down to him until they both sat on the carpet. In front of the fire, their tired bodies pressed close. Each exhale pushed them apart, each inhale brought them together. "I will stay. I am yours to command." And then, teasingly, he said, "Your magic doesn't frighten me anymore."

"Not even a little?"

"Well, perhaps . . . but only in the most intoxicating way."

She tucked her fingers under the collar of his coat, next to his skin. As she rested her head against his shoulder, the world receded, dim and distant and far away, until there was only this moment, only him and their hope.

The door swung open, and with it came a sigh of cold air.

Chandon stood in the doorway, lamp in hand. "How rude of me to interrupt! But there is no help for it, mes amis. Roland has finally shown his face and Foudriard—well, my darling has arrived with grave news."

"They're waiting in the great hall?"

Chandon nodded. "How much does he know, Camille? About the book?" He gestured toward Lazare.

"Not much, I'm afraid." she said.

"It doesn't matter. I'll help you in whatever way I can," Lazare said. "Even if it involves magic."

"Ah, Sablebois!" Chandon said with a sad smile. "Everything involves magic—it always has, and it always will. And if you are in desperately in love with a magician, it is practically inescapable. Now if you two will untangle yourselves, we should go in to the others. I fear we may be too late."

# 46

The mood in the great hall was tense. Foudriard, no longer in uniform but wearing a plain blue suit instead, shuffled maps spread out on a table. The Comte de Roland stood by one of the bookcases, bewilderment and shock etched across his pointy face. Foudriard left the maps to embrace Lazare, and they had a few quiet words between them. All the while, Roland sipped from a glass of wine.

He stopped drinking as she and Lazare approached. "The Vicomtesse de Séguin. And do my senses deceive me, or is it the aeronautical aristocrat?"

"Roland," Lazare said, bowing slightly. "I thought it might be you."

"Sablebois." Roland stooped into a bow. "I hope you have nothing against my being here? Strange times make for strange bedfellows. For the sake of this damned blur, I am willing to forgive you for beating me at every single game of carambola we ever played at Versailles."

"You are nothing if not generous, Roland," Chandon said evenly. "We must get to the point. Camille, will you tell us what has happened?"

For the sake of Roland, but also Foudriard and Lazare, Camille began with Chandon and Blaise's visit to the Hôtel Séguin. She told them how she'd discovered Odette listening at the door and thrown her out. How she'd received the package from Blaise, saying he had a book for her but also that he had sent other things, and the warning the house had given her that Lazare was in danger—and that somehow Odette was a part of it.

"Every minute we stay in Paris we are drawn further into peril," Chandon said, distraught. "The mob killed Blaise, who would never do anything to hurt anyone. They could take any one of us, at any time. They are everywhere."

"We are safe nowhere," Roland snapped. "But if we have the blur—"

"Once we get the book," Lazare interjected, "won't that provide you with safety?"

"If we could make enough of the blur, perhaps," Chandon replied. "But it's more than that. It's the Comité. It's the people of Paris."

"There can be no safety," Camille burst out, "not when the world is wrong! I had depended on hope, as if it were a lantern to light the way, when it was nothing but a ghost."

Hope had made her believe that change would happen. And it had, but not in the way she'd expected. The change she'd wrought for the girls had been good. But hoping that the leaders of France, king and revolutionary alike, would accept responsibility for their actions—that was a hollow wish. Despair and sorrow rose in her, numbing cold and swift, and she felt in her fingers the crimp of magic, the desire to change *something*.

"What else have we?" Chandon said. "Hope, our wits, beautiful clothes . . . no, wait—"

She refused to be cheered by his jest. "I am sick of hoping! After the violence at Versailles, I kept trying to believe. But I lost hope in the revolution when it murdered Blaise. It is tyrannical, bloodthirsty!" She dropped her head into her hands. "I have even lost hope in our country, its people—in France. There is no place for us here."

Lazare, his voice resonant with passion, said, "Mon âme, hope *is* dangerous. It is the most dangerous thing there is, because it helps us believe in the impossible. In balloons, revolutions, circuses—and love. None of it easy. What is the purpose of hope except to change things?" He waited until she looked at him. "And, yes, hope is terrifying, and hard, because believing in something is no guarantee it will ever happen, even if we work toward it."

In the silence that followed, the fire in the great medieval hearth danced and flickered. Fire that could light the way, fuel change, or destroy everything. Deep in her heart, she knew Lazare was right. What had she lived on when her parents were dead, she and Sophie starving, Alain beating her and trying to keep her down? Hope had been her food and drink. And though despair had shadowed her, it hadn't overtaken her. She thought of Blaise's mountain: two sides to everything. Hope was the sunlight, despair the shadow. Two sides of a coin, inextricable.

He added, "Without it we have nothing."

"Lazare, truer words were never spoken," observed Chandon. "Hope will take us a long way. But, if I may interject, mes amis—time ticks on and we do not yet have a plan."

*A plan would be something.* A plan was hope taking shape. She set her shoulders back, wiped away the tears that clung to her lashes.

"There's something else that adds urgency to our mission," she said. "On the oak from which Blaise was hanged, there a list. It had your name on it, Chandon, and yours, Roland. Blaise's was there too, but crossed out, and written beside it was the word *mort*. This is what they intend to do to all of us magicians."

Chandon's shoulders slumped. In his face was a sense of loss that mirrored her own. "Forget what I said about hope—they are calling for our deaths by *name?*"

"I would never have left for England if I'd known," Lazare said. "I cannot see how you—we—stay here any longer. We must all leave."

"But how?" Roland snapped. "We have no blur."

A faint smile played over her lips. "In my house I found a small case, with a few vials of blur that Séguin had made." Turning to Lazare, she explained as quickly as she could what the blur was and how it worked.

"Where is it?" interrupted Roland. "Are they authentic?"

"They are; there was one with my name on it, and I tried it. As for how I found it: the house showed me." She felt foolish saying it, but neither of the magicians seemed surprised. "I've sent a note to my sister, asking her to send the box here."

"The note's already gone by messenger," Chandon said. "He will be very discreet, and make certain he's not followed."

"How many vials, did you say?" Roland asked.

"Four or five, perhaps. Not enough."

"Not for all the magicians of France," Chandon said. "Or even for us, considering how quickly it wears off. We may have to reduce our aspirations."

"One last thing." As if she were following a thread that had been strung down hallway after hallway, she made her way through the labyrinth of all the things that had recently happened. She could only go forward by touch, but still, she was moving forward. "The book Blaise mentioned to me and Chandon? I believe it's still at his shop. Perhaps *that* was why he was attacked at his shop before he was murdered. Someone else wants it. We must go to Les Mots Volants tonight and find it. Once we have it, we can make enough blur to get ourselves and every other magician out of France."

"It's impossible," Roland sniffed.

"Why?" Lazare asked.

Foudriard tapped one of the maps he'd been studying. "The Comité has spies throughout the city, some of them with great knowledge of magic and how to find it."

It made a terrible sense. "Blaise was expecting a visitor the night he was murdered. Comité members, do you think?" she asked.

Foudriard nodded grimly. "And after Blaise's death, there will be additional watchers around his shop. They might be expecting us."

"Especially if they're also looking for the book," Lazare said. "They may trust one of you will lead them to it, and voilà, they have both the book and a captive magician."

Camille nodded, considering. "There is another way into the shop, one where people might not be watching. A series of alleys leads away from the door that opens into his apartment—there's a bookcase on hinges that acts as a door between the shop and his room. He led me out that way once, when he was worried about my safety."

"That sounds promising," Lazare said.

Chandon sat up. "And what if I have the key to that door?"

Everyone stared. "You do?"

"Blaise gave it to me the last time I saw him. *In case*, he said. I'm afraid I teased him mercilessly about it, which I now regret. I have it upstairs, quite safe."

"Bien. We go in that way, search the store—" Roland proposed.

"But surely he would have hidden the book," Lazare said, "if, as Camille says, he already felt threatened."

"It will be the needle in a haystack," Roland said. "I say we divide up the blur you found, work wards on our houses, and flee."

"We *must* at least try." Camille studied the faces of her friends, worn and harried by fatigue. "But it has to be tonight or we risk losing it forever. I can't fathom why Odette would want it, but in the hands of the Comité—"

"Burnt to a crisp," said Chandon drily. "Anything in the book that they can use against us, they will. And then it'll be thrown on a bonfire."

"That cannot be allowed to happen," Lazare said. "I'm going with you."

"I hardly need convincing to dust off my sword," Chandon said. "Strangely I feel as if I were born for this. Foudriard?"

"Of course," he said gravely. "It will be dangerous."

"But not to do anything will be even worse," Camille said. "And you, Roland?"

He raised his sharp brows. "If you insist."

While they had been talking, the messenger returned from Hôtel Séguin. He told them that Sophie and Rosier were both well, but that they'd searched through the wardrobe where Camille had put the valise and it was nowhere to be found. It was a hard blow.

It was possible the house had hidden it, somehow. Things went missing all the time. But the disappearance of the box they so desperately needed—especially if this planned failed—changed everything. There was no safety net now.

# 47

They left once it was full dark.

The crescent moon was rising, a scythe in the night sky, as Camille's carriage rolled silently away from Bellefleur. The wheels and the horses' hooves had been wrapped in rags and the quiet thump they made was unnatural, eerie. Inside, the curtains were drawn and none of them—not Lazare, Chandon, Foudriard, Roland or even Camille herself—dared open them. Only one lantern flickered in the carriage, and the shadows it threw made her companions' faces unreadable. Roland's white fingers danced nervously along his thigh, tapping out a rhythm only he knew.

They could no longer wonder *if* the watchers of the Comité would be there, but *where*. How they might be avoided, and if they couldn't, what those guards would do. Beyond that, she would not let herself think. Lazare was already wanted by the police. Chandon and Roland's names were on the list. And Foudriard, steadfast, and dashing, would end his career with the National Guard. And though Rosier and Sophie were safe at the Hôtel Séguin, Camille knew that whatever happened to her affected them, too.

But there was no other way. If they did not get the book, they would be trapped in Paris as the Comité's fist tightened around them.

As the carriage passed over the final bridge to the island, Lazare threaded his long fingers through hers. The warmth of him was all that tethered her to this moment, keeping her from racing through the wilds of her fear. It steadied her. She let herself rest her forehead on his shoulder and thought: *In an hour, we'll have found it. In an hour, we'll be on our way home.*

Soon the carriage came to a stop at the street that ran behind Les Mots Volants. The houses that crowded the narrow lane were silent, their shutters closed.

Roland peered out. "It's too quiet. Even for this late in the evening."

"This entrance is as concealed as we could hope for. If there are watchers," Foudriard pointed out, "they'll be at the front of the shop. We should go in now."

"I don't like it," Roland said with a frown. "I will keep a look out from the carriage."

Irritated, Chandon snapped, "There *is* the coachman to do that, Roland. But if you must, fine. I would rather have at my side someone completely committed to this adventure than someone secretly hoping to sneak away."

"A Roland would not sneak."

"He had better not." There was iron in Chandon's voice. "If anything were to go wrong, this carriage needs to be here, waiting, ready to run. Keep your eyes and ears open, comprenez?" He pointed to the bell that hung inside the carriage to alert the driver. "And if you need to warn us, open the door and ring the bell."

"D'accord," he agreed.

"We have the key, and the lanterns?" Lazare asked.

Camille held hers up. Once lit, it would provide only enough light to see by, but no more than that. Chandon showed them the key to Blaise's apartment. Brass, with a red warding ribbon threaded through the bow.

"We'll light them once we get inside," Foudriard said. "I have the flint in my coat."

Silent as shadows, they left the carriage. Two small alleyways, the last with a crooked gate, and they'd reached the doorway of the apartment. Chandon fitted the key to the lock.

"Strange," he observed. "It is already open." Blaise was always meticulous. Would he not have locked his door? Not if he didn't have enough time. Not if he were being dragged away—

"Careful," Lazare whispered. "Someone else may have gone in ahead of us."

As silently as they could, one after another, the boys loosened their swords in their sheaths and they went in.

As Foudriard lit his lantern, the tiny apartment flared into being around them. The air was bittersweet with the scent of magic. Bookcases towered all the way to the ceiling. His single bed haunted her: the pillows fluffed, the coverlet folded back as if he were about to come in, lie down to sleep, and dream of books. A sob caught in Camille's throat; Lazare squeezed her hand. They were doing this to save their own lives, of course. But she was also doing this for Blaise. What he'd worked for would not be in vain.

Between the apartment and the shop was a door that opened onto a short hall, two or three paces long. Slowly they crammed themselves into the passage, their breathing unbearably loud, until Foudriard finally pushed open the bookcase door.

Beyond lay the shop. Waiting. Foudriard held up his light.

It was as if a storm had raged through the room.

Books yanked from shelves lay torn in heaps on the floor. Papers littered every surface. Any order that had existed before was utterly destroyed.

"What now?" Camille asked.

A white cat emerged from behind the counter and pressed against Chandon's shins.

"Pauvre petit!" He picked up Blaise's cat, which scrambled onto his shoulders and lay there like an ermine collar, purring. "If only he could tell us what happened."

"It would help," Lazare said wryly. "But without him—now what? What does the book look like?"

"It's blue." On the floor alone were scattered so many volumes the search felt suddenly hopeless. Why hadn't she at least asked Blaise where it was? But then she remembered she had. She had asked him the second time he came to the Hôtel Séguin, and in reply Blaise had tapped his temple. "I remember now—he said it was in a safe place. I took him to mean it was in his head, but I hope I was wrong."

"It could be anywhere. Fan out," Foudriard said. Lighting their lanterns from his, they spread out in the small shop. "But stay together. Be aware of what the rest of us are doing at all times."

Camille went quickly to the shelves behind the counter. The magical atlas Blaise had shown her when she was there lay on the floor, its pages crumpled. She searched through all the books, piling the volumes against the wall. But neither did she find the book with the blue binding or—for she still hoped it might be there, somehow—*The Silver Leaf*.

The others had drifted into the far corners of the shop, sifting through heaps of books, making stacks to get through to the next pile, when Camille thought she heard a noise from the apartment. She held her breath and listened, hard. Could it be the book, calling to her? The way the house told her things?

It did not seem impossible.

Quietly she moved to the bookcase door. It was not entirely closed. Through the crack came a faint shuffling sound. Glancing at the others, she saw that they were absorbed in their searches. She'd be gone only a minute—it wasn't worth disturbing them. Opening the door, she slipped into the little hall that joined the two rooms.

Faint light shown in a line beneath the door.

But they had not left a lantern there.

There it was again: a shuffling, dragging sound. Suddenly she realized they hadn't locked the door. Someone had followed after.

Fear set her pulse to hammering. A Comité guard was in Blaise's apartment. She took a step backward, felt her skirts push against the closed door behind her. What should she do? For what felt like hours, she waited, hardly breathing. Then the presence in the apartment—whatever it was—stopped moving. It was *listening*.

She thought about running.

They would be forced to flee through the front door and risk being caught by the watchers. Even if they managed to escape, they would be hunted with more ferocity than they were now. And worse, their only chance to have the help of the blur would be gone forever.

To have any kind of chance, they needed the book.

Determined, Camille squared her shoulders. She was not powerless against whatever crept about in Blaise's apartment. Not yet.

Reaching into her pocket, her fingertips brushed past the wrapped package Lazare had given her to the crystal vial of tears. So small, so powerful. Prying loose the tiny cork, she held it under her nose. The scent of the trapped memories uncoiled: cold rain. Ink. Sadness and loss, the acrid smoke of burning leaves. If she thought too much about what was coming, she would not be able to do it.

*Now.*

# 48

She opened the door.

In the center of Blaise's apartment stood Odette. In her hand was a torch, its flame so hot and high it nearly licked the ceiling. About her waist hung her pistols, her black clothes absorbing the light so that under her plumed hat her face was ghoulish white, carved by shadows. Her gray eyes, so like Camille's own and yet not, were unreadable as stones.

"What a surprise to find you here," she said. "My apologies for the heat."

"If you put out your flambeau," Camille said carefully, "it would cool things down."

"I need some light to read by." Odette dragged her hand along the bookcase, tumbling a row of books onto the floor.

*Stall her.* Where could Blaise have put it? *Think!* Where was the safe place he'd mentioned to her? "Looking for anything in particular?"

"A magical book. Though that doesn't narrow it down very much, does it?"

"Why do you need it?" In the corner stood a bureau, its drawers yanked out, Blaise's clothes on the floor. "I could help you if you told me the title." Was it possible Odette was looking for the same book that they were?

"I don't need your help." Odette stepped closer. "I never have."

The light from the flambeau was too strong, and Camille had to shield her eyes or be blinded. She found herself staring at Blaise's bed. Plain and white. But no longer neatly made. The pillow had been pushed to one side. Perhaps she'd accidentally brushed it with her skirts, or Odette had. Now that it had shifted, the corner of a blue book lay revealed.

*It is somewhere safe.*

He had tapped his temple. Not committed to memory, as she'd thought, but even simpler than that: the book was safe under his head—under his pillow. But to get to it and then away to warn the others, she'd have to pass Odette twice. And she did not think she could. Not without help.

Bracing herself, she tipped the blur into her mouth.

One heavy drop. Then two, ice-cold on her tongue. Numbness crept along her cheeks, her throat, like frost under her skin. As the color bled from the walls, she said to Odette, "Adieu."

"Where are you going?" Odette waved her torch high as she searched the room. "Come back!"

Camille pressed flat against the wall as Odette ran past.

She had to hurry. Even as she rushed toward Blaise's bed, it faded from view, barely visible as the blur's sorrow-dream engulfed her. She found herself in an unfamiliar room, a dusk-filled library she did not remember. Was it a place Papa had once taken her? The bookshelves weren't white, as in Blaise's apartment, but black and barred with metal grates. Both *here*, at Les Mots Volants, and *there*, books lay scattered. Their pages flapped like wings as a door opened.

A silhouette stood in the doorway. "These books are forbidden!"

She crouched. Tried to disappear.

The figure stalked closer. A woman, her face creased with anger. In her hand, a riding crop. "What have you done?" she raged. "You are inviting the magic back in, when we have done so much to cut it out!" She grabbed Camille's arm, hauled her away. "We will get rid of the books, the magic lurking inside you, all of it!" A green book tumbled out of her hand—*here*, she knew it for *The Silver Leaf*, and her heart convulsed—and was lost.

Sorrow rose up insider her, an enormous, crushing wave. *My books!* she wept. Love and belonging and refuge torn away. Pain as her shoulder slammed into the doorway. Pain for what she knew was coming.

But this was not her memory.

She had taken Blaise's tears.

With that moment of clarity and understanding, the veil thinned, and she could dimly see through to the bed, and the book under the pillow. Only faintly now did she hear Blaise's sweet child's voice pleading, *Do what you want to me but spare my books, please aunt, please spare them please.* The magic was receding, and she had to move fast. Carefully, willing herself not to make the tiniest sound, she crept toward the bed. She was almost there when Odette returned.

"Come out, Camille!" The room was suddenly brighter as Odette held up her blazing torch. Camille could almost feel the books shrink away from its hungry flame. "I will find you, demon!"

*Not if I can help it.* One more step.

*There*, in the blur, Blaise screamed as his aunt tore pages from the books and shoved them into an open fire. "Be glad," she hissed, "I do not force you to eat them." His fury was an explosion. *Here*, in his apartment, her knees buckled from the pain of it. It was too much, the sorrow and the crushing pain—

"I see you."

Sagging against the bedpost, Camille watched as Odette came into terrible focus. In her hand she held a small blue book. Its cover was stamped with a crescent moon in silver. "Is this what you're looking for?"

Camille's heart lurched as she noticed the pillow had been thrown aside, the book gone. "What's it called?"

As if she had all the time in the world, Odette gazed down at the book's spine. "*On the Management of Sorrow.*"

In her hands Odette held the key to their freedom. Fatigue dragged at Camille as the blur ebbed. She had to act now or she would not make it. Far away, a bell was ringing. "I've never heard of it."

Odette's sneer was cruel. Calculating. "Then it will not mean anything to you if I use it for kindling? To light another torch? To set the world on fire?"

Everything in Camille screamed no. What choice should she make? Get the torch and save the whole shop, but risk Odette fleeing with the book? Or take the book and risk Odette burning them all?

Both. She would take the flambeau. Then the book.

As Camille lunged toward her, Odette hurled the torch into the air. Instinctively, Camille ducked as it hissed over her head and crashed into the books piled on the floor.

With a sound like a gasp, they caught fire. Flames snarled, and rose.

Like the books she'd seen on the barges, these too burned bright, and for a brief moment they dazzled like fireworks as a world's worth of knowledge vanished.

"No!" she cried out. "You cannot do this!"

"I already have." Odette flung open the door. The night air was fuel to the flames. As the fire roared, a monster unleashed, Odette laughed.

Camille backed up until she sensed the short hall behind her. Then she spun around and stumbled down it. The whole shop was burning now. Shoving the bookcase door open, she crashed into the bookstore.

"Run!" she cried.

The room was black with smoke and red with Comité guards' cloaks. The bell she'd heard had been Roland's warning; Foudriard and Chandon were nowhere to be seen. By the smashed-in front door, half-hidden by a bookcase, stood Lazare.

Waiting for her.

"Now!" he shouted. Jamming his shoulder against a bookcase, he pushed it over, trapping the men in the back of the shop. Screams of burning books echoed in her head. She ran toward him. Smoke burned her eyes; she could hardly see where she was going. Her foot caught on an open book and she stumbled. Before Lazare could pull her to safety, one of the guards grabbed her arm.

In the doorway, Lazare drew his sword. A bright line, hard and unwavering. Soot covered his face like a mask, and the mouth beneath it was grim. "Stand away from her!"

Over Lazare's shoulder, a shadow separated itself from the dark.

"Behind you!" she shouted.

Through the smoke she heard Lazare's muffled groan. Heavy hands yanked her away. "Camille Durbonne, in the name of King Louis XVI, we arrest you on the charge of being a magician and a traitor to France!"

Camille kicked at them, tried to twist away. "I have done nothing wrong!"

A bigger guard dragged her forward. She clutched helplessly at the wall, then the doorjamb, and finally at door itself. But her fingers slid and would not hold.

"Stop it!" she cried, beating at his shoulder. "I have done nothing wrong! You have no right—"

"Taisez-vous, magician," the guard said, and slammed his elbow into her head.

A thousand stars exploded. And then there was nothing more.

# 49

ake up!" cried a surly voice. "You have a visitor!"

Bleak light filtered through a shuttered window. Heavy stone echoed with footsteps, the metallic clang of a pail.

The throbbing pain in her head made it hard to think. She touched her jaw, tentatively. It was tender from her chin to her ear. Someone had hit her. *Hard.* That she remembered. The door to the room had a barred window in it, and through it she saw two figures, hurrying down a long, dim hall.

Sophie? Rosier? Was she in a hospital?

She pushed up onto her elbows and coughed. Beneath her was a narrow lumpy mattress covered in rough blue-striped ticking. In a corner stood a small wooden table and a straight-backed chair. One of her shoes lay on the other side of the room. Her stockings, she saw, were torn, the skirts of her dress scorched. She reeked of fire, as if she'd spent the night sleeping in the cinders. Slowly the evening came back to her. Bellefleur. The plan to get the blue book. The trap that had been laid for them. The shop, and everything in it, destroyed.

Beside her was a tin cup. Her hands shaking, she filled it from a clay vessel and drank. Were the others with her? Had they all fled? Lazare—he had tried to prevent them taking her. But what had happened to him?

The door creaked open and a man in a gray uniform stuck his head in. "Vicomtesse de Séguin?"

"Where am I?"

The man snorted. "La Petite Force."

*Prison.*

Numbly, she remembered when her family had lived on the rue de Bretagne, and then on the rue Charlot, the sprawling prison had never been far away. She'd never liked to pass along the streets where its entrances lay. *Superstitious*, Papa had called her, laughing off her fear. But it had never gone away. Now she was inside. A prisoner, charged with treason.

But how did they know to charge her with working magic? What proof could they have? "I've been wrongfully imprisoned!"

The guard made a scolding sound, as if everyone in the prison claimed the same thing and he was tired of it. "Save it for trial. A visitor is here to see you. I'll show her in?"

She tried to peer past the guard. "My sister?"

"Odette Leblanc."

It could not be. Though she could see that it made a kind of terrible sense. After all, Odette would have seen her arrested. But why come and gloat?

Odette stepped neatly around the guard and into Camille's cell. She wore her usual black clothes, pressed and clean, not at all reeking of smoke from the fire. "Leave us, please," she said to the guard. With a knowing smirk at Camille, the guard sauntered away, swinging his ring of keys.

"How dare you come here," Camille hissed. "Were you the one who called the Comité to the bookshop? What has happened to my friends?"

Odette crossed her arms. "So many questions! You will have your answers soon enough."

Her gloating smirk made Camille regret having asked her. It was as if she'd given her an unintended gift. "Tell me what you want or go."

"What I *want*?" Tapping her fingers against the stone wall, she pretended to think. "I want for all you magicians to die."

Camille stared. How had she discovered this? How long had she known?

"You think I don't know anything about magic?" Odette's voice was a blade. "Let me tell you—I do. And I want you to suffer as magicians have made the people of France suffer. But instead of being strung up from a tree, I want you to get your justice in public, so there can be no question about it."

"Justice?" The word burned on her tongue. "As if anything the Comité or the king has done has been just."

"Nothing can equal the pain your kind has inflicted on the people of France," Odette sneered. "You are bloodsuckers, sinners, and evildoers. You take what isn't yours and you bend it to your evil ways."

"You've been reading too many anti-magician pamphlets," Camille said levelly. "What have I ever taken of yours?"

"You don't even know?" she mocked. "It meant nothing to you, I suppose. *Everything* is easy for a magician. You simply happened to meet the girls, write a pamphlet using magic—and then!" She snapped her fingers. "Voilà, you were Jeanne d'Arc of the Revolution! Going to parties, draped in the tricolor!"

Dread churned in her gut. How did Odette know?

She stabbed her finger at Camille. "That should have been me. *I* worked for it."

This was a delusion. "Why couldn't we have worked together?" Camille asked. "The girls love you—"

Her gray eyes narrowed. "Not anymore. Did you seduce them with your magic and turn them against me?"

"Never! I only wanted to help—"

"Help? You are pathetic." Odette grabbed Camille's wrist and twisted it. "They'll remember who I am, once you are gone. While I struggled to pay for my pamphlets to be printed, I saw how many pamphlets you sold. I let myself believe you were better than I. Then I discovered it had nothing to do with what you said or what you wrote." Odette's voice burned with righteous anger. "You succeeded because you are a magician."

"Let go of me," she said, but Odette only hardened her grip.

How had she seen so deep into her heart? For wasn't this what she'd once believed herself? That it was nothing but a spell she'd cast, that whatever she created would turn back to scraps of twisted metal—less than nothing.

*No*, she told herself. Not anymore. That was not what magic was.

Bending Camille's wrist backward, Odette forced her against the wall. Her face was hard, and hungry for the pain she was inflicting. "How I love having you right in the palm of my hand. Some say Justice wears a blindfold, and only cares that the scales are even. I think Justice keeps her thumb on the scale."

Sophie had suspected this was who Odette was, but Camille had believed she could do good by being kind to her. "What changed? When you saw my house and what I had?"

"That?" Odette scoffed. "The money you got by a convenient marriage? I knew you had money from the beginning. I only had to get into your house to see if you actually were a magician," she spat. As if *magician* were poison on her tongue.

Camille tried again to wrench free, but only succeeded in pulling Odette toward her. Their faces were a hand's width apart, so close she could count the freckles on Odette's cheeks. See the gold and brown lines in the gray irises of her eyes. Feel Odette's breath on her own mouth.

"But why?"

"So I could write about it, of course." Angrily, she stepped back. She yanked at her sleeves, which had ridden up, exposing the black ink on her wrist. Camille had always thought it was ink from her pen, or her press. But it was a tattoo of a tiny bird.

Where had she seen one just like it?

The scrap of paper caught in the gates of the Hôtel Séguin. The anti-magician pamphlets she and Chandon had talked about, the writer's mark a little black bird. A flock of them, descending on Paris. "You?" she choked. "You wrote those pamphlets?"

Odette's mouth twitched into a gratified smile. As if she had been waiting only for this: for Camille to truly see her.

All this time, Odette had been working against magicians? But why? What had brought them together? How tangled it had become. She thought of the lines on her palm Séguin had read, the branches of the pear tree, the net of ropes across the printing room's ceiling: Was it fate or chance that made Odette cross Camille's path?

She shook her head. It didn't matter. Odette had no evidence. Only another magician could look at the objects at the Hôtel Séguin and say they were magical. And as long as no one broke the warding as she herself had done by inviting Odette in, the house and its people would be safe from the Comité.

Odette could play her games, but as long as they were safe that was all that mattered.

Stumbling to the pallet in the corner, Camille dropped wearily down on it. "Go away, Odette. I don't care what you have to say."

"You will when I see you in court. I imagine you'll be quite attentive then. And don't think the crowd has any allegiance to you. They will believe what they are told. You know that to be true, don't you?"

She did. And it filled her with dread. Rumor and gossip and lies—the fearful would believe anything that made them feel safe.

In the half-light, Odette's gray eyes had gone to iron. "My suffering will have been worth it when I watch you die. I wonder if they have figured out a special execution for magicians? An aristocratic death by sword is too good for you." Wistfully she said, "Whatever they come up with, I hope it is not quick."

# 50

From a window two floors up, the courtyard of La Petite Force looked like what it was: a prison. Walkers had trod paths in what was left of the insubstantial grass and only the topiary bushes, shaggy and unpruned, seemed solid and real. Back when it had been a rich man's house, it must have been beautiful. But now it was worn thin, ghostly.

Camille's fingers clenched the iron bars. Would Sophie come? Rosier? Soon they would find out what had happened. She imagined the street criers would be grimly satisfied to shout out the news of a magician—an aristocrat magician, no less—trapped by the Comité. What a prize!

And then the other, spiraling fear: What had happened to the boys? Foudriard and Chandon she felt certain had fled, warned by the ringing bell she'd heard; Roland, too. Perhaps all of them had escaped to the sanctuary of Bellefleur.

She tried not to think of what happened last night, but it came anyway: the choking smoke, the fire, the shadow that had loomed behind Lazare. Had he had time to run? Use his sword? And if he wounded or killed a Comité guard, what then?

Even if he'd escaped, nowhere would be safe.

She forced herself to take in the blighted courtyard below, the chill of the floor beneath her feet. There was no security. Not anymore. As she sat down on the pallet—to wait, because what else was there to do?—in the secret pocket of her dress, she sensed the weight of the bundled box Lazare had given her. She ran her thumb across the top of it . . . was there a stone set into the lid? It was tempting to open it, but not here. Next to the box were two tiny vials, both almost empty of tears: hers, made by Séguin through a process she would never know; and Blaise's. The torment he'd lived through when that woman threatened to cut the magic from him! She closed her eyes against the horror of what he'd wanted her to know.

*You cannot cut it from you.*

A sharp rap on the door interrupted her thoughts. "Visitors," the guard said. "A girl and a boy."

The door swung open and Rosier and Sophie rushed in, bundled against the sudden cold snap that had engulfed Paris. Sophie looked as if she had been up all night. The three of them embraced at once, hugging each other close.

"You smell like smoke!" Sophie coughed.

"Are you not sleeping?" Camille countered. There were so many things she wished to ask, and to tell them, but she was aware of the guard, listening outside the open door.

She shrugged. "I'm fine. It's you we've come to see."

Camille looked searchingly into Rosier's face. "Do you know what happened?"

He nodded.

"And?"

"It was such a silly mishap with the pigeons!" he said, exasperated.

*What?*

"I did not know you kept pigeons, Rosier," Camille said carefully.

"Oh, it is a new fad with him," Sophie replied. "There are four he particularly cares for."

*Is it a code?* "Which are those?" she wondered.

"I call them my oldest friends," Rosier said fondly. "They were all frightened by a fox last night! The excitable, toffee-headed one simply took off! And the other one who resembles a soldier with his blue feathers, he vanished too, in some other direction!" He stared at her, willing her to understand. "Both escaped the fox. As did the one who shrieked out the alarm. No doubt they're safe in a tree somewhere, surrounded by pretty flowers."

Beautiful flower: Bellefleur. And the pigeons: Chandon, with his hazelnut-colored hair, had taken off. Though Camille had thought Foudriard in his blue coat had escaped with Chandon, it seemed he'd fled separately. Roland had sounded the alarm. But why had Rosier not mentioned Lazare? She willed her voice not to break. "There was a black-headed pigeon that you loved well, wasn't there?"

His face crumpled. "We do not know what happened to him. Not yet."

"But you believe he will come home?"

"Of course."

"And I? I am not one of your pigeons, but I seem to have found myself in a very solid cage."

"First thing of sense you've said," laughed the guard, his face visible through the window in the door.

"You must be brave." Sophie took her hand.

"Why?" Their faces were very grave. "Tell me, what is it?"

"First, this new law is ridiculous. Who can show that a magician has ever hurt them?" Rosier said angrily. "The lawyer I spoke to assured me that he could get the charge dismissed. But it seems that we cannot avoid a trial."

He said more, explaining what had gone wrong, but there was a ringing in her ears over which she couldn't hear any other word but *trial*. Jurors, a solemn judge. Odette, eager to provide whatever evidence she could: her thumb on the scale, as she'd said. The prosecutor who'd use everything to argue for her death.

"Rosier, when will it be? I should like some time to prepare—"

"Camille, please sit." Sophie tried to bring her to a chair. "It's so sudden, I know—"

*I am being brave,* she wanted to scream. She was being as brave as she could. "When?"

"Tomorrow."

*Too soon.* "And if I am convicted," she said, dully. "When will I die?"

"That will not happen!" Sophie said fiercely.

Rosier took a hard drag on his pipe. "I trust you will not be convicted. Still, I plan for all eventualities. I will take good care of the pigeons. But to transport them, I'll need breeding certificates with their parents' names and—"

"Shut it—no one cares about your stupid pigeons!" the guard muttered.

*Passports.* Rosier meant to get them out of France. Somehow. "Henriette— the little one, with the fair nest of hair—is very skilled with those kinds of things. Writes a beautiful script."

Sophie squeezed his hand. "I'll tell you more afterward, Charles."

"I'll go today. And you, our dearest one, must speak with your lawyer, Dufresne, who is waiting in the hall."

"Try not to worry," Sophie said as she embraced Camille once more. Her chin trembled, but she managed to whisper, "You are in good hands."

After they left—Sophie wiping away tears, Rosier clutching his pipe in his fist—the lawyer came in. He was short, with busy eyebrows and a large mouth. His clothes were all black, and on his head he wore a gray wig.

He bowed. "Vicomtesse de Séguin."

"Monsieur Dufresne. Please sit." Restless, Camille went again to the window. Over the rooftops, heavy clouds threatened rain. "Where would you like to begin?"

He frowned, not unkindly. "I did not realize what a child you are. Very young to be charged."

*I have been working magic since I was ten.* "I'm charged just the same."

"Your youth will be a point in your favor, I am certain of it." He laid out papers on the table, sifting through them. "You are accused of using magic to undermine the cause of the people. For being a magician and ipso facto, a traitor to France."

"What does 'ipso facto' mean?"

"That simply by being a magician, you are a traitor." He cleared his throat. "Any truth to this charge? You may tell me anything in confidence."

Agitated, Camille left the window. "I never hurt the people of Paris. I tried to *help* them. You've heard of the Lost Girls who lived under the bridge and nearly lost their home?"

He beamed. "There was a public outcry over their treatment, and they were saved!"

"*I* wrote the pamphlets that rallied the people of Paris on their behalf," she said. "I never hurt them, with magic or anything else!"

Outside, rain tapped against the panes.

"But you do not deny you are a magician. Which, ipso facto . . ."

"What if I am?" She was gratified to see him flinch. "How can the prosecutor prove it? What evidence do they have that I am a magician?"

With the end of his quill, the lawyer scratched under his wig. "Because of the charge of magic, I went this morning to search the Comité records. In the last week, they were given something magical from your house."

"But they have never been inside!"

He consulted his notes. "A small valise, with glass vials in it."

Odette must have taken it. But how would she even know they were magical and not, say, bottles of perfume? "They are nothing that anyone but a magician would recognize."

He sighed. "Nevertheless, they have them."

"And they hate magic, that we know."

"It is not simply a matter of hate, madame. That has gone on for centuries. These days it is a matter of law. No hatred is required."

She spun to face him. "Did you know that Louis XIV executed the magicians who helped build Versailles because they threatened his power? This king is just the same—blaming magicians, good and bad—while he destroys the revolution!"

"Madame! I recognize that you are a pamphleteer, but you will not make these kinds of outbursts in court! They will not make a good impression on the jury."

"But they are the truth!" She wanted to pull the whole place down around her. "How can they judge me if they don't know the truth?"

He held up a patient hand. "You must leave that to me. And you must be as plain and silent as the grave. Answer only the questions that are put to you as briefly as possible. No pamphleteering—vous comprenez?"

She understood all too well. "I promise."

# 51

"Stand and state your name." A hush descended over the room as the prosecutor spoke.

Camille rose from the hard wooden chair. The air in the courtroom was stifling. In the gallery, Sophie and Rosier sat close together. Sophie wore a wide-brimmed hat to hide her face, but Camille could still see the frightened crimp of her mouth. Rosier caught Camille's eye and smiled, his hand clenched tight around his pipe. Both of them seemed prepared for the worst.

Behind them clustered the Lost Girls—the forger Henriette, glaring furiously at the judge; Giselle, nervously plucking at a tricolor corsage on her wrist; the always serious lock picker, Claudine. Otherwise there were not many she knew among the spectators. Two journalists crouched at the end of a row, quills in hand, already writing. An illustrator, his tablet against his knee, studying her and then his drawing paper.

Soon her face would be everywhere. On every street corner of Paris, the criers who'd once shouted the girls' stories would now shout hers. Wherever Lazare was hiding, was this how he would hear what happened to her?

But she was determined not think of that now. Instead, she would do what her lawyer had advised: speak as little as possible, and let him do the work so she would walk free.

"Camille Durbonne," she said, clearly.

"Are you not a widow? With a title?"

It was nothing, a title, a name. But the jurors sat forward, waiting. "I am also the Vicomtesse de Séguin."

"Aha," someone noted, as if she'd been caught in a lie.

"Madame la Vicomtesse, then." The prosecutor, a tall man in a white wig, approached. "Let us do this quickly, non? The good people of the jury and the observers in the gallery shall not be kept waiting to see justice done." With a flourish, he shook out his cuffs, as if to say: *Let's get to work.* "To the charge of being a magician, that is, practicing magic and hurting the people of France?"

"What of it?"

"Did you?"

"Did I hurt the people? No."

One of the jurors swore. Mutterings from the gallery.

"And of magic?" The prosecutor rubbed his hands together. "Be careful as you answer, Madame la Vicomtesse. Consider if you have ever consorted with magicians or owned prohibited magic objects. If you have, in any way, been helped by magic."

*Helped by magic?* She wanted to laugh. What did she have but her own magic?

Her lawyer, Dufresne, gave a tiny shake of his head. She knew what she must say, but the wrongness of it grated at her. A few short weeks ago she could have said no. But after Blaise's murder, how could she? After she had found her voice through magic and used it to advance the cause of the Lost

Girls? Magic was not the enemy. She remembered the horror she'd felt in the blur when Blaise's aunt had threatened to cut the magic from him, as if removing a cancer. But to deny magic would be to deny herself.

Calmly, as if it cost her nothing, she said, "I have not been helped by magic."

A snicker ran through the gallery. The prosecutor shifted lightly on his feet, as pleased as a street conjuror about to make a final reveal. "I call a witness."

Like everyone else in the courtroom, Camille's head swiveled toward the door. Odette strode in, dressed in her usual black riding clothes, her pistols tucked into a belt. Over her coiled red hair, she wore the black hat she'd worn at the march on Versailles. As she took her place at a witness stand, the brim cast her face into shadow.

"Please state your name, mademoiselle."

"Odette Leblanc."

"Occupation?"

She squared her shoulders. "Revolutionary. Pamphleteer."

The gallery gave her a round of applause; the judge called hoarsely at them to refrain.

"Do you know the accused?" said the prosecutor.

Odette nodded demurely. "I have lived in her house."

Gasps from the jury.

"Why?"

She wheeled toward Camille then. Her face was hard, as if she might grind her to dust with her stare. "Working for the Comité, I infiltrated her house in order to gather evidence about the activities of a club of antirevolutionary magicians."

Camille gripped the back of her chair, willing her face blank. It had not been just a personal grievance. For many long weeks, she had been working with the Comité to bring Camille down. She did not wear their red cloak, but she might as well have one slung over her shoulders.

"In your role as an investigator, did you find anything of note?"

"I did," she said. "I gave those items to the Comité."

"What were they?"

"A small valise, full of poison."

*Not poison. But how had she found it?*

"Anything else?"

Gleefully, Odette said: "A book."

"Ah. What kind of a book?"

"A magic one. I found it in a bookstore owned by a magician who was arrested by the Comité."

"And murdered before he could stand trial!" Camille burst out.

"Silence," the prosecutor hissed. From his desk, he picked up a small, rectangular package, wrapped in brown paper. Holding it gingerly by one corner, he brought it to Odette. "Was it this book?"

She picked it up as an eager hush ran through the gallery, everyone eager to see a piece of magic firsthand. "Yes. I found it when we raided the magician's bookshop. *Her* name is on it."

Hatred snaked through her. Had they raided the shop the night that Blaise was murdered? Had Odette been there when Blaise was accused? Perhaps she had done the accusing herself. Sneered as he was dragged into the snowy street, laughing as the horn blew to rally the mob, as if setting hounds on the scent of his fear. Imagine if he had put a stop to his magic. He would still be alive. She gripped the railing in front of her as the room swayed unsteadily . . .

"Attention!" Rosier shouted. "Madame is about to faint!"

There was a hard hand under her elbow, the sharp whiff of sal volatile. As the smelling salts revived her, the crowded room swelled into too sharp clarity once more.

Wasting no time, the prosecutor held the package high before handing it to Odette. *Camille Durbonne* was written on it in ink. It must be *The Silver Leaf*, which Blaise hadn't dared to send for fear of someone intercepting it. Despite everything, she longed for it.

"Will you open it and show the jury?"

Odette unwrapped the package. Inside was a book, which she held up so the jury could see. The cover was not green with silver stamps, as Camille had thought it would be, but black. The writing was not French, or any language that Camille recognized. Instead the pages were faintly covered with a series of tiny black marks, more like the scratchings of a knife. Her skin prickled. Why would Blaise have wanted her to have this?

"What language is that, mademoiselle?"

For a moment, Odette seemed chagrined. "Not good, honest French, that's for certain. It's a foul book of magic."

As she spoke, a slight breeze caught in the pages, rustling. The courtroom held its breath as one after another they turned, until eventually the book stood open to the very last page. On it was the sharp, red outline of a hand. Blood-warded. She knew instantly what that outline was for, and what it did.

"And what does the magician, the Vicomtesse de Séguin, have to say about that?"

Camille's lawyer spoke up. "She will speak after you have finished with your witness."

"You may sit down, Mademoiselle Leblanc," the prosecutor said.

"Before she does, I have one question for Mademoiselle Leblanc," said Monsieur Dufresne.

Odette looked as if she might laugh.

"The writing on that book—do you know for certain that it was the writing of the bookseller? The one who was hanged by a mob the same night the Comité raided the shop?"

She shrugged. "It was his shop. His package, ready to send out."

"Perhaps this one had been prepared, by him or someone else . . . and then Madame Durbonne's name found its way on it? Do you have a sample of the bookseller's handwriting, mademoiselle, so that we may make a match?"

"His shop burned to the ground," she said, dismissively. "I cannot help you."

Camille glared at Dufresne. Why hadn't he asked *her*? She could have given him Blaise's letter and it would have been proved that Blaise had not set it aside for her. For all she knew, Odette had taken the most frightening-looking book of magic in the shop and wrapped it up herself to discredit Camille. Her faith in this lawyer was steadily eroding.

"That will be all," Dufresne said, and Odette stepped down.

The prosecutor then wheeled toward Camille. "Tell me what you know of that valise that was taken from your house. Or tell me first, perhaps, about this clearly dangerous book."

*Stay quiet.* "Which will it be, monsieur?"

"Do you know what this book is? And why it has your name on it?"

She remembered Blaise's warm, cluttered shop. Books and teacups on every surface. The rolls of maps jostling in a cream-colored urn. His white cat curled up, pressed against the window. Blaise, working late. Determined, despite the risk, to save the books, and the knowledge they contained. That night, another collection was coming into his hands. And so he'd set a lantern on his desk and pried open crates and paged through volume after dusty volume, forgetting to be careful.

"I know nothing of it. Mademoiselle Leblanc was in the shop that night—perhaps she wrote my name on it?"

"Madame," warned Dufresne.

"Too bad she killed the bookseller, or you could ask him! He feared for his life, monsieur. People had come into his shop—we know who they are now—with the intention of murdering him. What was his great crime? Collecting books!"

"You stand accused of magic, madame," the prosecutor said. "Are you saying you consorted with a known magician?"

She gestured at her lawyer to say something. But he did not.

"Consorted? If you mean visiting his bookshop, then yes, I did. Have bookshops now been banned? Or must we stop reading, unless it is certain approved pamphlets and certain newspapers? And let me correct you, monsieur," she said savagely, "he was *not* a known magician—he was murdered before he could stand trial on that charge. It was rumor and the mob that convicted him."

"Counselor," the judge warned. "Your client must answer the question—"

"Quiet now, madame," Dufresne said. "I will ask the questions later."

*Would he?* He'd shown no signs of defending her and she feared he never would. Fury rose in her, rushing her forward. She faced the jury. "Do you not see what our King Louis has done? He's made an enemy for you to hate of the magicians. A dog to kick, someone to blame your troubles on." Camille's heart was in her throat, but she pressed on. "Has Louis signed the Constitution?" A rustle in the gallery: everyone knew he had not yet signed it. "He pretends to stand with the people, but he doesn't! While you blame magicians for your suffering, you let the king avoid any responsibility!"

"Counselor! Control your client!"

Dufresne made a frantic wave, but Camille ignored him. "I will not be silenced." Her voice was low, dangerous. "I will not sit quiet while this court—this revolution—pretends it is just, when it is not."

Odette began to laugh. "What a trial! What order we have in this courtroom! Why did I have to come here to testify against her, when she's practically admitted she's a magician?" Odette gripped the edge of the railing behind which she stood. "*I* know what they are. My own father was an aristocrat magician."

Shocked voices erupted from the gallery. "A great man, so they said. With his charm and his magic, he seduced my mother and set her up in her own little house where I was born." She was nearly wistful when she added, "We were happy then. My mother loved him, and he would arrive every week with armfuls of presents. But he tired soon of me. He fled, and my mother ran after him. Abandoned, I tried to sell the things he gave us. Only when they turned back to rubbish did I discover he'd enchanted them."

"Monsieur," Dufresne said to the judge, "please tell Mademoiselle Leblanc to stand down. It is not her turn! This has no relevance to this case!"

"Yes, it does," Odette sneered. "Wait and you will see what evidence I have gathered. You know what they were, once the magic wore off? Broken scraps of tin and paper and wood. Rien!" Her face grew keen as she remembered. "Everything he ever gave us was changed back to dust. The only things he could have given me that I truly wanted—his name and his *love*—were too precious to part with. He'd insisted I learn to read and write, and what good did it do me? It only taught me how little I was worth."

Despite herself, Camille's heart ached for Odette. To be abandoned like that!

"So how do I know, beyond a doubt, that this book is magic?" Hard pride gleamed in Odette's face. "Magic has a smell, did you know? I grew up thinking it was the scent of love, because I connected it with my father. Oh, how wrong I was! It is the scent of destruction and corruption! And unless we root it out wherever it may be, it will ruin us."

The gallery applauded, stamped their feet. Taking a shaking breath, Odette glared triumphantly at Camille.

"You are out of order!" shouted Dufresne. But the judge said nothing. He let it go on. It was no longer a true trial, if it ever had been one. It was a performance, and Camille feared how it would end.

Odette jabbed a finger at Camille. "Her whole house stinks of magic! The attics are full of it! I have gone over half of Paris, sniffing out magic with the Comité, and there was never such a foul nest of it as her house."

A hush fell over the room. In the emptiness, there was only the scrape of a shoe, the scratch of dead leaves against the windows.

Camille's eyes blazed. "I am truly sorry, Odette, that you had a father who did not love you. But bad people are not always magicians. They're everywhere, or haven't you noticed?"

"Enough, madame!" insisted the prosecutor. "Answer the question. Are you a magician and therefore a traitor to France?"

She was the bonfire, burning in the streets. She was fever and flame. And if she did not speak, it would consume her. "I am a pamphleteer for the revolution," she said, fierce and defiant. "I have used the magic of words to help the poorest among us, and if Odette Leblanc were honest, she would admit that."

"The magic of words!" she jeered. "It was more than that! Your spying, your vanishing, your magic-infested house—"

"How narrow your mind is, Odette, that you think no one else can do good but you. Has hatred made it so small?" She paused, and looked out over the gallery. The reporters scribbled furiously, and even from here, she could see the sketch on the cartoonist's paper: two red-haired girls facing each other. Behind the scribblers sat the Lost Girls, frozen, except for Giselle, red-eyed, rocking back and forth in her seat. Sophie's face was pressed against Rosier's shoulder. More people had come in to line the back of the courtroom. Hundreds of eyes and ears and hearts. Soon the papers and pamphlets describing the sensational trial would be printed and circulating all over Paris.

The only sound in the courtroom was the scraping of the quills. She would not let them tell her story—not that way.

"Magic," she said, "is not evil. That is like saying a hammer is evil. Or a scythe, because it can be used to kill as well as to bring in the harvest." As she spoke, Camille felt the fever-magic rise in her. Sympathy for the girls, the deaths of her parents, magicians hunted, Lazare gone—and whatever pain still awaited. "My magic helped print pamphlets that saved the lost girls from cruel eviction. It brought money to feed them and warm clothes. Magic," she insisted, her voice rising, "helped them see themselves as important."

"Quiet, madame, or we will have to remove you—"

She would not be quiet. She might never have an audience as large as this, and she would say what she must to convince them. Otherwise, what meaning did her life have?

"I am proud to be a magician!" she blazed. "Do you know where magic comes from? Not from evil, but from understanding. From great sorrow, great feeling at injustice and suffering. How can it be wrong? Sympathy is the fuel that changes the world, is it not? Magic *is* revolution!"

Someone in the gallery stood up, face crimson: "Magic is unnatural! The accused is outside the law, and therefore has no rights! Take her away!"

Had no one had heard her? Had her words had meant nothing?

The courtroom dissolved into chaos. After that there was nothing more to be said for the shouting down of the gallery, and the prosecution rested. Dufresne shuffled away, head down. The jury deliberated for ten fretful minutes while Camille sat in a room no larger than a closet. A fly buzzed against the glass of the barred window. Beyond it echoed the chants: *Magician! Magician!*

Dufresne stood behind her, and she listened to him wheeze. "You spoke too much," he said finally. "There was no order. You should have let me—"

"I did, monsieur. I waited, and you did not defend me."

When she returned to the courtroom, the jury had already been seated. Odette raised an eyebrow at Camille and dragged a finger across her throat.

Odette's gesture filled Camille with foreboding. The future of magic in France would be determined now. If Camille did not win this, more magicians would follow in her footsteps. They would sit in courtrooms just like this, be convicted on made-up charges, executed. The revolution she'd believed in would lose its credibility, and then the losses to the people would be even greater.

The judge cleared his throat. "Camille de Veaux, also called Camille Durbonne, Vicomtesse de Séguin, you have been found guilty of the charges levied against you. You will be hanged by the neck until you are dead." The gallery roared, and the judge banged his gavel for quiet. "Tomorrow at four at the Place de Grève."

She would be hanged like any commoner, a rope around her neck. The room swayed again, and she clung so hard to the railing her arms shook. She must stay standing. She must not faint, not now.

Dufresne slouched away, shaking his head. In the commotion, Camille saw Rosier stand, the Lost Girls behind him. Their faces were fierce, unflinching, their hands on their hearts. *You are one of us.* Rosier's face was blank with worry, but he mouthed at her: *Soon.* Raucous, the spectators pushed out of the courtroom, making plans to meet at the square tomorrow where the execution would take place. *Once I might have been among them,* she thought, applauding the death of the ancien régime, content never to consider the situation more deeply. Even Roland had been changed—for a moment—when he drank the unknown girl's tears and felt her pain. But to have sympathy you must let yourself feel vulnerable, and she did not think a crowd ever did.

A guard dragged her toward a side exit. Odette and the prosecutor made their way to the larger double doors, where a crowd of supporters waited for them. One girl stepped forward from the jostling group. It was Giselle. In her hand, she still held the tricolor corsage. Who was it for? For the briefest of moments, her eyes met Camille's. They brimmed with heartbreak.

Giselle waved and called out to Odette, "Mon amie! You did it!" She held up the corsage.

Giselle was now on Odette's side? Camille felt her betrayal like a kick in the gut.

Arms out, Odette skipped toward Giselle, her face lit with happiness. "It is over!" she crowed as the two girls embraced. "I made certain of the evidence, just as I told you I would, n'est-ce pas? Now she'll never trouble us again! We can go back to the way things were. All of us together again."

"Never again," Giselle said as she squeezed Odette tight. One of Giselle's hands was tangled in the sweep of Odette's red hair, the other close around her friend's waist. The crowd in the courtroom cheered to see the girls reunited. Camille ached to see Giselle overwhelmed by emotion—were those tears on her cheeks?

*No*, Camille thought. *Something is wrong—*

Suddenly Giselle smiled, wild and lost and grim, like a fox in a trap, ready to bite off its own foot. Her hand darted out—and wrenched a pistol from Odette's belt.

"Vive la révolution!" she cried.

"No!" Camille tried to wrench free of her guard. "Stop, Giselle!"

She hesitated. For one long moment, she and Camille looked at each other. In Giselle's hand, the black nose of the pistol shook. Then she closed her eyes and fired.

The gunshot shattered the world.

Women screamed. Men shouted for a surgeon. The crowd surged toward the girls. A dozen hands grasped Giselle and dragged her away. She did not resist, only crossed her arms over her chest and let them take her.

Odette lay motionless on the floor, a lake of blood widening around her.

Amid shouts for help, men in the courtroom gathered her in their arms. Her head tipped lifelessly back, red hair spilling free of her hat. The men carrying her slid in her blood. Under the light of the courtroom's many candles her dress gleamed, as slick as if she'd been dragged from the river.

Numbly, Camille said, "Is the surgeon not coming?"

"No surgeon can help her," muttered the guard.

"And the girl? Giselle?"

"They'll try her, and I warrant she'll hang—right alongside you." The guard grasped Camille's arm and yanked her toward the side door. "One more death on your conscience, *magician*."

# 52

The guard shoved hard between Camille's shoulder blades, and she stumbled into her cell. The door banged shut with a dismal clang. There followed the now-familiar jangle of iron keys before her jailer moved away. Did he stand outside, now that she was condemned? Or was a chair down the hall still acceptable for the guard of the first magician to be executed in Paris in more than two hundred years?

The view from the barred window had not changed. Prisoners still strolled their well-worn routes through the familiar garden. She envied them those tiny paths of freedom. For them this might be their home for the next few months . . . not, as it was for her, merely a rest stop on the way to the gallows. Damp radiated up from the floor; in her flimsy shoes her toes ached with the cold. At least she could still feel something.

At least she was still alive.

Returning to La Petite Force she had been heckled, taunted, ridiculed. The people of Paris had thronged the doorway of the court, jubilating in the promise of her hanging. "À la lanterne les magiciens!" they chanted. She couldn't shield herself from the rotten food they slung at her, and she tripped on the cobbles. The soldiers who marched alongside her took their time, trading knowing smiles.

No sympathy for the magician. She could hardly remember what she'd said in court when she'd tried to speak her truth. But what did it matter? Nothing had changed. Maman had told her only a few would ever understand magic. But did that mean she would have to go to the gallows?

She forced herself to consider it. The great square would become a sea, a heaving mass of spectators. Jostling, mingling, they would be out for the spectacle, there to enjoy themselves. She thought of the parties at Versailles, glittering and decadent. They were another kind of revel, but they too had been an upside-down world where different rules might apply. Even more so at a masquerade—

Her mind wrenched painfully back to the courtroom. To Giselle. Why had she done it? She struggled to think of Odette dead, to understand what had happened, and why. But there was only the slick of red on the floor, the corsage crushed into it, the acrid haze of gunpowder and distant screams. Giselle was here, somewhere in the prison. Was she cold, like Camille? Frightened? Or was she serene in knowing she'd accomplished what she'd set out to do?

Disguised as Odette's friend, Giselle had struck a blow for the revolution. It made Camille wonder if she might—

A sharp knock. The guard eyed her through the open door. "Visitors."

Sophie and Rosier came in, Sophie's face puffy from crying. Behind them marched the guard who sat heavily on a chair in the corner. "Five minutes."

"Camille!" Sophie cried.

"You mustn't cry, ma chérie." Camille pulled her close. Sophie's heart beat fast and hard and regular, and it gave Camille courage. She thought back to Les Merveilleux, the puppets flying away. She remembered all the different versions of the play Sophie and Rosier had devised. Could there not be one final retelling of that story?

She took a steadying breath and hoped that she could make them understand the plot unfolding in her mind. It would take skill and perception and much planning. The burden on them would be great to make it happen—and quickly. "All will be well. I only wish I didn't have to miss the spectacle."

Sophie seemed stricken, as if the events of the last few hours had caused Camille to lose her mind. "Whatever do you mean?"

"The Marvels, of course," she insisted.

The people she needed most to understand looked back at her blankly.

"Since I won't be there for the performance at the square, I had an idea for you. An innovation." *Please*, she begged silently, *please understand me.*

Rosier took out his pipe. "Do tell."

"What if," she said quickly, "instead of puppets, you used living actors?"

"Ah!" He took a drag on his pipe and she could almost hear the gears of his mind clicking. "I can see it now! Some of the actors might walk on stilts to give them the height the larger puppets had. And the *flight* of the white bird we call Mademoiselle l'Oiseau could be especially spectacular, non? To see her soar away?"

Like a mirror to Rosier's own, bright understanding flashed in Sophie's face. There wheels were spinning too, and in the midst of her own despair Camille was filled with a bright joy: whatever happened, the two of them were perfect together.

"It is really too bad!" Sophie exclaimed. "I know how much you wanted to be there in your dress with the white feathers."

The guard paid them no heed, but continued to pick dirt from his nails.

"Yes," Camille said, rapidly searching their faces to make certain they truly understood. "It is a shame I will not get a chance to wear it."

"And your gilt-and-cream carriage!" exclaimed Sophie. "How you will miss that!"

"She will miss many things, you pack of idiots," the guard said roughly. "Namely her own life."

"Of course, of course!" Cautiously, Rosier turned his back on the guard. "Still, I cannot forget how you said you wished to fly once more!"

"Exactly!" Camille said.

"She'll fly from the noose!" the guard guffawed.

Under cover of her hat, Sophie nodded seriously at Rosier. "We will be watching from the far side of the square! Just—look out for marvels. And think: lots of feathers!"

"Do not fear, we will advertise widely, by poster *and* crier," Rosier announced, "so that all of Paris will know when it is to be performed—even the flown-away pigeons! Who knows? Perhaps we can incorporate them into our show."

It was a brilliant idea. Advertising would let Lazare and Foudriard know to come to the performance. And there were enough roles for all of them to disappear into the show. "Thank you," Camille said. "Will the spectacle be traveling, after the performance? I had thought to give the house away."

Sophie frowned slightly, and Camille silently pleaded for her to make the leap. "Oh yes," she said finally. "I've already starting packing. The neighborhood just doesn't suit us anymore, does it?"

"Perfect." Camille kissed them both—Rosier knuckling tears from his cheeks—and bid them both adieu. She pressed her palms together, as if she might keep the warmth of them with her a little longer.

The guard turned the key in the lock.

Shadows filled her cell. The walls shifted closer until it felt as though they brushed against her skirts. Close, like the sides of a coffin. The plan they'd concocting was the best they could think of. But what if it wasn't enough? What if at the end of the square was not an escape, but the silent darkness of death?

This might be her last night on earth.

The last night she might be in the world with those she loved, even if they were far away. Her breaths might now be numbered. Each one subtracted from the total, like the ticking of a clock running down. This might be the last cold day. She might never again feel the sun freckling her cheeks. Be dazzled by the gold of Sophie's hair. Feel Lazare's body against hers, feel her own desire unfurling like slow fire. Never again feel magic transport her out of the ordinary and into the marvelous.

She clenched her fingers around the cold bars at the window. Her clammy fingers stuck to the metal and the pain brought her back to the cell. Whatever time she had left, she was not going to spend it thinking of death.

Instead, after dinner, she asked for a walk. One of the guards jeered, "It won't be your last time under the open sky, but it will be your last chance to enjoy it." Even at this hour, there were still a few women strolling the paths in the dusky courtyard. Camille kept to herself, relishing the kiss of the night air on her skin. But as she passed one of the tall shrubs that grew along the wall, someone slipped out from between their shadows and caught hold of her sleeve.

"Henriette!" Camille stared uncomprehending at the forger with her halo of fair hair. "Have they arrested you, too?"

"Shhh!" Taking Camille's hand, Henriette slid a small packet into her sleeve. "A boy with a pipe came to Flotsam House and commissioned four of those. When he told me one was for you, I said I'd bring it myself. Walk with me?"

Side by side they kept to the wall, like any other prisoners. "But how did you get in?"

Henriette's face shone. "Claudine."

*There is no lock that can keep its secrets from me.* Together these girls were formidable. "And she will let you out again?"

"She is waiting for my whistle." When they passed out of view of the guards, Henriette said, "I don't know what you and your friends are planning. It's better that I don't. I volunteered to come not only to give you the paper, but because I wanted to thank you for what you did for me."

"There's no need, truly—"

She held up her hand, ink-stained like Camille's. "Before you say it was nothing, let me speak. I've never been ashamed of what I do. But when we talked about my forgeries, you made a mirror and held it up for me to see myself. You gave me a new story."

"We all need that, sometimes."

"Well." Henriette smoothed her hair, blinking hard. "Whatever happens, thank you for that. I'll tell the other girls how brave you were in court. Like you were one of us."

It was the highest compliment she could have given her, Camille knew. "Thank you, Henriette."

She hesitated. "One more thing. Paris has your name in its dirty mouth and it means to see you swing. Whatever you do, be careful."

How could she be careful when she did not know what would happen? She would have to walk to her death and hope that it would, at the very last moment, be averted. Each step toward the gallows would be a step toward a possible freedom—or toward a certain death. Camille couldn't have admitted it to Sophie, or to Rosier. But she felt she could say it to this fierce girl who'd once stared death in the eye. "I'm frightened of tomorrow, Henriette."

Henriette's face softened. "Fear isn't anything bad. Fear is what keeps a rabbit still when the fox comes, and fear is what tells it to run. It's only a part of your own self, that wants to live. You can't let it take over, but I know you won't. You're strong. Let that fear live inside you right along with your bravery."

Camille exhaled. "I'll try."

"Good," said Henriette simply. "I'll go then."

Camille caught hold of her coat. "Have you seen Giselle? The guards would tell me nothing."

"I saw her an hour ago." Henriette stared into the distance, the horror of the visit plain on her face. "She may have lost her wits. She only repeats that Odette betrayed us girls at Flotsam House, betrayed the revolution . . . and betrayed you. All she'll say is that she'll accompany you to the scaffold. I don't think there's anything else we can do."

*Wasn't there?* "One more thing—"

Henriette stopped. She seemed very small in the lightless courtyard.

"It isn't much. You would have found out soon enough. My lawyer was instructed to tell you. Before I left the court, I made certain of it: I have given my house to all of you. It belongs to the Lost Girls now, each of you by name."

"*Your* house?" Her mouth fell open in shock.

"If you don't want it," Camille said in a rush, "sell it and divide the money."

Henriette laughed, gleefully as a small child. "Sell a house like that? Odette told us about it when she tried to convince us you were an evil magician. But all we could think of was the warm rooms and the feather beds, the cook, and a roof that doesn't leak." Wonderingly, she shook her head. "I can hardly believe it. Such a gift—thank you."

Was that a tear in the forger's eye? "It was never really mine, that house. Though in the end, I did love it. I hope you will be happy there."

"More than happy. Au revoir, then, princess, and bonne chance." Henriette gave Camille a secretive smile as she slowly crossed the prison yard. When she reached the ancient yew by the wall, she began to whistle.

In her cell that night, Camille carefully removed the object from her sleeve. It was a passport with a false name. She felt along the paper's fold. A tiny bump, where something had been hidden. With her fingernail, she slit the back of it. Inside lay a tiny knife. A gift from sharp-eyed Claudine, she was certain. A blade like that could pick a lock. Or slice a rope.

So much would have to come together. And there would need to be magic of a kind she had never worked. But the girls, at least, believed in her to escape.

The rest of her thoughts were malevolent with shadows. Lazare caught or hurt, in hiding somewhere, Chandon and the others gone to ground while Sophie and Rosier prepared for whatever, be it freedom or be it death, that would happen tomorrow. The city she loved, the city she'd believed in, was a city turned inside out, its ugly seams showing. Its streets and alleys and innumerable rooms were thick with ghosts she could not bear to listen to. Broken-necked and bleeding. Swaying from trees and lampposts, slain in courtrooms. Each day there would be more, rising on cold and silent feet. Murders and executions, hatred and righteousness, and rivers of endless sorrow.

It was right that she was going. Wherever that might be.

For in Paris, there was nothing left but ruin.

# 53

The red tumbrel clattered over the cobblestones.

In it, six prisoners crowded together. Shoulder to shoulder, knees pushed against knees. As the low-slung cart lurched along, their heads bobbed grimly. Each sat with their hands in their lap, their wrists tied. Some women wore only their chemises, having sold their dresses for food while they were in prison. Others wore their brave and gaudy best.

Stuck between two women convicted of having more than one husband sat Camille. When they took her from her cell that morning, no one had shoved a red traitor's coat over her head. Or cut her hair. Instead, she'd been taken to the executioner's assistant.

"You're the first magician," he told her as she was forced to sit in a chair in front of him, "but certainly not the last. I better make it good, for I'll be setting the standard for all that come after." Someone had given him a small pot of blue paint, and with his finger he drew a crude tear under her eye. Next he roughly rubbed her hands with coal until they were black. She tried not to think of the last time she'd seen these signs.

Fetching a shard of mirror, he held it up to her, as her hands were bound to the chair and she could hold nothing. "What do you think?"

Lightly freckled skin, sickly white. Lank russet hair. A purple bruise yellowing on her jaw, a blue tear spilling from a terrified eye. A magician. A ghost. "You satisfied?"

She swallowed.

"You know, I'm not." Unscrewing a jar of rouge, he jammed a finger in it. "I keep this for the ladies." On her cheeks he traced two bright circles. Then he pressed his filthy finger to her lips. She turned her face away.

It was no use. There was nowhere to go. He caught her chin with his free hand and wrenched it toward him. Slowly, excruciatingly, he painted her lips scarlet. And when he was done he held her tight and kissed her hard and long on the mouth. Tears leaked from her shut eyes.

*I am a ghost*, she told herself. *I am not here.*

"Fais de beaux rêves," he'd said as he stood. "Sweet dreams."

"Magician!" the crowd screamed as the cart rattled on. "Death to the bloodsuckers!"

Beside her sat Giselle. She still wore her yellow-striped dress, now stained rust-red with Odette's blood. Her quick smile had vanished. Instead her hazel eyes were wide as the sky, as if she were already gone.

"Giselle." When she didn't answer, Camille knocked her knee against hers. "Giselle!"

Giselle watched the buildings pass by.

"Listen to me, Giselle." Camille clasped the other girl's hands.

Vaguely she said, "What is it?"

"Come with me. I am going to escape."

"To what place?" she wondered. "There is nothing safe anymore, you know that?"

The cart jolted over a hole in the road, knocking their shoulders together.

"I'm going far away. You deserve better than this."

"I've been running my whole life. Now there is a price to pay. There always is, in the end." Fierce tears trembled on her lashes as she looked away. "I *knew* what the cost would be. I made that choice."

"Make another one!" Camille urged. "Your dreams are still waiting to be lived. If you don't want to come with us, I already told Henriette—my house belongs to all of you. A place for Céline to grow up, and for you to do what you want." She squeezed Giselle's fingers, hard. "Look at me."

Giselle did. As if, for a moment, there was something she might trust.

It was hard to believe when the world went against you. To keep making the choice to live, over and over again. To hope. "Do not throw away your chance."

Giselle clenched her hands into fists. "Won't they search for me at the house?"

"You never mentioned the other girls to the police, did you? Anything about Flotsam House?"

"*Never.*"

"In the beginning, then, be careful. Hide in the attics if you must. But the wardrobes are full of dresses, shoes, hats. Go out in disguise. Be whoever you wish to be. Perhaps they'll catch you. Or perhaps they won't. But it's better than giving up now."

Giselle paled. "We're nearly there."

Camille craned her neck. "Do you see a carriage?"

"Not that," Giselle replied, awe in her voice. "The gallows."

At the end of the narrow street, the open space of the square unfolded into sky. *Trust*, she told herself as her stomach clenched. *Trust.* They will be there. *You have the little knife*, she told herself, but fear clawed at her and the words wheeled away like frightened birds.

Everywhere, the crowd: seething and jostling and demanding. Hands grasping at the prisoners' clothes. A woman with scissors in her hand snatching at Camille's red hair, hoping to cut a souvenir. Just in time, Camille yanked it away.

"I'll get it when they cut your body down, traîtresse!" the woman spat.

The cart lurched, and Camille struggled to see. Where was the carriage?

"Please," she begged. She only realized she'd spoken aloud when Giselle rested her head on Camille's shoulder.

"Are you waiting for the sign?" Giselle asked.

"It will be a golden carriage." It sounded impossible, like something out of a fairy tale.

"It shall come."

The tumbrel rattled into the square, and a deafening roar rose up from those gathered for the execution. Men, women, and children so small their mothers held them by the hand. A man was selling meat pies, the aroma delicious and sickening. Several girls sold tricolor rosettes made of ribbon. Through the crowd ambled a juggler in a black-and-white striped suit, calling singsong, "Marvels are coming! Pay attention! Marvels are coming!"

Beyond the juggler rose the platform, and on it, the gallows' ebony beams, its keen circle of rope. Nearby stood the broad-shouldered executioner, his hood thrown back, large hands easy at his sides. There should have been no one else there on that grim stage with him, but there was. Four scarlet-cloaked guards of the Comité, like crows come to the gallows to watch her die. At their feet, the silent, waiting hounds.

The tumbrel jolted to a stop. Giselle swayed, caught hold of Camille's shoulder.

"What's happening?" one of the women said, hope in her voice. "Why have we stopped?

An old woman grunted. "A carriage, all white and gold, that's blocking the way! The horses are rearing up!"

Relief flooded through Camille. *Now.*

She raised her eyebrows at Giselle, who nodded. Héloïse's little knife lay tucked in her sleeve, and she shook it out into her lap. "Quick," she said to Giselle, "cut the rope!" Taking the tiny knife, Giselle sawed through the bindings. In a moment, Camille was free, and, willing her hands not to shake, she sliced the ropes that bound Giselle. "Now run," she hissed as she cut through another set of cords and gave the knife to the startled woman next to her. "This is your chance!"

Without a backward glance, Giselle stepped out over the edge and dropped into the crowd. Camille stood, swaying, and then leaped away, the other prisoners overturning the cart as they jumped after her, the spectators in an uproar. Dogs howling like wolves. The jailor shouted for help, but the people, who'd come for entertainment, cheered. As they roared and pounded their thousand feet, Camille fled.

People got in her way, and she went around. The platform was empty and the Comité crows scattered. Red flashed as the guards moved through the crowd, fanning out. Hunting their prize. Not daring to draw attention to herself by running, she forced herself to walk, agonizingly slowly, pretending that she too was enjoying the spectacle. Inside she trembled with the terror of knowing they were an arm's-length away. If she were caught by the Comité they would make an example of her, she had no doubt.

Very close, a scarlet cloak snapped in the wind.

*Fear is what keeps a rabbit still when the fox comes, and fear is what tells it to run.*

She ran.

Wishing she had but a drop of blur, she raced through the edges of the crowd until she found a reeking alleyway no wider than her arms outstretched. She didn't dare go farther before changing—she had to make it to the stage at the square's far end, and she couldn't be dressed like this. She was so clearly a prisoner. Desperately she hoped her friends would be there, masked and ready to take over the puppets' parts. What roles they'd play she did not know, only that she was to be the white bird. Mademoiselle l'Oiseau.

From the square, voices echoed, shouting for the magician to turn herself in.

*Steady now.* She had made it out of the tumbrel. That was the first step. She had freed Giselle and the others. Second step. Now, the third. Transformation. Her stomach convulsed, and she was sick in the alley. *Almost there*, she told herself, as she wiped her mouth with her sleeve. She spat in her hands and rubbed the painted tear off her cheek and the prison grime from her forehead. *Almost there.*

Out of long habit, Camille raised her hand to her shoulder, where she had always pinned the diamond brooch. But her fingers touched only silk. In her confusion, she'd forgotten she wasn't wearing her enchanted dress.

How had she thought she would change this dress? It would need blood, she knew. What had she done with Claudine's little knife? A wave of panic coursed through her as she looked at her empty hands. That too was gone. For one dizzying moment, she stared at the filthy ground for something, anything, she could use.

In the manure lay a black nail come loose from a horseshoe.

She picked it up, then spat on it to clean it as best she could. Beyond the alley, the crowd exulted. She must hurry.

The nail was so small. Only a bit larger than the point of the brooch. But it was also dull and dirty. Gagging, she set the point against her arm.

What had Blaise written to her? *Magic is not in the blood.*

She'd thought he meant magic was not in the family, not something passed down. That it was not something inherent in her, but instead, something she could choose.

But he might have meant something else. She let the nail fall from her fingers.

In the bright square, the gilded carriage had trundled away. Police were spreading through the crowd, offering shouted rewards for the escaped convicts. And somewhere, everywhere, was the Comité, tightening its net.

So little time. Pressing her palms against the bodice of her dress, she steadied her breath. She stared at her blackened fingers. They had been this way before, dirty from digging up nails. Before she'd worked the glamoire, before she met Lazare, before she had changed everything. Had it been only a dream and now she was back where she'd started, with only empty hands and a burning desire to transform?

*No.*

Something *had* changed. She had become someone new. Stronger, more whole. She thought of the magicians' blackened fingers in the portraits, the way the gold leaf had worn off over time to reveal the sooty underpainting. That darkness hadn't faded; it had always been part of them.

Blaise hadn't worked magic with his hands. The blood she had seen him spill to read those warded books? It was only an outward sign. She'd been wrong to believe that magic was in *that*. It was something much deeper that had cajoled those books to speak and made paper rise and burn like stars. He'd worked magic with his generous and sympathetic heart. He'd worked it with his whole being.

Deep inside, her sorrow rose.

At times she'd lost her way. She was flawed, no Jeanne d'Arc. Nevertheless she strove for good amid this sorrow.

As feeling fevered through her, like fire in her veins, she felt her magic soar.

*White*, Camille imagined. *White, glittering with glass and set with pearls.* She pictured the doves that swooped from the rafters in the workshop and the glad flash of their wings. Like the crystals of snow in Blaise's hair. Like her pamphlets floating over Paris.

*Feathers without number.*

She spilled no blood. She didn't make the dress turn anymore than she sent blood to her heart or squeezed her lungs when she ran. But where her palm touched the bodice, the silk began to change. Around the shape of her dirty hand, the silk lost its color: white as ash.

*I am this*, she told herself. *This is who I am, this is my story.* Listening to her, the dress made itself over: snow-white silk, overlaid with hundreds of dancing white plumes. Lengths and lengths of it shimmering ghostlike in the alley's gloom.

Until the Comité realized she'd worked magic—and the Comité would, if they caught her—she'd be safest as part of the spectacle. She had only to get there. The crooked lane led away into the gloom, along the twists and turns of Paris's labyrinth.

There was no time to waste. She picked up her skirts and disappeared.

# 54

The white-and-gold carriage had come to a halt at the far end of the square, near a low wooden stage. Over it was raised a red curtain; behind it stood a painted backdrop of a gray sky dazzled with snow. A white fawn pranced across the platform, paused on nimble hooves, blew a horn, and ran on.

In the crowd of spectators, a little girl pulled on her mother's skirts. "Tiens, Maman! A play!"

For on the square's opposite end, far from the gallows, a band of players had begun to perform. Les Merveilleux were known for their extraordinarily lifelike puppets, and if the performers today were not puppets but flesh-and-blood actors, no one seemed to mind. Dressed in flowing white garments, they stepped disjointedly on slender stilts. Their faces were painted alabaster and decorated with pips from every suit—hearts, diamonds, spades, and clubs—like the beauty marks women at court used to wear in another age, long ago. From behind the snowy sky, sheer curtains billowed and parted. A princess appeared. She wore a gold crown on her golden hair, and when a masked highway man appeared, she curtsied low to him, making the crowd applaud. He wore a white mask and a red beard. When he drew his sword, the princess swooned on her spindly stilts as the people shouted: *Ahhh! Be careful!*

Behind the curtain, Rosier briskly hooked Camille into a harness and clipped it to a line. "Up!" he commanded. "Do not think twice!"

The rope pulled her and she flew. As an enormous white bird, she snatched the golden crown off the princess's golden head before soaring away. The crowd roared its approval. The princess fainted into the highwayman's arms. He bent and kissed her. Behind them grew a forest. From between its black trunks tiptoed a ghostly wolf who disappeared as the lovers stared at one another, deeply in love.

Between the princess and the highwayman unfurled an enormous bouquet of the reddest roses. As if they were spent dandelions, the princess blew on them, and the crimson petals floated out over the crowd in a rain of red paper.

The players took their bows. The crowd applauded: *Encore! Encore!*

*A rain of rose petals,* Camille thought from her dizzying perch on a window ledge. *Or blood.* The window beside her was open; Rosier had promised it would be when, far below, behind the golden carriage, he'd strapped white wings to her back. *You're almost there. Madame who lives upstairs was happy to help make the players' performance a success, as long as I gave her a front-row seat. They will all be entranced,* he'd said when she'd choked out that the Comité was there. *Trust me—they will never see you in this feathered dress.*

Below her on the cobblestones, the white-costumed players were already stepping into a carriage, waving adieu. She had only a minute to join them. Through the holes in her snow-white bird's mask, she took in the square, where every red-cloaked man might be a guard of the Comité. Casting one last look over Paris—dirty and crowded, dangerous and beautiful, her beloved city of marvels—she unclipped herself from the line and slipped through the window into a stranger's apartment. A tea set sprigged with pink roses waited on a polished table, like at the queen's tea parties at Versailles. A thousand years ago, in another life.

Down the stair's tight spiral she ran, the tips of her wings trailing behind her. Dashing through a courtyard where a dog frantically barked she was suddenly in the street, where her own carriage, now painted white and gold with a banner spelling out LES MERVEILLEUX, waited. Bowing to the spectators who applauded her, and calling out brightly, as Rosier had suggested, "Next show in half an hour!" she made her way through the throng.

As she approached the carriage, Rosier, the masked highwayman, jumped off the driver's box and flung open the door with a flourish. "Entrez, Mademoiselle l'Oiseau!"

"I'm coming! Perhaps I should fly instead, if you are so impatient?" she said, flapping her wings in the air. She dared not look past the spectators in the first few rows for fear of seeing black hats. *Play the part*, she told herself. *Disappear into it.* Pulling a tiny crown from her hair, she tossed it into the crowd: one final piece of misdirection.

"Mine!" someone shrieked, and soon they were all scrambling for it.

"Get in," Rosier urged from under his highwayman's mask. "We're leaving immediately." He pulled a cord on her harness that collapsed her wings, and she scrambled inside, pulling the door shut. Through the window she saw him leap onto the box and take the horses' reins. The whip snapped. She hadn't time to sit down before the carriage jolted forward and tossed her against the wall in a flurry of feathers.

"Ouch!" cried Sophie from behind her princess mask. "You're crushing me!"

"Pardon," Camille said, finding a spot next to the white wolf. The carriage picked up speed. Buildings shuffled past the window, faster and faster. "We did it," she said, slowly, as if she didn't yet believe it. Tears pricked behind her mask. "And everyone is here?"

Sophie's smile wavered. "How beautiful your dress is!"

Taking a steadying breath, Camille took in the carriage with its familiar green upholstery. Had they truly done it? Risked all, and escaped? There was Sophie, untying her princess mask, and there was black Fantôme in his wicker basket, curled like a comma alongside Blaise's white cat. Beside her sat the wolf, his furred mask a hood that covered his entire head. She reached out and took his white-gloved hand, felt its answering squeeze.

He was here! Her heart soared. "My love, wherever have you been?"

The wolf's head tipped back, as if surprised.

She laughed and threw her arms around him. "Oh, it doesn't matter now—I am only so glad you made it in time!" But in her embrace Lazare did not feel like himself. Too narrow, too compact. "Lazare?"

Sophie reached for her. "Camille—"

There was, she saw now, an empty space next to Sophie. Where was the bear from the forest scene? "Someone is missing! Where is the white bear? Was that Chandon's role? Or is he on the box with Rosier? And— Foudriard? Is he riding postillion?"

He couldn't be. She would have seen him astride one of the carriage horses when they'd come into the square. Bewildered, Camille stared at Sophie, then at the wolf, trying to grasp what was happening. "Why do you not say anything? You're frightening me! Tell me what's happened!"

Wearily, the wolf pulled off his hood. But instead of Lazare's amber-flecked eyes, it was Chandon's hazel ones she saw. "We don't know where they are. We left word as best we could, but we had no sure way to tell them the plan." He swallowed hard, as if not saying the words could keep them from being true. "We waited all morning. But Lazare didn't come. Neither did Foudriard."

*No.*

"Camille," he said warningly, "I've decided to believe that they are together, and they will catch us on the way. Do not say different, I beg you."

Camille banged her fist against the ceiling. "Stop!" she shouted. "Stop the coach!"

But the carriage hurtled on. Sophie dragged her down to the bench. "Sit, or you'll only hurt yourself!"

Camille reached for the door handle, but Chandon held her back. "Let me out!" she cried. "I cannot go without him! Why did you not wait longer?"

Anguish contorted Sophie's face. "Rosier feared we'd be arrested if we waited. Lazare is wanted by the police! His face is plastered on posters all over the city. And the Comité," she said helplessly, "made it impossible to linger. It was you or them."

As Paris rattled by beyond the window—tilting houses and brash new buildings and ancient churches and squares—Camille's head sank into her hands. As she wept, she felt the dress stir around her, breathing more extravagant white feathers into being. It was beautiful magic, but it was no consolation for the desolation of this. To have finally escaped, and to be leaving him behind.

"Be brave of heart, mon petit oiseau," Chandon murmured as he wrapped an arm around her shaking shoulders. "The game is not yet over."

# 55

As the carriage hurried through the city, Camille peered out the circular window in the carriage's back wall. No red cloaks, no police. Perhaps, Camille considered, they were still searching the crowd at the Place de Grève. Perhaps they had given up.

They had nearly reached the western gate when suddenly the coach slowed. The horses' hooves thudded on packed earth, their harness jingled as they tossed their heads, pulling against the reins.

"What is it?" Camille wondered. "Shall I'll open the window and ask Rosier—?"

Chandon held her back. "Careful."

She lifted only the edge of the tasseled curtain. Outside loomed a stone wall with a closed wooden gate set into it. Beside it milled several policemen who were inspecting the carts and riders ahead of them in line. "They are speaking to everyone who wishes to pass through."

"They will be checking our passports." Sophie opened her purse and pulled out the forged document. Her hands shook and she dropped it in her lap. "What if—"

"Our passports are perfect." Camille trusted Henriette knew her trade. "But we must appear as performers who travel like this often." She tied the white bird face on so it sat on top of her head, its fall of feathers covering her conspicuous hair. Sophie did the same.

"Not I." His cheeks flushed, Chandon flung his wolf mask across his knee. "With the windows closed it's so hot in here that no one in his right mind, player or not, would wear this loathsome hood for any longer than he had to."

The carriage crept forward and stopped again. "How many more are there ahead of us?" Sophie asked.

"One cart, and a group of riders." And there, beside a wagon full of wine barrels, two guards in black hats and crimson cloaks. "Dieu," she said low as fear clawed through her. "They're here."

"Stop that!" Sophie yanked the curtain closed. "We are players on a stage, bringing marvels to the people. There's no reason for us to be afraid of the Comité."

"But if they recognize me—" Camille tried to push back the terror that rose in her as the carriage trundled closer to the gate. Guards dragging her away. And what would happen to Sophie, Chandon, and Rosier for traveling with an accused magician? In that moment she was glad that Lazare, at least, was somewhere else.

"They won't." Chandon rummaged beneath the seats and uncovered a bottle of wine. Sloshing it about the carriage, he drenched her and Sophie's dresses as well as the fur of his white wolf costume. "Addendum to the plan: we are to be drunk, and foolish, though respectful, and they will be so annoyed with us that they will leave in disgust—"

The door was wrenched wide by a policeman. Behind him, their hats shadowing their faces, loomed two Comité guards. One of their monstrous dogs pushed his head into the carriage and, as his black lips pulled away from his yellow teeth, inhaled. His nose twitched, as if scenting for magic.

*The wine.* Fervently she hoped it would be enough to cover the bitter ash scent of the magic she had worked.

"Passports, s'il vous plaît."

In his hands, the papers dwindled, insignificant and powerless. Cursorily, he paged through them. "You are all performers?"

As one, they inclined their heads. Chandon burped. "Pardon!"

"Drunk and debauched," one of the Comité guards said as the dog growled. "And what is your play?"

*What could they possibly say? Well, monsieur, it is a fantasy, a fairy tale. A story of love and wishes and a longing for beauty—a play about hope and possibility.* She knew they would consider it antirevolutionary in the extreme. Hadn't Sophie and Rosier already been warned?

She remembered how in the Tennis Court at Versailles the members of the Assembly had raised their arms in a Roman salute. That was the kind of thing they valued. Virtue. Reason.

Before she lost her nerve, she said, "It is an ancient play, messieurs. Popular in the time of Caesar, it's a story of a transformation and hope, a virtuous parable for our time."

The Comité guard shoved the policeman out of the way and leaned into the carriage. "Those costumes are an insult to progress. Fantastical. Magical." He spat the word out as if it would kill him. Beside him, eager saliva dripped from the dog's mouth.

*Steady,* she told herself, but she could not stop her frenzied, galloping heart.

"But, monsieur!" Sophie gave him her most winning smile. "The only magic in the play is true love. In my role as the princess, I give up my crown to marry a reformed highwayman. *He* is taught a lesson about being honest and hardworking, and *I* am humbled to see the wrong in my royal life."

The guard grunted. Camille clenched her hand in her skirts to keep herself from screaming. They were so close. To go back to the terror of the jail, or worse than that, back to the black shape of the gallows—

"Here," Chandon slurred, taking a huge gulp of wine and holding the bottle out to the guard. "Want a sip?"

The guard's lips thinned in disgust. "And France is to be transformed for the benefit of you costumed fools? Take your play out of Paris. It is not wanted here." He threw their passports at them and, yanking his dog away, closed the door.

Chandon put a finger to his lips and they sat in silence as, on the box, Rosier clucked at the horses. The carriage jerked forward. As the ancient walls of Paris rose up around them, the crowd parted, the gate creaked open, someone shouted, "Look! A circus!" But no one stopped them. It felt like years that they sat in the hot carriage, not daring to move, as the wheels rolled on. When they finally were out of sight of the gate, Rosier cracked the whip and sent the horses into a gallop, racing west.

For six hours, they traveled toward the coast. The landscape was flat, autumn fields shorn to stubble, grapes ripening on rows of leafy vines. Clusters of broad oaks and chestnut and hazelnut, woolly sheep on a hill facing in the same direction. A wide-open sky such as she'd never seen before, only now and then pierced by a church steeple. Every hour, Camille peered through the back window, each time certain she would see the black horses of the Comité storming after them. But for now their luck held.

Only once did they stop. At the inn where they'd waited for fresh horses, running grubby children, guests, the ostlers and stable boys caked with grime, the scullery maids and the washerwoman, her laundry basket on her hip—all of them stared at the players in their white costumes. When they drew close, Camille wanted to rush back into the carriage and hide. The crowd made her skin crawl.

But Rosier made a grand flourish, exclaiming: "We are Les Merveilleux! One week from today, at this inn, we will perform for you—bringing you wonder and delight!"

The people laughed and cheered. Camille and Sophie curtsied deeply, and Camille let her wings unfurl, making the children gasp. But once the new horses were hitched, they scrambled into the carriage, relieved to pull tight the curtains and head west to the sea.

Each little town they passed, Camille searched its narrow streets for a sign. Was Lazare there, somewhere? Were he and Foudriard waiting around some corner, watching for the gilt carriage? She begged Rosier to go slowly, in case the boys were waiting somewhere, *anywhere*. He obliged her a few times before putting an end to it. "We left word for them, Camille. They know where we are going," he reassured her. "We'll wait for them there. Slowing down only exposes us, and we're already alarmingly conspicuous as it is."

The farther west they went, the more the towns fell away, until there was only waving grass, the sky's washed-out dome, and the white road running toward the sea. It was nearly nightfall when in the distance, they spotted a smudge against the horizon. "Could that be it?" Sophie asked.

"Duprès told me we couldn't miss it." Chandon had been the one to arrange their lodgings—a favor owed to his mother, called in. "As long as we bore left onto the smaller road, we'd end up at his inn in Wissant." Impatiently he pushed down the window. A cool sea breeze swept into the carriage. "There's nothing behind it but endless water and endless sky. It looks as if it might be the very last house in the world."

For now, their journey had come to an end.

# 56

The inn at Wissant was a rambling, low-slung building, its thatched roof dotted with windows like sleepy eyes. A tow-headed boy was playing with a stick next to a high wall of gray stone. When he saw the carriage, he waved them on, running ahead through an archway opening onto a stableyard. As the carriage clattered over the cobbles, the boy pulled stout wooden doors closed behind them. Only when he lowered a massive wooden bar into place did Camille finally exhale.

Safe for now. They could take off these costumes, wash, edge slowly away from what had happened as they waited for Lazare and Foudriard to arrive. She felt as though she'd been holding her breath since the Paris gate.

Despite everything, there was a bright note of excitement in Sophie's voice when she said, "This is my first time staying at an inn, did you know, Chandon?"

"I suspect there will be more in your future," Chandon said, his voice colored with melancholy. "I do hope you like it."

Where the carriage had come to a stop stood a man well into middle age. His clothes were very fine, but of a fashion already vanished from Paris. He opened the carriage door, and as he handed Camille out, he said, "Welcome to my home, madame, the last inn before the sea. I am Jean Duprès, and this was once the house of my ancestor, the Marquis de la Tourendelle, who was something of a pirate. I do a little in that way, myself, but mostly I am an innkeeper." His sunburned cheeks said otherwise. "We do what we must, n'est-ce pas?"

Clapping Chandon on the shoulder, and asking after his mother, Duprès brought them all through the stables, where horses nickered softly as they passed. At the front of the inn, the shutters were fastened over the windows. Duprès pointed to a sign hanging on the glossy blue door: CLOSED FOR RENOVATIONS.

"You see? We will not have any trouble, and you will be perfectly at ease here, I trust. Please sit while your baggage—and the cats—are removed to your rooms." Beckoning them on, he led them to a cozy, low-ceilinged room where a fire crackled in the grate. The ceiling was laddered with chestnut beams; Turkish carpets warmed the flagstone floor. Oil paintings of boats on stormy seas hung on the walls. White curtains trimmed with cotton lace covered the windows. From the kitchen came the rich scent of a roast cooking. A maid came into the room, holding a large tray with wine and tea and soft cakes on it, which she set on a low table by a sofa plump with pillows. Something in Camille's tight heart eased.

Duprès smiled at them as if they were his own children. "You must be very tired, mesdames and messieurs. The Marquis de Chandon wrote me a little of your troubles. We're not free of that madness here, but, nevertheless, think not of it now. You will be very safe."

"Thank you, monsieur," Camille said, "for all of this." The inn seemed very large. Wasn't it possible that in a far wing, Lazare and Foudriard were already resting? "There are two more in our party. Have they already arrived?"

He shook his head. "If they are coming from Paris, rest assured they will be here soon. And if not," he added, "we will keep their plates warm for whenever they do arrive."

*And what if that is never?* He meant to comfort her, but what could he know of what she was fleeing, or her worry for Lazare? They had only just arrived, she told herself. There was time, still. She did her best to remember how grateful she was for this. They had escaped with their lives.

Not everyone was so lucky.

Once they'd washed, they found their way down complicated staircases and narrow halls to the dining room. Supper was laid on a long table where brass candlesticks crowded between sparkling crystal and plates decorated with blue-and-white peacocks. It had not been that long ago she'd seen real peacocks at Versailles.

But all of that was gone. The palace gardens would soon be overgrown, its yew hedges gone shaggy and feral, thorny vines scrambling from the château's roofs into its windows. The peacocks flown, Versailles' magic gone and faded to nothing.

Platters of food flowed from the kitchen as Duprès regaled them with tales of pirates and buried treasure. She should have felt relief, but instead she found it harder and harder to smile, to appreciate Sophie's animated replies or Rosier's questions about life on the other side of the Channel. Unfailingly her gaze went to the two empty chairs at the table's far end. Every now and then, she caught a desperate grief in Chandon's face she recognized as her own.

After dinner, they rested by the fire. Several hunting dogs came in and lay down, resting their long-eared heads on Rosier's feet. Herbal tisanes were served along with a plate of chocolates in the shape of ships. When it was time to go to their rooms under the eaves, Sophie asked if she should leave a candle lit in their room, or would Camille be coming up now, too?

She attempted a reassuring smile. "I may sit here instead—it'll only be a few hours until it's time to get ready to leave again."

"You needn't wait," Sophie replied firmly. "He *will* come."

Chandon was the last to go up, as if he'd been waiting to speak to her alone. "Bonne nuit," he said, stooping to kiss Camille on the cheek. "Promise me you won't fret? If anyone can arrive here unscathed by the time we leave in the morning, it's our handsome boys. Try to sleep instead. It'll be a rough journey over the sea tomorrow."

She said nothing, too afraid her voice would crack.

"What a fool I am!" He took from his bag a small parcel, wrapped in brown paper. "In the rush I nearly forgot. This was delivered to Bellefleur, addressed to you, moments before we left. Now might be the perfect time to open it."

Numbly she wondered why something for her would have been sent to Chandon's house, and set it next to her on the sofa. On the floor above, she heard her friends saying good night, opening and shutting doors, the floorboards creaking and then fading into quiet. The inn drowsed as the sea wind rattled in the windows. It reminded her of the Hôtel Séguin. It would be missing her, she knew. Searching for her in its rooms. Wondering. Could it know that it had helped save her life, and Lazare's? That it had shown her who she was? Her throat constricted. The girls would bring it life, but of a different kind. The house would always be waiting for its magician.

Blinking back tears, she picked up the package. As she cracked the wax seals, the paper fell open. Inside lay a small green book that looked as if it had fallen out of her memories. Hardly daring to believe, she ran her fingers over the silvered patterns of twining vines and stars. Just as they had done then, the curving letters of the title—*The Silver Leaf: A Primer*—seemed to unfurl in the firelight. Underneath was written: *As You Water the Roots, So Does the Tree Bear Fruit.* The ends of the pages were marbled pale green and blue, and when she held it to her nose, it smelled of burned wood and ash and magic. A book of magic created for small children . . . or those who'd never learned enough.

A blue ribbon marked a place toward the end, and she opened it there. She expected to find the working for the magic called tempus fugit, but it was not there. Hurriedly she flipped to the page on the veil. Only one short paragraph. As she read, disappointment stabbed at her. There was even less information in *The Silver Leaf* than there had been in Saint-Clair's journal. Here were only warnings of how dangerous it was. She supposed it was because it was a book for children. Though, she thought, frowning at the page, weren't children the ones who most needed to know the dangers?

She turned back again to the place marked by the ribbon. In the margin had been drawn—by Blaise?—a pointing hand that indicated a short passage.

> . . . *yet for reasons we do not know, there was a change.*
> *In our earliest documents, the source for magic was called*
> *"avec-le-sentiment," because of magic's absolute reliance on*
> *powerful emotion as its fuel.*

She knew from the portrait that it was her ability to feel deeply that had drawn Séguin to her. It had also been what had drawn Camille to write about the girls, and so put her in Odette's sights. Both times feeling deeply had thrust her into grave danger.

> *Over time, "with-feeling" was seen to come from only one*
> *of the strongest emotions, which we call "sorrow." It is*
> *impossible to pinpoint the exact moment when this change*
> *occurred; the earliest reference to magic worked from*
> *sorrow is in the diary of magician Henriette Louise de*
> *Clos in 1475. She ranks all the emotions in terms of their*
> *power, and concludes that the source for transformation*
> *resides most deeply in sorrow. It was a simple theory, and*
> *a dangerous one.*

A draft from the window shivered across the back of her neck, and she pulled her cloak higher. One woman and her writings had changed everything.

> *What had once been sympathy was reduced to sorrow. It*
> *was powerful, and therefore taught to children to use in*

*times of crisis. But there was a cost to this change. Instead*
*of a connection to others, magic became a dark thing to be*
*feared. Soon magicians created ways to contain their too-*
*painful sorrow: the veil, or blur, which cut a magician into*
*parts by separating one emotion from the whole; and the*
*sorrow-well, which allowed one magician to use another*
*magician's pain. In both instances, the magician who relied*
*on these would, in the end, cease to feel. The heart is a*
*muscle that must be used.*

Since she was a child, she'd been told the wrong story. And she'd believed it: that magic was wrong. That *she* was wrong. She'd believed she was doomed to live in sorrow if she used magic. A tear glinted diamond-like on her lashes, and she blinked it away.

*Remember, children: the strongest magicians are those who*
*are brave enough to accept the whole of who they are and*
*what they feel.*

The last sentence was underscored, and beside it, in the margin, was penned: *For Camille. Our secret history.*

She closed the book and pressed it to her lips. *Merci mille fois, Blaise.*

Upstairs, she found her way down the corridor and into her room. Sophie was already asleep. Her golden hair spread over the pillow; gently the coverlet rose and fell. So long ago it felt like a dream, Camille had woken in her own bed to find Lazare sleeping beside her. The sheets had fallen from his tawny shoulder. Around him his hair had flowed, dark as the ink she loved, the fan of his lashes resting on his cheeks. That day, the dawn had been full of promise and hope.

She did not know how to hope any longer.

Beyond the window lay the stableyard, a walled garden, the thatched roofs of the inn's long wings, pale and vague in the moonlight. Alongside ran the road on which they'd arrived from Paris, like a long white finger pointing home. Great oaks that had grown beside the road for centuries cast deep shadows over it, and she tried to imagine Lazare and Foudriard taking refuge in those pools of gloom. Trying to be invisible, trying to stay safe.

But all she could think of were field mice and tiny voles, hunted creatures that hid from the owl under cover of night, unable even to hear death as it swooped close on silent wings.

# 57

In the morning Lazare and Foudriard had still not arrived.

As luck would have it, the sea was too rough to make a crossing to Dover, and so it was decided that the travelers would remain at the inn one more day. Like Camille, Chandon did not want to leave without them, but they also feared that, given enough time, the Comité would find their way to Wissant.

Sophie tried to distract her by showing her what she'd packed from the Hôtel Séguin. In one trunk was nestled Camille's enchanted dress—*I was afraid it would try to bite me*, Sophie said, *but I managed*. The other trunks were packed with clothes, a few keepsakes, books, and papers. Then, with a triumphant flourish, Sophie poured onto their bed the contents of a large burlap sack: earrings and ropes of diamonds, necklaces set with pearls and emeralds and sapphires like shards of night, and more bejeweled snuffboxes than she'd ever seen in the house.

"Where did you find all of this?" Camille asked in amazement.

"When Odette first came to stay, what did you think I was doing, sneaking around the house? I was scooping up as much as I could to hide it from her." There was a note of triumph in her voice. "My suspicions came in useful, as you can see."

"I should have listened to you."

"True," Sophie said. "But you let her in because of your feeling nature, and it's hard to fault that." Scooping up a collar set with diamonds in the shape of daisies, she draped it around her throat. Turning so that the morning light dazzled in the stones, she regarded herself critically in the mirror.

"What do you think—shall I wear these at my wedding?" She caught Camille's gaze in the mirror. "When *all* of us have arrived in England."

Camille didn't trust herself to reply. On the bed also lay the strange little packet, wrapped in faded red cloth, that Lazare had asked her to keep safe. Temptation to unwrap it gnawed at her, but instead she slipped it into her dress's hidden pocket to keep it with her. A small magic, a charm to bring him back. She imagined how it might be in the seaside town, every day walking the cliffs in the brisk air. Checking the boats in the harbor, searching for a sign that he'd landed. The days ahead of her were a despair of doing nothing, a long gray fog of powerlessness. How could she simply wait?

While Camille tried to keep her despair at bay, Chandon's mood grew only darker. Never much of a drinker, he was up at dawn with a bottle in his fist, his eyes red-rimmed.

"Bellefleur," he muttered, "my things, all of that gone—fine. Well and good! Who needs ghastly medieval furniture and portraits of one's ancestors? Take it all! But my beloved Foudriard? That is a step much too far." The bright color had gone from his face, and he'd refused to change out of his white wolf clothes, which were now stained and dirty. "I am sad beyond all reckoning," he admitted to Camille, "and know not what to do."

After lunch he'd thrown himself onto the bench in front of the pianoforte and begun, idly, to pick out a tune, a saraband by Handel. Its slow, melancholy chords—and the handsome grieving boy playing them—brought the maids to tears. The whole busy house stilled, listening. But when he began to play it a fourth time, Camille couldn't bear it. She had to go out.

She carried the song's minor key with her to the cliffs. There the sea breeze was fresh and fierce. Over the sea the sky was the gray of iron, and far off, on the other side where the white cliffs would have been if she could see them, rain fell in heavy sheets. Lazare would have liked to have seen it.

Lazare had told her the sea was like the sky, endless. It *was* wide and endless, but it was also deep. She sensed the valleys he'd described for her, so far below that they might as well be bottomless. The sea was like a living thing, moving and changing, its currents powerful and unknowable. It was unlike anything she had ever known and yet, it was also very familiar.

Once Papa had told her water rose in droplets from the sea and the rivers and the puddles to be collected in clouds. Then, as rain, the water returned to the sea or the lakes or the Seine before it was drawn up again, over and over, forever. *Though we called them by different names, the sea, the rivers, the puddles are all one thing: water.*

Magic, she understood now, was like that.

How could she ever have thought to cut her magic from herself? Could you cut the rain from the sea and keep it separate? Just like the sea lived in the clouds, magic lived in her. It would always be there, uneasily tending toward transformation.

She walked on, buffeted by winds but grateful for them. One more day, and then England. One more day for Lazare and Foudriard to arrive. What kept them? Perhaps they hadn't gotten away. Perhaps he'd had to fight and was now injured, dying. The wind snatched at her hair and she brushed it back. She refused to think those thoughts. He *would* come. If not today, then tomorrow. And if not then, he would find them in Dover.

Sleek black birds, their necks curved like snakes, drifted on the water until, as one, they dove, disappearing under the waves.

But if he didn't?

She vowed to return to France. Rosier could stay with Sophie. Perhaps she'd set up another shop, making whatever she wanted. They would be happy together, she knew.

And Camille? She would use her dress and her magic to disguise herself once more. She'd scour the streets of Paris, the prisons, all the hiding places she could uncover. She would be a thousand different people, each one a stranger, inquiring about a tall, brown-skinned boy with hair like a blackbird's wing. *An inventor,* she might say to encourage them, miming pockets full of things he'd gathered to fuel his dreams. A cloud-watcher. Elegant, clever hands, and a lazy, swoon-inducing smile. Maybe they'd have seen him, and she would go in the direction they told her. Sorrow would be a lonely companion, but it would fuel her search.

Below the cliffs, waves rolled in. In the moment before they crashed and dissolved on the sand, they became like molten glass, an unearthly blue. One after another, never ceasing.

She too would be relentless. She would not give up.

Even if it took her whole life, she would never stop searching.

# 58

They left in a skiff at dawn, the tide running out.

Duprès had told them they'd be less conspicuous leaving from the beach below the inn, rather than the harbor at Wissant. From the beach, a smaller skiff would take them to a fishing boat in which they'd cross the Channel. Melancholy and dispirited, they'd followed him down a narrow path that wound through waving grass and rippled sand to the water. Off the beach waited the flat-bottomed skiff, a lone figure at her oars. Duprès had sent their trunks to the dock in town, from which, if all went as planned, the fishing vessel would depart and wait for its secret passengers.

At Duprès's insistence, they removed their shoes and stockings. Camille and Sophie carried their skirts over their arms, the icy water numbing their feet as they waded to the skiff. They climbed in awkwardly, pants and skirts now soaking wet. As if he'd done it all his life, Rosier walked the boat out until it cleared the sand before he jumped in.

As the sailor put his back into the rowing, and Chandon and Rosier each took an oar and began to pull, Camille waved at Duprès, who stood on the far dunes, solemnly watching them depart. On the strand, the footprints they'd left were already erased.

At anchor, a good way from shore, lay the fishing boat. Her two masts poked like fingers into the brightening sky. On her hull was painted her name: *Estelle*. As soon as the fishermen spotted the little skiff, they lifted the anchor and began to raise the sails. Camille looked back toward Wissant, the forest of masts in the harbor.

The boys had not come.

With an aching heart, Camille clambered up a rope ladder to the deck of the *Estelle*. The captain said gruffly that she might find the passage less troublesome belowdecks, for the sea was still rough. It was dark in the belly of the boat, and it smelled of rotten fish. She found a narrow cabin where a lantern swayed on a hook and sat down on a bench. She didn't want to watch France recede behind her.

Paris would still be the place where good and terrible things had happened, all the pieces of her life. The glorious balloon flights with Lazare, the stars seen from the tower at Notre-Dame, the terrible oak tree like a gallows, cozy Flotsam House under the bridge and the muttering Hôtel Séguin protective behind its gate, her printing press and her memories of her family, the silver-black river always running away. Paris was where she'd become who she was. It was inside of her, forever.

And England?

She couldn't grasp it. Lazare had told her about the cliffs of Dover, but seeing them without him—she shook her head. She knew already she would not stay there very long. Once Sophie and the others were settled, she'd return to search for him.

At first the crossing was rough, the stout vessel rolling as it raced ahead of the wind, but it didn't take long for the sea to change. Through the port-hole she watched the waves shrink until only small puffs roughed the water's surface and the sailing became smooth.

Suddenly Sophie appeared in the doorway of the little cabin, her eyes sparkling. "You're not feeling seasick, are you?"

Camille shook her head.

"Then you must come up on the deck! Quickly! The sun is breaking through the clouds and dancing on the water. You must not miss it! I promise you'll find it quite extraordinary."

Reluctantly, Camille took her sister's hand. Together, kicking their skirts out of the way, they climbed the ladder to the deck. Around her, the sea spread out in storm-gray hues. She'd seen it on the map, and knew that compared to the great oceans of the world this was only a narrow strait, but nevertheless it felt enormous and endless. The air was alive as it rushed cold over her skin, full of tiny water droplets. She inhaled the fresh, briny scent, and it felt as though it cleared something in her.

"See? Isn't it wonderful?" Sophie squeezed her hand. "Take it *all* in."

"Very well," she said, smiling at Sophie's enthusiasm. "It *is* magnificent to be at sea." Ahead fog still hung over the water, but now that the sun was shining, she hoped it would burn off, revealing the English side. "Do you think the cliffs will be as lovely as they say?"

"I cannot wait to see them! Though there are many beautiful things in the world."

"Oh? You seem quite captivated by the sea journey," Camille observed.

"Perhaps I am. It is full of surprises, don't you think?" Sophie shaded her eyes and looked back toward Wissant. "I never imagined there would be so many ships. Though ours is a paltry enough thing. Don't scold me! It reeks of fish guts and is slippery with scales, while others are dashing and sleek. There," she said, pointing, "the one with the yellow hull—see how fast it comes!"

Following Sophie's finger, Camille spotted a small sloop cutting across the water, its sails so full of wind that the vessel heeled low over the waves. Three people moved back and forth on deck. "It's nearly in the water!"

"How fearless they are!" Sophie winked at Camille. "What if they are pirates?"

"I'll fetch my cutlass!" Camille laughed, despite her sadness trying to play along. "I left it belowdecks."

"Not yet," Sophie said, catching ahold of Camille's sleeve as if she actually would go. "I wish to see what happens next."

For several long minutes they watched the vessel cut through the water. Spray leaped from its bow, frothing into the air and hiding its crew from view. With its large triangular sail and two smaller, narrower ones in front, it looked like a flock of flying white birds. Now and again Camille glimpsed the quickly moving figures on deck. When it seemed it might pass beyond them, the nimble sloop tacked, changing course as swift as thought. It had been going fast before, but now it ate up the distance like it was nothing.

"They *are* coming toward us!" Camille gasped. Were there really pirates in the Channel? She thought of their belongings in the hold, the sack of jewelry. "Does the captain know?"

"I suspect he does—they're pulling up beside us! The fishermen are throwing them lines!"

The little sloop had let out its sails and was gliding along the *Estelle*. The sun off the water made it hard to see—but one of the young men on board, clearly the captain, wore a naval uniform. With a practiced motion, he grabbed a line as it sailed through the air and, hand over hand, pulled them closer. One of the others was tall, and lean, and something about his easy movements reminded her of Lazare. The memory of him hurt, like a hand crushing her heart.

"Camille, do you see?"

She held her hand up against the glare as another line was thrown to the yellow-hulled sloop. The tall one caught it effortlessly, as if ropes were everyday things to him.

"Sophie? That boy—he is so familiar to me." She felt faint, and the cries of seagulls and the plash of waves seemed very far away. "Do not tease me anymore. Tell me true—is it him?"

Sophie's eyes shone with happy tears. "That's why I fetched you from the cabin! The captain had just got the signal from a navy officer—a Baron de Guilleux?—that they were coming."

It was Lazare, and she thought she would splinter to pieces as he pulled in the line, drawing the sloop closer. In that unguarded moment, she saw how his ragged clothes, the same ones he'd been wearing the night they'd gone to Les Mots Volants, hung from his shoulders. How dirty and raw-boned his face was. The yellowing bruise on his temple. "Lazare!"

He spun toward the deck of the *Estelle*. The fatigue vanished from his face as joy overtook it. As if they'd only just parted, he shouted, "Did you see how fast we were?"

When she nodded, hardly able to speak, he gazed at her with such intensity she felt she might burn to ash in the heat of it. Taking the line in his hands, he leaped.

She held out her arms. He slipped as he scrabbled for a foothold, but then he caught himself and slid across the deck into her embrace. The fisherman whooped. She ran her hands down his damp cheeks, his neck, his shoulders. Solid and warm and *real*.

"Where have you been?" Relief made her voice shake. "I wanted to believe you were safe, but it was so hard—"

"Mon âme." He held her close, his arm cradling her. "Shall I tell it all to you now?"

She nodded gravely.

"We came as soon as we could. That night, at Les Mots Volants, when you were taken by the Comité, I fought with the guards to free you. But it was impossible. Foudriard and I were nearly caught ourselves. I didn't dare return to my parents' house. My tutor once had taken me into the sewers the Romans built under Paris, and there we hid. Under Paris, in the filth, cut off from the world above. I didn't know what had happened to you until I crept out at night to speak to your gatekeeper, who gave me a message Rosier had left with him. But by then we had already missed the performance of Les Merveilleux, and your escape." He didn't look away from her, not for a moment. "My parents were willing to loan us horses, and on them we fled to Wissant, only to arrive at the empty inn this morning." He shook his head, though if it was in despair or wonder at their luck, she didn't know. "I vowed I would not rest until I had found you."

"I vowed the same, you know. Walking above the shore of Wissant."

"You didn't doubt?"

"I didn't doubt you. I doubted the *world*, Lazare. I thought it would tangle you in its web and keep you away." She didn't care if he saw her tears as they spilled hot over her wind-cold cheeks. She'd been brave long enough.

Slowly, lovingly, he kissed away her tears. "The old world is flawed. But the one we make will be different. Better."

"Do you promise?"

He pressed her to him, close to his heart. "I promise."

Then Foudriard climbed aboard to be warmly embraced and kissed by everyone, while Chandon laughed through his tears. Then the fishermen were pulling up anchor and trimming the sails as the *Estelle* sailed onward to England.

They were approaching the far shore when Lazare took her hand. "Régardes! Do you see them?" he pointed excitedly off the stern of the boat, where the waves curled and frothed.

There was something in the water. Something alive, something moving. A gleam of silver, tiny bubbles—and then a silver-gray creature leaped clear of the foam. It cast itself into the air, its short narrow snout playfully raised, before diving back under the water. Another one followed behind, swimming sideways beneath the waves, its sweet black eye facing them.

"She sees us!"

Lazare slipped an arm around her waist. "*Adventurers*, she's thinking."

Entranced, Camille watched as the sleek creature kept easy pace with the boat. "She's going as fast as we are! She must be a dolphin, non?"

"Just like the ones I saw from the balloon when we sailed along the coast from Lille."

He had kept his promise.

Behind them, the sky was storm and rain. But across the narrow sleeve of water, the light transformed. The clouds had been torn apart by the wind and now the afternoon sun gilded the high chalk cliffs. Rosier was laughing, pulling heavy nets with the fishermen, while Chandon and Foudriard had disappeared to stand at the stern, Chandon's hands warming inside Foudriard's coat. It was as if nothing else in the world existed. They seemed hardly to speak, but both were smiling—one grave, one teasing—as the *Estelle* drew closer to its destination.

"You don't happen to have that package I gave you?" Lazare asked.

"Of course." She reached in her pocket and handed it to him. "I carried it with me always . . . I felt I couldn't set it aside."

His inquiring gaze met hers. "You never opened it?"

"It's yours, n'est-ce pas? I also had the strangest feeling, that if I did as you asked, you'd return to me."

"And so it came to pass." His voice was rough, unsteady. "Here, I'll show you."

Pulling at the knots, he unwrapped the fabric layer by layer, the ragged ends of it flicking in the wind, until the box was laid bare. It was a tiny silver snuffbox. It would have fit in a circle made by her thumb and forefinger with room to spare. On its blue-enameled lid winked a constellation, each star a tiny, glittering diamond.

Seeing it in Lazare's hand, his long brown fingers cradling the vulnerable and valuable object, the memory of another snuffbox came to her. The one she'd found on the stairs at Versailles in the spring and lost to Chandon in a gamble she'd hoped would change her life. And it had. She hadn't known at the time what would happen when she slipped it into her dress's secret pocket. It had been a golden key that had unlocked everything that came after. Such a small thing, to set her on this path.

Lazare polished the top of the snuffbox against his coat. As he did so, the wind caught in the edge of the fabric and tore it out of his grasp.

"Oh no!" Camille cried.

But the wrapping was gone; they both watched the fabric sail away, winking red, before it disappeared over the water.

"It doesn't matter," Lazare said. "What's important is what's inside." He flicked the lid open.

Camille stood on her toes but couldn't see. "Snuff?" she teased. "Is that what I've been carrying all this time?"

He plucked something out of the box and showed her. Between his fingers gleamed a ring of yellow gold, set with a scarlet stone as big as her thumbnail. In the watery light, it flickered like slow fire.

She'd never seen anything like it, not at Versailles or anywhere else. "How beautiful it is!"

"It's the only one of its kind. It was commissioned by my Indian grand-father, a gift to his daughter on her wedding day. After she died, it was one of the few things that traveled with my father on that long voyage from Pondichéry to Paris."

"You're not thinking of selling it, are you?" she demanded. "We don't need to do that. Not yet."

"I've got another plan for it." He took her hand, brought it to his lips. "Camille?"

Her heart startled like a bird in her chest.

"There is nothing I love more than you in this world. While we were hiding under Paris, it was so dark, but still we knew the day was over, when night came, for there was a grate through which we could see the first star rise. It told me one more day had passed and that we'd heard nothing, knew nothing, had done nothing . . . do you know what haunted me then?"

She shook her head only the slightest bit, afraid to break the spell.

"That I would die in that wretched gloom without ever seeing you again." His breath was ragged and raw. "I could not endure knowing that this revolution—this fight for the things we both believed in—had taken you from me. You had feared the revolution had failed us, and in those tunnels, I believed it had. I believed it had destroyed all the happiness in the world, all the magic. All that I loved."

She turned his hand over and kissed his palm, heard his breath catch. "But it hasn't, has it?"

He shook his head. "Still, I wanted to tell you," he said softly, "in case it mattered to you."

"Nothing matters more." Once she had feared they were growing apart, like the branches of the pear tree at the Hôtel Séguin. How wrong she had been. And now that they were together, she did not ever want to be away from him again. Could she say to him, *Shall we marry?* Did she dare ask: Would you walk this new path with me, wherever it takes us?

She steadied herself. *To be true to yourself is to be brave.* "Lazare, I wish to ask—would you—"

"Camille," he said, searching her face. "Will you—"

"—marry me?" she said.

He threw his head back and laughed. "You run fast, Camille Durbonne! Yes, a thousand times, if you will have me."

An inarticulate moan escaped her as he drew her close. Her tears were falling fast, and she felt them dampen the warm skin of his neck, his cravat, his hair. "Yes," she whispered in his ear, her lips on the tender place where his pulse beat. "Yes, I will."

He slipped the ring on her finger, where its ruby shone like a heart of flame, and then he bent to kiss her. His mouth tasted of salt and fire and yearning. She kissed him back, aching and desperate, as if this kiss could undo the loss and pain they had suffered. As if a kiss could unwind the past and make a new world. As his hands slid around her shoulders, she twined her fingers into his hair, and there was only this moment, the two of them together.

In their kiss, time ceased to exist.

As did the sea, the wind, and the sky. The boat and the people on it. The dolphins and the birds. There was nothing but the press of his body against hers, his sweet mouth, his hands cradling her face, and the rising of her own desire.

Suddenly he pulled away, the corner of his mouth curling in a smile.

"Why are you stopping?" she gasped.

"I'm sorry, my love—it's Rosier, as always."

"Enfin!" Rosier cried out. "We have all had enough of waiting!" He strode forward, Sophie's hand in his. "I thought you would never get to it, either of you!"

"My nerves!" Sophie laughed. "I wanted you to spot the sloop yourself, Camille, but I had so much work in getting you to see it!" And then Chandon was stepping toward them, followed by Foudriard, champagne bottles like bouquets in their fists, as Sophie skidded along the slippery deck to throw her arms around Camille.

"Fetch the ship's captain!" Sophie called to Foudriard. "He must marry them immédiatement!"

"*Them?*" Camille exclaimed. "I wish none of us will ever be parted."

Like the master of marvels he was, Rosier produced wineglasses from the pockets of his coat and handed them around. Chandon poured the champagne, filling their glasses so they overflowed. First he embraced Lazare, congratulating him on his good fortune on marrying a brave and lovely magician. Then he stooped to kiss Camille and said so that only she could hear, "See? Good magicians always get what they wish for."

Then he turned to the others and cried, "To magic!"

"And to hope," Lazare said as they clinked their glasses. The golden wine that bubbled and danced was like her heart, dazzled and too full.

As happy conversation buzzed around her, the smoky blur of land that was France disappeared behind her. Gone from sight was the magic-threaded Hôtel Séguin that had protected and encouraged her as best it could. Adèle and Daumier and the others who had seen fit to care for the house's magic and history and had given her shelter. The joyous and fierce Lost Girls who'd seen in her a friend. Lasalle, who had taken a chance on her. The brother she had lost, and her parents, Paris's rooftops and the silvery Seine, the friends she had made at the gambling tables at a vanished Versailles—all were beloved to her. Not long ago she'd vowed never to leave, but now she was an émigré: homeless, cut adrift. There were so many unknowns ahead of her she thought she might drown in them. Lazare must have seen the troubled emotions play across her face, for he put his arm around her shoulders, drew her close.

"It's hard to leave, isn't it?" he mused. "Even when there is so much joy, and the chance to finally be free to be who we truly are."

"It is very hard," she acknowledged. "You know what it reminds me of? When a balloon is ready to fly, it strains at the ropes tethering it to the ground, as if it wishes to be free. But when it's airborne, it can only go where the wind blows it. And when the fuel runs out it may crash, get tangled in a tree, fall into the ocean—"

"Mon âme, look at me."

When she did, she saw the conflict in his face mirrored the one in her heart. What Giselle said once came back to her: *You saw me.* Then she hadn't understood what it meant to the flower seller. But now she did. In Lazare's deep brown eyes, she saw herself as whole. It had taken her accepting her own magic for that to happen.

"We can go back, you know," he confided. "Or we can stay. No matter where we are, I know you will write, and I will learn the clouds. We will still work for change. For anything is possible."

She took his hand—strong, steady, alive—in hers. "As long as we are never parted."

Ahead of them, the white cliffs rose up, taller than cathedrals. The water that had seemed so broad and wild diminished and was gone. As they neared land, a flock of gulls, flashing white and black in the sun, sheered once over the boat before they winged away.

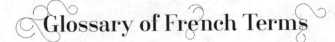

# Glossary of French Terms

À bientôt—See you soon

À la française—In the French style

Bien sûr—Of course

Bienvenue—Welcome

Bonne chance—Good luck

Brava/Bravo/Bravi—Good, well done! A word of praise, often for performers (Italian)

Citoyens—Citizens

Comme ça—Like that

Comprenez—Understand

Continuez—Continue

Dieu—God

Émigré—Emigrant

Enfin—Finally

Entrez—Enter

Fais de beaux rêves—Sleep well

Fantastique—Fantastic

Hélas—Alas

J'arrive—I'm coming

Je ne sais quoi—Something extra special (literally, "I don't know what")

Liberté, Égalité, Fraternité ou la mort—Liberty, Equality, Brotherhood or Death (Revolutionary motto adopted 1793)

Ma chérie—My dear (feminine)

Marchande de mode—A stylist

Merci/Merci mille fois—Thank you/Thanks a million (literally, thank you a thousand times)

Merde—Shit

Mon âme—My soul

Mon ami/amie/amis—My friend (masculine/feminine/plural)

Mon Dieu—My God

Mon petit oiseau—My little bird

M'selle—Contracted version of Mademoiselle or miss

M'sieur—Contracted version of Monsieur or sir

Naturellement—Naturally

N'est-ce pas—Isn't it

Ne t'inquiète pas—Don't worry

Oh là là—Oh no! (what your friend would say if you slipped on a patch of ice)

Protegée—A person who receives special attention and instruction from someone more experienced

Régards/Régardez—Look (at that)

Rien—Nothing

Salut—Hi

S'il vous plaît/S'il te plaît—Please; literally, if it pleases you (formal/informal)

Taisez-vous—Be quiet

Tiens—Well/look/see here

Vive la France/la nation/le révolution—Long live France/the nation/the revolution

# Historical Note

*This is a desperate time, when desperate games are played for*
*desperate stakes.*

Charles Dickens, *A Tale of Two Cities*

Dickens famously began his novel about the French Revolution by saying, "It was the best of times, it was the worst of times . . . it was the season of light, it was the season of darkness, it was the spring of hope, it was the winter of despair." And it really was. Spanning five years (1789–1794), the French Revolution is a complex historical event, full of extraordinary people and actions that set France—and the world—on fire.

Because this is an alternate, magical history of the French Revolution, I've taken some liberties with the historical record. For example, I've put figures like the Marquis de Lafayette and the king and queen of France in situations they were never in. I've also used magic and magicians as a way to raise certain issues, such as emigration and state-sanctioned secret police, that hadn't yet come to the fore in 1789.

A few anachronisms to note: Today, we'd call Lazare an amateur scientist. But he would have called himself a "natural philosopher," since the word "scientist" wasn't coined until the 1830s. For ease of understanding, I've used the word "science" instead of "natural philosophy" in this book. Similarly, in this series I've used the name "Place des Vosges" to refer to the beautiful park where many of the stories' events take place, so that readers, especially those unfamiliar with the history of Paris, can follow Camille and Lazare's wanderings on a contemporary map. Before 1799 it was called Place Royale.

In case you're curious, here's a bit more about the people, places, and events that figure in this book.

*A brief time line of the events of 1789:*

| May | Meeting of the Estates General at Versailles |
|---|---|
| June | Tennis Court Oath |
| | French and mercenary troops sent to Paris |
| July | Riots in Paris |
| | Fall of the Bastille |
| | The Great Fear |
| Aug. | The Great Fear continues |
| | Nobles renounce their feudal rights in the National Assembly |
| | Declaration of the Rights of Man and of the Citizen |
| Oct. | March on Versailles |
| | Royal family brought to Paris and installed at the Tuileries Palace |
| | Distinctions made between "active" and "passive" citizens |
| Nov. | Church property seized as property of the nation |
| Dec. | Paper money called "assignats" issued by France to prevent its bankruptcy |

*The French press:* Before the Estates General met at Versailles in May 1789, there were only a handful of state-sanctioned newspapers in Paris. By June, there were more than three hundred newspapers in Paris, not including a deluge of pamphlets and magazines. Historians estimate that 70 percent of men and 80 percent of women in Paris had some basic literacy; those who couldn't read had the news read to them by street criers or friends. Jean-Paul Marat printed 3,000 copies of his newspaper, *L'Ami du Peuple*; Jacques Hébert's *Le Père Duschesne* had a print run of 80,000 copies in a city of 600,000 people. Since each copy of these radical newspapers was probably read by more than one person, their influence was vast.

*March on Versailles:* On October 5–6, 1789, a group of about six thousand women marched the fourteen miles from Paris to Versailles to protest the price and scarcity of bread. Among them were women who ran market stalls, sex workers, middle-class and working-class women, as well as men dressed as women (some sources say they were agitators in the pay of the duc d'Orléans). Before they left Paris, they were joined by fifteen thousand sympathetic members of the National Guard. Fearing they would desert if he did not let them march, Lafayette accompanied them. The women ransacked Versailles, threatened to kill the queen, decapitated several guards, and their protests led the king to agree to sign the new constitution. Sixty thousand people marched alongside the king's carriage as it made its way back to Paris: a sign of the people's new power.

*The Great Fear:* In the summer of 1789, people displaced by famine roamed the French countryside, looking for food and work. The revolutionary events of the spring, most important the meeting of the Estates General and the storming of the Bastille, had given peasants hope, but they also feared aristocratic payback. Fueled by fear and lightning-fast rumor, peasants mobilized in large groups and attacked anyone who threatened them (vagrants, peddlers, the homeless, nobles). These attacks fueled more panic, which in turn fueled more attacks. As historian George Lefebvre observed, "What matters in seeking an explanation for the Great Fear is not so much the actual truth as what the people thought the aristocracy could and would do."

*The poor:* I drew inspiration for Camille's pamphlets from Henry Mayhew's important series of articles published as *London Labour and the London Poor* (1849–1852). Mayhew interviewed hundreds of poor Londoners, from an eight-year-old girl who sold watercress to a disabled Black boy who, for a coin, swept a clean path for pedestrians crossing the street. Although Mayhew wasn't as enlightened as he might have been, he brought attention to the plight of his city's poor. Edmé Bouchardon's "The Cries of Paris," (1737–1746) a series of drawings of people who worked on the streets of Paris, also inspired me. You can view them at www.getty.edu/art/mobile/interactive /bouchardon/index.html.

*Balloons:* Strange as it may seem, when I dreamed up a balloon corps for Lazare to lead, I had no idea that such a balloon corps had actually existed. But it did! In 1794, the French Aerostatic Corps (Compagnie d'Aérostiers) was created to aid the French government with gathering information, communication (through signaling), and the distribution of propaganda. As far as I know, Lafayette was never involved with it. The balloon corps saw action in Napoleon's imperial battles in Egypt before it was disbanded in 1799.

*Revolutionary women:* The ghosts of several real-life women of the French Revolution whispered in my ear as I wrote this book. Their names aren't as widely known as Robespierre's and Danton's, but they deserve to be. The first is the playwright Olympe de Gouges, who in 1791 wrote the *Declaration of the Rights of Women* as a corrective to the *Declaration of the Rights of Man* after demands for equal rights for women were repeatedly ignored. De Gouges was also an abolitionist. Her beliefs were seen as treasonous, and on November 3, 1793, she was executed by guillotine. The second is Charlotte Corday, who murdered one of the Revolution's leaders, Jean-Paul Marat, in his bath when she was twenty-four. Few believed Corday herself was responsible, though she insisted she acted alone for the good of the revolution to kill the "monster" Marat. She was guillotined on July 17, 1793. You can read more about these and other revolutionary women in Lucy Moore's *Liberty: The Lives and Times of Six Women in Revolutionary France*.

*Émigrés:* After the fall of the Bastille in July 1789, members of the queen's household, such as the Duchesse de Polignac and the king's brother, the duc d'Artois, fled France. Early on, émigrés were mostly royalists like them, worried about revolution. But the exodus continued and in 1791, a law was passed demanding that émigrés return to France. If they did not, their property would be confiscated. By the end of the French Revolution, more than 100,000 French people from all walks of life had left their homeland for England, Austria, and even the United States, most of them never to return. My own history as an immigrant as well as my father's experience as a refugee (and a three-time immigrant) make me particularly sympathetic to the émigrés' plight, which is reflected in Camille and Lazare's search for home, belonging, and the hardships they're willing to endure to achieve it.

# Acknowledgments

When the performers in Les Merveilleux soar through the air, it's possible only because of others who, working tirelessly and generously behind the scenes, make magic out of the ordinary. No spectacle gets off the ground without them, and I've been lucky enough to have an entire troupe to help give this book wings.

First to my agent, Molly Ker Hawn—though I make my living with words, I find there aren't enough to thank you for all you do for me. Merci beaucoup for your understanding and advice, your advocacy and sharp sense of humor, and for encouraging me to keep dreaming. I'm lucky to have you in my corner.

Un grand merci to my editor, Sarah Dotts Barley—for your patience as I wrote and rewrote, for the space you gave me, and the questions you asked.

At times, writing this book felt like crossing the English Channel in a boat made of paperclips and wishes; your belief in this book (and me) was the beacon on the far shore toward which I rowed.

Thank you too, to all the wonderful people at Flatiron Books: Sydney Jeon, Megan Lynch, Cristina Gilbert, Bob Miller, Claire McLaughlin, Jennifer Edwards, Chrisinda Lynch, Vincent Stanley, Jordan Forney, Katherine Turro, Nancy Trypuc, Kelly Gatesman, Keith Hayes, Anna Gorovoy, Toby Yuen, and Stephanie Umeda. In the United Kingdom, thank you to Rachel Petty, Rachel Vale, Helen Crawford-White, and the rest of the team at Macmillan Children's, as well as Venetia Gosling. I'm awed by how many people it takes to get a book off the ground, and I'm grateful for your hard work on my behalf.

While a spectacle is about dazzling and wondrous performances, behind the curtain it's something else entirely: the disheveled dressing room with its cracked makeup pans and tangled wigs, costumes and candy wrappers and wilted bouquets—reminders that there's both a public writing life and a private one. I'm incredibly fortunate to have writing friends who come sit in that dressing room with me to discuss the show (and what could make it better) while chatting about writing and hopes and fears. And when I need it, they unfurl the safety net below me, saying: *Don't worry, we've got you.*

To Heather Kassner and Gabrielle Byrne, I wouldn't have survived this series without you and our daily—hourly!—chats and vats. Your love, friendship, and support made this book possible. To Lillian Clark, for understanding, and reminding me always to punt into the sun. To Karin Lefranc and Rebecca Smith-Allen, whose insight and friendship means so much. To Julie Artz and Jessica Vitalis for believing I could do it, and helping me get there. To all who read drafts of this book, and kept me going with your positively clairvoyant notes and caring: I couldn't have done this without you. When I thought all I needed to fix my book were a few more note cards, Robin LaFevers reached out to suggest there might be a deeper issue, and that the soul of my story might be found in a fairy tale. And when I wandered lost through the thorny brambles called Book Two and Publishing, Stephanie Garber so kindly lit a lantern and looked out for me. To Jo

Hathaway, Kelly Roell, Sara Faring, Emily Bain Murphy, Kip Wilson: you brighten my days. Thank you *all*, you wonderful coconspirators.

Thanks too to Zander and Kate of the beautiful schooner *Guildive*; when asked what would be the best way for my ragtag band of émigrés to cross the English Channel undetected, Zander didn't hesitate: a fishing boat.

To the dear friends and family who supported me when I was only half in this world and who tugged me back into it, especially Sonja, Jeff Giles, Sabine, Karen, Mike, Dennis, Dina, Dad, Kim, and Mary. Thank you for holding a place for me, and for asking how it was going.

As this series comes to a close, I'd like to salute those who helped roll out the red carpet for these two books: Stephanie Beaver, Jessica Cluess, Rosalyn Eves, Stephanie Garber, Alison Goodman, Alwyn Hamilton, Margaret Rogerson, Christina Russell, Sami Thomason, and every author, librarian, bookseller, reader, book blogger, and Instagrammer who loved these books and shared them with others. Merci mille fois! And to those of you who have taken the time to tell me—via messages, social media, and reviews— how much you loved this series, thank you. You kept me writing long after the curtain fell.

To Tim, strongman, lifter-upper and encourager of writers, thank you for carrying me this long way. And to Lukas, plot magician and wizard of insight and advice on birds and boats and other things, thank you. I can't wait until you write your own book. I love you both very much.

Finally, to those of you who see injustice and take action, however small it may be: you are my heroes. Your determination and daring, your righteous anger and your courage give me hope. This book is for you.

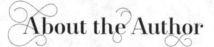

# About the Author

Born in Sweden to Indian and Swedish parents, Gita Trelease has lived in many places, including New York, Paris, and a tiny town in central Italy. She attended Yale College and New York University, where she earned a Ph.D. in British literature. Before becoming a novelist, she taught classes on writing and fairy tales. Along with her husband and son, Gita divides her time between a village in Massachusetts and the coast of Maine. She is also the author of *All That Glitters*, the first book in the Enchantée duology.